A SIMPLE ACT OF KINDNESS
AN OLD-FASHIONED LOVE STORY

MICHAEL A. WAY, SR.

A Simple Act of Kindness – An Old Fashioned Love Story is a work of fiction

Copyright © 2023 by Michael A. Way, Sr.

All rights reserved. No part of this work may be reproduced in any form without written permission, except by reviewers, who may quote brief snippets in review.

Published in the United States of America – Morning Prayer Publishing: For questions, email: morningprayerpub@michaelalvinway.net

Visit author's website at: michaelalvinway.net or email: mike.way@michaelalvinway.net

ISBN: 979-8-9867743-1-2 (hardcover)
ISBN: 979-8-9867743-0-5 (softcover)
Subject: Romance – Christian – Fiction – Mystery
Printed in the United States
First Edition
Interior Book Design by Brady Moller
Cover design by Emmanuel Ebirehri

Disclaimer

This is a work of fiction. Names, characters, events and incidents are the products of the author's imagination. Any resemblance to actual persons, living or dead, or actual events is purely coincidental. Certain long-standing institutions, agencies, and public offices are mentioned, but the characters involved are wholly imaginary. All of the businesses and places mentioned are real and serve as the fictional backdrop to this novel. Lastly, space and time have been rearranged to suit the chronological flow of the book. The names of musicians, artist, and product names are real and are used under fair use statutes.

    The opinions expressed are those of the characters and should not be confused with the author's. All passages relating to therapy and psychoanalysis have no factual basis but are expressed as opinion by the fictional characters using them.

> Scripture quotations are all from the KJV of the Holy Bible,
> Cambridge, 1769

For my real-life Audrey

CONTENTS

Foreword — xi
Author's Preface — xv

Prologue in Heaven — 1
Prologue On Earth — 5

PART ONE
~ LOVE AT FIRST SIGHT ~

Chapter 1 — 15
Ships Passing in the Night

Chapter 2 — 23
A Friendly Battle of the Sexes

Chapter 3 — 29
Ethan off Course

Chapter 4 — 35
Kindergarten Radishes

Chapter 5 — 39
No Thanks; I'm Not Interested, But I Should Have Been

Chapter 6 — 45
A Mother's Advice to Her Son & More…

Chapter 7 — 51
Are We Friends or Dating? Going it Alone

Chapter 8 — 63
Life Goes on and on and on…

Chapter 9 — 69
Audrey & Clair; Which Could Be the One?

Chapter 10 — 79
My Love From Another Star – Seoul, South Korea

Chapter 11 — 91
'All By Myself' – The Song in Real Life

Chapter 12 — 97
Friends… I think?

Chapter 13 — 103
Only the Lonely; Couples Ministry & Clair

Chapter 14 *The Shrink*	121
Chapter 15 *You Two Are Under Arrest!*	127

PART TWO
~ THE FRIENDSHIP ~

Chapter 16 *The Accidental Friendship*	135
Chapter 17 *The Kiss That Was More Than a Kiss*	157
Chapter 18 *I Would Die For You, and I Don't Know Why*	171
Chapter 19 *The Side-stepped Love, Opioids & Forced Honesty*	185
Chapter 20 *They Know, but We Don't. Huh?*	201
Chapter 21 *Friends With Benefits*	207
Chapter 22 *The Nice Guy Paradox in the Modern Dating World*	213
Chapter 23 *Reading Each Other's Minds on Christmas*	223
Chapter 24 *The Talk – Feelings & Emotions*	231
Chapter 25 *The Talk – Sex, Intimacy, & Confession at the River's Edge*	239
Chapter 26 *Life's Kaleidoscope*	251
Chapter 27 *Finding Chuck*	261

PART THREE
~ REVELATIONS ~

Chapter 28 *Friends Become a Couple*	267
Chapter 29 *Dreaming Our Lives Away; Dreams & in Dreams*	277
Chapter 30 *Tangerine Joanie*	299
Chapter 31 *In Her Own Words; the Recording*	311

Chapter 32 *When Harry Met Audrey; Again*	315
Chapter 33 *The Fight & Heavenly Intervention*	321
Chapter 34 *Aria's Intervention*	329
Chapter 35 *Friends No More*	335
Chapter 36 *Dreamland; Dreams Become Reality*	345
Chapter 37 *Infused Dreams & Future Memories*	351
Chapter 38 *Thanksgiving With the Sawyers*	359
Epilogue	371
Acknowledgments	385

Foreword

As a former Vice President of technology companies and Chief Information Officer for government agencies, I have had the pleasure of leading and mentoring many, many individuals. However, in the motley group of project managers, programmers, system administrators, and computer security analysts, I can only point to one individual that I can categorize as a romantic Renaissance man. We will get back to this description later, but I assure you that only Mike Way would fit this description in telling the story of Audrey and Jonathan.

Mike is both a former employee of mine and a friend. I actually met him at the gym in my small southern Maryland seaside town. Often a gathering place and a way to meet others, one would take time between workouts to get to know each other. After meeting Mike, I learned about his computer programming skills and encouraged him to apply for a job opening at the company where I worked. We also became friends after I invited Mike and his wife to a crab feast at my house. As I got to know Mike over time, I noted that he was a romantic. He and his wife have a close and unique relationship, so it's not surprising that he stepped away from his coding career, deciding to use some of his many talents to write this book.

When Mike first told me that he was writing a book, he caught my attention. He explained his desire to write a simple love story. But I was surprised at his topic. Being a lifelong reader *(I read every single book in my school library)*, I began to appreciate Mike's interest in writing.

I admit I was at first surprised at the topic chosen by Mike. A romantic novel written by a computer programmer? However, given his longtime personal romance with his own wife, his compelling writing style, and his desire to tell a simple, romantic story, the idea of the book was exciting. In addition, I was shocked but intrigued at Mike's transformation from a computer geek to a storyteller. I read *A Simple Act of Kindness* when it was just a manuscript. The novel engages and excites you in a way that is as unique as the author. You will feel like you're viewing a movie as you read; that's remarkable.

—Allison McCall, CIO

Mourning doves were chosen as the symbolic logo for this novel. Did you know that Mourning doves mate for life and the bond is so strong it can extend, for a time, beyond death? Their love is an endless love. These doves have been known to watch over their deceased mates attempting to care for them, and to return to the place where the birds died.

You are about to read a story of a possibly endless love between a very rare couple.

Author's Preface

Have you ever longed to read a good old-fashioned love story where hope was all that carried best friends through the hazardous waters of a budding romance? Perhaps you've dreamed of a story steeped in the simplicity of love and not lust. Maybe you want to observe how great loves begin with the protagonists never knowing the outcome for their futures together. Is it possible you would like to learn how love was supposed to be even in your own life?

A Simple Act of Kindness is such a story, a tale in which we observe a developing romance distilled down to the simple concept of answering the questions: "Do I like this person? Do our hearts like each other? Are they my soulmate?"

My journey to write this story began with my love of romantic movies and books packed with the substance that included the essence of what we all seek; love, companionship, understanding, and intimacy. I think we all crave to be with someone we can depend on and nurture each other. This book offers modern couples hope to go the distance.

The human love story is as old as time, but how exactly do we

AUTHOR'S PREFACE

learn how to love someone? Precious few today spend their whole lives with the loves of their life. Why? Because keeping romance alive is a lost art. Often, movies and media present infatuation as love leaving real-life couples disappointed with the hard work of staying in love in the real world.

In *A Simple Act of Kindness*, we see a thoroughly modern woman, Audrey Sawyer, and a self-sufficient professional man, Jonathan Dawson, in a unique situation where friendship bloomed. Both accidentally see a sneak peek of what love between them could be.

It terrified them, so they settled on a buddy-ship that lasted until their souls took over, insisting on a soul-mate-ship. Do you want a true soul mate? This novel is a fascinating glimpse of what love could be.

This book is for anyone who's ever been in love, wants to rekindle an old love, or longs for a new real romance. This novel is your story if you wish to fall in love as people once did. You will be treated to view what a strong, intelligent, and feminine woman has the power to achieve with or without a man.

With our male protagonist, you will admire a self-assured professional man, not someone looking for any opportunity to get laid. Instead, you will get inside the mind of what this type of high-value man looks for in his prospective partner for life.

This novel sees marriage as a unique partnership where achievement together is ordinary, and a couple does not compete in the dangerous game of one-ups-man-ship, a recipe for disaster.

Lastly, I purposely wrote this novel similar to how a movie screenplay is created. I wanted readers to visualize scene descriptions that place them in the center of events as they happen. If you want an additional emotional charge, *YouTube* the songs mentioned throughout; their titles are in *Italics*.

If you listen before or after each song mentioned, you will immerse yourself in the story's emotions along with Jonathan and Audrey. I've never seen it done this way; I like it and hope you will too.

Enjoy,
Michael Alvin Way, Sr.

Prologue in Heaven

A Simple Act of Kindness
Angels Walk Amongst Us Unaware – Guardian Angels

The board of elder angels in heaven gathered around in conference. Some stood, some paced, while other lower-ranked angels were annoyingly pondering the outcome of the earth, which they called third from Sol. Great care had been taken to create ecological balances that could sustain carbon-based life, called humans, created directly by God.

For eons and after various animal and plant life iterations, humankind was created as a self-replenishing, self-reproducing creature, eventually called human.

At first, the man was created and given dominion over all the earth. Next, the Master created a helpmeet for man. The man named her woman because she was made from his very bone and flesh. Together, their mission was to produce hybrid humans called children, to live in a peaceful organizational unit, first called tribes, then family, all in the free-will service of the Creator.

Soon, after a serpent polluted the bloodlines, disobedience to the Master's only rule occurred. The man and woman consumed fruit from the only forbidden tree. Soon, with the knowledge of good versus evil, humanity found itself steeped in tumultuous emotions of a violent outburst, including murder, theft, falsehood and chaotic activity, self-will, avarice, envy, and carnal destruction.

Within generations, the children of the original humans, Adam and Eve, came to destroy the perfection of the creation. Their disobedience, including their son's first act of murder, was evidence of the fall from grace. Finally, a great flood destroyed humanity for the good of the planet. Only eight would rebuild the earth's population in the image of the Creator's original plan.

Sadly, ill-gotten intentions crept in through the daughters of Noah. Sin again began the cycle of lust, envy, avarice, greed, vanity, and wickedness again and again and again.

Through evenly divisible units of time humans called weeks, months, and years, various men and women were born to be inserted into the timeline. Their purpose was to offset the ensuing environmental and spiritual destruction that classes of men and women would create among themselves in future generations of their species, a species designed by God to be a little lower than the hierarchy of angels.

Humankind would create this environmental destruction without regard for the prospect that their actions would bring about their eventual misery, death, and the fall of the planet on which they live, which sustains them.

This event, if allowed, would be the catastrophic end to the planet called earth.

And so, under God's guidance, the elders decided to introduce a concept of original love that flowed from agape-to-romance-to-family love. This action was designed to create for the world to see as a sustainable model of His original union the Creator envisioned.

It was decided that the product of this union would produce a male child to be called Kenneth, and he would, in his time, produce an environment where humanity sought love instead of power over each other.

A SIMPLE ACT OF KINDNESS

The problem amongst the elders was to select two would-be humans, a man, and a woman, as parents who possess DNA that will most likely produce the male child offspring needed to invent the technology to save the world from itself.

It was determined that not one existing adult man, not one already born adult woman, had the combination of four-letter DNA code sets to create the forty-six chromosomes in a future child.

The elder angels studied the A, C, G, and T, the "letters" of the DNA code. Then, an exhaustive search began for the right combination of chemical proteins adenine (A), cytosine (C), guanine (G), and thymine (T), respectively, that made up the nucleotide bases of DNA.

Pouring through the billions of living human DNA pairs in the correct age range, many close sets were found, but the only perfect match was found in two children, a five-year-old girl, Audrey Sawyer, and an eight-year-old boy, Jonathan Dawson.

Fortunately, both lived in the same geographical region of Maryland. Still, both Audrey and Jonathan exhibited anti-social tendencies combined with extreme stubbornness and willfulness. The irony was that neither Audrey nor Jonathan could be swayed by peer pressure; neither cared what others thought was right for them because of their steadfast personalities. Instead, while not particularly religious, their internal GPSs were locked on God and on doing the 'right' thing at all costs.

The elder angels agreed these non-cooperative personalities made the likelihood of these two children ever knowing each other, much less becoming a couple, virtually impossible.

At first, the idea was given up until one of the senior angels, Clarence, spoke. "I have long experience at this. Although I helped our last target, George, I have a newly minted protégé, Ethan, who can help Jonathan and Audrey find, know, and eventually love each other. We need an *Old Fashioned Love Story*, something innocently invisible to the parties. Both Audrey and Jonathan have one thing in common we can use; they're both susceptible to 'a *simple act of kindness*.' It can work, I tell you because they're nice people.

Clarence assured the council of elder angels. "All we need is the skill and finesse of Ethan-the-angel's personality."

And so it was that the junior-grade-angel Ethan was dispatched as a human. Ethan was stripped of the knowledge that he was an angelic being. The elders felt that he would be more effective for this critical mission if he walked among humans, not knowing he was an angel.

Ultimately, Ethan's job assignment is to protect and guide the chromosomes of Audrey and Jonathan to produce the child, Kenneth. Then, he, Kenneth, born of pure love, would grow into manhood and save the earth's environment, granting the planet a third chance to avoid destruction.

Kenneth, the offspring of this new and genuine love between Jonathan and Audrey, will, through the effectiveness of his charm, leadership, and willpower, combined with his unique genius, will create a firewall against the destruction of the irreplaceable environment of earth.

The journey of a remarkable and unique love between his parents begins.

Prologue on Earth

Audrey & Jonathan

Audrey was thought to be a strange girl all her life. In high school, she is classified as socially awkward and even one who does not like boys. Why? Because she is popular among the guys, as they talk sports, mechanical stuff, tools, or whatever. Her counselors think she is an unsolvable conundrum because she exudes unique femininity with just a touch of tomboy baked in. Audrey is known to laugh when around her friends, but no one has ever seen her smile as an everyday facial demeanor. This countenance gives Audrey the reputation of being stoic, standoffish, and unfriendly. Audrey knows of her reputation among others; some say she enjoys it.

The school counselor, Gwen Atkins, calls her parents to a private parent-teacher meeting to discuss Audrey's oddness.

Audrey's parents, Graham and Elise Sawyer, come to the school during the fourth period to meet Mrs. Atkins, the school's female advisor.

Mrs. Atkins begins, "Thank you for agreeing to see me. Now

there's nothing academically wrong. Your daughter is the pride of our school. She's a straight A student," she pauses, extracting a folder from her desk, and then continuing, "In fact, she is only one of three 'A' students out of six hundred and twelve."

Graham interrupts, "Then tell us; why did we take off from work to hear this? Audrey is an amazing, kind, and thoughtful daughter. What exactly is the issue?"

"This is awkward," comments Mrs. Atkins. "Perhaps because you've been around Audrey, you haven't noticed, but Audrey is unusually attractive. I've never seen a girl in my years here that never had a boyfriend. She gets along with all the students but never wants to form a serious relationship. I believe this is the age when students learn to spread their social wings. This semi-mating ritual allows young people to make better choices as adults. A few protected social bumps and bruises prepare young people for real life. Don't you agree?"

Graham and Elise show no emotion but continue to listen.

Mrs. Atkins proceeds, "Audrey exhibits all the girly activities one would expect, but unlike most girls, she elected to take all the shop classes traditionally enrolled in by boys. Don't get me wrong, and I'm not suggesting that Audrey has a different sexual orientation…"

Elise interrupts, "Are you suggesting…?"

Gwen responds defensively, "Of course not. It's just that anti-social behavior leads to later problems, and we're trying to head it off now."

Mrs. Atkins opens the folder and says, "Are you aware that in the sixth grade, Audrey cut a girl's hair sitting in front of her in Geography class even before junior high? You must understand that we wouldn't be here today if her behavior had been corrected back then. All I'm saying is that Audrey loves the guy activities as much as the female electives. She was terrific in all the home economics classes like cooking, sewing, writing, and performing. Audrey also possesses a phenomenal singing voice. After completing those classes, she enrolled in a wood, metal, and print shop and excelled in all three. She has a natural mechanical ability; her shop teachers say she can fix anything."

Graham responds. His tone is both proud and direct. "Yes, we know about the hair incident. Does your folder inform you that the young lady in question had long hair that fell almost to her butt? Does your folder tell you that she spent half a semester flipping her hair and that the mop landed on Audrey's desk? Did you know we met with the school and the girl's parents to ask them to ask their daughter to refrain? The parents quibbled, *'But my daughter has such beautiful long hair; perhaps Audrey is jealous.'* The next day, Audrey cut the girl's hair that lay across her desk whenever missy flung it. Finally, Audrey cut it off with scissors and stuffed the loose hair into the lunchbox we gave her. So yeah, we knew and were quite proud of Audrey; we even took her out for ice cream later to reward her."

Mrs. Atkins says, "And you call that socially responsible?"

Elise stops Mrs. Atkins, saying, "I've heard enough. Allow me to give you the lowdown on my daughter. She has a perfect fairness meter; she absolutely knows right from wrong; fair from unfair treatment. She acts quickly and decisively when you mess with her. And yes, she's pretty, but we trained her never to trade on her natural attractiveness. We believe inner beauty trumps transitory exterior good looks. So we raised Audrey to be a nice person without guile or vanity. She has helped Graham with car repairs since she was four. She often prepares a four-course meal to treat us now and then. She studies hard and has a beautiful singing voice and a heart of gold. However, Audrey is super stubborn. No power on earth can influence her to do something she does not want to. She is one-hundred-percent resistant to peer pressure of any kind. Audrey thinks for herself. She will consider anyone's advice but will only act on it if it makes sense to her. Lastly, Mrs. Atkins, boys have been trying to bed her down since she was fourteen; Audrey insists she will wait until she's married for reasons that make sense to her and, quite frankly, to us too. We know that young women Audrey's age are banging guys like bunny rabbits, but we are pleased that she chose to live her life this way."

Graham jumps in. "My only fear is that she won't find a man she considers good enough. My daughter is a plain and straightforward girl; what you see is what you get. She loves God but is not religious, mainly because she has observed the hypocrisy in many churches and prefers a direct relationship with God. She's been hanging around me since she was knee-high, so she has a bit of a potty mouth and sharp tongue if you piss her off, but I consider that her benign defense mechanism."

Graham and Elise stand. "If that's all, we will go. We appreciate your concerns. Our little girl is just right for us. So you have nothing to worry about; we got lucky and brought a genuinely good girl into this getting weirder by the minute world."

As the door to Mrs. Atkins' office closes, she speaks the last word to Audrey's parents. "Now I see; the problem is not with Audrey; it's with you two."

Gwen Atkins hasn't been aware of Graham's acute hearing until Mr. Sawyer turns back, re-opening her office door. Audrey's mother tries to stop her husband, whispering to him, "Ignore her; come on."

Graham re-opens the door, saying, "Oh hell no!" to Mrs. Atkins. He continues, "You don't know anything about our daughter. Didn't you hear me say that Audrey's fairness meter points true north, and she is never inconsiderate, nor is she afraid to stand up to mistreatment? At seventeen, she purchased a piece of a used car; we fixed it up together. Audrey paid for it with her part-time job earnings. We gave her a curfew of ten o'clock on weekdays and midnight on Friday and Saturday. One Tuesday night, she came home ten minutes late. I was furious and grounded her; she calmly placed her keys on the kitchen counter, informing me that her car was now my car. She explained that she was tutoring another student at the library on differential equations. Differential equations at seventeen; amazing," Graham growled. "How many kids do you know of at that age that can do that? Audrey very calmly explained that I was being unfair. She asked me if we trusted her. She informed me that we raised her not to know specific rights from wrongs but the knowledge of how to determine right from wrong. She said to me, *'Didn't you and mom say that I would be better armed to deal with any situation with the judgment of good and evil?'*"

He continues, "What could I say? She was correct. I handed her the keys back and apologized. Do you know what she told me, Miss Gwen? She said, *'It's okay, Daddy, we all make mistakes, but I will never lie to you or do anything that shames you, mom, myself, or God. I'm glad we had this talk.*' On that day, I learned how wonderful my daughter is and how good parents we had been. Audrey has never let us down. So perhaps we are not the problem; maybe it is the rest of the world that…"

Graham takes Elise by the hand and leaves Gwen Atkins dumbfounded.

JONATHAN DAWSON NEVER KNEW HE GOES TO THE SAME ELEMENTARY school as Audrey. Franklin and Allison Dawson, his parents, brought two sons and a daughter into the world. The Sawyers and the Dawson's never knew each other in the Dunkirk neighborhood; they learned they were neighbors when each family independently moved to Davidsonville, Maryland.

Harold 'Harry' Dawson is half a year younger than Audrey and attends the same school as Audrey, while Jonathan is two years ahead of them at the same Whitehall elementary school. Harry has never noticed Audrey as he is always lost in his own little world. He loves milk cap pogs and slammers, checkers, chess, and his favorite, Chinese checkers.

Jonathan is a more serious student and a loner. Jonathan possesses farm boy mid-western chiseled good looks. It would be easy to compare him to a Greek statue as he came into his college years because of his unassuming handsomeness.

Jonathan grew up protecting his little brother from the myriad of bullies populating elementary through middle school. Jonathan had to be forced to fight, opting instead for talking out a disagreement to a non-violent resolution. But, if pride tempted the offender into a physical confrontation, Jonathan would not hesitate to grant the other person a deliberate beat down, often apologizing to the recipient after the fight, the other person on the ground with a bloody nose.

In college, Jonathan began to notice women, but since childhood, Tyler, his friend, said to him, "Johnny, why is it you only like pretty girls who never smile? The girls you are attracted to all seem to be sad."

Jonathan answered in the oddest way for such a young man. "A girl who smiles for anyone will smile for everyone. I want a girl whom I make smile. I want her to see my heart, and I want to feel her heart in my heart. Most women's smiles are fantastic and alluring. Only when they don't smile can my heart's eyes see their heart's eyes first. I'm looking for a woman who can make my heart quicken, not one who can only cause me to react with desire. Do you understand, Tyler?"

"Dude, you are weird," Tyler said. "You're never gonna get laid with that attitude. Man, college is where the action is. Listen, Man, get with a chick, a bunch of chicks, and figure out what turns you on. Hit it and quit it. Sooner or later, you'll find the one woman that rings your bell, and then you can make a go of it and maybe find a potential wife. I'm doing that; I'm sowing my wild, very wild oats."

Jonathan laughed, saying, "You live your life your way; I'll do me. No drugs, booze, smokes, or chemical experimentation. When I meet the girl I want, I will instantly know. I don't want love; I want the love of my life the first time I fall in love. I'm sort of old-fashioned that way; I guess it is because of all the love songs of the past that have influenced me. I listen to the great songs by the Carpenters, Foreigner, REO, Nolan, Sinatra, Orbison, and so many others and realize what those songwriters must have felt."

He then said, "Tyler, have you noticed that there are no love songs anymore? People today are hooking up without even knowing their sex partners' names. Young people swipe right to get laid and left to pass. Social media is exposing everyone's body count and relationship history. I'm not feelin' that, my friend. I don't want to carry that kind of baggage into a lifetime of love. I never understood folks who marry multiple times. Guess it makes sense to them, but not to me. So, I'll wait, be patient, and keep my heart's eye open to spot the girl of my dreams."

Jonathan graduated and was recruited right out of his Master's program into a six-figure salary as a programmer for a secret Federal government agency.

Even though it was way out of his way, he would often visit his friend, Chuck, a line manager at the small hometown grocery store his parents liked. Jonathan worked there as a stock boy starting in eighth grade. Chuck was in the produce department, and they became fast friends and remained so, even when Jonathan left to attend college and Chuck advanced to become one of the store's managers.

As both boys became men, Chuck often tried to connect his handsome friend with pretty girls frequenting the store. Jonathan always chuckled, refusing the prompting, careful not to hurt Chuck's feelings.

Today is an early day home from work, Jonathan, smartly dressed in a business suit, shirt, and tie, and London Fog topcoat, stops by the Market for a Saratoga Sparkling, his second favorite soft drink, and a salad for tomorrow's lunch. Jonathan loves earth-tone clothing; he's sporting brown and tan socks under his pant leg into a buffed Mezlan dress shoe.

It's a fateful day because Audrey's mother calls Audrey's cell, asking her to stop at any grocery store for a handful of ingredients her mom needs to make her father's favorite homemade chicken soup.

Audrey has been performing security patching for the network servers at the Naval Academy that day. Unfamiliar with the area, Audrey opens the Waze app to search for the nearest grocery store and is led to Graul's in Cape St. Clair.

SOME WOULD CALL IT HAPPENSTANCE, LUCK, FATE, OR SERENDIPITY; Ethan and Clarence called it perfect timing. Neither Audrey nor Jonathan knew that these events of that day would create a relationship, love, and the vehicle to save the world from its ignoring of an inconvenient truth.

And so the adventure begins.

Enjoy!

PART ONE

LOVE AT FIRST SIGHT

One

SHIPS PASSING IN THE NIGHT

Late Winter: Christmas Season

An upscale professional man, Jonathan Dawson (20s), is a well-rounded cosmopolitan man living in the Downs neighborhood of Annapolis, Maryland. He needs his vehicle serviced at the massive auto park off Route 50 east on exit 29A. After picking up his truck, he heads for the nearby suburban semi-rural community of Cape Saint Clair, Maryland, a few miles east of Annapolis's Maryland state capital, before returning home.

Growing up near here when he was young, his parents loved the *ruralness* of the community before moving to Davidsonville near Riva. Jonathan has fond memories of working at Graul's part-time while in middle school and stops by the 60s-era local Market on his way home from work to pick up a few groceries. He is a bachelor who enjoys cooking his meals and hates fast food.

As he glances around the Market, Jonathan enjoys the subtle Christmas decorations placed around the store; we can tell by his whimsical smile that the site brings back memories of his early teenage years working there.

Expertly moving around his old stomping ground with a handcart and a few groceries, he squeezes by the crowded deli counter. The store's PA system plays Sirius 80s hits, softly blaring REO Speedwagon's *'Can't Fight This Feeling.'* Jonathan, a pianist who loves the old songs, pretends to play an imaginary keyboard as the song progresses.

Unexpectedly he sees a young woman, Audrey (early-20s), near the deli counter. She is wearing an elegant knee-length camel-colored cashmere coat with a decorative Christmassy scarf and woven knit hat with beautiful shoulder-length hair strands poking out just behind her delicate ears. Jonathan abruptly ceases pantomiming keyboard mimics.

Audrey is standing with two girls, 6 & 8, and a little boy, about 4. She is standing there as if she is waiting in line; she is holding a produce bag with three shallots and seven baby-red bliss potatoes with a receipt inside the bag with the veggies.

Jonathan notices the odd countenance between the four of them. He comments to the young woman, "Shallots and potatoes; someone's making a soup. I'm sure it will be great, and your kids will love it on a rainy day. You know it's supposed to rain today?" he asks as a statement attempting to entice Audrey into a casual conversation.

He smiles kindly at her, glances down at the four-year-old, and notices Audrey's colorful stocking-like knee-high socks. He smiles at her again, pulls up his right trouser leg, and motions to his bright and stylish socks.

She never parts her lips, but a smile is tightly held behind her emotionless facial expression.

He kneels to the little boy, asking him if he likes apples. The boy and the older girl nod 'yes.' The younger girl says, "Hi, mister, my name is Joanie; what's your name? You're very nice. Will you get me a tangerine, please? I'm not too fond of apples; they're boring. By the way, she's not my...." Joanie is interrupted by the deli manager shouting, "Next!"

Jonathan acknowledges the smile from the little boy and answers Joanie. "My name is Jonathan." He then proceeds to complete his shopping and places two apples and a single tangerine in his basket after paying for the rest of his groceries.

Saying 'hello' to Chuck, the front-end manager, Jonathan peers down each aisle but does not see the woman or her children. Chuck asks Jonathan if he has lost something. Jonathan nods an "*I'm good*" to his friend Chuck.

He waits outside near the exit door to give the apples and the tangerine to the children as they exit the store.

A seemingly eternal ten minutes pass, forcing him to glance at his watch. Then, finally, he heads to his truck, and just as he starts it, he sees the three kids emerge from the store's exit door.

Surprised, Jonathan does not see the young woman but a fiftyish grandmother, the three children, the two oldest carrying a single grocery bag.

He grabs the fruit and approaches the children. Jonathan inquires as he hands the apples and tangerine to the children. "I promised your children treats when I saw them in the store with their mother. Is she still inside?"

The woman seems puzzled and responds, "I'm not sure what you mean, sir."

Jonathan repeats his question as a statement, "I saw them at the deli count…"

The grandmother answers, "Oh no, you've got it wrong, mister; I had to use the restroom and asked the young lady who had just checked out to watch the kids. So I guess I took a little longer than I thought. When I returned to collect the munchkins here, I thanked her, and she left the store."

"Did you know her?" Jonathan asks.

"No, never seen her before, but she was pretty, wasn't she? And I love those adorable socks she was wearing."

Disappointed, Jonathan drives off. Arriving home, he parks in his driveway with a water view of the Magothy River that connects Annapolis, Gibson Island, Cape St. Clair, and Severna Park.

Audrey is a programmer and cyber security expert. She rose through the ranks at CISA because of her attention to detail and concerns about accuracy and minor clues. As a result, many of Audrey's coworkers nicknamed her *'Fastie,'* a shortcut acronym for fastidious.

Known for her inquisitive nature, she would even defy her supervisors if she thought there was a hint of a cyber-attack looming. When she was told, *'…Oh, that's nothing; just a standard DDOS attempt,'* she would run it down to its source, often creating illegal honey-pots to catch the culprits.

Many of her micromanaging supervisors wanted her fired for a zillion acts of insubordination, but her accuracy and nose for danger were too good to risk losing her. Eventually, the division chief created a one-person department just for her. Within two years, she had stopped sixty-two ransomware attacks and nearly impossible to find malware attempts.

Some call her cyber-Beethoven because she could see the attack just by glancing at the code. It's difficult for her because she is plain pretty, which makes her irresistible to guys on the unit, but her rigid professional demeanor keeps all potential suitors at bay.

On occasion, she finds herself lonely for a man's companionship, but other than her college friends Mateo and Ethan, she has no friends and hated the drama-filled pettiness of her so-called female friends all through school, college, and the work world. Some say she hates women, but the men understand Audrey does not care for the pettiness and gossip often displayed by her female work associates.

Audrey is a beautiful feminine girl whose personality is skewed male. She can change her own sparkplugs, change her oil, and no service advisor at any dealership dares talk down to her after their first encounter with her. Audrey is intelligent and intuitive, and just because she's attractive, folks learned that she was not to be trifled with. Audrey never used her inherited good looks to trade on; she earned everything the old-fashioned way; with hard work.

The boys called Audrey 'Mr. Sulu' in college because if a guy approached her salaciously, one could almost hear her mind say, *'shields up; yellow alert.'* Audrey had never shown anything other than friendly banter with any guy. Her parents gave up on marrying her off, and she was daddy's little girl, and he was painfully proud of her calling her his chip-off-the-old-block.

Audrey's mother was a professional designer; she retired early from the firm after she and her husband designed, built, and then purchased their aging-in-place home, complete with elevators.

Audrey's father had his wife work with the architect to give her exactly the home she wanted. Audrey's mother retired while still young, at forty-five. If asked why, she responded, "Why would I have such a beautiful home and only spend sixteen hours a day in it with eight going to sleep? No, I want to live in my house, not just come home to it."

It was nearing Christmas, and Audrey's mom wanted to make her famous homemade chicken soup for her husband and best friend, Audrey's dad. Not wanting to leave burners in full flame on the range, she asked Audrey to stop by any nearby store to pick up three shallots and six baby red-bliss potatoes on her way from work. Who knew this simple request would forever change Audrey's life and the world's future?

Audrey was angry with herself after picking up the vegetables her mother needed. Why? Because for the first time in her life, she had a heart-fluttering reaction to a man, and of all places, in a tiny little grocery store in the middle of nowhere. How could a simple act of kindness get to her like this; it was impossible. The thought of genuine feelings for a perfect stranger angered her, but upon examination of what her mind had just whispered with the single word, *perfect*.

Audrey, still driving, is shocked by the man's approach. His encounter surprised her that she could react to a man that would make her run away. Quibbling and disappointed with herself, her mind's voice is angry. *"He obviously likes kids. No, wait. Perhaps he thought those were my children, but no way, I'm too young to have kids that age. Maybe I will see him again. Guys like that don't grow on trees. Audrey, what were you thinking? You could've at least said hello, but no, you couldn't even do that. You are so pathetic when it comes to guys. Couldn't you at least give him a glimpse of a smile? Audrey, you're killing me here."*

Suddenly she stops talking to herself, seeing that a sudden downpour of rain has made the street to her parent's house slippery.

"Mom asked me to pick up a few things for her. So that's the only reason I went to that dinky little store; Mom and her shallots. I'm going to get soaked getting these to her."

Audrey made a mad dash for the side porch door, jumping out of her SUV with no umbrella. She fumbled for the keys and was drenched when her mom opened the door. "Oh my, honey, look at you. I didn't want you to get wet. Here, darling, give me your coat, hat, and scarf. And take off those silly Astro Club socks you love, and I will get you some dry clothes."

"Mom, what's with the shallots and potatoes?"

"I'm making your dad a homemade chicken soup. The shallots and potatoes make the soup a whole meal in one pot. Your dad loves my single-pot meals."

Audrey frowns, asking her mother, "Hmmm, I wonder how he knew a soup was in the offing?"

Then, Audrey mumbles to herself, *"I cannot believe you did that to yourself, Miss Audrey Sawyer; that guy was charming, friendly, and handsome. He was obviously interested in you, and you just ran off before he could make a direct approach."*

"Who, darling? What are you talking about?"

"Oh, it's nothing, Mom. I'm changing, and I've gotta run."

Her mom volunteers to get Audrey's coat cleaned. Audrey has dried her hair and face and has changed. Her mom carefully makes Audrey button up in one of her raincoats. They talk for a minute, and then Audrey is off, saying she has to get home for a Zoom/Teams late afternoon meeting.

The following day, Audrey's mom takes the damp clothes to her local dry cleaner as promised.

G<small>RAHAM AND</small> E<small>LISE</small> S<small>AWYER WERE EXCEPTIONALLY PROUD OF THEIR</small> daughter, Audrey. She was an unusual daughter; not quite a tomboy and not quite a debutante, but something perfectly in between.

Audrey was a geek who excelled in academics but was judged by the world for being too pretty for such an intelligent woman. Audrey hated the relationship between attractiveness, femininity, and intelligence, feeling that one could have all attributes without the fuss and muss of being thought of as an object of affection.

Audrey insisted that she be loved strictly for who she was. But, unfortunately, that was increasingly becoming a tall order.

Graham sits at the table as Elise serves him a colorful bowl of her famous boiled chicken soup. Graham waits for her to get a bowl, and together they dine and talk.

Elise begins, "You must thank your daughter when you see her; I could not have made the soup without her getting me a few ingredients I thought I had here."

"How is my little girl these days?" Graham asks.

Elise answers wryly, "She's not a little girl anymore. When she changed her drenched coat, let's put it this way; she has a stunning little figure and the cutest face. Even as her mother, I can see she's a knockout."

Graham gets up and kisses Elise on the side of her face. "What's that for?" Elise asks.

"Because you're my knockout, Mrs. Sawyer, every time I look at you, I wonder why you married a regular guy like me."

Elise blushes and responds, "Because not only are you dashing and handsome, you're kind. You have no idea how rare that is. Of course, anyone can do a kind thing, but not many people are kind as part of their nature. I adore your kindness, how you consider and treat me, and how I know you'll always be there for me and me for you. You're a perfect husband, Mister Sawyer."

Elise asks, "Do you think our daughter will find the happiness we've found with each other?"

"I don't know," Graham says. "That boy Ethan has been sweet on her since middle school, and he's a nice, good-looking boy who I think would be a great son-in-law, but Audrey ain't feeling him; I'm sure of that."

Elise responds, "I think she met someone today at the store; she seemed a little dazed today and kept talking to herself, mumbling about some guy she met, didn't meet, that made her heart flutter. I didn't want to push her, but I think cupid had his arrows out today, and one of them nicked our little girl. Poor Ethan may never have a chance now. Finish your soup, and let's look at our show in the family room."

Two

A FRIENDLY BATTLE OF THE SEXES

Early Spring:

After running errands, Audrey stops at a coffee shop in Bowie Town Center, Maryland. Two guys, Mateo and Ethan, and Audrey, are at a table in a robust conversation on the question of patriarchy v matriarchy. The two men are arguing that women have achieved full equality. At the same time, Audrey responds that while women control access to dating, sex, and relationships, men have ultimate control of marriage if a woman wishes for a husband. She argues that Sadie Hawkins may be appropriate for a high school dance, but women do not propose to men on bended knees with a sizable precious metal/jewelry ring.

The friendly argument continues, and Audrey's friends ask her why she's not married. They cite her beauty, femininity, and intelligence but disregard her because she rarely smiles or laughs.

Audrey responds that she would like to be married. Still, she cannot find the one quality she seeks that is more important than him being attractive, athletic, a stud, handsome with a full head of hair that dresses well and can get her the 'bag.'

Instead, she states she is looking for a kind man with a penchant for mutual consideration and willing to lead without being a dictator.

She further states that she seeks a man who will treat her as Christ treats the church. Finally, she looks at each of them one at a time and asks if they have ever met such a man. Mateo groans. "There she goes again with the God stuff," with polite sarcasm in his voice.

Sipping her coffee, she informs them that she did meet such a man a few months earlier during the Christmas season in a rural grocery store. She ignores Mateo and turns to Ethan, explaining his approach and her shock at his simple act of kindness that made her freeze and unable to respond.

Audrey says, "He was a nice looking man; I could tell he was interested, but I ran away before we could properly meet."

Mateo interjects, "What do you mean, properly meet? Why didn't you exchange contact information? Was it due to fear of being disappointed again?"

"Yes," Audrey answers. "My parents are worried that I'm heading for the life of a single, never married spinster. But, I think I will find the right guy. Take what happened a few weeks ago. I'm hopeful that when the time is right, the time will be right."

"Huh?" Mateo says.

"I believe in divine providence," Audrey explains. "I've lived a mostly charmed life; I'm sure God will grant my wish for the right guy. I have the patience, tenacity to wait, and hopefully, the vision and wisdom to recognize him when he shows up."

Ethan asks, "The grocery store guy, will you try to find him or someone who knows him? You know I've had a crush on you since junior high? You always blow me off. Are you sure you're not ignoring the man who's been right in front of you for years?"

Audrey rubs the back of Ethan's hand. "You're a family friend, a super buddy to me, you've protected me, and you're quite cute, but Ethan, you don't make my heart flutter. I'm not trying to be cruel. It's not wasted on me how much you care, and I hate keeping you in the friend zone, but that's all I can do."

Mateo speaks up brashly, "What about me; you dig me at all?"

"No, Mateo, I'm crazy about you," laughing, "you're my favorite male-chauvinist-pig/person."

Mateo grabs his chest. "I'm hurt. I love you too, Sister Audie of the Sacred Heart Abbey."

She responds, "So, back to my mystery man, no, I'm saying a guy like the one I saw at the market has got to be married; besides, his approach was not directly to me, but to the children I was watching while their mom or grandmother used the store's restroom. He was too good with the kids not to be married and a father; there's no way he was single. All the good men are taken."

Ethan chimed in, "Audrey, I've never known you to have an emotion about any man. Are you serious; have we, meaning you and me, do we have a chance to enjoy a romantic relationship? I'm deadly serious here, Audrey; what's keeping you from loving me? Your parents like me. I think I'd make a good husband and want you to be my wife."

Audrey asks, "Why do you want me to be your wife? Answer that for me; your answers will reveal the answer."

Ethan ponders her question. He looks to Mateo for help; Mateo quips, "Do you realize you just proposed to Audrey? Do you realize you just asked her to marry you? This may be your only shot to get her to say yes; make it good, my friend."

Ethan looks at Audrey. "You're beautiful; what man wouldn't want to be with you? You're sexy and pretty. You'd be a good mother; you're the woman I want to come home to every day because I would never betray you! You can count on me to provide for our family. I promise I will love you forever if you give me a chance."

Audrey takes his hands and says, "Those are all wonderful reasons that any woman would want and expect, but they miss the mark completely."

"Then tell me what the bulls-eye is," Ethan demands.

"That's just it, the bulls-eye is the key to any woman's heart, and if she has to tell you the combination to the lock, it is of no effect but a counterfeit to what should come naturally. That's what makes love so profound between couples; when two people hold the keys to the other's heart, they will know instantly. As crass as it may sound, it's the reason why people who are considered unattractive by others manage to find love. Something about their personality holds the key to love for the other person regardless of esthetics. That is why so many so-called beautiful people in cosmopolitan cities like New York and LA marry and divorce. Their love never makes the jump from infatuation, which is sometimes a prelude to love, to actual love. So, Ethan, while you want me to be with you, part of your primary desire is sexual, not romantic. Once you realize the difference between the two, you'll be ready for the love of your life. But know this one thing, Ethan, you may not find love because I sense there is more to you. I can't prove it, but you're closer than a friend to me; you, my friend, are my guardian angel. You just don't know it."

Ethan, disappointed, understands what Audrey is suggesting, and at someplace within him, he realizes that she is correct. Finally, Audrey seals the deal by slamming a kind yet intensive question over the intellectual net. It stuns him, and he cannot return the ball.

"Ethan, you're in your early 20s; now imagine me at fifty-nine. I've aged and I'm just coming out of menopause. I still look good, sort of MILF-like, but not like I am now. Can you still see you and me growing old together; you as a twenty-something, me as a fifty-something? Naturally, you can't see that now because your eyes, flesh, see me as your equal, hot and young. Is it possible for your heart to see me as I will be then? Nope, you can't. I'm saying that while our bodies may be equally yoked, our hearts are not. I am looking for the man whose heart loves my heart; the rest, including our bodies, will follow suit. That's the start of what I want in a man."

Ethan nods with deep respect for what she had said, and her honesty made him admire it even more, saying, "Well, when you find your mister right, I will be there to protect you and vet him as your guardian angel."

Mateo covers his eyes as if a flash-bang had gone off. "Holy smokes, Audrey, that was brutal. You left the poor boy with no hope. Ouch! That was merciless. What about me; what do you think of me?"

Audrey gives Mateo a slippery smile, saying, "You are the epitome of the playboy I see all the time but avoid. I trust you because, while nuts, you are one of the more honest men I have met. I trust the easy way you express yourself, and I glean a bit of truth about men from you, truths I need to protect my six. Guys are always trying to figure out how to get the un-gettable girl. Your antics make me aware of how far a man will go to snare his prize, notch his belt, and claim any new cherry he can. You, Mateo, taught me how to tell which men play the long game versus the short game to a woman's heart."

Audrey grabs both men by the arms as they prepare to leave the coffee shop. "But I love you both; you're two halves of a similar coin. Thanks for your advice about the grocery store boy; it's just what I needed to hear; a man's perspective."

Three

ETHAN OFF COURSE

Ethan had a single task when sent to ensure that Jonathan and Audrey kept their hearts aligned, just long enough for their natural courses to bring these two passing ships into the same port in the waters of love.

Clarence raced down the corridors leading to the council of elders. He burst into the chamber where he had not entered ten minutes ago in celestial time but was between fifteen and twenty years earth-time.

Clarence had watched his hand-picked protégé, but something strange happened on the road between puberty, adolescence, and young adulthood; Ethan began to develop romantic feelings for Audrey. Naturally, this was a strict no-no for all angels on assignment.

At first, Clarence wasn't sure of Ethan's understanding of his assignment or his failure by stripping Ethan of his awareness that he was a heavenly being with a specific job to perform. However, Ethan had begun to believe and act like a human, and even though he was in human form, he showed all the signs of developing an old-fashioned crush on Audrey while serving as her protector.

The success of having Audrey meet Jonathan while she was only five sowed her attachment in her heart that was to last a lifetime.

So, it was that Jonathan and Audrey became innocent, fast friends at eight and five, respectively; they only liked each other as schoolyard pals. Jonathan began to walk home with Audrey to protect her at first from Rodney-the-bully. Jonathan stayed by Audrey's side until they separated because he graduated from middle school. At the same time, she remained in elementary school for two more years.

And that became the problem; Ethan was handed the baton to continue protecting Audrey because they were the same age. Ethan and Audrey remained friends through high school; at that time, Audrey adored Ethan as a great friend, but Ethan demonstrated all the signs that he was falling in love with Audrey.

While a freshman in college, she met Mateo, an insanely crazy and funny guy friend who knew all the relationship ropes as a seasoned junior upper classmate.

One day, while at the Quad cafeteria, she shares her problem with Ethan's affection, making her increasingly uncomfortable, but she has no desire to hurt him since they have been friends for so long.

Mateo introduces Audrey to Lydia, who knows how to handle pleasant and unpleasant boys. Next, Lydia and Audrey meet in Audrey's private dorm room for advice on the 'Ethan' problem.

No one knows that Clarence has arranged to have Mateo make the introduction.

Audrey explains her dilemma over sandwiches and Mountain Dew. "Ethan and I have been buds since elementary school. He's great, kind of cute and nice, but I ain't feeling him like that. Ethan keeps hinting that he wants me to be his girlfriend; Ethan keeps saying he wants to marry me one day; it makes me uncomfortable. He's a sweet and serious guy who would never hurt me, but I don't see him as my man. What should I do, Lydia?"

Lydia takes a swig of her drink with a mouthful of food. "I got just the solution for you; you have to gently put him in the 'friend-zone'."

Audrey asks, "The what?"

Lydia sits straight up as if she is about to share nuclear launch codes. "The friend zone is a woman's best tool to keep a guy on a variable-length-leash. The nice thing about it is that you can shorten the leash or let it out to control how close a relationship you want with him. If you want to be wine-and-dined, you have to establish the friendship first with words, then take him out to dinner, and pay your half of the bill. Even if he tries to pay, don't let him. This attitude sends the unspoken signal that you do not want to be obligated, but every other part of your countenance at dinner is charming, elegant, and guiltless. He will enjoy your company so much that he will think there's hope of romance one day. So you have to play him like a fish; reel him in; let him out. Eventually, he will find his comfort level find a girlfriend, and once the two of them form a relationship, he will tell you, hoping you will become jealous. At this point, give him your best forehead kiss and congratulate him with a bright smile. Tell him how happy you are for him and how lucky she is. He will bond with the new girl and become a true friend only to you, keeping in the back of his mind that you will be with him one day. At this point, you will have a long-term friend who will do anything for you and, even when he gets married, will never forget your friendship. That, my dear Audrey, is the friend zone."

Lydia continues, "The second method that works is simple, won't cost you time or a meal, and will put him in the friend-zone within two to three weeks. It goes like this; while in the palsy-walsy mode, politely complain to him about one, two, or even three guys, like Alex, Joe, and Tom, who he may know, are hitting on you. Tell him how uncomfortable it makes you. Ask him earnestly why men can't just be friends with females. He will immediately cease to show romantic interest in you soon after that. Over the next few times he sees you, and you are looking good, on one of those occasions, he will take the chance to hint that he wants to be more than friends with you. When he does, tell him, '…stop joking; I know you're not like Alex, Joe, and Tom.' He will recoil like he's been caught and bitten by a snake. At this point, because of his pride, he will never hit on you again. And if all that doesn't work, there's the ice-cold friendship. What you do is never smile in his presence; men hate that. Never laugh at his jokes and never, never, never ask how his day was or show excitement about anything he wants to share with you. Never encourage him but tell him he's a good friend once a week, plus or minus a day. His pride will eventually make him lose hope, and ultimately, he will realize the only reason he liked you in the first place was your beauty or his desire to have sex. All men are simple and easily programmed if you know the code that manipulates them. They all want the same thing. Some will take the long road; others will become frustrated early and leave you alone. As soon as another woman he wants shows the slightest interest, you are history until they get the urge to rekindle the flame that never existed in the first place."

Audrey looks disgusted and troubled. "That's horrible! I would never want someone to do that to me. It's so mean and deceitful. But, I will tell him how I feel; I will be honest. I don't play games, especially with people's emotions. If that doesn't work, I won't see him again."

Lydia looks at Audrey, considering the following suggestion in the arsenal. "You may not ever need this one, but if there's the guy you meet; he looks good, and you want to give him a little taste; maybe once or twice, and then friend him, do this…."

Audrey interrupts, asking, "What? A little taste; what are you talking about? A little taste of what?"

Lydia laughs. "Honey, you are a bona fide antique. A booty call, sex, getting your rocks off, getting laid, a hook-up. Please don't tell me you're a virgin; that's crazy in the twenty-first century. Are you?"

Audrey speaks imperiously, "Yes, but not for any reason you could conceive. Yes, I was raised Christian, but sex was always going to be my choice. Most people don't realize that for every person they have sex with, they carry the spirit of those partners into the next relationship. Depending on the body count of the so-called lovers, there are hundreds of ghosts in the sack with the two in-the-present lovers. Yikes, I don't want that. I'd rather wait to meet 'the' guy who is waiting to meet 'the' girl, and if we are compatible, imagine what the Irish used to call 'first-night' will be like. I think it's worth waiting for."

Lydia responds, "Suppose you don't meet Mr. Right; you marry and divorce several times; what is the ghost count like then? Audrey, you're way too old-fashioned, and you're gonna die alone with that attitude. You're going to miss out on all the fun of having many men appreciate your goodies; your beauty, your sexuality, is that what you want?"

"I just don't want the heartache of thinking about my past lovers when I'm with my husband; ghosts of past lovers can be a terrible thing to endure. I know several men and women who wished they had been more conservative with the cookies. If I die a virgin, I can live with that; nuns and priests have been doing it for centuries."

Lydia smirks. "Okay, I hope it works out for you, but I suspect you will endure a lifetime of feeling, then ignoring this guy's longing for you. If you can handle that, it's your play."

Audrey asks Ethan to meet her at their favorite burger joint the next day. She pays for his meal and, after eating, takes both his hands and says, "Ethan, my friend of friends, the boy-now-man who protected me all these years, I must now have a very difficult-for-me conversation about you and me. Are you up for a serious conversation? I need to speak my heart, and what I may say may hurt you. Will you let me tell you what's been on my mind?"

Ethan nods 'yes.' He continues, "I know what you want to say; I do. You want to tell me that you know I have feelings for you, but they are not reciprocal. You want to say that you do not want to jeopardize our relationship and that you're not in the market for a boyfriend or significant other now. Am I right?"

Audrey is straightforward. "You're a Godsend and a very nice person, but I have no romantic interest in you or anyone else. If you harbor hopes that we will become a couple other than friends, I need you to abandon those thoughts. Can you do that for me?"

Ethan never knew that he has skewed from the course set for him and that his mission as friend and protector of Audrey has been surreptitiously restored.

He stays a true friend in the noblest sense of the word until the day he meets Mateo and Audrey at a coffee shop. He learns during that meeting that for the first time in her life, Audrey met a man at a tiny grocery store that made her heart flutter with feelings of love and desire.

Ethan's old feelings of longing for Audrey return in a deluge of awkward emotions to hear his buddy of more than a decade talk of love and heart and emotions for the first time. And even though she did not know, speak, or care for the man and the feelings he generated in her, she said that his simple act of kindness overwhelmed her, and she hoped never to find this mystery man who had the potential to bind her heart for her good and his.

Ethan festers in pain, and the nearly hateful jealousy instantly tormented him with the possibility that his hidden love would be lost forever.

Four

KINDERGARTEN RADISHES

Seventeen Years Earlier:
Audrey Is Nearly Six Years Old And In Kindergarten
Whitehall Elementary School – Bowie, Md

Miss Job, a kindergarten teacher, has taken her class to the school's garden patch, where each student planted three red radish seeds six weeks ago.

The garden has rows for each grade and each class in the grade. A 2nd grader is in a row several yards from the kindergarten row. About 7 or 8, a young boy is weeding his single cherry tomato plant. He is about to leave when he sees the kindergarteners march down their row like penguins. He notices a young girl whose demeanor is one of purpose and self-assurance. She notices him noticing her and offers a kind yet petite and hardly noticeable wave of 'hello.'

Miss Job tells the children that they will pull up the radishes each student planted, brush off the dirt, and explain how food is grown and that what they pull up is the freshest food they will ever eat in their entire life.

Each row has placards with each student's name.

Each student gently pulls up their green carrot-like sprouts to expose not carrots, but three clustered radishes. In turn, each eats their radishes. Suddenly, class bully, Rodney, whom some know by his middle name, Ronald, grabs Audrey's radishes, eats one, and throws the other two into the wooded area outside the garden patch.

Audrey is stunned, angry, and close to punching Ronald just as Miss Job grabs Ronald, shouting at him, separating him from the other students.

The second-grader sees what has happened and approaches the bully-jerk with anger. He considers the heartbroken young girl and asks his brother Harry to share one of his radishes with her in her kindergarten class. He takes the radish from his younger brother and gives it to the young girl. She wipes her defiant tears and bites into the radish. A distinct crunch and she smiles joyfully, thanking Harry, her classmate, and his older brother, whose name she does not know.

Miss Job is incredibly proud of Harry and his brother. She announces to the class, holding Harry and his brother close to her, "You've all learned how to grow and benefit from the food you created, but more importantly, you've witnessed a simple act of kindness by Harry's brother and Harry." Miss Job interrupts herself, "Young man, what is your name?" Harry's brother, not wanting attention, makes up a name on the spot. "I'm Kenny."

Miss Job continues to the class, "Boys and girls, carry this lesson in your heart; remember, a simple act of kindness will serve you well for a lifetime.

The children march back into the school, and all is silent in the garden until Jonathan notices Ronald-the-bully waving an angry fist at the young girl. She is concerned about the danger because no one else has caught his threats.

After school, the various students in destination orders are lined up to board the dozen school buses waiting in the school's parking lot. Ronald gets behind the young girl. "You just wait; you got me in trouble, and you're going home with a bloody nose today."

The young girl turns to Ronald, shouting, "You will be the one with a bloody nose. Now leave me alone."

A SIMPLE ACT OF KINDNESS

On the school bus, Ronald shoves the young girl to the back of the bus out of view of the driver. Just as he raises his hand to hit her, a firm hand grabs Ronald's hand in mid-slap. "Touch her, and it will be the last thing you touch. The young boy kicks Ronald in the shin, demanding, "You go up front and sit by the driver; if I see you near her ever again, it will be the last thing you see. You got me?"

Ronald fearfully nods 'yes,' grateful to have escaped the situation. The young boy sits beside the little girl, wordlessly holding her hand in a protective arc. Finally, he says, "I will make sure you get home every day safely."

She asks, "Why?"

He responds, "Because you and I are not friends. I don't like girls as friends, but I hate bullies; I can't let that guy hurt you. So I will protect you as long as you want me to."

The bus stops a block from her home. She rises to exit the bus. He watches her through the window as the bus pulls off. He notices her looking around with caution. The young boy asks the driver to stop. The driver says, "But Jon, your house is two stops away; that is a bit of a walk."

The driver stops, and Jon gets off and jogs back to the little girl, grabbing her book bag. "Let me take that for you. I don't trust that Ronald guy; I'll walk you to your front door from now on."

The little girl blushes and smiles a 'thank you, Kenny.'

Just as Jonathan walks the extra blocks back to his house, Harry's bus is just arriving. "What are you doing walking home, Big Bro?"

"I didn't like the looks of that guy; I thought he might go after her; I couldn't let that happen. By the way, I don't want people to think I'm some hero; I told her my name is Kenny; keep my secret, and don't you dare tell Mom or Dad that I almost got into a fight over some little girl. They will never let me hear the end of it."

"You got it, Big Bro. Did you know that another girl, Clair, likes you? Jonathan chuckles, "yeah, right, she's too weird, always staring at me." Harry responds, "I dunno, big bro, she's kinda cute to me." To which Jonathan says, "Okay then, take her, she's yours."

Neither Harry nor Jonathan know that this conversation and the events of that day would affect the rest of their lives in a way they could never imagine. And so it is that Harry's big brother, Jonathan, walks Audrey to her door every day. Even after he graduates elementary-to-middle school, he makes it his business to check on her safety every day, asking former schoolmates about her. Then, early in the next school year, Ethan takes the baton and begins walking with Audrey.

During those elementary school days, Jonathan and Audrey never say much, but those who watch them can tell they like each other. As she approaches home, her father is there, proudly snapping photographs of his daughter with the first boy she has ever shown an interest in.

After Audrey graduates top of her class at Whitehall Elementary, her family moves, and to his lament, Jonathan, her protector, never sees or hears anything about Audrey ever again. And while Jonathan has never known, Clair keeps a secret eye on both Harry and Jonathan, and those who know Clair can't tell which of the brothers she has the more enormous crush on.

Five

NO THANKS; I'M NOT INTERESTED, BUT I SHOULD HAVE BEEN

Present-Day:

Audrey cannot forget the man she calls John Doe Christmas just passed, and she decides on her regular Sunday morning drive to A.A. County Farmer's Market. This exhilarating experience always clears her head. She's been coming here for years and knows most of the vendors by their first names.

Audrey is a farm-to-table minimally processed food nut. She is strict about not consuming anything GMO or treated with pesticides.

Moving through the rows of vendors with names like Good Luck Farm, Bowens, Egg Barn, and others, she fills her reusable Trader Joe bags with eggs, kale, scones, and assorted seafood. Then, saving the best for last, she stops at the crab truck run by a mother and son duo. The mom, Aileen, greets her. "Audrey, I thought you'd be here today and saved you a half dozen number ones."

Audrey shoots Aileen a 'thank you' smile, hoping to avoid her friendly push to find Audrey a boyfriend; today would be no different. "Audrey, honey, I've got a customer who'd be perfect for you. You're a pretty girl; you should have a boyfriend. He's one of my regular customers; the fact is he will probably be here soon. Do you want to meet him? He's really good-looking and nice."

"Aileen, I keep telling you, modern men are not for me. I want a nice man who's not self-centered, someone kind and thoughtful. Unfortunately, those men are already taken or married. So, unfortunately, those decent men just don't exist anywhere. They're all caught up in their careers, sports, harems of women, and all the nookie they can get; that's not for me; I'm too old-fashioned. But thanks for the crabs."

"Audrey, I've told him about you, and he doesn't want to meet you for all the same reasons. Doesn't that mean you two would be perfect for each other? He's really a good catch. So, when I see him today, I'm gonna try to convince him to at least meet you."

Audrey waves a nonchalant 'goodbye' to Aileen, exiting with her haul of farm stand goodies back to her Crofton townhome at Beazer Homes Riverwalk.

STILL TIRED FROM A LONG SATURDAY, JONATHAN FALLS INTO HIS COUCH that evening with the television on and doesn't wake until Sunday morning. He listens to a voicemail and returns Chuck's call.

Chuck asks him if he's still thinking about the sock girl. They talk about the serendipity of the situation, but Chuck says, "I don't know, man, I know she was special, but you might have to move on. But you'll be the first to know if I ever spot her. I'm heading up your way this morning to the farmer's market. Do you want to grab a coffee?"

Seated in a booth at the IHOP in Edgewater, Jonathan asks a question he knows he cannot ask. "Do you think I'm crazy for hoping against hope to meet this one in a million girl?"

Chuck answers briefly, "I've only seen her that one time you saw her; I will give it to you, she's gorgeous, but there are lots of pretty women out there. What's so special about this one?"

Jonathan, sipping his coffee, says, "I see beautiful women all the time too, but it was like my whole being was shaken seeing her. It was like the image of her was already in my heart as its missing piece. It wasn't sexual but something much more. If I believed in reincarnation, I could swear she was someone I loved from a past life. I never felt anything like that before; I've got to find her and settle this phenomenon if I am to move on." He says with trepidation, "I almost hate to go to the farmers market with you. One of my favorite vendors, Aileen, is a crab and seafood seller; she keeps trying to hook me up with one of her customers. Aileen says we're perfect for each other. I don't want to even think about the woman she has in mind for me. But let me man up; let's go get your stuff."

Driving into the parking area, Jonathan sees there is not a single space available. Suddenly he sees the backup light of an SUV exiting a prime spot in the next lane. Nearly peeling rubber, Jonathan just makes it to the now empty parking space as another driver had been trolling for the exact location. Jonathan feels a sensation of tingling he has not felt since seeing the sock girl in Graul's.

Jonathan does not know that he has just parked in the spot where the woman he has been searching for has just exited the market.

Chuck grabs various produce items before making his last stop for striped bass. Now at the seafood truck, Aileen comes out of the back where she has been sorting crabs by size. Seeing Jonathan, she hugs him, saying, "Jonathan, Charles, you two almost never come here together. How are my two favorite adopted sons doing? What can I get you today?"

Aileen ducks inside the truck, returning with Chuck's sixteen-inch rockfish and half a dozen jumbo crabs for Jonathan. While she wraps and bags their orders, she speaks to Jonathan without looking at him. "Jonathan, I know you're making crab soup today, but you're a fool and stubborn. The woman I've wanted you to meet was just here; you took her parking space as she left. You'll never find a girl like this, but I ain't mad at you. I asked her for the last year or so if she wanted to meet you and she gave me the same silly answer you gave me; *'you're both waiting for a special someone whom you don't know.'* She says modern men ain't bleep, and you say you can't stand modern women; you two should be perfect for each other. I give up playing matchmaker. She's the best you'll ever find, and you're the best she'll ever find, but neither one of you wants to meet." Frustrated, Aileen says, "I don't get it."

The next few months seemed to fly by. Clarence was frustrated with dozens of near-misses between Audrey and Jonathan. Clarence was especially hopeful about utilizing Aileen at the farmer's market, but Audrey and Jonathan seemed happy going about their lives.

Audrey is engrossed in her job and hobbies, including hiking, photography, droning, and swimming. Unfortunately, she can't bring herself to include working out at the local health club since hobbies were to be enjoyed, and she insists that exercise is not enjoyable.

Audrey is careful not to overdo it or use too much weight at the club as she works the circuit. She stays away from free weights as if they are Kryptonite. Finally, one of the trainers, Patty, asks her, "Audrey, you could work more intensely and become a hard-body."

Audrey responds with an answer that the trainer finds reasonable, but for some reason, she also finds Audrey's response offensive. "Patty, I prefer a soft firmness to my body, muscles, and overall physique. When a woman works out too hard, she becomes 'cut.' I don't want to have a man's musculature; I prefer a woman's softness."

Not wanting to offend a client, Patty rebuts by saying, "Are you saying that I look like a man?"

Audrey is still working out on the recumbent bike, saying, "Of course not. A man's body is hewn with mildly defined muscles to perform the necessary duties of a man. A woman is necessarily softer, nurturing, and is the weaker, strength-wise vessel. I believe the man that I would want would appreciate his wife being more on the feminine side. Patty, you're oozing with femininity, but your occupation requires you to demonstrate the strength of someone more powerful, muscle-wise, than me.

"Your husband adores you the way you are. That is all that matters. I believe a degree of female body fat is most desirable to the average man. But in reality, to each their own."

A SIMPLE ACT OF KINDNESS

Patty accepts Audrey's answer, but she still feels deeply offended at some level she could not define, causing her to feel self-conscious around other traditional women who frequent the club. She likes Audrey but could not explain her awkward envy of Audrey's goddess-like body.

Because Jonathan and Audrey have never used the same health club, Clarence dismissed the idea of a chance meeting while exercising. Clarence tried to scheme, but he, not being earthbound, there was little an angel-first-class could do directly beyond injecting an idea into a subject's mind.

Clarence sought the advice of counsel and was instructed to wait-and-see, to give fate a chance to get these two together. And so, free will was restored to Jonathan and Audrey. Clarence defiantly shouted into the nothingness of the cosmos, "Audrey, he's looking for you; Jonathan, she's looking for you." On earth, both Jonathan and Audrey think they heard *'something'* but quickly dismiss the sound from heaven as a fluke.

Now home, Jonathan prepares a new batch of his famous crab soup while watching a Netflix K-Drama on the kitchen television.

His soup ready, Jonathan prepares a take-out bowl for tomorrow's work lunch and eats a hearty meal for tonight's dinner with a Mountain Dew chaser.

And as usual, Jonathan meanders to the corner of the great room, pulling out the seat to his Yamaha Baby Grand piano. But before sitting down, he glances at the Korg electronic keyboard; he is torn between the two, eventually straddling the grand piano, playing an old REO tune, *I Can't Fight This Feeling Anymore*.

Audrey steams two ears of corn at her home, inserts corn stickers in each end, settles into her favorite chair, and eats the butter-slathered maze while watching a K-Drama on her beloved Viki network.

After an episode, Audrey secretly loves her singing voice. However, she had never heard her voice until her seventh-grade teacher asked her to sing in a school play. Audrey, terrified and shy, refused. Finally, her father encouraged her by asking her to sing a pop tune with him.

Her dad recorded it, and when she heard her voice on the recorder, she was stunned and pleased.

Her father explained that no one likes their voice because they do not hear the voice internally the way others listen to it externally. She smiled and, forever after, had confidence in her voice. Audrey eventually sought a voice coach's tutelage as a college freshman.

Tonight as often happens during the morning shower, she sings to herself. Tonight she chooses *"All By Myself"* with a sing-a-long karaoke CD. The song is sad and haunting; she wishes she had a significant other who unconditionally loved her.

That night, both go to bed, wondering what voices or noise they heard from the cosmos. Then, falling near to sleep, Audrey whispers, "Was that him, I wonder?"

Jonathan falls asleep with the television still on, the sleep timer set to thirty minutes, after performing his nightly hygiene, crashing peacefully with the last thing he said to the universe, "Was that her, I wonder?"

A voice neither Audrey nor Jonathan know shouts in a whisper back to them simultaneously, "YES!" Neither understands it is the sound of a frustrated angel, Clarence.

Six

A MOTHER'S ADVICE TO HER SON & MORE...

One Year Later:

Jonathan had frequented the store where he first spotted his dream girl several times in the passing years, but never on the day when the manager, Chuck, was on shift. Finally, after a year or so, Jonathan sees his friend, Chuck, who informs him that a year ago, the woman he had been looking for based on his description was there on the same day and nearly the same time that he, Jonathan was there. Chuck says, "…Ships passing in the night, huh?" with shrugged shoulders, stating a silent *'que sera'*. He continues, "…But she was something to look at, an unmistakable quiet type of beauty. Unfortunately, I couldn't call you because my phone died, taking all my contacts with it. Sorry, my man."

Home Of Jonathan's Parents, Franklin & Allison Dawson: Davidsonville, Maryland

Jonathan Dawson parks his luxury pickup in the home's driveway where he grew up during his teenage years. It is a beautiful day, and his mother, Allison, is watering a fantastic array of shrubs, flowers, and greenery in her house-side gardens.

Jonathan approaches her, leaning down to kiss her cheek as he is much taller than her. She squirts him with water as he tries to evade. Now seated on the porch, his mom brings him a sparkling water, saying, "I always keep one for you as I never know when you will drop by."

Allison studies her son's face, then asks, "What's bothering my oh-so-serious son; you look a bit stressed?"

Jonathan relaxes in one of the comfortable porch chairs. "Mom, how did you and dad know each was the only one for you for a lifetime?"

Allison smiles. "I wondered when you'd ask me that. Your dad said he always knew from the moment he met me. Me? I didn't like him, but the more I got to know him, his character, even to this day, won my heart to him. You see, son, he was, is, handsome and all the things girls want, but his character…"

"What do you mean, character?" Jonathan frowns. "Are you saying he was a character, an odd fellow?"

His mom sees her son's trouble explaining. "Yes and no. What I mean is that in college, guys were always hitting on me with one goal in mind. Some guys tried for a few weeks and gave up; some took the long approach, waiting months to see if I would. It's not that I was so good, but I wanted a man who wanted me for the real woman I was, not my-then smokin'-hot-body. So yes, my son, your mom was very desirable, and I learned to keep all those potential suitors in what they now call the friend zone. Back then, we called it 'keeping the boys at bay'."

She laughs while Jonathan blushes. She continues, "Your dad had game, but he was a gentleman. He allowed me to get to know him, feel comfortable and was insanely honest. There was never a question I could ask him that he would not answer. So, eventually, I trusted him with my heart and body, and then we got engaged and married, creating you, Harry, and your sister, Willow. If you ask me, I'm the lucky one; I wasn't sure then, but I made a great choice of the person to share my life with. Anyway, after you and Harry were born, I decided to stay home because I wanted to raise you. So when you were eight, and your brother entered first grade, I went back to work, picking up my career right where I left it. Your dad and I worked together, paid off this house in seventeen years, put you guys through school, and now enjoy empty-nesting while we still have careers. We work because we want to, not because we have to. All these questions lead me to suspect that you, my son, are thinking about settling down. Have you found someone? Tell me."

Jonathan looks at his mother and slowly turns away, unable to confess his feeling. "Mom, a year or so ago, I almost met a girl down at Graul's one day. I don't know what happened, but just the sight of her and her demeanor swept my emotions to a place I've never been. I dismissed the feelings because I thought she was married with three kids, and then I found out later that she was single. I've searched everywhere, even with Chuck at the store, and no one has seen her. The problem is that I meet wonderful women at work while I'm droning, at professional events, and the occasional time at the bar with friends after work. I've even attended a few churches, hoping to find the right girl, but I can't move past the feeling I instantaneously had when I met this crazy wonderful girl with the crazy socks."

Allison interrupts, "Socks?"

Jonathan ignores her interruption. "That, my dear mother, is another story. So, what should I do? I feel I can't move forward, and I can't time-travel backward to meet her again. What should I do? I'm serious. Mom, I'm a mess; I can't get this girl out of my head or heart. I think about her all the time. I'm afraid to commit to so many nice girls. There's this girl at work, Clair, who's crazy about me. People call her my work-wife, and she's a really great catch. What if I do, and then I discovered my sock girl when I'm already in a relationship with Clair, married, and have a family? That would kill me, Mom; I've got to meet her again; just once, that's all I need, and then I can move on with my life."

Allison Dawson sips her coffee and ponders her son's question for a minute. Then, she looks at him, pauses, and touches both his hands.

"Son, I'm sorry that you have inherited your father's curse, and I am broken-hearted for you and the girl. Your father denied himself from the moment he met me. I could feel his love whenever he looked at me, and the look wasn't sexual desire; it was a genuine feeling of love, as one could imagine. It was a burning, searing love that made me uncomfortable. I wanted to be liked, maybe even loved by guys, but I did not want a guy to be in love with me. At first, I felt suffocated, and I friend-zoned him, fixing your dad up with my friend. They became close; he gave up on me and eventually lost all hope of me accepting him and proposed to her. My friend asked me to be her maid of honor because I had introduced him to her. I accepted initially, feeling that I had dispatched him to a good girl whom I knew would be a fantastic wife. They were happy as we helped plan the wedding together, but then a funny thing happened on the way to the forum; I had a dream that I was godmother to their firstborn, and in that dream, I saw their whole life ahead; it was enviable. But I also saw or felt the sadness in his heart that he was to spend his life with an alternate choice for the woman he loved."

She continues, "I saw my life at 37 having lived the way I thought I wanted to live in rebellion to my upbringing, having a dozen hot-girl-summers behind me and a body count that I am too ashamed to believe I thought wished to be that reckless young woman. I was about to throw away my future to my friend, what God had presented to me, all for something that had no value beyond the moment. Son, some days when I'm alone, I cry to God for sparing me the life I thought I wanted. A while ago, Garth Brooks did a song called '*Thank God for Unanswered Prayers*'; I thank God nearly in tears every day for not answering my prayer to remove your dad from my life. Some years have been tough, but I wouldn't trade what your dad and I have together. I'll go so far as to say I'd like us to die at the same time and date because I don't believe either of us wants to live without the other."

Jonathan is moved by hearing his mother's confession of her almost mistake for the first time. He replies, "So, what are you saying I should do? And how did you get dad back? Did you break your girlfriend's heart? And, where is wandering Willow these days?"

A SIMPLE ACT OF KINDNESS

Allison responds guiltlessly, "To the last question; we don't know what Willow is doing. Every now and then we get a postcard; we gave up; she's too stubborn, so we had to let her do her thing after she graduated from university. I'm sure she's okay; she just has to find her purpose in life. To your first question about my best friend, the short answer is yes, I broke her heart, and your father rejected me for playing games with all our lives. I thought he hated me, and he did. Still, we saw each other a year later, and the look in my eyes and the way he hugged me said it all, and today he credits me with having the courage to put our destination lives, the lives we were supposed to live, back on track for without which we would not have you and your siblings. My girlfriend; I went to her the night of the rehearsal, grabbed your dad, and told them both that I had made a mistake in getting rid of him, hoping to stick him with her because she was such a good person. I felt that their love would grow but that my soul would wither like a weed if I didn't at least tell them. They both cursed at me; she grabbed his hand and pulled him away, saying they were getting married the next day and that I was not invited. He pulled away from her, 'I hate you for this. I can't marry her now, and you sicken me,' and he stormed out of the church, and she never saw him again, and I saw him almost a year later, and by a miraculous act of God, here we, and you, and your siblings are. So with this girl, you might have heart-love for, give yourself some time, and try to find her. God will assist you if she's the one. And if after a reasonable time to be determined by you, thank God for the unanswered prayer and go live your life. Perhaps Clair is the girl you're supposed to be with. Maybe you can't feel Clair's love for you because you're preoccupied with the sock girl, but on the other hand, love is indelible when it writes on one's heart. True love is always better than ordinary love. Give it some time; remember son, Que Será, Será (*Whatever Will Be, Will Be*)."

Seven

ARE WE FRIENDS OR DATING? GOING IT ALONE

While working, Jonathan looks up from his desk, feeling lonely even more after talking to his mother. He thinks about the thousands of female coworkers in his division, many of whom have shown an interest in him. He dismissed them all after talking to the old-timers.

At a lunch-&-learn internal get-together on cloud security, the subject amongst the married men brings up the issue of the prospects at work.

Raymond carries the conversation, "Just don't do it. There are thousands of single, married, separated, and divorced women here. Most are very nice, but a workplace relationship can go south in a nanosecond. You have a disagreement offsite, and it can quickly become an embarrassing work problem, and you will have no defense if she decides to lower the boom to keep you in line. Worse, she can cost you your job if she can prove you harassed her."

Nathan jumps in, "What used to flatter women can be deemed a respectful approach by one woman and harassment by another. So leave your emotions at the door and keep it strictly business around here."

Charlene adds, "I wish it weren't true, but I've seen and heard of disasters with work-wives and work-husband scenarios. After the loving is over, I'm telling you that all bets are off, and everybody loses. Disciplinary actions are severe and permanent on your record. I'm a woman, and I hate saying this, but guys around here would be wise not to even compliment a woman on her outfit, shoes, hair, or anything; doing so could wind you up in personnel, I've seen it. And sometimes a guy will indeed come on strong, but that's rare. So please take my advice and do your fishing in different waters."

Raymond and Charlene add, "Are you aware that folks around here think of you and Clair Hansley as a work couple?"

Raymond goes further, saying, "Clair is no fox, but she is definitely wife material. No man would ever mind waking up to her every morning. She's sweet, kind, attractive, and smart. If she dressed a little better and did her hair, she'd be irresistible."

Charlene interrupts angrily, "Now that's just like a man. What do her hair and clothing have to do with anything?"

Derrick joins the group, saying, "Charlene, men are visual; they see first. If the package looks good to them, then it's on. I saw Clair at the company beach party last year; she has a smokin' hot body to die for, and with no makeup, she's pretty, but around here, she wears those drab-looking church clothes; no one will notice the beauty she is."

Charlene fires back, "Are you saying she has to dress like a 304 to get noticed?"

Raymond says, "Nope, but even business casual would be an improvement. No one knew Cinderella was beautiful until she dressed for the ball; then, she caught the eye and the prince and became the queen. Notice I said 'caught the 'eye.' That's the point. And a woman does not have to meet the so-called European standard of beauty, because beauty is truly in the eye of the beholder."

Charlene turns to Jonathan, further advising him, "Derrick is right; Clair would be a great wife, mother, and lover, but if anything goes wrong while you're dating, you'll regret it. So take my advice, be her friend but keep her your friend-girl until one of you is no longer working here."

Jonathan absorbs all the advice, asking, "So, where do you find a single unattached woman who is approachable?"

Eric chimes in, "No bars, clubs, or local watering holes. Try upscale gyms near-professional enclaves. The church is always good, especially medium to large churches with robust singles ministries; there are a few good dating apps but stay away from the 'hook-up' sites; they are just for folk looking to get laid or a casual booty call. Some are hoping that call will convert to a long-term relationship. It rarely does. Then there are places like upscale coffee shops where singles go to read, talk, and gossip; bowling leagues, celebrations, and friendly concerts. Even a zoo can be a place to attract and find someone of interest. Going with a workgroup to an upscale bar and restaurant always attracts after-work happy hour singles looking to meet someone nice. Other than those places, you'll have to depend on dumb luck and happenstance."

Over the next seven weeks, Jonathan attends all but the zoo and meets three very nice ladies he begins to see casually.

He meets Victoria at Coffee Café at their usual Thursday night jazz concert. It is a popular place with lots of atmosphere and women in lovely dresses and men wearing expensive suits from the local K Street and Connecticut Ave lobbyist crowd.

Victoria is elegant and high-powered. She tosses Jonathan a look that let him know she is interested, but he becomes disenchanted as a coworker of hers greets her. "Hi, Vicky."

She replies curtly with a smile. "I prefer to be called Victoria," dismissing him with a petite wave. Still, she is refined, pretty, and sophisticated.

They go out a few times, and he thinks she likes him, but all she talks about is her career, cachet, and track she is on to reach her dreams. She never asks a single question about Jonathan, and he soon finds that while she is attractive, the effort to have an equitable relationship is too much for him.

Victoria is great on his arm, and the guys are stunned everywhere she goes. She appreciates that Jonathan drives a King Ranch luxury truck, but when he arrives at her condo to take her to a Kennedy Center concert, she asks, "Are we going in that? No darling, we'll take my Lexus." She never realizes his truck cost more than her Lexus; she only saw it as a truck.

Victoria is sexy, and any guy would love to be with her that way, but she isn't committing to any long-term relationship. Perhaps Jonathan is wrong, but he senses she is more into casual intimacy with a clean break looming in an uncertain future. He wasn't raised that way, and they just amiably drifted away, never to date again.

Jonathan also meets Claudia nearly the same time he meets Victoria. She is an unusual woman in that she doesn't talk much, but it is always something profound when she does.

Once, they take a tour of the Baltimore Aquarium to see the Human Body exhibit. She marvels with child-like joy seeing the beautiful display of human anatomy. However, she remarks when she sees how the brain is protected, "Man is so stupid. Considering everything God had done to protect the brain, we humans call boxing a sport where the winner causes a concussion. How long will humankind consider the gladiatorial game a source of entertainment? The sport is barbaric and counters the creator's extraordinary attempts to protect that individual organ from damage." She shakes her head in disgust, and Jonathan is amazed as she saw something that few neither saw nor understood.

The exhibit of the muscular two ice skaters stuns her. She comments, "Now that gives me a new appreciation for the Olympics. Consider what it must take to train every muscle in one's body to perform that maneuver; magnificent."

He comes to appreciate Claudia's intellect and appreciation of the ordinary. He finds her wise, engaging, and brilliant, but she cannot emotionally connect to anything or anyone. She is pleased with herself and has every right to appreciate her own abilities but is wholly unable to see beyond her considerable wisdom. Jonathan finds her to be intellectually narcissistic.

Jonathan tries to hold her hand once; her reflex makes it clear that touching of any kind is not allowed. Claudia puzzles him because she is generous in terms of calling to wish him a good day. In addition,

A SIMPLE ACT OF KINDNESS

Claudia would text friendly little emojis, showing that she is thinking of him. Jonathan wants to become closer to her and asks her hypothetically whether she could see herself being with him as his girlfriend or significant other. She replies, "Certainly not. You would make a wonderful occasional man I'd like to see, but you're not interesting enough to commit to a relationship with. Obviously, you make great money and have had a good upbringing, but Jonathan, not to hurt your feelings, you're boring."

That shot across his ego's bow is enough; he never sees her again and blocks her contact information from his phone. He is mentally exhausted after trying to work his way into her life.

Jonathan finds himself thinking once again about the girl with the socks.

He lays in bed at night trying to remember her face; he can't. He generally remembers what she looked like, but he can no longer pick her out of a police lineup. Instead, he sees her height, weight, hair, camel cashmere coat, and beautiful legs wrapped in those colorful sock-like stockings in his mind's eye.

He begs his brain to remember her face, but after years, the image of her face is lost to the oblivion of faded memories.

The only memorable feature he remembers about her is that stoic smile and his heart going crazy, saying this girl is the one. How is he to find her? He thinks of his heart as a Geiger counter and her heart as a particular isotope of plutonium.

Jonathan aches to see her again. He even went to Graul's every Christmas on the chance she would be there, but year after year, he disappointed himself. He never paid much attention to the lyrics of *Every Year, Every Christmas* by Luther Vandross until he began this merry-go-round of looking for his seen-then-lost-love.

While Jonathan is pining for his sock girl, Audrey experiences a different type of courtship game, for in most instances, she is the prey, and men are the pursuers. Virtually no men she met, even when she wasn't looking, found her and came with a myriad of come-ons, most designed to get her in the sack.

The only emotion that can touch her heart is genuine kindness, the type she saw with the man in the grocery store; the guy that didn't try to come on to her and hit on her but was respectful and kind.

Audrey thinks she might be in league with this middle-aged guy she sees at the dry cleaners. She tells the clerk that the blouse is not hers, but all the other pieces are correct. The clerk examining the computer-generated label insists that the blouse belongs to her. The gentleman steps to the front of the pickup line, saying to the clerk, "Let me see the tag for the blouse and one of the articles from her clothing."

Taking out his phone, he opens an app and scans both articles of clothing. "Ah-hah, while the numbers are the same, the barcodes are different. Here, look," he says to the clerk. "This blouse belongs to the grouping with this number."

The manager verifies it, thanking the man and apologizing to Audrey.

The middle age man steps back to his place in line. Audrey waits outside to thank him. "Sir, I appreciate your help. How did you know?"

The man says, "I'm Walter; I am a programmer and specialize in bar and QR codes. Often the code and the numbers are buffered and don't print simultaneously. A checksum should be added to the software they are using. It's probably homegrown software that has not been *IV&V'd* (independently verified & validated) like commercial software."

Audrey says, "Can I buy you a cup of coffee to thank you properly?"

Sitting in a nearby Starbucks, one cannot but notice that Audrey is half the age of her benefactor. He does not look old and is quite distinguished but is closer in age to Graham Sawyer, Audrey's father. Walter seems genuinely interested in her, but the age difference is more than Audrey can overcome. Yet, strangely, Walter's kindness touches her and makes her think of the grocery store guy.

Audrey and Walter talk about computers and current events at the small table. They are genuinely enjoying each other's company.

The conversation becomes difficult as several customers stop by the table, saying some version of, "You and your daughter look great; you must be so proud."

Walter says, "I wish I were young enough to date you; you're amazing."

Audrey thanks him for his help at the dry cleaners. They depart, shake hands, and never see each other again.

Walter looks back at her, pained by the age difference. "Life is so unfair."

As Audrey drives away, she says aloud, "So, there are still perfect gentlemen in existence; they were all born a generation or two ago. That sucks. Aren't there any nice men my age? Oh, man, where are you, my grocery-store-lover?"

Audrey's next try at love comes from a totally unexpected place. During high school, she dabbled with dirt bikes. Now a grown woman, she decides to buy a motorcycle.

She makes the deal at the local Honda dealership and signs up for the MSF Motorcycle Safety Foundation class at Arundel Community College. To her surprise, she is not the only woman to decide to satisfy the urge to ride like the wind.

The class has twenty-three students, eight women, and fifteen men. Six men are in her age range, and two, Thomas and Gerald, two very handsome guys, quickly make their intentions known by jockeying to sit on either side of her to win her attention.

The class lasts two days in the classroom and two days on the outdoor practice course.

Audrey loves everything about the class and enjoys Tom and Jerry, the nicknames she gives them as they playfully fight for her attention.

She dismisses Tom and Jerry, working to keep them in the friend zone Lydia taught her to use. Audrey despises herself for using the technique but has no choice since she does not want to embarrass her classmates by rebuffing them harshly in front of others in the class. Nevertheless, she understands camaraderie and friendship are meaningful.

The class ends, and she rides with a few classmates until the summer/fall riding season is over in Maryland. They all promise to get together next season, but everyone returns to their usual lives and forget their playful promises to each other. It is just as well since work is amping up, and she finds herself often too busy to ride, waste time, or much of anything else. Audrey is somewhat grateful because it takes her mind off the grocery store guy, that is, until she runs into a most unusual man while getting her car washed.

A year later, while at her favorite carwash, a man walks up and sits next to her in the inside waiting area. He gets a free coffee and politely shouts to her, "Can I get you a beverage?"

She offers him a stoic smile with a hand motion that means, 'No, thank you.'

He gets his coffee and plops down next to her, leaving a single seat between them. He opens with an unusual line that she finds interesting because it resembles what did not happen at the grocery store all those years ago, leaving this numbing ache of uncertainty in her heart.

"Don't mean to be rude, but I have to introduce myself. I am Charles Darwin; like the evolution guy, I don't believe in evolution; I think God created everything. Now, I am not stalking you, but I saw you drive in here, and your face stopped me in my tracks. So, I said to myself, '*Self, if you don't meet this girl, you'll regret it forever.*' So, here I am. I cannot live with the regret of not knowing the angel who enters my heart at first sight. Sure, I'm being pushy, but suppose you're the one that is supposed to complete my life? So what if we miss out on each other 'cause I was too chicken to offer to meet you?"

Audrey, startled, says, "Does this line work for you with most women? How lucky have you been using that approach, and why would I or any woman fall for it? You're nice and charming, but perhaps you're a few months early laying this on a woman you've never seen or met before. Don't you think?"

Charlie Darwin thinks about it for a minute and responds with a thought she could not dispute. "Firstly, what's your name?"

"Audrey."

"Okay, Audrey; imagine this. You're standing in line to buy the mega-million lottery ticket for an opportunity to spend two dollars and possibly win 867 million dollars; that's nearly 600 million dollars in a lump sum after taxes. And let's say you get an apprehension attack and step out of the purchase ticket line calling yourself stupid for even thinking you could win. You look at the guy behind you wearing the orange baseball cap and plaid hunters' shirt who will now purchase the ticket you were supposed to buy. The next day or so, you see him holding a four-foot check for 867 million on the local news. You, Miss Audrey, have just missed the once-in-a-lifetime opportunity to win the rarest prize of all."

Audrey says, "So, what does that have to do with me; I'm just getting my car washed?"

Charlie stands and somewhat crouches down, facing her head-on. "Don't you get it? You are the multi-million dollar prize. If I didn't come in here, insist on meeting you, a one-in-a-million girl, how would I feel to know that you spent your life euphemistically with the guy in the orange hat and plaid shirt instead of me? I could not live with that, so, no, it's not a line; if you tell me to drop dead and leave you alone right now, I will. But at least I will not spend the rest of my life wondering if my apprehension cost me a lifetime without you. Do you get it now?"

Audrey is amazed by his logic and replies, "Can I buy you a cheap meal? Your words have affected me, but not how you might think. Can I tell you my story over some fajitas?"

Charlie follows Audrey to a nearby restaurant on Forest Drive, Jalapenos. The waitress draws a menu of sorts on the craft paper covering the table and suggests the lunch portion of Shrimp Fajitas sautéed with poblano pepper and onions, served with rice, beans, and condiments.

They accept and begin a casual conversation.

Audrey is anxious to tell her story. "Now listen, Charlie, I invited you to lunch because what you said touched me; it has been the story of my life for the last few years. Mr. Darwin, strangely, you remind me of one of my best friends; his name is Ethan. Anyway, I've got to clarify this so you won't misunderstand our lunch. Charlie, you will never become my boyfriend, lover, or casual date. I just need your honest advice. Still, I need to confide in you about a dilemma I face, and your explanation back there at the carwash leads me to believe you can help me understand and assimilate my own personal orange baseball cap. Will you lend me your ear, your understanding, and your advice?"

Charlie nods 'yes,' still mesmerized by her. "I still can't believe I'm sitting here with you. God is good. Go ahead; bend my ear."

While enjoying their meal over the next hour, she tells Charlie about the stranger she met and the missed opportunity. She explains that she can't move on, feeling the meeting will come again. She insists she cannot explain why but has to wait for him.

"So, Charlie Darwin, what is the evolution of my dilemma? Will my mystery man ever leave my heart? What's your advice?"

Charlie sits there for a while, saying nothing. She watches him, and he watches her. Neither display any emotion. The waitress clears the table, and he orders cheesecake for two. Audrey smiles, wondering how he knew she loved the dessert he picked.

Charlie plays with his dessert, starting and stopping to speak. Then, finally, he pushes the cheesecake away and says solemnly.

"Audrey, I have a solution, but it contradicts my beliefs. I have decided to be truthful or selfishly dishonest for the last few minutes. I will start with selfishly dishonest. I am sure that over time, I could skillfully make you comfortable enough to forget this guy and take my time to replace him in your heart, and it would work. But it wouldn't be the right thing to do. Your emotions are still raw, and it might take a year or more, but I could replace him in your heart and make you happy. Would that be fair to you? No. Would I get what I want, you? Yes! But that would rob you of your intended virtue and would be a slick version of the guy in the orange hat pushing you out of the way, knowing the winning ticket would come up next. So, my dear Audrey, if I were you, I would take the next few years to seek out this man of yours, and if you find him or someone close, go for it, give him your heart, and live a great life. You deserve that. Consider your biological clock and physical requirements, factor everything together, and go forward. I am a big believer that God will help you. Trust Him with purpose. Perhaps he sent me to you today not to fix my loneliness but to help you improve yours. And in the end," he gives her his business card, "no matter what happens, even though we've only met once, I will be your friend whenever you need me. And now, when I feel that tug from the woman I am supposed to be with, I will recognize her pull because of you."

Audrey drives away that day, spinning her head, mentally asking herself, *'What just happened? Who was that guy? How did he know exactly how I felt? And yes, he could have taken advantage of me. For a minute, I almost forgot about my mystery man. Sheesh, that was a close emotional call.'*

What is more important now than anything is that Charlie's words stuck in her conscious mind, and Audrey sets out from that day forward to be open to the possibilities, and God would direct her path to the man she first loved at first sight based on a simple act of kindness.

Eight

LIFE GOES ON AND ON AND ON...

A Year Later:

Time moves on, and Jonathan and Audrey forget about their chance of almost meeting summer after summer. Yet, now and then, something reminds each of the momentary encounters they could never define.

Both have now completely forgotten about the encounter and end up at a corporate rah-rah session hosted by their respective employers, one a Federal employee, the other a Federal contractor with a major government agency.

Audrey is the first to take the dive into the relationship world. Several years have passed, and she has been a bridesmaid to college friends each May, June, and July for the last two summers.

Fate is cruel, since she is often the prettiest woman and catches the bride's bouquet-toss six out of seven times. Many attendees know each other from their associations. On occasion, the 'mean-girl syndrome' manifests itself as she hears the gossip collectively. "What's wrong with

Audrey; all that pretty, and she can't get a man." Another would say, "Maybe she doesn't like men."

Audrey especially hates when she runs into Juanita and the cruel-girl-crew at the hair salon; she tolerates their teasing because she loves the way Anton styles her hair.

She is accustomed to ignoring people; peer pressure is useless on her, but it bothers her to see her parents and relatives be hurt by her apparent inability to secure a boyfriend. As a big fan of Korean Dramas, Audrey is attuned to single adult children's stress inflicted on parents. And while Americans are not sensitive to this global family dynamic, Audrey decides to indulge her mom and dad by at least bringing home a friend-boy.

Audrey determines that during this spring, she would be open to dating. She is aware of her beauty but hates women who capitalized on that single aspect of femininity. Even when Audrey wears knee-length dresses, she can stop traffic. It annoys her, but still, she appreciates her gift.

Audrey decides to accept an advance from a guy who suggested that he be her male girlfriend a few months earlier. At first, she thinks it an awkward suggestion, but as he explains it, the more it makes sense. Harold is a funny guy, always quick with a joke. He is charming and never makes her feel uncomfortable; he enjoys her company.

It is impossible to determine if they are a couple; his protectiveness around her keeps would-be suitors away.

Audrey suspects that he is a long-termer, meaning he would settle for years of friendship in hopes of one day becoming her man.

Harold and Audrey's pseudo-relationship lasted nearly a year. However, his subtle pressure to convert the friendship to actual dating worries her. Knowing she is a strong candidate to be sent to South Korea, Audrey passively allows the relationship to lapse, hoping for a clean break.

Feeling desperate for time invested with Audrey going up in smoke, Harold makes a move that angers her.

Audrey has accepted his invitation to a movie at an upscale theater with restaurant-style seating. She enjoys the film until he does something he had never done in the two years of their *buddyship*; he tries to hold her hand all through the film.

Audrey pretends to need her hand to get popcorn; time and again, he keeps reaching for her hand, squeezing it to make it difficult for her to let go. Finally, she asks him, "What do you think you're doing; why do you keep touching me?"

His answer offends her, but she had suspected such for the last few months. "Because I want more than to be your male girlfriend. Audrey, I've had a thing for you; you must have felt it. I want more than friendship; I want to be your man."

"Harold, I appreciate your admiration and adore your friendship, but it's not reciprocal. I don't feel that way about you. So please don't be offended."

Harold becomes sullen and doesn't say anything for the rest of the movie. Audrey begins to feel threatened. He had driven, and now he is responsible for driving her home. Slipping into the ladies' room, she slips her hand-held taser into her jacket pocket, praying that she'd be safe.

The ride home is difficult. He becomes curt and argumentative. She says, "The weather is so nice tonight, just a little cool."

Harold's response is stern. "If you say so." Then, suddenly, he says, "You've made a fool of me. You've been teasing me all this time. You must have known I was falling for you, and now you're declaring yourself 'not-interested'. That's bull, and you know it. All the dates and the money I've invested in a future with you is what I get. I even met your parents and friends, helping you pretend to be in a relationship. Do you think I'm stupid? You can't use a guy like that."

At this point, Audrey can sense this is going south fast. So when she gets to the next traffic light near a busy intersection, she cleverly waits till the opposite traffic light is about to turn red and grabs the door handle. "I'll Uber from here."

Harold screams, "Get back in here; I'll take you home." But the traffic behind him begins violently blowing horns, forcing Harold to move forward. He curses at her as she flags down a taxi trolling for fares.

Sitting back in the car, she asks the driver, "Can we just sit for a minute; I need to catch my breath."

The driver says, "I saw that back there. I was behind you for a few blocks, and your body language made me think you might be in trouble. Let me know where you want to go, and I'll take you at no charge. I have a daughter your age, and I hope someone will help her if she ever needs it. You're safe now, ma'am; pay it forward one of these days."

As promised, he plays relaxing music on the entertainment system and is quiet to her front door. He hands her a card and says, "If you ever need a ride, feel free to call. Have a blessed rest of your evening."

He drives off. Audrey reaches her home safely, opens her cell phone, and blocks Harold's number forever.

Still shaking from the event, she carefully looks out to all the windows of her home, ensuring that Harold is not stalking her. She is fortunate to have a townhouse with an attached garage. Exiting the garage, Audrey drives to work, still shaking and a bit nervous. She tries to talk herself out of the feeling that last night was the prelude to a physical attack of much worse.

The idea of having a man-friend for the sake of appearances was just too much.

Then, suddenly, after a two-year respite, she wonders for the first time in forever about her mystery man at the little grocery store in Cape St. Clair.

At work, everything is safe and ordinary. Audrey wraps up in her career; she daydreams until her boss asks to see her.

Audrey is an excellent analyst and has never been called into the big boss's office. Nevertheless, she controls her nervousness and enters the execs office.

Gwendolyn Chambers is near retirement and admires Audrey. They have a unique simpatico that Mrs. Chambers hides well, not wanting other staff to believe Audrey is her favorite.

Gwen starts, "Firstly, there's nothing wrong. I asked to see you to thank you and to give you something special. Of course, I'm being a bit biased, but you deserve it. You and I had a conversation a few years ago; we talked about movies, television, sports, etc. Do you remember?"

Audrey tries to look as if she remembers, but she does not. Audrey rarely shares anything personal about herself, but she plays along as Gwen continues. "My first K-Drama was *Healer*. By episode 6, I was hooked. After that, I Netflix binged *Crash Landing on You*; amazing. After enjoying a few more, I became annoyed with American television. It seems that Korean television shows like *Misty* have higher production value, better actors, and storylines that keep you in suspense until the very end. I love the time travel and I.T. storylines."

Audrey asks, interested, "What was your favorite time travel story?"

Gwen chuckles. "Too many to count, but *Tunnel*, *9 Times Travel*, and *Familiar Wife*, which made me reexamine my attitude toward my husband. Then there's *Eternal Monarch*; amazing! But that's not why I called you in here. We are working with a major electronic organization in Seoul. I'm sending you as our best specialist. They will provide housing for you in one of their corporate apartments. Would you like to go?"

Audrey thinks about Harold and everything she's been through lately and answers with a grateful, "Yes, I'd love to see where they shot *My Love from Another Star*; one of my favorites."

Gwen hands her a folder complete with itinerary, tickets, and per-diem in Won, the Korean currency. Then, she asks, "I assume you have a passport, do you?"

Stopping by her parent's home that evening, she mentions to them, "I'm flying out to Korea the next day after the cyber conference at the Dulles Expo Center. Scored an assignment from my boss to help PGP."

Her mom asks, "Do you have time to have dinner with us? It will be ready in twenty minutes."

Audrey follows her dad to the back deck; he can sense she wants to talk.

"Daddy, that guy I brought home, Harold, became violent with me when I turned down his romantic conversion. He said he didn't want to be friends anymore. I was actually scared and thought I'd have to use the taser you gave me in college. I've never seen him like that; I trusted him. I felt he would've forced himself on me if the conditions were right. That's one of the reasons I accepted the Seoul assignment. Am I right to be angry; you're a man; tell me?"

Audrey's father answers solemnly. "Separating myself from being your father, I'd like to kick his you-know-what. No man has a right to impose his desire on any woman. I understand libido, and even my contemporaries told me to get a gun when you were a teenager. Why? They said, *'Your daughter is so pretty, you will have to fight the suitors off.'* I laughed then, but as you got older, even I, your dad, could understand that you inherited what made me crazy about your mom. Still, it would be best if you didn't have to deal with that. My advice: never see him again; don't take his calls, apologies, or anything. Why? Because if he would work on you as a friend for nearly two years, he's a long-con vs. a short-con. He's the type that will make you his goal, and if you let him in the door, he will consider you the one that got away. He will suck you back into his web, and when he thinks your guard is down, he will either gently court you or rape you. So, please don't do it. And if I ever see him again, I will tell him a thing or two; I promise he will never bother you again."

Dinner with her mom and dad is great and comforting. Audrey kisses her parents, and they wish her a safe and fun trip with loving parental hugs. Audrey tells them, "I love you guys. Sometimes when you're grown, one doesn't think they need their mothers and fathers; you guys are the best. Goodnight."

Nine

AUDREY & CLAIR; WHICH COULD BE THE ONE?

Love triangles can be nasty little things, but what happens when two potential lovers are unaware of the third party?

Jonathan and Audrey both attend a cyber security conference, unaware of whom the other is because of the COVID masking requirement. Something in both their eyes suspects, but unsure, and in the ME-2 age Jonathan is afraid to approach her. Lydia, Jonathan's coworker, observes his interest in the mystery woman, urging him to make a move. She also warns Jonathan that he has a work-wife he is unaware of. Nevertheless, Jonathan decides to approach the mystery woman. But before he can, he hesitates, freezes, and before deciding to go for it, she exits the building, possibly losing his opportunity forever.

MICHAEL A. WAY, SR.

Present-Day:
Air & Space Museum: Dulles Campus

A VARIANT OF COVID HAS REAPPEARED AFTER YEARS OF REGRESSION, forcing the return of preventive measures for large gatherings. Entering the large facility set up for a convention, several thousand mask-wearing professionals are wandering the venue during the meet-and-greet session of the cyber security portion of the conference.

The conference coordinator, Aaron Kendrick, views the crowd from the catwalk above the convention hall floor. He remarks to his assistant, "It is impossible to distinguish any particular face." Looking through his binoculars, faces of the attendees become clearer. Aaron sees Clair Hansley, a coworker, and friend of Jonathan Dawson.

Mr. Kendrick, just three years older than Clair, has admired her for years and has developed an innocent crush on her that he cannot express. So he moves down to intercept her at the Adobe booth.

Clair is confident, intelligent, and awkwardly beautiful. She is a collage of so many great aesthetic features but combined seems just a bit off. Claire is 5'6" at about 120 pounds. She is thin but not skinny. Her eyes are warm and beautiful and betray a kindness remarkable for her beauty. She has a small mouth with perfectly shaped lips and a nose that is cute beyond cute. She wears her hair up and dry, with no sheen, bounce, or apparent softness. Still, she is adorable, and most men find her pleasant and approachable, but few offer to date her. Clair has only two interests, her work, and Jonathan Dawson.

Jonathan and Clair have been coworkers and friends for several years. They work in the same division and often have to coordinate on the same projects. Clair has subtly let Jonathan know she is interested, but he is stuck on his sock girl and only confides in Clair as his female buddy and confidant. Clair knows she is in the unintentional friend zone, but the more Jonathan shares about his broken heart over the market girl, Clair becomes even more frustrated.

Still, she takes every opportunity to have lunch with Jonathan; she brings him coffee in the morning and comes to sit in his large manager's cubicle three times a week.

Aaron approaches her at the Adobe booth, asking her to step

aside. Clair does with a smile. "Hi, Mr. Kendrick, sure, let's step over here. What can I do for you? You did a great job pulling together such a diverse group of vendors; you should be very proud."

Aaron Kendrick starts by saying, "What I have to say is personal, and I hope not inappropriate. Clair, I've liked you for some time now, but with all the workplace rules, I am frightened to death to tell you that I would like to date you. Stop me now because I don't want to be called to personnel for even asking you this."

Clair is startled and slightly embarrassed. She replies, "This is flattering, and I completely understand. Firstly, we can't date because my heart is with someone else. You and I are in the same dilemma because the guy I like works with me in the same division and is friendly toward me. Still, I want to begin dating him, but he only sees me as a coworker and friend, and I am afraid if I approach him romantically, I may end up in personnel. He is a manager. I hope I am not hurting your feelings, Mr. Kendrick; you're a very nice man, and any girl would be lucky to be with you like that, but sorry, my heart is already taken."

Clair shakes his hand, thanking him for being discreet and respecting her position. Clair does not notice Aaron's sharp disappointment as she walks away, mingling into the crowd.

Lydia, the socialite queen of this agency, sees and observes everything. She notes the exchange between Aaron and Clair and chuckles, saying softly, "He struck out with her; Ouch!"

Watching Clair, Lydia notes the grace and ease with which Clair works the crowd till she finally gets to Jonathan after glad-handing with people from other agencies who were invited to the expo. Lydia notices the beauty in the room, Audrey Sawyer. Audrey has a reputation for being one of the best cyber detectives on the planet. Audrey's beauty throws many people off because they cannot reconcile her attractiveness with her abilities. Many wonder why she is still unattached.

Finally, Clair reaches Jonathan and decides to use Aaron's approach on him to test the waters she has been afraid to try at work. Jonathan recognizes Clair even through her mask, saying, "Hi, Clair. I didn't know you'd be here. What's up, my friend?"

Clair says, "Jonathan, since we're away from work, I need to ask you something. Can we steal a corner somewhere to chat for a bit?"

Clair leads him from the main hall to the museum alcove and sits near the retired Space Shuttle exhibit. So, seated, Jonathan asks, "What do you need, Clair? We talk all the time at work; why here?"

Clair inhales deeply and touches his hands; Jonathan gently pulls away, trying not to embarrass her as he pretends to scratch his ear. She continues, "Jonathan, at work, you told me a bit about your girl you found then lost at the grocery store. I've tried to advise and help you both find her and get over her, but something funny happened while helping you."

Jonathan is puzzled and looks at Clair, mystified by the nature of this conversation. "Clair, I'm not sure what you're trying to say. Are you saying that my confiding in you has made you uncomfortable? If so, I'm sorry; it's just that I like you and trust you. You're kind and sweet and practically the only woman I trust."

Clair asks, "Do you think I'm pretty? Am I physically attractive to you? Could you see yourself dating me?"

Jonathan's answer both pleases and hurts her. "Any guy in his right mind would think you're pretty, unless they are blind. Physically attractive, sure; I wouldn't call you sexy. But I can easily see that you would clean up real nice if you decided to go that way. Could I see myself dating you? Perhaps if you and I didn't work together and I didn't have my sock girl in my heart, you'd be fun to hang out with. You're brilliant and funny. Clair, what's this all about? Why are you asking me all these questions?"

Clair hesitates and then answers, "I don't want to get myself fired over this, but I have to tell you that you are the kindest, most thoughtful, and genuine man I have ever met. I know you hold out hope for the sock girl, but Jonathan, I developed feelings for you somewhere along the way. I think I might love you. I am not some desperate female looking for a handsome guy, which you are; I'm looking for a man with a beautiful heart, like yours. I hate to go all Sadie Hawkins on you, Jonathan, but would you consider becoming my boyfriend?"

Jonathan feels trapped and does not want to hurt Clair's feelings. He considers the situation and his options, answering her succinctly.

"Clair, let me think about it. I'm going out of the country soon for vacation, you know, just to clear my head about the sock girl. But I will do this; nothing between us at work will change. I know that people call us work-wife and work-husband; I'm a little flattered because I learned that you had nothing to do with spreading that rumor. I know people admire seeing us together and the way we work. So I'm okay with that, but there are some ground rules you must follow if I decide to continue our… whatever this is. Number one, As you know, I fell in love at first sight with this girl from the market; she is still in my heart. I have no intention of forgetting her. Number two, we can do fun stuff, eat out and have fun away from work, and even though it may look like we're lovers, we are not. That brings me to number three. We, meaning you and I, will never have sex unless we're married. Sex complicates things. If we ever get to that stage, I want to be in love, not just love you or be in lust. Don't try to seduce me. I know this sounds like the girl's role, but I only intend to sleep with my wife whenever that happens. And lastly, if I ever find my sock girl or another enters my heart, I cannot, will not continue this relationship; we are to be simple friend-girl and friend-boy to each other. Clair, can you live with that?"

Clair stands and says, "That's all I want. I only want a chance to win your heart."

Jonathan says, "Okay. When I return from Korea, I will call you with my decision. But I'm telling you in advance, don't get your hopes up; you'll never win my heart. Kapish?"

Clair walks back to the convention hall; Jonathan shouts to her, "Clair, I'm honored; you're a nice woman, and I am truly touched. See you back at work."

Jonathan reenters the convention hall, where he is pulled over by Lydia, who is oozing with curiosity, asking Jonathan, "Did she make her pitch? Did you break her heart? You must know she's smitten with you? Everyone at work calls you guys work-mates."

Jonathan chuckles and moves through the crowd toward the snack table. Audrey is also at the opposite end of the snack table as people push and shove to grab the assorted goodies.

Soon, Audrey and Jonathan lock eyes, unaware they have been

looking for each other for years. Their KN-95 masks, combined with their fading memories of the other's face, hide their ability to recognize each other. They exchange the usual corporate banter and handshakes, moving on without showing any particular interest in one or another. Upon the handshake, both react as if they've felt and touched something oddly familiar. They smile beneath their mask.

During the break, both head to respective ends of the snack bar full of drinks, coffee, pastries, and gourmet drinks like Perrier, Spindrift, Saratoga Sparkling Water, and Topo Chico.

Simultaneously, Audrey and Jonathan reach for the last Saratoga on the buffet. Their hands touch, they both laugh and tell each other, "It's yours, enjoy!"

Both look at each other's name tags, saying simultaneously, "Do you hear or feel that high-pitched whine?"

Both nod 'yes'. Audrey comments, "I only felt that once…" She does not finish her statement. Instead, Audrey concentrates on what this man says; she extends kindness.

She insists he has the last bottle. He picks it up, opens it, and hands it to her. "No, it's for you. My pleasure to meet someone who likes and also has an eccentric palette preference for a second favorite drink. I will have the Topo Chico Lime; it's almost as good, but not as sweet as you."

She laughs politely. "Now that's a line if I've ever heard one. I'm actually smiling under this mask, and I wanted you to know that." Then, putting the bottle down, she forms a heart with her hands and a slight bow that he takes as a hearty thank-you. Finally, she directly looks into his eyes, asking, "And what is your first favorite drink?"

"An ice-cold Mountain Dew," he says as he returns the bow, saying "*Gomapseumnida*."

"No way, can't be; I love Mountain Dew, but I can't quite figure out the taste notes, but it is *soooo* good. Oh well, I have to get back to my group. Bye. You're nice." She turns to him, saying, "Unreal, an American who knows how to say *'thanks'* in Korean." She gives him a thumbs-up and continues on her way. Surprising herself, Audrey turns back to face this man.

She decides to probe this man a little further. "So, what do you do for fun back at home? Most IT people are the boring sort; tell me."

"I'm not boring, and I love doing outdoor stuff. But I'm a bit of a loner because I just don't like what people my age think. No morality, no decency, no kindness, and only what they want and want right now. I know, I know, I sound preachy."

Audrey interrupts, "No, not at all; it's great to hear 'old fashioned in a new package."

Jonathan continues, "Hmmm, anyway, my parents claim that I am an old soul in a new body. I don't enjoy superficial BS, and I'm not too fond of modern dating rituals wrapped up in social media. An hour ago, one of my coworkers, a girl, asked me to be her boyfriend. I thought it was supposed to be the other way around. I let her down easily, so it wouldn't be uncomfortable at work. She refers to me as her work-husband, expecting me to see her as my work-wife; not gonna happen. I also don't get swiping right or left, I don't get the whole 'DM' thing, and I hate that people put their whole lives on Facebook. You could say that I am a cool-head, self-sufficient introverted extrovert. When I really get fed up with things as they are, I go to the Awakening to clear my head. When I fall in love, I'm looking for a woman who touches my heart, not excites my body. I want you to know that I've learned to recognize and love lovely eyes in this face-mask world. So, even though I can't see your whole face, I will never forget your beautiful eyes."

Audrey nods to him, and while we cannot see her full facial expression, her eyes betray that she is impressed by what he's said. "I usually hate these events, but meeting you has been the high point. And to be sure, I love your eyes too. Thank you for letting me have the last blue bottle. Bye."

They both wander off separately, mingling with coworkers from their respective groups.

Lydia, Jonathan's coworker, observes Audrey and Jonathan as they occasionally look back at the other as they join their respective groups. She smiles, enjoying the moment.

Jonathan is bothered by his instant affinity for her as the event ends. In a subtle panic, he searches the crowd, but the 139,000-

square-foot campus is overwhelming. Jonathan catches a glimpse of Audrey talking briefly to Clair and other women outside the 15,000-square-foot conference center, and just as quickly, they all disappear from his view. The crowd thins more and more, minute-by-minute. Finally, he dashes outside to the massive 2400-space parking lot, but he cannot see Audrey and curses himself for his apprehension in asking for her contact information.

In an UBER, heading back to his office, Jonathan laments to Lydia, who is the same person who watched his awkward exchange with Audrey and Clair.

Lydia tells Jonathan, "It's none of my business, but you blew it. That girl at the soft drink table looked you over with a keen interest in her eyes. A woman can tell, while you stupid guys would never notice. And from the looks of it, you were checkin' her out too; I've seen her before at other conferences. I don't know her or her name, but the word on the street is she is some kind of cyber genius. She hardly ever smiles or engages in conversations at these events; I'm surprised she talked to you. I think she'd be a great catch for you; guys hit on her all the time, but no one ever gets the attention she just showed you. Why didn't you ask for her number? I'm sure that she wouldn't have been offended, especially since it was a business social event; that's what people do at these things. Here, look."

Lydia hands him a stack of nearly an inch thick business cards. "That's the only way to build and extend your LinkedIn network. You get and give a biz card, reach out with an invite, and voila, you've got contacts; you'll never know when you'll need what they offer."

He hands her back the stack of cards. She adds, "I even get e-cards directly on my phone; makes contacts even more accessible."

Jonathan looks out the window, mumbling, "The truth is, Lydia, my heart just wasn't in it as I'm still stuck on the girl my heart flipped over in a chance encounter a few years ago. The girl I met today reminded me of her, but I was too terrified to be more forward. Nowadays, if you make an approach to a woman and you run for political office 20 years later, she can say you harassed her, and you have no leg to stand on. It's your word against hers. I don't want some lady lawyer on my case for an innocent approach to a woman I'm interested in. Seriously, I don't know how men and women meet. It seems like online is the only verifiable way to prove mutual consent to even meeting someone."

Lydia studies his face. "Tell me about this woman you met; how many years ago did you say, and where?"

Jonathan explains; Lydia studies his face and offers her sympathy. "More than a couple of years ago now, wow, that's tough. You say she was in her early 20s, and she'd be about 23 now, probably married; you say she had a quiet 'pretty' about her but didn't smile much. Hmmm, and you can't let her go in your heart or mind?"

He tells Lydia he doesn't believe in instant affinity for a stranger, but he cannot shake the romantic feelings. "Since then, I've had several friend-girls, and I thought about getting engaged, but I didn't go through with it for any good reason. Worse still, over the years, I've imagined, dreamed of, and wished for what I saw as 'our' life together, our children... everything, kind of a weird version of the Nick Cage movie, *Family Man*, in reverse. Now that's sick!"

Lydia asks, "And what about the Saratoga girl you just almost met, what was that like?

He responds, "First time in a long time that I felt my heart race over a woman, but I was too big-of-a-chicken to do anything about it. So I've faced it, Lydia; I'm going to die a lonely old man consoled by my younger brother's family and nieces and nephews as a complete relationship loser."

Lydia comments, "Jonathan, you should consider hooking up with Clair. I saw her talking to you; a woman knows; she wants you. Perhaps you should pursue being friends with benefits or a work-wife arrangement if you don't already have a main squeeze."

Jonathan answers with self-assurance, "Lydia, I just ain't wired that way."

Lydia tries to console and push Jonathan. "You're too old-fashioned, Johnny Boy; you're gonna miss out on a lot that life has to offer if you don't get with the program. Life is as good as you let it be; you're only human."

Jonathan appreciates Lydia allowing him to vent. He thanks her and mumbles, "I'm out of the country for a week soon; perhaps I will come back with a clearer focus. Thanks, Lydia."

Lydia stops Jonathan, "You'd better come back with a clear head, Jonathan; a bird in the hand is way better than two in the bush. You're behaving as if you've got forever. The best women are closing in on their men; they know they have a biological clock. Women's attitudes are shifting. They want education, a simple romance, love, and marriage, and some want family by their mid-twenties. That way, they can raise the kids and return to work in their early thirties, resume their careers and together with devoted husbands, combine their strength for their children's college expenses. Get the right girl now, build a life and family, and then enjoy the fruits of your efforts. You don't have forever to play the field or wait for the 'perfect' wife. I know Audrey is a wonderful woman, and Clair will make you a perfect home; you won't lose with either of them, but if you don't make it happen, you will lose both. I'm just sayin' life is a series of choices, so choose before you lose."

Lydia's sage advice hits Jonathan like a torpedo hitting a battleship. Jonathan instantly distills Lydia's words into *'find sock girl; if not, forget her. Work to re-meet Audrey today to confirm that instant affinity we just felt or lastly, build a relationship with Clair, the woman who demonstrated the courage to tell you how she felt, then go on with life, Mister Dawson.'*

Now with renewed purpose, Jonathan searches the crowd for the girl with the Saratoga water in her hand.

Ten

MY LOVE FROM ANOTHER STAR – SEOUL, SOUTH KOREA

Audrey is a big fan of South Korean television drama, often referred to as K-Dramas in the 'states.' So she was excited when she was selected to be a cyber security liaison between her company and a sizeable Seoul-based computer firm. Seoul, halfway around the world, is where accidental strangers become friends who have no idea they've already met before at a cyber expo.

Late Spring:
BWI Thurgood Marshall Airport – International Departures:

AUDREY ARRIVES BY BUS FROM THE LONG-TERM PARKING TO BOARD A Korean Airlines plane bound for Incheon, with a final destination for Seoul.

Audrey gets comfortable in first class. Then, the plane takes off, and after a meal, she comfortably falls asleep in her pod.

She is awakened by the flight attendant indicating the plane is on final approach, asking her to engage her seatbelt and prepare to disembark.

She strolls into "Arrivals," where a driver holds a placard with her name on it. Then, he drives her to the PGP Electronics office complex in downtown Seoul.

Audrey has been in Seoul for nearly a week. Little does she know that a friend she doesn't know is a friend who has departed America for Seoul today.

The familiar tower on the horizon is unique to DULLES INTERNATIONAL AIRPORT; Jonathan's taxi drops him at the sign saying KOREAN AIR DEPARTURES.

KAL-1302 takes off, heading for South Korea.

The flight attendant, Alice Park, ensures that each passenger is comfortable in business class. Then, she greets Jonathan. "Is there anything I can get for you?"

Jonathan responds by saying, *"Annyeong haseyo,"* with a slight bow of his head.

Alice is immediately impressed by his perfect conjugation of her native language. She grins with respect and admiration. "How did you learn our language?"

With a friendly smile, Jonathan speaks in English, "I adore K-Dramas; seen a few hundred in multiple genres and sort of picked up on the phrases. Unfortunately, I can't read Hangul, nor can I speak it very fluently, but I understand most of what I hear."

Ms. Park asks eagerly, "What's your favorite drama? What will you be doing while visiting my country? I'd love to show you around if you'd like?"

Jonathan appreciates Alice's friendliness and responds, "I'm on holiday, or as you would say a vacation. I want to spend a week in Itaewon and Gangnam district, exploring. I haven't had a vacation in years; it'll be fun to burn some of my savings. After Seoul I'm going to Jeju for a few days; your Hawaii. As for my favorite series, too many to list, but my first was *Full House*. I liked it so much that I researched and discovered the wealth of older stuff out there, including *Jumong, Stairway to Heaven, Winter Sonata,* and *Jewel in the Palace*; amazing! Within the last few years, it would be *My Love from Another Star* or *Crash*

A SIMPLE ACT OF KINDNESS

Landing on You, maybe *Healer*, *Forecasting Love & Weather*, *Misty* and strangely, *The King's Affection* was better than I thought it would be. *Sky Kastle* was intense and go-gobs of historical series, but don't get me started. Oh, and *Beauty Inside* was cool. I didn't like the Netflix version of *Back to 1989*, the Viki version had more detail. The Tiawanese are stepping up their game; Korea better watch out."

Alice Park responds, "Well, you know your stuff. That's impressive. Not many Koreans could rattle that many dramas off the top of their heads. Tell me, what's your cell? I will text you my contact info; I know just the place in the Itaewon district to take you. I will bring a few friends, trust me, you'll have a ball; oops, I'm ignoring my other passengers; gotta go."

Her smile is genuine and awkward as she reluctantly moves forward to care for other passengers.

KAL-1302 lands at Gimpo International. Entering a taxi, he requests, "300, Olympic-ro, Songpa-gu 76-101F, Lotte World Tower, Seoul."

A taxi drops Jonathan at: SIGNIEL SEOUL. Jonathan is escorted to his suite, where he plops down on the bed and is asleep in minutes.

Next Day: Morning:

AS A MONTAGE OF VIEWS, JONATHAN SPENDS HIS FIRST DAY TOURING all the places he's seen on Korean television. Using his cellphone camera, he snaps a series of panoramas of downtown, shopping districts, food stands, restaurants, parks, bike paths, saunas, watching a drama shoot, evening prayer at a church, and many other exciting sites.

PGP CORPORATE HQ - the PGP Twin Towers building in Yeouido-dong, Yeongdeungpo District, Seoul :

Many Korean security specialists surround Audrey. They are discussing methods of offsetting ransomware attacks from the north. She suggests double-blind enclaves with redundant check-sums for zero-day incursions. She explains using her hands and the whiteboard how zero-day attacks escalate. She combines a ghosted IPv4/6 addressed honeypot as the first-line redirect to a secure intranet. The honeypot clone is constantly check-summing, searching for the slightest alteration via tracerouting and reverse intrusion to punish the potential invaders severely.

A PGP Vice President approaches Audrey with a CAC/PIV card. "This will allow you to stay at one of our corporate apartments at the main entrance's far right door. It is a luxury suite that is fully stocked. Please do not lose this card, as it is your only way to access the apartment. Even the 24/7 security personnel in the lobby will not allow you in without this card." He bows to her and says, "Enjoy your stay, and we look forward to seeing you tomorrow."

The week flies by, and each project Audrey works on is completed ahead of schedule. Finally, it is Friday, and the PGP regular employees invite her for drinks and table BBQ during a break.

Lunch at the bistro near work is excellent. Then, announcing that since it will be a beautiful Friday night, a splinter group offers to take Audrey to Itaewon for a taste of hip Korean nightlife.

A PGP salaryman proudly boasts, "We'll show you the best, and you'll love the cuisine at Jonny's HD and Maple Tree, good stuff!"

The gang is casually strolling through the shopping and food stands. Audrey loves the environment and hearing the language indigenously. Rallying together, the employee accompanying Audrey unanimously shouts, "Let's go to Jonny's Dumplings."

At night, the streets of Itaewon – dong is loud, robust, and festive, reminding Audrey of a minor Mardi Gras parade. People have fun and mingle in the nightlife.

Inside the restaurant are various tables set up informally. The ethnic mixture is robust and friendly.

A group of three men and three women, including two Americans, one of which is Tyler, the other, Jonathan, is at a table, enjoying a variety of dumplings when Audrey's PGP group enters the restaurant.

Two of the entering groups spot friends in the already seated group. They greet each other in Korean, and upon observing the Americans in the seated group, they switch to English.

"Alice Park, I thought you'd be in Canada for another week; did

KAL screw over you? You should've called me, and you know how much I love the dumplings here."

Flight Attendant Alice Park stands to greet her PGP friend, saying at first in Korean, then switching to English, she says, "No, I traded with an American crew to get here early to celebrate my Mom's birthday." Next, Alice turns to introduce her new friend. "This is Jonathan; I met him in first class and promised to show him around; he is a K-Drama groupie, so I had to bring him here." And that's Tim and Janice; Jonathan is on vacation, Tim is attending a conference, and Janice is my friend here, so I asked her to join us so that two guys would not have to fight over me."

Jonathan smiles warmly.

Alice's PGP friend responds, "I didn't know we were coming here. We just wanted to show our American coworkers a bit of our nightlife. So, everyone, this is Audrey; she's from Annapolis, Maryland, and this is Peter; he's from Kansas City. They are both cyber geeks helping us to firm up our security."

Those already seated, stand to greet the newcomers. Jonathan bows graciously.

The restaurant and the night out are pleasant. The Koreans in the group continuously watch the Americans, almost as if they expect them to be instant friends. In particular, they work to maneuver Audrey to the open seat next to Jonathan.

Peter is attracted to Audrey, but she shows no particular interest in him beyond general courtesy. One of the Koreans starts in English, "They don't look like…" he cuts off his words and completes his thought in Hangul, *"They don't look like a couple. I like Jonathan and Audrey."* The Koreans do not know that Audrey and Jonathan have an excellent comprehension of the language, even though speaking Hangul was difficult for the American linguistics ability.

The other Koreans nod in agreement.

Audrey and Jonathan note the Koreans' keen interest in them. Both smile at the crowd and then at each other. Jonathan winks his eye at Audrey; she smiles happily and flashes back as if they both have a secret.

As the conversation between the Koreans continues, Jonathan and

Audrey pick up on phrases to say how attractive a couple they are. They hear in Korean questions like, *"Do you think they like each other? They're both attractive with kind personalities. What can we do to nudge them to become a couple? Americans are supposed to be cool. Can't these two see how perfect they are for each other?"*

Jonathan smiles at Audrey; she returns a stoic smile which puzzles Jonathan. Both are clearly embarrassed, but Jonathan is less so as he begins observing Audrey's beauty and demeanor. Surprisingly, Audrey's aura touches his heart.

Alice, seeing this, makes the offhand comment in Korean, "Jonathan is going to be my boyfriend when I'm back in the States; he just doesn't know it yet."

Audrey picks up the comment but ignores it, showing no reaction. It is evident by the sudden tightness of Audrey's face that Alice is marking her territory. Audrey smiles as if she does not understand Alice's comment. Under the breath of her mind, Audrey can hear her mind almost screaming *'why you little…'* in Korean.

Streets Of Itaewon:

The group tours the night spots, enjoying the activity and Mardi Gras-like atmosphere.

The group thins out after each bar. Jonathan and Audrey refrain from drinking the green bottles of soju at every stop. At each stop, their Korean host, including a slightly befuddled Tyler, call for drivers, taxis, and rideshare till Audrey and Jonathan are the only ones left after they duck out from the dwindling crowd and find a cab back to their respective hotels.

Inside the cab, the driver asks for destinations. Audrey responds, "PGP HQ building number-two on Yeouido-dong, Yeongdeungpo." Jonathan speaks in Korean, "Signiel Seoul." Audrey and Jonathan engage in polite conversation, but not personal. They chuckle a bit about how the host thought they were a couple. The general conversation continues about the unexpected beauty of Seoul.

Audrey responds, "It's like an Asian New York City. Korea was never on my bucket list, but now that I've seen it, Seoul should have been on the list along with my other favorite cities, Hotlanta, Temecula, Austin, Sedona, Versailles, and Christ Church, to name a few. I did Atlanta a few years ago, but I keep adding to the list. What's on your bucket list, Jonathan?"

Jonathan grabs his chin, thinking, and says, "I just added you to my bucket list. If you were going to be here a little longer, I'd love to take you to Jeju; M.C the Max is performing. They're my favorite Korean group. But I know you can't stay; I heard you say that back at the bar to your PGP comrade. As for my regular bucket list, I'm just happy that God has kept me. I feel so blessed to be on this side of six that I don't complain about anything."

Jonathan continues, "But if I did have a bucket list, it would include seeing the pyramids at Giza, the Parthenon; I'd love to see a Rieu concert, Grand Canyon, and time travel if it were possible. And after that, find the most beautiful woman with a wonderful personality to build a family with. I guess you could say that I want to be an old-fashioned husband with an old-fashioned wife and together as one half of an old-fashioned love story."

Audrey nods in approval of his grateful attitude as she studies his emotionless handsome face.

Arriving at PGP Plaza, Audrey exits the cab to Tower Two. Jonathan asks the driver to wait until she is safely inside the locked side entrance to the tower. She appears to be looking for something in her clutch.

Jonathan exits the cab, asking the driver to wait.

"Is something wrong?"

"I think I left my CAC/PIV card in the building. I can't get to my company apartment without it."

"Is there anyone you can call? Any way I can help?" Jonathan asks.

"As a foreigner, without the CAC, they will not be able to help me. So I'll check into a hotel around here."

Jonathan ponders her dilemma and tepidly offers a solution. "Why not allow me to escort you till you find a hotel? I don't feel comfortable leaving you alone at 1 a.m. May I assist you?"

Audrey reluctantly accepts his offer. However, she looks worried and realizes that she is at the mercy of fate.

They reenter the cab, asking the driver the best choice for hotels. He looks at both of them with a disappointed expression on his face.

Jonathan speaks without hesitation, "No, nothing like that. She's locked out, and she needs a place to stay. We're just friends."

The driver responds, "There are several large conventions going on here this week. There's not a single nice place within miles of here with a room available. I would not suggest she stay at the available places, if you know what I mean. There's *"Oh Pal Pal"* in *Cheongnyangni 588*, not a place for a pretty lady like her. No, sir!"

"Take us to my hotel; I'm sure I can get her a room there."

Arriving at the SIGNIEL SEOUL tower, Jonathan pays the cab driver. Then, inside at the registration desk, he says, "I'm in the east tower; "Do you have a room for my friend here? Something nice, please."

"I'm sorry, sir, but we are all booked up through the week, several major conventions here in Seoul, all at the same time. Other hotels are calling us looking for accommodations. I'm so sorry, sir."

Jonathan escorts Audrey to the luxurious seating area, motioning her to sit down. He catches his breath and looks directly into her eyes.

"Look, this will sound crazy, but I am not going to leave you in a lobby like this. It's dangerous, and you're in a foreign city. I insist you stay in the sitting room in my suite. It's safe and comfortable, and I swear, I promise that you will be safe with me. I have no other intentions other than to keep you comfortable. Besides, if you're not secure, I will never be able to sleep. Will you allow me to help you? I know we're strangers, but I insist. I promise I won't bite." He extends his hand as a gesture for a handshake, saying, "Deal?"

Audrey hesitates, saying, "I can't stay in a strange man's hotel; it's not right."

Jonathan shows understanding, but then shocks her a bit with his next statement. "Perhaps we're not complete strangers. I know your eyes. I think you and I shared a sparkling water at an I.T. expo not too long ago. I remember telling you how pretty your eyes are. With the mask, that's all I could see of you. I saw your nametag; I believe your name is Audrey Sawyer; am I correct? I remember shaking your hand and feeling an instant friend connection. Did you feel it too?"

Audrey speaks, surprised but now more relaxed. "You're Jonathan, Jonathan Dawson, aren't you? I love your eyes. This is uncanny, our meeting like this halfway around the world." She shakes his hand, saying, "Nice to see you again. I do remember feeling an instant connection."

Audrey, now tired and frustrated with her situation, studies Jonathan's face and mannerisms and continues holding his hand.

Jonathan sighs, closing his hand around her and escorting her up the elevator, down the curved corridor to the door of his room. Inside, he gives a tour of the luxury suite. "This is the bathroom, and this is the master bedroom. You may have it, and I will sleep in the adjoining sitting room; I insist."

"But I thought you said I was to use the sitting room?"

"That's true, I did say that, but I'm sure you'll feel more secure taking the master suite; it has a lock on the door. I want you to sleep well without any worries. I will see you in the morning and treat you to breakfast if you like."

Jonathan exits the room and plops down on the couch, catching his breath. Within ten minutes, he is fast asleep.

Audrey washes her face and brushes her teeth with the hotel-provided utensils, soaps, lotions, and creams. She cracks the door to the bedroom to thank Jonathan. Tip-toeing out, she observes he is sleeping soundly. She sits in a chair across from the couch, observing his slumber. She watches him sleep for nearly ten minutes, and now for the first time, we see Audrey smile widely, warmly, and with great affection. She is beautiful.

She goes to the master bedroom and returns to Jonathan with an extra blanket. Audrey gently covers him as he sleeps.

Again, she sits across from Jonathan, watching him for minutes more. Again, we see her eyes following his face, down to his chest, his long crossed legs down to his feet, still wearing comfortable shoes.

She walks over to Jonathan and sits at his feet, watching him to ensure he is asleep. A few minutes pass, and she lifts one leg at a time, placing his right leg in her lap. Then, she gently unlaces the shoe-strings and gently removes his shoes, setting them on the floor beneath the couch.

Something jars her as she observes his colorful earth-tone socks hidden beneath his cuffed khaki trousers. Audrey whispers almost imperceptibly to herself, "So this is what it would be like to take care of my husband." His socks remind her of the socks the guy in the little grocery store wore. She smiles as if she remembers something extraordinary.

Pulling the blanket down to cover his feet, Audrey stealthily strolls back to the master suite, continuously watching Jonathan until she is safely inside the room. Then, closing the door carefully, she reopens it again, watching Jonathan sleep.

She retires in the master bedroom, undressing and putting on the oversized silk pajamas he has left in the chair next to her bed. She snuggles in for a night's sleep with a kind stranger in the next room. As she falls asleep, she kneels beside the bed to pray in whispers to the air, to no one, to God. "This is special. Thank you, Lord, for always protecting me."

Audrey barely sleeps as she tosses and turns and checks on Jonathan. Fighting the urge, she comes to the sitting room; she reaches for him to wake him but stops inches from touching him. Her expression betrays a tortured confusion that could be confused with fear and longing. She sits in the chair across from him, her face full of anxiety. Finally, she whispers, "No, it's wrong; I can't, I won't, but I want to."

Audrey wraps herself with her own arms as if she is clinging to her body for strength and protection while Jonathan remains asleep. Then, finally, she rises from her seat, accidentally kicking the small waste basket near the chair. Jonathan hears it and starts. She smiles brightly and then frowns as Jonathan falls back into his sleep. Then, with the softness of a feather landing on a pillow, she walks over to him; Audrey kisses Jonathan's forehead and returns to the master suite, happy and disappointed simultaneously.

The next morning, Jonathan sleeps curled up on the couch, the blanket still covering him. Audrey reaches for the door but then, seeing the hotel-supplied notepad on the telephone table, decides to write Jonathan a thank you note. As she places the note on his shoe, she sees his cell on the telephone table. She writes a longer, more personalized message in the 'NOTES' section of his iPhone. *Jonathan, you're wonderful. Thank you for being so kind last night. I didn't know such men still existed. Your girlfriend, Alice Park, is fortunate. If you find this note and I am not intruding into your life, and you want a woman strictly as a friend, my number is…';* she keys in a number that we cannot see. She completes the note, *'It was fun hanging out last night. Thank you for coming to my rescue. Have a great rest of your vacation and a safe flight home. Audrey.'*

Pgp Hq:

AUDREY EXITS THE BUILDING, BOWING TO HER HOST AT PGP Electronics. She enters the reserved Genesis Town Car but pauses to look around, hoping to see Jonathan; she does not. The chauffeur says to her, "Traffic will be bad; we must leave now to make your flight." The driver takes her to **INCHEON INTERNATIONAL AIRPORT.**

Audrey boards her plane, heading for Baltimore, Maryland, to Annapolis, home and away from a man she met twice. A kind man who made her heart flutter, protected her and whom she wished would reach out to her when he returned to America.

Eleven

'ALL BY MYSELF'
– THE SONG IN REAL LIFE

Signiel Seoul:
Signiel Hotel, Seoul:

Jonathan tosses and turns, finally waking up and heading straight to the bathroom. Standing there, he moans, grateful to relieve himself from a full nighttime bladder. Jonathan stumbles out of the restroom, half awake. He approaches the bedroom and knocks softly, calling Audrey's name. He listens at the door, and after a few seconds, he gently opens it and discovers the bed is made, pajamas laid out on the end of the bed, and his guest, Audrey, is nowhere in sight.

As Jonathan dresses, he sees a post-it note stuck to his shoe. Sitting on the couch, he reads its simple message holding the note against his chest.

> The note reads: *'Thank you, Jonathan, for protecting and caring for me. A simple act of kindness goes a long way. My flight leaves early. I hope someday we meet again. Audrey.'*

MICHAEL A. WAY, SR.

Same Day: Jeju Island

Jonathan and a friend from America, Tyler, who hung out with them on the Itaewon night-on-the town de-boarded the commuter flight just landing on Jeju. The two guys spend the day paling around the tourist spots, seafood joints, and boat excursions to the island's volcanos. Jonathan's mood is upbeat with a twinge of sadness. Tyler attempts to pry what's bothering Jonathan, but Jonathan resists.

Halfway up the last mountain trail, Jonathan turns to Tyler, commanding him to separate from the group to a nearby seating area.

Tyler barks at Jonathan. "What, Clamshell?" he asks with indignation. "So now you wanna talk."

Jonathan, puzzled, asks, "Clamshell?"

Tyler: "Yeah, you've kept your lips as tight as a clam since dinner last night. You ain't fun no more, not even a little bit, and I can guess what's bothering you, having known you so long."

Jonathan: "Okay, genius, go for it."

Tyler interjects, "The girl, I mean woman you met last night, Audrey, made your little bruised heart quiver. She reminded you of the grocery store girl back home you've been pining after for all these years. You flipped over her, but you are too scared to meet and love someone else for fear of *England Dan and John Ford Coley*. You're becoming a coward, Jonathan, that's not like you. I've known you since third grade, and you've never backed away from anything or anyone. You're gonna waste your life looking or waiting for a one-in-eight billion girl on the planet. You're so sure that grocery girl is the only one for you that you are throwing away your whole life. Audrey is not just a beauty; she's got that 'something' beauty that flows from the inside out, unlike the superficial good looks most women exude today. Even I can see that in her, and women say I'm a dog. She spent the night in your suite, and you never made your feelings known?"

Jonathan answers, "I just met her formally; I saw her with a mask on at a conference. We shared a hello and soft drink. How would that have come off if I pursued a first-date relationship? Love at first sight? She'd look at me like I am a fool."

Tyler gave a quick retort, interjecting, "Not love, my man; how 'bout just becoming friends? You are so darn serious sometimes; you've gotta loosen up! So, am I right?"

Jonathan replies with sadness in his voice, "You're right, but what does it matter now? I'll probably never see her again. I called PGP; she flew out this morning, back to the U.S. of A. Worse still, I tossed all the business cards I collected, including hers when we first met at the expo; now I feel stupid."

Tyler pats Jonathan on the shoulder with reassurance; "Look, bro, you'll find her again when you least expect it. Fate and Karma work that way. It's like when you lose something in your car or home. You look for months but never find it. Then, within hours or days after you forget about it, stop looking, it pops up in the folds of the couch, beside the dryer, and in the coat you haven't worn since a year ago. I promise you, you will see her again, and if she's not attached, or even if she is, make your feelings known. Don't choose for her; offer her the choice to be with you or not. Don't hit on her or come off as Mr. Suave; just be your naked self. I like you, and I'm sure she will too if you let her see the side of you I've known since we were in the third grade. And what about Clair, your work-wife? She's good-looking and smart."

"Clair is infatuated with me. She thinks she loves me but doesn't toggle my heart like Audrey or my other girl. Yeah, Clair will make a great whatever for some guy out there, but I want something special. If I got with Clair, it would only be about sex. I'm not saying she's a fast girl, but I can tell by how she looks at me that if I gave her half a chance, she'd give me her all with no regrets."

Tyler asks, "Do you think she's a 304? Do you think she'd cheat on you?"

Jonathan thinks about it for a minute, answering, "Naw, she's not that kind of girl. She's a one-man woman. At worse, she'd be a little possessive and clingy, but I'm sure she'd be a faithful lover for life."

"So, what's wrong with that, Jonathan? That's more than most men would pray for. She's pretty, smart, fit, and sort of hot. She could stand to dress a little better and highlight her cute face. She may look plain, but underneath she is stone-cold beautiful. You would never regret…"

"Tyler, I'm not interested in just sex; I want intimacy. Sex is just two horny people satisfying their desires. Intimacy is comingling of two hearts and souls as well as physical bodies. When two lovers have an intimate simpatico blessed by God, there is nothing like it. I see my mom and dad; when they are watching television or doing yard work, you can feel the love between them. You can't put your finger on it, but it's there for sure. That's the love I want, not sex for sex's sake. I want to miss my girl even when I'm sitting right next to her. Does that make sense to you, Tyler? Other than that, what's the difference between an animal's sex and hooking up with a prostitute? There's no love there, just sex."

"Believe it or not, I know what you mean about intimacy. So when we get back, I want you to go to church with me. Excellent teaching, preaching, and lots of lovely young ladies there. We have a terrific couple's ministry."

Jonathan chuckles sarcastically, asking, "Then why aren't you married?"

Tyler continues, "We're close to jumping the broom; you just have been too busy to realize who she is. You've talked to her a million times, but you never bothered to see us as a couple as you like being lost in your own little world. When we nail down a date and venue, you will be my best man. Jonathan, now that I've found my soulmate, you could never get me to betray her like the me of the old days. Why have hamburgers when you can be married to a ribeye steak?"

Jonathan seems puzzled, then snaps his fingers, shocked and amazed, yelling out, "Olivia? I thought she was just your buddy, your best friend and such."

Tyler smugly says, "Exactly; I'm the lucky one; I get to marry my best friend. Look, buddy, things run hot and cold in a marriage, but friendship never wanes. Besides, it's human nature to be more considerate to your friends than your relatives. If I were you, Dude, I would be Audrey's friend first; get a feel for her; see if you like her. Then, after an honest friendship is certain, explore your possible feelings for her. I gotta tell you, man; my dog days are over since meeting, friending, and loving Olivia; it's amazing."

Jonathan looks puzzled and asks, "Tyler, what changed you? When did you become so spiritual?"

"Johnny, you and I have known each other since grade school; you know how I am, was. So, anyway, I met Olivia at an Orioles game; she was buying a brat and coke, and I was in the adjacent line buying a beer and a cheeseburger. We laughed at the concession stand; it was magic, and we left for our seats. During the fourth inning, I saw Olivia two rows in front of me with no one in the seat next to her. So I strolled down and sat next to her re-introducing myself. We enjoyed the rest of the game, exchanged numbers, and the rest is history, our history. And the odd thing is that the ticket I got came from a friend who had to go out of town. I'm telling you, Johnny, karma, I mean, God, is something else. Yeah, I know you're not used to me talking about God, but Olivia took me to church. The preacher asked all the young people to listen to Eric Carmen's *All By Myself*. I listened to the song maybe six times. Then, I Googled the song and listened to Celine Dion's version, and saw my present life through the words. If you've never heard it, it will change your life, well, maybe not you; you were never a dog like me."

Tyler mumbles, struggling to remember the exact lyrics but then remembers, singing the song's haunting words of perpetual loneliness. Jonathan is touched as he listens to the words as Tyler sings. When done, Jonathan smiles, saying to his friend, "Wow, Tyler, you've got one helluva great voice, and I love the song's message.

Twelve

FRIENDS... I THINK?

A Month Later:

Audrey is cleaning her townhouse dressed in overalls with her just-below-shoulder length hair tied in a scrunchie. She wears elbow-length cleaning gloves when her two closest male friends, Mateo and Ethan, stop by.

Audrey brings Mateo a Mountain Dew. While Ethan goes through her fridge looking for leftovers, Mateo plops down on the couch, but Audrey leads Ethan out to the deck with her sparkling water; Mateo follows. Audrey slumps, saying, "Glad you guys dropped by. Sometimes I don't know when to quit, and I'm too cheap to hire a maid. My mother would kill me if I hired a maid."

Ethan asks: "So, my friend, how was your trip to Soul?"

Audrey answers with little enthusiasm, "It's not Soul, it's Seoul, and it was pretty good. I got to see some of the nightlife, and the techies at PGP are great. If I could speak the language better, I could see myself living there."

Mateo jumps in, "And what about the North; they're working on nukes, and Seoul could end up like Ukraine."

Audrey explains, "There is no way America would let that happen; the place is too beautiful, too USA-zy. I did, however, meet a guy over there. I haven't been able to stop thinking about him. The longer I'm away from him I miss him, his character, and his kindness. I'd be scared to get to know him; I'm sure he'd disappoint me sooner or later. He's too good to be true. Nobody, and I mean no one, is that nice a person."

Mateo, surprised, asks, "You mean you haven't been in contact with him since Korea?"

"Nope, I snuck out of his hotel as quietly as a mouse. He said the night before that he sort of wanted to take me to breakfast. I liked him instantly, but I was not ready for a new entanglement with a good-looking guy. He was charming, sweet; you know, all the things a proper girl looks for in a man. He was nothing like you two, especially you, Mateo; he was a true gentleman. But, I left him an obscure message on his phone and put a general *thank-you* post-it note in his shoe. I suppose he didn't want to follow up; he never contacted me."

Ethan chimes in jealously, "Wait a minute, you slept with him? I thought you were a nun; wow, miss goodie-goodie-two-shoes; he must have been something else. What's wrong with me; I'll sleep with you!"

Audrey sternly approaches Ethan, punching him in the upper arm, and he howls, "That hurt!

Audrey is exasperated. "I don't know why I bother with you dirty-minded boys. She is visibly annoyed by Ethan's comment but quickly lets it pass. She spurns him with the words most hated by men. "That's exactly why I keep you in the 'friend zone.' I value your company and want you around, but I want nothing more than to be your friend. Besides, didn't we already have this conversation a while ago? You promised to stay within your boundaries; I thought you wanted to protect me, not jump my bones. It bothers me that you would never dream of sleeping with Mateo if he were a female; he's your friend. Why can't you and I have the same relationship as you do with your male friends? Pretend I'm your sister, niece, or cousin. Do you want to sleep with them?"

Ethan squeals, "Yikes, when you put it that way... Ouch! That's just nasty. I can't even imagine that crossing my mind. But, Audrey, I am a man, you can't blame me for thinking like a man, plus you're hot!"

"Well, that's how it feels when you, who are supposed to be my friend, suggest sex with me. I love you both, but not in any romantic way, so stop saying suggestive things to me. Just be my friends, my best friends."

Audrey explains further, "As to me staying in Jonathan's room, it wasn't like that. I got locked out of my corporate apartment after a night out. There were no vacancies anywhere. He offered to let me stay in the sitting room of his luxurious hotel room, promising me he wouldn't bite me. He was so charming and trusting. I could feel his heart and mind and knew instantly that he would never hurt me, unlike you." She smiles derisively. "When we got to the room, he gave me the master suite and slept on the couch. If it weren't for memories of my first love-at-first site occurrence a few years ago, I could see myself with someone like him. I actually miss him, and I don't know why. I've never been interested in any guy. I like you two, but you're both so full of crap!"

Mateo and Ethan give her a *'who-me'* look.

Mateo asks, "Now that's a mouthful. Did you get his DM, numbers, email, anything?"

Audrey shrugs her shoulders, "No, but as I said, I did leave him an obscure breadcrumb on his phone. I guess he never found it, which means fate says 'no.'"

Mateo interjects, "That sucks, Audrey, and you're wasting valuable time, and the clock is ticking. I don't want to sweat you, but I'm texting you my girlfriend's therapist's contact info. Her name is Dr. Campbell, Doris Campbell. She's amazing to talk to and blow off some steam. She can guide you; help you use your own history to make it better. She's not expensive, but to show how serious I am, I will send her payment for your first session, and if you like her, you can book a follow-up. But trust me, my buddy, you're too smart, too young, too pretty, and have too much to offer to run headlong into Spinster-Ville. So promise me you'll see her."

Audrey seems puzzled and fascinated simultaneously. She sharply turns to them with a question. "Hey, guys, why is it that guys never tried to engage me in conversation, invite me on dates; they just stare; what's up with that from a guy's perspective? I'm curious."

Ethan answers first. "For one thing, Audrey, you are too attractive to be approached; you look too good, and most guys that see a girl like you assume you already have someone. So why bother? Why shoot your best shot and have it go down in flames? Trust me; all guys think this way."

Audrey frowns. "I look okay, but I'm no beauty queen; I don't get it."

Mateo cracks back, "That's because you're girl-stupid. You cannot distinguish your own sexual-marketplace-value, SMV; no woman can. That validation comes from those who evaluate you—men! Listen, Audrey; your eyes, mine, and everyone else's eyes can only see outward; your eyes cannot see what the world sees. So other people's eyes, in particular, men's eyes, are what determine your SMV. Many ultra-skinny and super obese women call themselves divas, queens, and boss-chicks because they don't see themselves in reality's mirror. Trust me, reality's mirror is harsh. When a woman has four-inch twisting fake fingernails, the guy is thinking straight-up, 'how does she type, shower, or anything with those claws? And I certainly don't want her cooking for me with nails like that. When a guy sees obviously fake hair, eyebrows, and padded apple-bottom undergarments, he hates it because it is only that woman's interpretation of what she thinks looks good to a man; it's not what a man wants."

Ethan chimes in again, "Audrey, not to blow up your ego, but you are what men consider a natural beauty. With no makeup and nothing special, you look wonderful in jeans and a simple shirt. However, you would dazzle most guys wearing an after-six gown with stylish pumps and polite makeup. There are two kinds of girls guys pay attention to, the Mary Anne girls and the Gingers."

"What!" Audrey screams.

"Way back when there was a sitcom called *Gilligan's Island*. The two females were attractive; Mary Anne was an innocent school-girl pretty, while Ginger was movie-star glamorous. Most guys, if honest, would say they'd like to sleep with Ginger, but most would say that Mary Anne was the one they wanted to marry. Why? Because she is fresh-out-the-shower beautiful, while Ginger was only as alluring as her makeup, dress, and sultriness. You, my dear, are a perfect blend between Mary Anne and Ginger, leaning 75% Mary Anne and 25% Ginger, making you just about perfect. You only have one flaw that takes you to zero, and that is why you don't have a boyfriend."

Audrey sits straight up between the two as they say almost simultaneously, "You never smile."

"What?" she states. "What do you mean?"

"Audrey, we've known you the longest, and you never smile. Don't you know that a woman's smile is the most potent tool in her arsenal? It's not like you have to give a big goofy grin, but a modest smile shines your light in a way nothing else can. It sends the non-verbal signal that you are a nice person who shuns drama instead of creating drama. A smile exhibits your inner joy, the joy most, even other women, are subconsciously attracted to. George Strait sang about it in his hit, '*You Look So Good in Love.*' Check it out; it will become self-evident unless you're a total blockhead. Are you?" Mateo asks. "Ethan and I love you because we have known you long enough to see through the semi-grim façade, we know you, but no one else will take the time to learn how wonderful you are. But, seriously, the only time you've smiled today is when you talked about the guy you met in Korea. Then you were beaming like a million candlepower searchlight; he must be quite a guy to get you to smile. And to be clear, I'm sure Ethan will agree; you will re-meet the guy you met in Korea again; God works that way. You need only be patient, give it a little time, and when you least expect it, God will present Mr. Korea to you if it's in His will. Trust me; I know these things."

Mateo summarizes the conversation by saying, "No bull, you've got it all, but you come off as sad, depressed, and often grim with no smile. The worst of it is that you're really cool, and only a few people you know well see that side of you. So, get it together, chickie, before you become an unrequited old maid with a pretty face. Get mad at me all you want; one day, you'll thank us for giving you a clue."

The three settle back in their respective deck chairs, silently enjoying the tree-lined view. Audrey silently ponders her friend's advice, simultaneously remembering and thinking of Jonathan, and hoping what Mateo and Ethan are convinced of, that she will meet Jonathan again.

Thirteen

ONLY THE LONELY; COUPLES MINISTRY & CLAIR

A Week Later: Sunday
Brookstone Church & Worship Center

Jonathan has accepted Tyler and Olivia's invitation to church. The morning service is lively and joyful, filled with friendly people who seem to love Olivia & Tyler and warm to Jonathan graciously as Olivia introduces him to many people.

After service, Tyler takes Jonathan to greet the Pastor, greeting other parishioners as they exit the church. Then, interrupting the hand-shaking session, Tyler pulls the Pastor aside to meet Jonathan.

Tyler: "Jack, I mean Pastor; this is my friend I mentioned to you. Please, when you get time, can you meet with him?"

Tyler turns to Jonathan. "I've told Pastor Jack your backstory; he knows our history, and I know he has some sage advice for you.

Pastor Jack shakes Jonathan's hand, saying, "Jonathan, Tyler has been bending my ear about you for a while now. He says you're the last of the good guys. I want to chat with you to explain that more than half of our singles have found God and love and are planning a life together. If you have time this week, let's do a crab cake sandwich at Mike's on the Bay and discuss what is bothering you over a seafood plate."

Mike's On The Bay Crab House:

JONATHAN EXPLAINS SINGING KAREN CARPENTER'S "TRYING TO GET that feeling again", describing the chance encounter with the girl with the cute socks. He laments that he cannot forget her for many of the same reasons Audrey shared with her male friends earlier.

Pastor Jack: "Have you sought her out? What is it about her that makes her the 'one'? Is it lust? Do you want to tag her because she's unattainable?"

Jonathan responds with restrained anger, "What exactly are you implying? Do you think I'm a stalker or crazy?" Then, angry, Jonathan stands. "This lunch is over."

Pastor Jack remains seated. "Calm down, Jonathan. I had to discover your true motives. I needed to know if you are trolling me to learn a way to get a good girl laid. Your reaction is exactly what I needed to observe. Often, I have to push one's buttons to get to the core. Now tell me what's so special about her and talk to me, really talk to me; don't tell me what you think I want to hear, or we are wasting each other's time."

Jonathan sits again, his anger disappearing, telling the Pastor, "It's hard to describe. Yes, she's beautiful, but not like a made-up movie star, but in this soft feminine way that calms something in me. When I looked into her eyes that day, I could see my whole future—kids, tuitions, diapers, Saturday night mom and dad dates, us shopping for back-to-school. I saw a life I could never imagine in her eyes, and I wanted it. I know it sounds crazy; heck, it sounds crazy to me, but it was like 'something-at-first-sight'. It was something I can't explain. That's why I don't want to hook up with the next pretty girl. How would I feel if I married and had family and saw her and she was available? Do you remember that old song by John Ford Coley? The lyrics say, *'It's so sad to belong to someone else when the right one comes along.'* I don't want that to happen to me… or her."

Pastor Jack replies, "All excellent reasons, Jonathan. My only fear is that you may miss life, waiting for a life that may never materialize, and then get to the end of your life, having had no life at all. I understand you're stuck on the girl that moved your heart, but what about exploring new opportunities, you know, just as a distraction? You know the allegory about misplacing something only to find it just after you stop looking for it, do you?"

Jonathan whines, "Yes, sir, everyone has heard that one. Why do you ask?"

Pastor Jack excitedly replies, "There is this new woman who joined our couple's ministry three weeks ago. She's a plain-pretty girl, but there is something wonderful about her just under the surface. I would love it if you would come to our next meeting and check her out. I'm not saying to form a romantic relationship, but she could be just the diversion you need till both her and your dream person appear. I think it would be a win-win if you got to know her. You won't be able to tell at first glance, but I'm sure the guys that get to know her will be the winner. Will you meet her?"

Jonathan reluctantly agrees.

Having overheard much of the conversation, the waitress scribbles her name and phone number on Jonathan's receipt, saying, "My name is Veronica; I'm single and would love to go out with you. Call me when you get a minute; you won't be sorry." Pastor Jack notes the advance and winks at Jonathan as they leave. "You see that, Jonathan, you'll have no problem meeting nice women; promise I will see you at the Wednesday meeting."

Wednesday Couples Meeting.

THE CHURCH CONFERENCE ROOM IS NEARLY FULL AS SEVENTEEN WOMEN and eight men gather around the table. Pastor Jack has everyone stand and state their names and age. Unfortunately, Jonathan is not here, and there is only one open seat as the session starts. Halfway through introductions, Jonathan comes in, takes the empty seat, looks around, and is surprised to see he is seated next to Clair, his so-called work-wife.

Clair speaks first, almost in a whisper. "Hi, I had no idea you'd be here. When did you get back? You said you'd call me; did you have fun in Korea?"

Jonathan is passively annoyed but plays along as he listens to Pastor Jack moderating the session. "You are all here because you know how difficult it is to find remarkable love in today's dating environment. This place and ministry provide a safe place for men and women to mingle without pressure, but more a group friendship. Hopefully, with a little commonality, some of your budding friendships will sprout into a relationship that may grow into dating, love, and maybe even marriage. There are refreshments at the corner table; grab something and someone to mingle with. God bless you all. I will be circulating the hall if you have any questions."

Pastor Jack works the crowd, working his way to Jonathan, saying, "I'm so glad you decided to join us, and you are sitting next to the woman I wanted you to meet. Jonathan, this is…"

Jonathan interrupts him, saying, "Clair. Yes, sir, I know Clair. We work together, and she's an amazing coworker I treasure."

Pastor Jack asks Clair, "You mentioned when you joined three weeks ago that you were waiting for the man you like to return from Korea. Jonathan just returned from Seoul; is there something I should know?"

Clair answers Jack directly, "Pastor, I've worked with Jonathan for a few years. People at work think of him and me as work-wife and work-husband. He's the nicest guy in the world, and I asked him nearly a month ago to be my boyfriend. He said he'd think about it. Jonathan promised to call me upon his return. Seeing that he's here and didn't call me, I guess I'm not the girl for you, Jonathan."

Jonathan does not appreciate Clair's insinuation, saying, "I told you I'd think about it, Clair. I'm here not because I'm looking or have discounted your feelings; I'm here because Pastor Jack is helping with the problem I mentioned. He felt a friendly distraction would get my mind and heart off of the girl I fell in love with at first sight. It's nothing personal, Clair; you're a wonderful woman any man would be proud to be with; it's just that my heart is taken for now."

Pastor Jack interrupts, "Jonathan, take Clair out for one date, something casual, you know, a cup of coffee, a movie, something simple. Please get to know her as a person, not a coworker. She is extraordinary. I'm not suggesting you forget the girl in your heart; I'm merely saying Clair is an unusual woman of superior integrity. Would you at least consider being her friend?"

Jonathan, thinking he can scare her off, turns to Clair. "This Friday, after work, let me take you out on my motorcycle. We can ride to Hunt Valley north of Baltimore. I know a great little coffee and pastry shop there. You game?"

Jonathan expects Clair to refuse as most of the women he knows are frightened to death to ride on the back of a motorcycle. He thinks for sure she would turn him down and begin to view him as reckless. Then, he'd be rid of her forever.

But instead, Clair says, "Sure, I'd love to ride cupcake with you. I get to wrap my arms around your waist and snuggle close to you for protection. I will wear jeans and bring a jacket; it sounds like fun."

Jonathan drives his bike a little wildly and almost twenty miles-per-hour over the speed limit up 97 to 695 to 83 north. He thinks she'd be frightened, but instead, she holds on singing inside her helmet. Finally, Clair shouts above the relative wind blowing past their helmets, "I love this, and I love you, Jonathan. I can't believe you're taking me out. I'm the luckiest girl in the world. This is so much fun!"

At the coffee shop, both enjoy cheesecake and coffee. Clair laughs at all his silly jokes; she smiles with pleasure in her eyes and touches his hand every chance she has. However, she would not stop staring at him, and her gaze betrays her long-time wish to be in his company.

Jonathan tries not to notice that she is adorned differently than he has ever seen her. Clair is wearing L.L. Bean Women's True Shape Straight-Leg Jeans, revealing a shape he has never observed before. The jeans stun him, and seeing her petite sexy buns throw him off his defiant game. The jeans perfectly drape over the tongue and strings of her rose-accented Cariuma white leather Salvas sneakers. Clair covers her top with a matching pink and white flower print 3/4 sleeve stand collar blouse with bone buttons and an Iroquois navel-length necklace. The open top two buttons reveal a flawlessly soft décolletage, showing just a hint of her perfect breasts Jonathan has never noticed. So many coworkers joke about Clair's awkward dress style; Jonathan wishes they could all see this extraordinary beauty now.

Clair, for once, has worn her hair down in a long ponytail that drapes over her shoulder to just above the length of the necklace and, without effort, shines and shimmers as the light bathes her face. She's wearing a hint of blush, eyeliner, and a nearly invisible flesh-tone lipstick.

Jonathan gulps hard and tries not to look as he realizes for the first time in his acquaintance with this girl for nearly two years that she is beautiful.

Clair blushes as she notes him noticing her. Then, she says something to him that blows his mind. "I dress down at work, and nearly everywhere I go. I never want any man to notice me as anything more than plain-Jane-Clair; it's my defense mechanism against guys hitting on me. You, Jonathan, are the first and only man so far that I want to see me as a woman. I know this is premature, Jonathan, but I've had a crush on you since elementary school."

"What are you talking about, Clair? I've only known you since you started in my division at work. I never knew you before."

Clair responds, "Oh yes, you did. I was in the same class as you when you grew the cherry tomato plants. I was there when you helped that girl Rodney, the bully, was picking on. I was there on the school bus with you every day. I was there when you took to walking that girl home from school every day. I was there when we went to middle and high school, and it bothers me that you didn't give me the time of day. Your brother sort of liked me but was too shy to even say hello. You and I went to different universities, but I kept up with you and worked very hard to qualify to join your division at work. I never had the nerve to tell you how I felt then. I thought you'd notice me one day, but when you began to cry on my shoulder about your grocery store girl asking for advice, I decided I better mark my claim. That is why I asked you to be my boyfriend at the I.T. Expo. I am not some flighty little girl with a school girl crush; I think I've loved you my whole life. And while I don't expect you to choose me to be your life and your wife, I could not live with myself if I didn't tell you that you were my love-at-first-sight. So, even if you don't choose me and find your market girl, I can live with that because I want you to be happy. What I couldn't live with is not knowing if you could have been mine. And the oddest thing is that you motivated me to make my feelings known. How? Because when you told me that you were too chicken to make your feelings known to the market girl, you lost her, perhaps forever. I realized that if I didn't approach you, even though it was uncomfortable and risky for me, I couldn't imagine suffering like you because I didn't at least try. I love you, Jonathan Dawson, and I'm not taking it back. And lastly, now that you see the real me and you know that I am what the world would consider beautiful, I don't want you to want me because I am attractive, I excite your libido, look good on your arm, or you want to have sex with me. I only want you to want me because you feel that I am worthy of your love, and you are worthy of mine. The physical stuff will take care of itself if you ever truly love me as I love you."

Jonathan, now stunned, is speechless. He tries to process what she has said but has no words.

Mumbling, he says, "Clair, You've got to give me some time to process this. You say I've known you for nearly twenty years. Unbelievable; are you saying...?"

"She interrupts, "Yes, I am still a virgin. Aaron and Cory from work have asked me to date them, but until and unless you turn me down definitively or meet your girl from the market, your sock girl, no random guy will ever have me. I'm not against sex; it's just gotta be the right guy, you or someone with your qualities and personality, if that's even possible."

Jonathan drives Clair to her apartment complex and waits until she enters the building before leaving. She returns his spare helmet, kisses him on the cheek, and as she walks to the complex door, he looks at her, never having a clue that his work-wife was this gorgeous.

At home that night, Jonathan is bothered by his cowardice and Clair's bravery. Part of him feels Clair deserves to be his girlfriend because she spent her short lifetime staking her claim in his heart. Clair Hansley knew what she wanted and pursued it.

Jonathan feels a little guilty because as he observed her hidden beauty, he thought about how nice it would be to have sex with her. However, he quickly dashes the thought, realizing that the idea is purely about possessing her physical body and not because he loves her.

Jonathan ponders the idea of allowing himself to fall for her. Still, again, he discards the idea, knowing that he would only do that because he wants her physically at this moment. He dreads the thought of actually falling in love, marrying Clair, then discovering his sock girl after giving his heart to Clair. Jonathan's morals and self-respect would not allow him to hurt any woman, especially Clair, his sock girl, and Audrey, the new girl in his heart from Korea.

Clair bounces into his cubicle a month later with a cup of coffee while at work. She has never mentioned anything relative to what they talked about on the first date, but neither bothered to attend Pastor Jack's couple's ministry.

Clair sits in his cubicle talking about the projected budget for the upcoming server replacement project when Jonathan turns to her, saying, "Clair, do you like seafood?"

Clair answers quickly, "I'm a seafood nut except for octopus, squid, and raw tuna. So, why do you ask?"

Jonathan says, "Because I'd like to cook for you at my place this weekend. Maybe a movie after dinner?"

Clair answers with most unexpected words, "I'd love to, but I'm not having sex with you, even though I want you. Are you okay with that?"

Jonathan laughs, saying, "You're a funny girl; sure, I'm fine with that. I will text you my address but never come over without calling me first; are we clear on this?"

The following Saturday, Clair knocks on Jonathan's door at four o'clock. Inside he is nearly done preparing two lobsters, corn and rice pilaf. Clair is wearing an A-line dress that loosely shows her figure as she walks around his home, admiring the cleanliness and neatness. Her hair is straight and curled simultaneously with a slight shimmer and bounce. The dress is just above her knees, and her bare legs descend into a Spanish-style cork-heeled pump. He watches her every move, shaking his head from side to side.

She shouts from the living room; "I can't believe you invited me to your home; I never dreamed this would happen."

Jonathan comes out of the kitchen wearing a chef's apron. "Dinner will be ready in ten minutes. And I never knew you were this beautiful. I feel shallow saying this, but for someone your size, you are breathtaking. You know, I've only seen you as my buddy and coworker; it's not fair that you look this good."

Jonathan sits at the breakfast bar as he speaks to her again. "And why is that? Why would you never believe I'd invite you over? We've been friends for two years."

"With ME-2, it's not easy for men and women who work together to have a friends-only relationship. Besides that, with you knowing how I feel about you, I thought you'd be afraid to have me over."

"Well," Jonathan begins, "after that no sex proclamation, I lost all fear."

She laughs, saying, "Are you sure that's wise? That could have been my reverse psychology ruse to get you into the sack?"

"I thought about that, and the one thing I'm sure of is that you're genuine, and you don't lie. So I'm safe from you, and you're safe from me."

Clair responds with a comment that throws Jonathan completely off. "Jonathan, while it's true that we're not going to have sex tonight before I leave, I will fulfill one of my fantasies with you. I am going to kiss you with all the passion I can muster. Just once, but when I'm done, you will know how much I love you and a foretaste of my passion for you. Fair warning."

While Jonathan is sitting out plates, Clair wanders over to Jonathan's Yamaha baby grand piano and plays Ballade pour Adeline. Each note of the famous tune is played perfectly, and she hums the song as she plays with her eyes closed.

Jonathan is mesmerized and comes over to the piano, touching her on her shoulders. Clair continues playing to the last note, then stands to face Jonathan, saying, "I love your piano."

Before she can say another word, Jonathan pulls her to him and kisses her with all the passion she's been hoping to kiss him with. Clair explores his mouth with her tongue as if she is consuming his very being.

When they pull away, he stares and says, "I'm sorry. I love that song. You played it beautifully. Forgive me for doing that."

And with that, she returns his aggression by kissing him with equal passion. Jonathan, embarrassed by his actions with Clair, returned to the kitchen to finish the lobsters. Clair, hoping to entice Jonathan into another embrace decided to show-off her musical talent a bit more. She wandered to his Korg keyboard, uncovered it, and played *Non-Dimenticar* adding electronic accompaniment as she played the famous song. Jonathan glanced from the kitchen, amazed by the musical range of his so-called work-wife. He waited for the melody's conclusion and then called her for the meal he set before her. Jonathan asked Clair, "I'm an old soul, but you, Clair, are too young to know that song; how can you know it?" She blushed appreciatively, answering, "Because the words Martin put into that song are exactly how I feel about you."

Jonathan, always the gentleman pulled her chair out for her, and they sat at the spread before them. Clair bowed her head, saying grace, and then looked up at Jonathan, thanking him warmly.

After dinner, Clair helps clean the kitchen. Finally, Jonathan says something that pleases her to her bones while disappointing.

"Clair, I don't think we should do a movie tonight. So let's call it a night."

Clair answers as if she could read his mind. "I agree. I didn't plan on this; I want you… See you Monday at work."

And with that, Clair leaves Jonathan for her apartment.

Jonathan goes to his piano, playing the same tune, then banging on the keyboard, asking himself, "Sock girl, where are you? Audrey, I need you; where are you? It's you I want, not a substitute."

Surprisingly, as Clair and Jonathan pass each other in the hall, both greet each other pleasantly, but she slips a post-it note in his hand as they pass. The message instructs Jonathan to meet her near her car in the underground garage.

Inside her car, she says, "Are we still friends? I know Saturday was as difficult for you as it was for me. I spent Sunday wondering if you hate me."

Jonathan replies, "I feel mixed up, Clair. I never dreamed I'd want to be with someone like that who was not in my heart. I'm not saying you're not worthy of my heart, but Saturday was my animal's lust for you. I haven't had a chance to love you, but the dinner, the dress you wore, your hair, and then Ballade pour Adeline on the piano was over the top. Can you forgive me for kissing you like that?"

"Are you kidding me, Jonathan? You made my dream come true. You should know that while you don't love me, I do love you, so for me, it was not an animal's lust; I desired to have the man that's in my heart. I'm good, so don't worry about me. If you think I'm trying to precipitate something or move your girl out of your heart, I wouldn't…"

"No, I don't think that, after all, I invited you to dinner. So, are we good?"

Clair nods 'yes,' and both go back to work.

A Month Later:

CLAIR CALLS JONATHAN PROPOSING A DATE. "JONATHAN, HOW WOULD you like to go on a unique date where you get to stare at my legs and my booty?"

Jonathan screams with glee through the phone. "What are you talking about? You're crazy!"

Clair again asks with insisting sarcasm, "Do you want to stare at my legs and booty or not? If you do, meet me at the Bass Pro Shop Sunday at 10:30. Wear some shorts and hiking tennis shoes."

Arriving at Arundel Mills, Jonathan heads inside, looking around for Clair. Not seeing her, he assumes she is running late. Jonathan walks over to the giant aquarium and stares for a while. He then meanders to the rock climbing wall, peering at the giant stuffed bear. Suddenly he hears his name called. "Hey, good looking, Jonathan; I'm up here."

Looking up the rock wall nearly forty-five feet, he sees Clair near the top, screaming, "Come on up!"

As Jonathan negotiates the jugs, slopers, pockets, and pinches, he climbs closer and closer; he is stunned by her legs, thighs, and hips as her shorts barely cover her upper thigh. As he gets closer, she asks him, "So what do you think, you like what you see? I only asked you to come on Sunday because the place is always empty. I couldn't show you my goodies at your house or my place; I didn't want you to lose your mind. I just wanted you to see what will be yours one of these days if I'm lucky."

Jonathan is unsure this is the same woman he's worked with for years. He says, "You bring out the dog in me; a dog I've kept in his cage. How in the world could you work with me for two years and I never got to know you were a goddess?"

Clair laughs happily. "'cause you only had eyes for your girl, but I ain't mad at you. I think I'm winning you over. Come on up to the top."

Jonathan reaches the top and, standing next to her, looks at the whole store from above. Clair grabs her auto belay cable and harness and releases her foot from the nearest pocket, swinging six feet through the air next to Jonathan. Clair kisses him, saying, "Hi, lover. Let's go down, and I'll treat you to a hot pretzel."

Jonathan does not want to admit it, but Clair's open honesty and steadfast affection tempts him. He cannot believe he is walking around a mall with Clair showing her gorgeous legs while he holds her hands as a couple. Jonathan is troubled by the guys passing in the opposite direction glaring at him, saying, "Dude, your girlfriend is beautiful; you're so lucky."

Clair blushes with appreciation and holds Jonathan's arm even tighter, saying to him, "People think I'm your girlfriend. I hope you're my husband one day."

A SIMPLE ACT OF KINDNESS

Nearly four months have passed since Jonathan and Clair began their unofficial dating. Jonathan would not claim her as anything more than his friend-girl, even though Clair thinks of herself as his girlfriend. During the time since the rock climbing, Jonathan agrees to see her nearly every three weeks and would not allow her to feel he is obligated.

It bothers Jonathan that he looks forward to seeing Clair because it takes his mind and sometimes his heart away from thinking about Audrey.

Every time Jonathan hears anything about Seoul or watches a K-drama, he misses his Audrey, thinking about how much he wants her. The combination of the attention from Clair and his desire to see Audrey just one more time erases the ache he feels about the girl he met in the grocery store.

Jonathan admits to himself that he'd like to meet the grocery store girl to see if he could solidify his heart's feelings for her into true and robust love. He also notes that since Korea that he does, in fact, love Audrey. Jonathan feels terrible that he only likes Clair, but Clair's femininity and devotion to him would place him in the danger zone if he ever finds Audrey. It confuses Jonathan since seeing Clair while rock climbing, combined with her stunning beauty the night he prepared dinner for her, was beginning to overwhelm his emotions. As to Clair's sweet and devoted kisses, Jonathan tries desperately to talk himself out of liking them, but his efforts fall flat as they kiss more and more on subsequent outings.

Jonathan loves her embraces so much that he once makes an excuse to see Clair on two consecutive nights. He hates himself for loving her sweet kisses. Their early kisses were gentle pecks and polite smooches to the forehead and cheeks. However, the night she played Ballade changed everything as Jonathan had an unexpected physical reaction to her body's beauty and tender embrace.

Clair and Jonathan have suggested a myriad of weekend get-togethers with activities like long walks, short road trips, conversations around his fire pit, miniature golf, and watching the sunrise on the Chesapeake Bay at five a.m.

Clair once hears Jonathan say he likes Bay fishing. So she goes to

Herrington Harbor, probes to find the best charter captain, and surprises Jonathan by taking him out on the Bay for a two-person charter for a boat designed to host a dozen anglers. She pays to charter the whole ship, saying she wants to spend time with her Jonathan all alone.

The captain and helper assists them in baiting their lines. The captain whispers close to Jonathan, "Man, your girlfriend is crazy. She paid for this whole boat just for you two. She told me she loves you and you're worth it. Do you know how much it costs to rent this vessel for a day? She paid the whole price for just the two of you. I've never seen that before; that girl must be crazy about you."

Jonathan and Clair return to the dock with rock, perch, a few blues, croakers, and flounder. The captain's helper scales, cleans, and dresses them, putting them on ice in a Styrofoam container.

That night, Jonathan fires up the outdoor grill and prepares Clair a seafood dinner fit for a queen.

Clair helps him clean up and then asks Jonathan, "I know you're going to say no, but can I stay the night with you?"

Jonathan, feeling trapped, asks her, "Didn't we agree that we said no sex? So if you stay here tonight, what do you think will happen between us? Just sleep. Right."

Jonathan doesn't realize that she has set him up to learn his true feelings and motivations.

Clair begins, "I didn't say I wanted to sleep with you; actually, I wouldn't mind. I meant I want to stay and do a little binge-watching, and then I will sleep in your spare room. I didn't realize that you're willing to and want to sleep with me in your heart."

Jonathan feels caught as his first statement reveals what he has suspected all along; that he could be convinced under the right conditions to make Clair his.

Clair cleverly lets him off the hook, grabbs her stuff, kisses him more deeply and passionately than ever before, and says, "Good night, Jonathan. I'm glad you enjoyed my gift today; it was so much fun. And I thank you for the gift you just gave me, the gift of knowing that you want me. I feel so good. Bye."

Clair leaves without discussion, knowing she has left Jonathan with his head spinning. Nevertheless, Clair's womanly intuition knows that he would be hers with a few more outings, as he calls them, despite his rigid objections.

Clair and Jonathan are called into the Division Chief's office two weeks later. They sit at his small conference table, and he greets them warmly.

"Clair, you've done an amazing job helping Jonathan run his ship. Your budget process has made him the star of the division. As a result, I'm promoting you to COTR. You're being reassigned to Lexington, Kentucky, at the GSA building on Barr Street. Jonathan will accompany you and stay for two weeks to help set you up. You start October 1st with a huge salary increase, a grade, and a four-step wage increase. You will not be subject to the cost of living decrease moving from DC to KY. Your detail will be for two fiscal years, after which you can return here with another grade increase. What do you say?"

Clair is both pleased and disappointed, sheepishly saying, "Yes, sir; I'm honored that you trust me."

The chief says, "Great, I will email you both all the dope you'll need. Some of my people there have already found you a great place to live. Take a week off, go down, and see the condo. We've given you a travel and expense voucher; it won't cost you a dime, well, maybe a little upfront, but you'll be reimbursed. Now get out of here, you two. Make plans and keep me in the loop."

Outside the chief's office, Clair almost collapses as Jonathan has to catch her. He looks at her face, sees tears, and says, "I know you are happy about the promotion; you'll do great."

Clair pulls Jonathan by the hand, with many people looking, to guide Jonathan to a private conference room around the corner. Then, he hears Clair scream angrily at him for the first time. "I'm not upset because of the promotion, you blockhead! Can't you see? You really don't understand? You, my dearest friend, don't get it; I've wasted my time. This is unreal!"

Jonathan is startled and tries to console her without touching her, asking, "What's the matter with you? Anyone here would be happy with what they just gave you. You're single, unattached, pretty, and smart. You're staring at a unique opportunity here. I don't get it."

She screams, "Of course, you don't. I'm going home for the rest of the day. You'll figure it out, genius."

Clair leaves for the day, and when she returns the next morning, she is composed and purposeful as she informs Jonathan of their itinerary and thanks him for volunteering to go to Kentucky with her.

Still unsure of what upset her, he decides to grab some quiet and private time with her to help sort out her emotions. "Clair, I will take you to Kentucky myself. I will be at your apartment tomorrow morning around seven."

Jonathan picks her up and drives on what seems like back roads to Old Annapolis Road. Clair is pleasant but not talkative. She tries not to pout, but the frown persists. Finally, he winds and curves off 450 and onto Church Road, arriving at Freeway Airport. The field attendant fuels Jonathan's Beech and has the airplane seated on the compass rose.

Clair perks up a bit and enters Jonathan's plane's large and spacious cabin and cockpit. After a few preflight checks, Jonathan taxies and takes off within minutes of his arrival.

Now at cruising altitude, Jonathan turnes to Clair with his most tender and concerned voice, asking, "Now, what's bothering you? Why do you look depressed and angry?"

Clair is perplexed as she is enjoying this surprise from Jonathan but disappointed at the recent turn of events. She finally opens up, saying, "I never wanted a career. I've known you since second grade. I've tried to keep my dignity about this, and I know one can't make someone love them, but it can't be turned off so easily. Look at your sock girl and Audrey from Korea. You can't forget them, and I can't forget you. God knows I've tried. Since my teenage years, I saved myself for you and you only when all the other girls were having their fun. And now, just as we are getting closer and closer, this promotion! But, I'm not stupid; I know you want me, and I am willing to respect your wish to be married. And now, with this two-year separation, we're sure to lose all our progress over the last six months. I can see that the pain you felt missing Audrey has lessened month by month. I know you love kissing me; I know you lose yourself in our embrace, and I have retrained myself from taking what I want from you to preserve your wish to do things your way, the right way. But, if I leave now, I can feel it in my bones; you're going to meet Audrey again, and I will lose you to her forever. All I ever wanted was to be your wife, have our children, and help you reach any goals you desire. I wanted to grow old with you. I wanted to feel the depth of your love for me in our most intimate moments; that's all gone if I take this position. Will I lose you, Jonathan? Say I won't."

Jonathan can feel her pain as she bawls her eyes out. Jonathan is torn between being honest and preserving Clair's dreams and dignity. At this moment, he is forced to examine his genuine emotion for her. Jonathan is terrified, knowing that this could be his last shot at happiness with someone who truly loves him.

Jonathan reaches over and moves a few loose strands of hair from around her face to behind her ear. He says, "You sure give a boy a lot to think about. But, the fact is, Clair, I've been afraid to tell you what I am about to say for fear you'd take it the wrong way. I'm not being disingenuous either, but I love you as a friend. I am not 'in love', but I do love you. That's a big deal for me. But, Clair, I am also a man. What I mean is that the man, I mean the man-only part of me, perceives you as one of the most beautiful women ever. I admit that when I saw your body while rock climbing, the man part of me wanted you right away. But, Clair, everybody can say that. So many people today are having sex because their flesh cries out for the flesh of the person they want. Yes, my flesh wants you, but I control my body, not the other way around. The only rules I have set for intimacy is that number one, I will be in love, and number two, that I am married to the woman I am in love with. That's it. So, Clair, I love you, but I've been transparent and fair; I am not in love with you. Do I want you physically? Yes, I do, but only under the right circumstances. Clair, I don't want to enjoy a sexual relationship with you, and then we don't marry each other for some strange reason. I am one-hundred-percent sure that sex with you would rock both our worlds; there is no doubt. Now suppose later on in life after our breakup, we marry or are with another. Can you imagine having sex with your husband all the time thinking about the sexual acts you and I performed for each other? Do you want to think about me when responding to your future husband's touch? How would you like it if we were married and I moaned another woman's name while enjoying an orgasm with you? It would devastate you, and I know it would kill me to hear my wife calling a ghost from her past's name while making love with me. So, yes, this separation will change our relationship. You may lose me; I may lose you. I have no way of knowing who you will meet in Kentucky. I promise to visit you as often as possible and not for business. It will only be to see you and you alone when I visit. I'm not in love with you, but I love you. Don't sweat it; just be my friend and let nature take its course. Besides, I've been looking for Audrey for years now and my market girl even longer. I'm never going to find them, and the only thing I want to find in the short run is those wonderful wet and sloppy kisses you give me. Gosh, I love kissing you. Are we good now?"

Clair smiles with subtle confidence, feeling reassured in the candid truth Jonathan has just revealed. She takes great pleasure in knowing that her feminine wiles have changed Jonathan's emotions from like-to-love. Clair now knows all that is needed is a nudge to push him from love—to in love—to marriage. Clair consoles herself, knowing she has waited since she was eight years old; she consoles herself, knowing she could wait another two years.

Fourteen

THE SHRINK

Annapolis Professional Center:

A udrey finds a parking space, enters the first floor, reads the legend of tenants, and takes the elevator to the office of Dr. Doris Campbell, Mateo's girlfriend's therapist.

The kind receptionist brings Dr. Campbell and Audrey a hot cup of Oolong tea.

Therapy Session For Audrey:

AUDREY ENGAGES IN A SERIES OF VISITS. AT THIS APPOINTMENT, DR. Campbell asks Audrey for permission to record her session, informing her that she always records for notes and later analysis. Audrey consents, and the candid sessions begin.

During the counseling sessions, Audrey explains her apprehension about forming a relationship with men. Then, she talks about wanting to meet again, someone she never knew but was touched by a simple kind act.

She is adamant that she will not commit to a relationship until she feels that way again. She explains her observed cycle of a relationship. They talk about seeing the good-looking guy, only to discover later he is a self-centered jerk.

Then, Audrey remarks infatuation is a precursor to unrealistic expectations in love and is too dangerous to risk one's relationship future. Finally, she bitterly talks about the former high school sweethearts she knew years earlier, most of whom came to hate each other a few weeks, months, or years later.

Audrey destroys love at first sight, having determined that it is lusting at first sight. She gives a detailed overview and calls it a syndrome.

"Seriously, Dr. Campbell, the only time a complete stranger moved my heart occurred in a random grocery store somewhere in Maryland, which I only frequented once; I don't even remember where. And this guy was really handsome and polished. I've met many guys who would be the first-class choices any woman would appreciate. But I want to face every day for the rest of my life with that same heart-moving emotion. So far in my life, he is almost the only man I've experienced that sensation for. Something similar happened while I was in Korea. Physical beauty is skin deep and temporary, but a person's heart will always be the heart of my future partner and will remain even when I'm older. That's the love I want, and only that love."

Dr. Campbell has been patiently listening; she now interrupts Audrey. "I want to give you a list of scenarios to think about. Parse through them before we meet again. I believe we can have a more enlightened session if you open yourself to these traditional mores. Write them down, and they will stick in your mind that way. Here's a pen and paper. Ready?"

Dr. Campbell waits for Audrey to take notes, then begins. "During my years of practice, I have gleaned the following from many-a-woman's point of view."

"Great women are attracted to a man's character before his physical assets."

"Women with character respect honesty."

"All women watch how men treat them in a public setting, determining how important she is to them."

"A woman who bonds with a man as a ride-and-die friend will likely never sleep with him. Instead, she will be with him as a friend until the end; and him, her."

"A woman who feels an affinity for a man's character may be threatened or unnerved by the unexpressed feeling she is developing for him. As a result, she may resist if she is not ready for this type of romantic bonding at this particular time."

"Her past experiences will come into play as she decides to jump in or run away."

"The following situations are often relevant, particularly in the case of your mystery man. If you are ever in a situation where your male friend is hurt, sick, or in danger, you, his buddy, will organize your life to care for him without prompting. Of course, there will be no hint of romance, but both of you will experience a deep non-sexual affection for each other, I promise you. Then, after he heals, you will abruptly return to your normal life, yet you both will detect the subtle 'missing' of each other within yourselves. Finally, when you least expect it, a discussion ensues via carefully manipulated innuendo between you both about the nature of your relationship and whether or not it should escalate. Neither of you will want it to overwhelm the other. Neither of you will dare to approach the forbidden idea that you may be 'in love' instead of 'just' friends who love each other. You will also develop a creeping wonder about sex with each other that will, if unbridled, turn into full-blown intimacy before you are ready. Always remember, Audrey, the heart wants what the heart wants, and just as dangerous, the body wants what the body wants. That is why no person can hold their breath or ignore hunger pangs for sustained periods. Your body will plead with you both to give each other what it wants; each other! *'Danger, Will Robinson.'* It will be a terrifying and awful conundrum for you both. But, hopefully, this little chat will give you the tools you'll need to navigate love on that scale if or when it happens. You're both playing with love's fire; it can singe and destroy you or make your life the best life ever. See you next session, Audrey."

Dr. Campbell's Office:

It has been a few months and a few therapy sessions for Audrey with Dr. Campbell, who begins somberly, "Audrey, there will be no tea today as I will do all the talking. I want your undivided attention, as what I will say may alter the rest of your life. Are you ready?"

For some strange reason she cannot define, Audrey lets her guard down and simply says, "Yes, ma'am," a term she has not used since middle school.

"Audrey, we have only two choices here. I will declare them, and you will decide the path. You are not a stubborn person, but you are incredibly stubborn about your perception of your love-life. Perhaps it's not professional to say this, but I think you're right about your heart's love. You've had several experiences, but only two left an indelible imprint on your heart. First, it was as a kindergarten student. The second, and the event that made the most dramatic impression on you, was the grocery store event and the comment about your adorably cute and ridiculous socks. You were a fully functioning adult, and you froze, then ran away from the feeling and the guy before he could engage you because you were afraid and overwhelmed by the raw brutality of heart-love at first sight. Too many people obscured the third occurrence."

Audrey interrupts her, "What third? There was no other occasion that I know of?"

Dr. Campbell interjects, "Mateo's girlfriend mentioned your Topo Chico/Saratoga moment at an I.T. expo and someone you got to know in Seoul."

Audrey answers, "Oh, that was just some nice guy I ran into at the snack table; it was nothing. I promise."

Dr. Campbell continues: "Did you bother to tell your heart that? The heart wants what it wants. This is why both men and women have unexpected affairs after marriage. They meet someone wildly attractive to them, become infatuated, and then have sex. Sex seals the deal; soon after the cocaine effect sets in. Both narcotics and orgasms pulse in the same pleasure center in the brain, and soon after that, one cannot do without the other in their life. As for you, Audrey, you have had the heart rush that most never achieve. It is more potent than the orgasmic rush so no other man will do for you at this point in your life. That's a good thing, but it could leave you a disappointed woman who will die alone without sharing your life with a partner. So, should you just find a man you like, settle down, have a family, and live a great life? I can't answer that question for you. There are many lovely men out there who will make fine husbands, boyfriends, and partners. The question for you and your heart is, can you live with the regret and longing for your original love? Most people do. Can you? Personally, from what you've told me, the guy you re-met in Korea fits the bill, if not a close second, to your grocery store guy. He didn't try to have sex with you when an opportunity and your vulnerability were on the line. Most men would have at least tested the waters to see if they could score."

She continues, "I hate to be so crude, but that's the reality of today's dating scene. Your guy did not try; he gave you his room, respected you, and rescued you in a situation where he could have pressured you. This person, Audrey, is an unusual and classy man. And make no mistake, he knew you wanted to have sex with him; he's not stupid. But no, he respected you enough not to create an emotional moment where you would give in to your lust and not your heart. So he spared you the pain of regret, even though he wanted you. He wanted you, but he wanted more than your body; he wanted your heart. He wanted to enjoy your body's pleasure, and I suspect if you two ever meet again, he will not sleep with you until he becomes your husband, and you, his wife. But, from the way you described him, both your hearts want the same thing, true and unconditional love. It's not a bad future, Audrey; you should consider grabbing on. It's your call."

Fifteen

YOU TWO ARE UNDER ARREST!

Laurel, Maryland:
Merganser Pond, Patuxent Wildlife Research Center.

It has been a quick month, with spring just over the seasonal horizon. The sky is a brilliant blue, cloudless expanse over the research center. Suddenly, an employee of the center who is inspecting a 'hide' sees two drones flying at opposite ends of the pond. The employee grabs his walkie-talkie.

Moments later, we see a Laurel Police SUV and a DNR Pickup cruising along both sides of Route 198, Laurel-Bowie Road.

The DNR officer pulls off the road and approaches a female with a drone controller in her hand. He asks, "Do you have a drone flying over Merganser Pond?"

She responds, "I don't know what Merganser is; I'm just getting great footage of the tree line and power lines," she points, "...over there about a mile away."

"Miss, bring your drone home. It is illegal to fly over a federal research reserve." Then, with a stern voice, he repeats, "Bring it in now."

He instructs her to get in his officially marked government truck. She tries to explain it is recreational flying as a hobby. As he pulls into the administration building's parking lot, they see the Laurel police SUV with another drone pilot sitting in the back of the vehicle. The pilots are instructed to go inside with their drones, gear, and controllers.

They hardly notice each other as the officer examines their gear. Then, finally, the center's security officer warns them about flying in a restricted area, directing them to photos showing the "no drones" warning signs.

For the first time, both intruders look at each other. Audrey speaks first. "Hey, it's you. Long time no see; Jonathan, right?"

He responds almost with glee, "Audrey, you remember my name; it's been a minute since Seoul. So, Audrey, what are you doing here?"

"Same as you, Jonathan, flying my Mavic; you've got a Phantom. Awesome!"

Annoyed, the officer speaks, "Nice that you two are acquainted. It's clear you didn't intend to break the law. Both of you should consider getting your 107-A, Drone and Trust certificates, and learn where you can and cannot fly. I'm giving you a warning this time, but if we catch you droning here again, the law allows us to confiscate your drones and fine you five hundred dollars apiece. Are we clear?"

DNR officer Nelson gives them a warning citation while asking the other officer to release them.

"Joe, take them back to their respective vehicles; get them out of here."

Jonathan politely asks the officer, "You can just take us back to my truck; I will take her to hers."

Back at his truck, Audrey and Jonathan are thrilled to have met by sheer happenstance this way. Neither can stop smiling. He takes her to her SUV, inviting her to a cup of coffee, to which she agrees, and they enter a nearby Starbucks.

They sit in a quiet booth, each happy and terrified. Jonathan begins: "Oh my God, I thought I'd never see you again. Meeting you again like this is crazy, I've only met you one and a half times, and I have missed you like you wouldn't believe. I have prayed to God that he let me meet you just once more… and I wasn't even supposed to be droning today. Oh my God."

Audrey replies with equal excitement, "I still can't believe you protected me in Seoul, let me stay in your suite, and never made a move on me when I was frightened to death, even though I tried to be cool about the situation. I was terrified, and you made a horrible situation wonderful. I asked God to let me meet you just once more to say thank you. I left without waking you or saying goodbye for fear of developing an emotional attachment to one of the nicest men on the planet. By the way, do you ever use the 'memo' section of your phone?"

Jonathan wonders where that question came from; he gives her an involuntary, "Huh?" But then, he sees she is serious and continues, "Never used it; I can't thumb type at high speed like most; I use the voice memo when I want to take a quickie note. So why do you ask?"

Audrey answers, "No reason in particular; it is where I keep all my drone adventures so that I can easily remember them. I am sure to have a few interesting notes about you soon." She smiles almost with glee.

They sit there, talking for nearly two hours, both looking at their watches, knowing they have to leave but not wanting to go. "Audrey, you and I keep looking at our watches. I was supposed to be at an important meeting an hour ago, and I suspect you had something more scheduled than sitting in a coffee shop with me, but I have to tell you something insane."

Audrey is intrigued and says, "Yes, I was supposed to meet my friend Mateo, but I know that if I mentioned it or called him to say I'm going to be late, you would release me to go, and I just am not ready to leave you yet. So tell me, what do you want to say."

Jonathan clears his throat, saying, "My heart is pounding sitting here with you. I've only known this feeling once in my life. Promise me that you'll become my friend. This emotion is crazy, but I love this feeling I'm getting just from sitting here with you. You've got to feel it too, do you?

"Jonathan, this is confusing to me too. After Seoul, I missed you like someone I'd known for years. My heart actually ached to see you again; that's only happened once in my life, but that's a long story. What you did for me in my most vulnerable situation was unforgettable. Mateo and Ethan are my male buddies, and I told them about you. Both said to have faith, and if God wanted it, He'd allow me to run into you one day. I feel like I can breathe again now that you're here. You know, back in Itaewon, when Alice introduced you and Peter from Kansas, she mentioned you were from Annapolis. Did you know I held out hope of seeing you again because we sort of live in the same geographic region? So I made up excuses to go to stores in Annapolis in hopes of running into you. You should know this about me, that I don't believe in love-at-first-site. But missing you the way I have, makes me believe in like-at-first-site, so, if you're up for a male/female friendship and nothing more, I'd love to be your friend, one of your best friends, Mr. Dawson."

Jonathan is surprised by Audrey's straightforward honesty and responds. "I will take being your friend any day on any terms; who knows what may blossom? But as long as I get to see you, breathe the same air as you, talk with you, I will be grateful for any time I get to be with you."

Audrey asks, "Do you really feel that way? Most guys I've met are always trying to figure slick ways to become intimate; you're the first guy I've met; well, to be accurate, you're only the second guy who has approached me with honest intentions. Jonathan, this is your third time; first at an I.T. Expo where you gave me your Saratoga water. Next, at a luxury hotel in Seoul where you saved me from a terrible situation and saved me from myself, and now, the third time, at a coffee shop here in Laurel. Jonathan, I always trust my instincts. Because of the vibes I am getting from you, I'm pretty sure you're someone I can trust with my heart. You won't break my heart as my friend, will you?"

Jonathan extended his hand to shake her hand. As they touched hands, something visibly quickened in both of them, and both loved the feeling, and both were scared of what this feeling meant.

Finally, Jonathan thinks about what Pastor Jack instructed him to do, and without asking, he says, "Don't be frightened, but I'm going to hug you; I need to. I hope, no, I pray that you and I can become fast friends."

Audrey stands and tepidly hugs Jonathan. The look in both their eyes betray the connection that both wants and need but know could never happen until they find the feeling they once had in a little grocery market in Cape Saint Claire.

And so, their friendship begins on as solid a footing as possible. Both are equally relieved to meet again. Jonathan and Audrey decide to renew the friendship that started in Korea; each is too proud to let the other know how much they were missed by the other.

Both believe they are to become friends, just friends, for life, or so they thought. But fate has other things in mind for this new friendship.

PART TWO

THE FRIENDSHIP

Sixteen

THE ACCIDENTAL FRIENDSHIP

A year has passed with Jonathan and Audrey enjoying the love of friendship without the love of love. After the drone incident, Jonathan and Audrey have become friends, not lovers. As they experience each other more, both want to reluctantly take their buddyship to the next level to become best friends. Audrey likes the idea but makes it clear to Jonathan that they are not boyfriend and girlfriend. Jonathan sours a bit because he has become accustomed to her company. He is partially ready to forget the grocery store woman he's been pining after for years and lets Audrey know so.

Audrey is invited to the wedding of her college roommate, Sondra. She is not a fan of weddings or funerals and asks Jonathan to be her date at the ceremony.

Jonathan attempts to hold Audrey's hand as they enter the wedding site; however, she is dead set against even a hint of romance and pulls her hand from Jonathan's hand. Finally, Audrey whispers with a touch of kindness, "Jonathan, I am uncomfortable having to remind you that I will abandon our friendship if you persist in being lovey-dovey with me. I love you, but not like that; do you understand?"

Jonathan releases her hand and tries to lighten his hurt in his answer. He places his hand over his heart, saying almost sarcastically, "I'm hurt, and here I thought we were becoming an item."

Jonathan accepts the non-romance thing, but to protect his emotional integrity, Jonathan suggests that they argue to flesh out how they will handle their first argument on their opposing views on something; anything. He is daring her to balance her emotions versus her logic and reasoning. He knows, but she does not realize he wants to engage her in an emotion-based chess match. Jonathan knows that irreconcilable differences cause most breakups, even among friends.

Jonathan says, "Are we having our first disagreement here? Perhaps we should talk about this and other stuff."

During the reception dinner, both question and ponder the things they disagree on.

Audrey asks, "So you want to fight? Are you sure you want to spar with me? I'm pretty stubborn; you won't like fighting with me."

"Yes, I will like fighting with you, Audrey; why; because you mean that much to me. Understand this; most couples never learn how to fight, disagree, and compromise. Fighting fair will teach one how to reconcile differences, allowing the relationship to go the distance. Audrey, I've got my issues, and I have no idea where you and I will end up. But this I know, when I thought I'd never see you again after Korea, for some silly reason, I was broken-hearted. Your friendship is a treasure to me, and as long as you are never disingenuous, I will be by your side in whatever capacity we allow each other. We will individually set boundaries and learn to comply and honor the other's wishes from this moment on: (in Spanish) '¿*Entiende usted?*'"

Audrey nods in agreement. She shows her frustration, pouting. "We are so in sync, Jonathan Dawson; you're no fun." She laughs, as does he, but neither understands why this arrangement annoys them both.

As they leave the reception venue, they continually stare wordlessly back and forth at each other. Neither realizes that they are getting comfortable with compromise. Neither understands that each would rather give in than lose this precious budding relationship. Finally, Audrey says the unthinkable, wishing she never said, "Jonathan, we need to stay in our lanes. We're emotionally drifting into something more than we bargained for."

Jonathan answers, "You just figured that out; you'd have to be blind not to see what's happening to us; scary stuff."

Almost back to her townhouse, Jonathan asks Audrey, "Tell me what you think of the traditional wedding vows?"

Audrey answers directly, "I understand what they are supposed to mean, but I feel the vows bond women to a subservient life."

"I believe," starts Jonathan, "that the vows are semi-literal."

Soon what starts as a friendly argument becomes a full-blown revolving disagreement that strains and almost breaks their relationship as friends during the following few weeks.

Both Audrey and Jonathan subconsciously abandon the formerly background thoughts each has been pondering of them being married to each other.

The resolution of the disagreement is both melancholy and surprising to both of them. Yet, without permission from their owners, their hearts dictate the solution to the friendship.

Neither Audrey nor Jonathan is aware their hearts have decided on compromise independent of the brains that created the predicament. The hearts decide to take charge, but Audrey and Jonathan's brains fight back. The friends are unaware that their hearts are working to solve the problem and encumbrances to them romantically loving each other.

The strain between Audrey and Jonathan continues. They try to force-fix things, but to no avail, but the hearts have a plan.

Passively pleading, Jonathan calls and says he'd like to kayak with her.

Audrey responds, "Jonathan, I'm not in the mood; but I will come down to the bay and help you get out of the boat ramp and watch you for a while. Where do you launch?"

Something suddenly comes back to Audrey's memory, something her mom and dad had said to each other since she could remember. Whenever her mom or dad started to disagree, one would remind the other, *'The heart wants what the heart wants, and my heart still wants you. Let's stop this foolishness; it's not important anyway.'* That was how her mom and dad sustained their marriage through the worst of times. They loved each other enough to give in, but she can't, she will not do that.

Audrey departs to help Jonathan, and it annoys her that her heart hurt wanting to be with him despite his offending her on her view of wedding vows. *'Why that subject of all things?'* she thinks.

Audrey meets Jonathan on the Riva ramp of the South River. She helps him unload his Orange and Blue kayak, tying the boat to the mooring post until he parks and returns.

Jonathan looks at her; he is still troubled by the spat they had at the wedding a few weeks ago, asking Audrey, "How long will we keep behaving this way? I know you miss the old us of just a few weeks ago."

Audrey answers sternly, "Yes, I miss us, but those vows are for cavemen. They completely negate a woman's point of view as if she's her husband's property."

Jonathan's response surprises her. "You are correct, but your understanding of the premise is where you are mistaken. The man's vows are equally if not more binding. He is pledging his life and being to protect, honor, and love you. He is the leader of the family, not the boss. He becomes the property of his wife. The husband is not the commander-in-chief; he is the leader and partner if he has the correct perspective. He will honor his wife and consider her in everything. Audrey, consider this; in an ordinary car, no front-wheel-drive or anything unique; an automobile has front wheels that steer and guide the vehicle while the rear wheels provide movement and motion. The car, which is the marriage, needs front wheels to guide it and the rear wheels to make it go. Front wheels can do nothing without propulsion; the rear wheels will only go in circles or crash without the front wheels. Both are necessary to move through life. I know you were raised a Christian even if you don't practice. I know you know a thing or two about God. But, consider this; God leads man, a man leads his woman, and they together teach their children in the mandates set by God. Yet, we see the world emerging as a chaotic mess out of order outside of that formula, eventually destroying itself. Today's relationships have four front or four rear wheels with no clear direction. And while both partners assume those roles, the relationship goes nowhere in circles or sits idle, achieving nothing. An army has a few leaders who guide millions of lesser rank. They need each other to win the battle; the generals lead, the others follow, yet the victory belongs to all while the responsibility rests on the leaders' shoulders.

He continues, "You would never feel subservient or less than equal if I were blessed to be your husband. All life comes through the woman; only she can create and sustain life. So I will never forsake you or lead you down the wrong path. And for every decision I make on our behalf, I will seek your advice, wisdom, perspective, and guidance. I may overrule you a time or two, but my intentions are always to protect and serve our family. That is what the vows mean to me. Those vows I make not only to you but to God. Do you understand that people often break promises to others, but I will not break my promise to God to love, honor, and respect you in sickness or health? Whether you or I am rich or poor, I will obey our heart's desire for each other until the moment I am no longer on earth. So I am giving you a lifetime guarantee sealed by God and my love for you that I will never break your heart, and I hope you will never break mine. If that sounds like a bad deal for you, then I am not your guy, but I will always be your friend. I love you that much."

Audrey is wordlessly considering what Jonathan has said as he launches the kayak. She knows she is moved by what he has said, and knows she is being stubborn.

As he paddles his boat further and further from shore, she watches him, saying to herself, "Careful, girl, do you realize he just proposed to you? The man loves me and wants me as his wife. So all that crap he was talking about was a cunning way to let me know his intentions and to let me know his expectations of me as his wife. So why would I want to be a wife? I'm an independent woman; I don't need a man to provide for and protect me. I make crazy money, and I'm respected in my field. What does he expect; me to be barefoot and pregnant bound to a kitchen? I can match and sometimes exceed any man's competence. No way! But he didn't say that; he talked about an order of things without chaos. He spoke about how he would adore and treat me, his wife; he already does that as my friend. And suppose we do disagree on something? Why should his be the final word? That's bull; I'm just as intelligent, if not more. But he is a decent guy; cute too. I need to think of a strong rebuttal to this guy; my heart already likes him too much, and what about my grocery store man? Slow down, girl; don't go down this path with this man; you might find yourself at Kleinfeld's saying 'yes' if you're not careful."

A few weeks have passed, and Audrey decides to test her new resilience and resistance to the attraction she feels for Jonathan.

Calling Jonathan the night before, she says gaily, "Jonathan, we've lived in the DMV all our lives and never been to the Lincoln Memorial. Don't you find it odd that people travel thousands of miles worldwide to see what is right here in our backyard? So if you want to meet me at the Arlington Cemetery Iwo Jima site, we can bike over the bridge to the memorial. Let's be tourists tomorrow."

Audrey is on North Fort Myer Drive at the soldier's memorial. She looks up to the statue of the soldiers planting the flag on Iwo Jima and is genuinely moved. Two men approach her on foot as she observes the words engraved in the wreath on the base of the massive pedestal. She reads the words aloud, "Uncommon valor was a common virtue." Then, Audrey walks her bicycle to another side, reading another inscription, "In honor and memory of the men of the United States Marine…" She stops, startled by the men that seem to be following her.

Audrey's reading of the solemn words is interrupted by two cat-calling men's voices standing behind her. One of them says, "Yo, baby, you lookin' good. You want to hang out with us?" The other one laughs, saying, "You are so fine. Can we hang out with you?"

Audrey is shocked and a little frightened as she looks around to see if Jonathan is nearby. Not seeing him, she passively panics as the men move closer, saying, "What's your name, baby? we just want to be friends." The other states to the other man, "Oh look, she's scared. Pretty girl like you shouldn't be out by yourself. What, you think we're here to rob you?"

Audrey thinks fast, telling them that her husband will be there soon. Then, she replies, "I'm waiting for my husband; could you please just move along."

One of the men walks up to Audrey nose-to-nose, saying, "I think you're disrespecting us. You got any money in that Fannie-pak?"

Jonathan rides his bike toward them, hearing and observing the situation. Then, next to Audrey's bicycle, he greets Audrey with a peck on the cheek, saying, "Sorry I'm late, sweetheart." Jonathan looks at each of the men individually and then back to Audrey. "Are these guys bothering you, Audrey?" Finally, he turns to the men saying, "You wouldn't be hassling my wife, would you?"

The younger of the two voices with loud objections, "Your wife! Man, you're playing us; she ain't your wife. Don't even try to be no hero; why don't you move along?"

Jonathan gets off his bike and gently shoves Audrey behind him to protect her; he says curtly, "I'm asking you to leave my wife alone; we got no beef with you two; we're just out for some fun."

The older man laughs devilishly. "We out for some fun too, and she looks like just the kind of fun we want. Look, man, you better mind your business; this here is between the lady and us. Get the," he uses an expletive, "…out of here. Neither of you is wearing rings; you ain't married. If you know what's good for you, you'll…"

Before either man can complete their threat, Jonathan executes a flawless roundhouse kick to one and punches the other on the bridge of his nose. Both men are on the ground. Jonathan places his foot on the chest of one of the men. He is seething with anger, saying, "I love this woman; you ever see her anywhere ever again, don't even speak."

One of the men attempts to wipe the blood from his nose as he tries to apologize. "We didn't know; we were just messing with her." Jonathan responds, "Apologize to her, NOW!"

Both men sheepishly offer apologies. Jonathan takes his foot off the man's chest when nearby Park Police see the disturbance and approach. Jonathan explains, "This is my wife, Audrey; these two were intimidating her as I rode up. They didn't want to back off, so I dropped them."

Jonathan turns to Audrey, holding her hand. "Are you okay, honey?" Then, turning to the officers, he says, "Can we leave now?

We won't be pressing charges. Jonathan glares at the men currently being detained by the officers, saying, "You ever bother my wife again, you're dead."

Audrey looks at Jonathan. She feels awkward because without even being her husband, he has protected her without regard for his own peril. She is puzzled because Jonathan behaves as if nothing happened.

A few minutes later, Jonathan turns back to admiring the Iwo Jima statue solemnly, telling Audrey, "It is incredible what they did to ensure democracy and freedom survived. I thought Memorial Day was for picnics and Bar-B-Qs when I was a kid. I was about fifteen when I saw the celebration at the Tomb of the Unknown Soldier; then, I understood the sacrifice, never thinking of Memorial Day as a holiday but a day set aside to revere those who paid the price. Audrey, those men and women and those whose names are on the wall across the street had the same dreams for themselves as you and me. But they laid down their goals for homes with picket fences, adoring spouses, and bratty children to leave us the legacy we have. We, all of us, owe them everything. Their sacrifice allowed the circumstance whereby I got to meet you and my sock girl. I can't imagine life without you as my…"

Audrey is confused about Jonathan's protection, but she is still determined to be defiant, saying, "So, Jonathan, are you saying you got that sock girl out of your mind; am I a substitute?"

Seeing the hurt on Jonathan's face, Audrey instantly regrets saying that. She asks herself silently, *"Why am I being so snarky? He just saved me; what am I doing to this kind man?"*

Audrey knows he cannot hear her thoughts, but then he answers her directly, "You're cranky and ornery because you're fighting falling for me. You don't want to submit, but your heart does. I am already open to the idea of giving you my heart; you're not. So stop being so mean and be my friend. I can see the hurt and pain on your face whenever you mistreat me. I promise I won't ask you to be my wife until you're ready, so stop worrying."

Audrey gives Jonathan the biggest smile, gets off her bike, and kisses him on the cheek. "I hate you, Jonathan," to which he replies, "I know. Let's ride across the bridge and check out the sights."

They are on the steps of the Lincoln Memorial. We see him attempting to hold her hand, but she pulls away and then takes his hand. Audrey drags Jonathan down to the reflecting pool. They stand there, gazing at the reflection of the Washington Monument and the thousands of tourists. Finally, Audrey says to Jonathan, "Wow. We're a great country."

Next, they tour the Vietnam memorial; Jonathan points out the name of his grandfather's best friend, who died in the war many years ago.

To break the sadness, Jonathan leads her across Constitution Avenue, where they take selfies in front of the statue of Albert Einstein.

Back at Jonathan's house, Audrey gets out to bid Jonathan goodbye. She sits on the front steps; he joins her but does not say anything.

Long silent moments pass when Audrey abruptly turns to face Jonathan. She cannot look at him eye-to-eye but speaks at him instead of to him. Observing her discomfort, Jonathan makes it easy by moving down one step as she remains on the step above.

"Jonathan," she begins, "I've been an awful person trying so hard not to love you for the last month. I'm a bright girl who is in control of her emotions. We have some weird kind of accidental friendship; it's crazy. I've never thought about any man this much except for the guy I saw at the market... Gosh, I wish you were that guy; this would be so easy. I love you as a friend, and I don't want to love you as anything more. I hate you for making me feel this way. Nowadays, I only feel joy when I'm with you, thinking about you and dreaming about us. This situation is impossible. You keep saying all the right things, and my heart loves it, but I don't. And now a new wrinkle; I never considered my man's protection of me until today. Still, if we never become... if that never happens, I won't have to suffer when you cheat or leave me. I won't have to fear that you may strike me with your fist one day. It happens! I can't give you my heart, even though I want to; I can't let myself be hurt. I've seen the pain suffered by women I know; it's terrible.

Do you know why I don't have a dog? I feel this way because I have seen coworkers' agony when their pet dies. Some have to take a vacation, some are never the same, and I understand. However, I love dogs and decided to avoid that hurt by never having one. I've seen friends almost want to commit suicide when they broke up with their boyfriends; I decided that would never happen to me, so I never had a boyfriend, only friend-boys. Jonathan, this accidental friendship has a mind of its own. I know I sound weak and pathetic, but every little piece of my heart I give you scares the *you-know-what* out of me. So please stop pursuing me, telling me indirectly that you love me; I know you do, but I don't want to love you. Can you understand me? Can we please just be friends, huh?"

Jonathan reaches up to the step above and takes her hand, urging her to stand. He, at six feet tall, and she, at five-foot-four; they stand there eye to eye. Jonathan never says a word; he simply wraps his arms around her and holds on to Audrey for endless minutes.

When he lets go, she notes his eyes are filled with tears. As he looks at her, he, too, sees her silent tears he knows would be there by the subtle convulsions of her body as he holds her. Audrey pulls the sleeve of her jacket over the lower palm of her hand and wipes the tears from Jonathan's eyes.

Jonathan tries to wipe her tears, but she stops him, saying, "No, let them dry on my face. I want to remember the way I feel at this moment. I will never forget you calling me your wife, protecting me as your wife, and loving me as your wife. It felt so good, and I hate it. I'm not ready to fall in love, my love. Good night, Jonathan; thanks for a great day."

Time has moved from summer to fall. Both enjoy the razzle-dazzle show of lights and waterjets as they are transported through Annapolis' Chesapeake Carwash tunnel.

Emerging from the carwash drying station, Audrey drives them to an empty parking lot near the carwash exit. Audrey tosses Jonathan a fresh microfiber towel, and they perform a second wipe down, joyfully removing the few remaining water spots.

A mile away, at Annapolis Harbour Center they stop at Sweet Frog, enjoying soft serve with outrageous toppings. They are talking and laughing when a young woman comes to their table, saying, "Are you two a couple? I never see couples get along like you two."

Audrey responds: "No, we are not," she holds up two sets of fingers as quotation marks, "a couple? Why do you ask?"

The young woman giggles, saying, "It's just that he's so cute, and I didn't want to assume you guys were lovers and throw away a chance to meet a gorgeous guy." She grabs her cell, asking Jonathan for his number. She dials it, and instantly Jonathan's phone lights up with an unknown number. The young woman says, "Now you have my number, my name is Penelope, but you can call me Penny. Ping me one day; I'd love to take you out." To Audrey: "Sorry to interrupt."

The woman leaves the table and the eatery.

Audrey is surprised by her reaction: "You better delete that number right now. Can you believe the nerve of that brazen chick? That's just rude hitting on my guy when I'm sitting right here."

Jonathan looks surprised. "Your guy? Are you saying I'm your guy now? Are you jealous? Wow, I've moved up in the world. And I didn't know you had such a hot temper; when you get mad, you'll call someone out of their name in a nanosecond. Ouch, I hope you don't get mad at me!"

Audrey speaks with pouting anger: "Even if I can't commit to you yet, she darn sure can't have you. You're my... you're my..." now speaking sheepishly and stammering, " you're almost mine. Yeah, my dad says I have a bad temper too, but only when I get riled up. Dad says I inherited it from him; he's quite proud of it; I'm trying to get rid of it; I am supposed to be a lady."

Jonathan smiles, seeing this first emotional reaction from her, and he is pleased. Audrey catches his slight smile and affectionately punches him in the shoulder. He laughs and says, "Let's get outta here."

The following Saturday morning, Audrey joins Jonathan at the top of the driveway outside his home. His truck is parked facing forward, half in, half out, just in front of the garage door. Audrey slips Dickies coveralls over her street clothes.

Audrey, wearing canvas work gloves, cranks the hydraulic jack handle raising the front of Jonathan's truck. Jonathan is sitting on the ground near the front wheel he has taken off. Audrey hands him various tools as if she were a nurse assisting a surgeon.

Together they replace the disc brake pads on both sides. Audrey enters the truck and presses down the brake pedal as Jonathan, still on the ground, bleeds the brake valves onto a drip pan. Audrey signals that the brake pedal feels firm, and they are done.

Audrey's wrists are soot-filled, and her forehead and hair are disheveled with black brake dust.

Jonathan compliments Audrey. "We did it and saved a bunch of money."

Audrey, looking soiled yet beautiful, says, "Yes, we did. I'm hungry. Let's go get something to eat."

Jonathan replies unexpectedly, "Nope. You're too dirty. Come inside to clean up, and I will fix you lunch."

Audrey smiles and gathers Jonathan's tools and heads for the garage. "Well, who knew my friend could cook? So what are you serving, cold cuts on white bread?"

Jonathan shoves her toward the bathroom. "Take a quick shower, and I will have some food ready when you come out. Spare towels and stuff are in the linen closet."

Audrey quips, "Are you crazy? I'm not taking a shower in some man's home; no way!"

Jonathan replies, "Look, if I didn't try anything in Seoul… Just shower and get your butt back out here in twenty-five minutes or less."

With a polite but serious smile, she smells her wrist, wrinkling her nose from the smell of brake dust and brake fluid on her hands. Audrey showers, washes her hair, and comes out of the bathroom wearing a floor-length terry cloth bathrobe that is obviously too big for her petite frame and her hair wrapped in a towel-made turban. She is a stunning natural beauty.

Awestruck, she comes to the kitchen where Jonathan is just setting out two bowls of pasta with shrimp, andouille sausage, peppers, parsley, garlic bread, and two Mountain Dews. As she approaches the table, she jokes about him actually being able to cook, saying how delicious the food looks. Audrey is oblivious to the way Jonathan is looking at her.

Jonathan is fighting not to say anything, but unable to resist the urge, he blurts it out, "I had no idea you were this fine." Finally, he catches himself and apologizes. "I'm sorry; I didn't mean to say that. Oh yes, I absolutely meant it; you've got it going on, girl; I don't know why I never noticed before."

Audrey graciously acknowledges this compliment, saying, "That's because of the grocery store girl you're stuck on; but no worries, I understand. Let's eat; looks good. A man who can cook; some lucky girl will be happy to be your wife."

They enjoy the meal as they talk about everything, but he can barely hear or pay attention as he continues to sneak a peek at the fresh-out-the-shower beauty sitting across from him.

She helps him clear the table and changes into her street clothes. Audrey comes back in a moment; she passively hears his mumbling. Audrey blushed with appreciation.

As Jonathan washes the dishes, he mumbles to himself, "Wow, that's the first time my heart has raced like that since the girl with the socks. Jonathan continues mumbling and thinking, *"I'd love Audrey to be my wife one day if she could only get past... If I could only get past my own weirdness."*

Jonathan drives Audrey home. He is quiet and somber. She tells him how much she's enjoyed the day and how pleased she is to have a male friend who doesn't constantly think about jumping her bones. She rubs his hand in gratitude.

Jonathan turns to her, asking, "You mean I'm in the dreaded friend zone?"

Audrey is surprised by Jonathan's reaction, saying, "Isn't that what you wanted when you asked me to be your buddy? Don't change up on me now; I would hate to lose you as my dearest friend. If it's any consolation, Jonathan, you should know that while I don't think I'm in love with you, I do love you with all my heart. I've never said that to anyone, ever. I love most of those I call friends, a simple, spiritual love. But, Jonathan, I love you something more than platonic but less than in love. Mr. Dawson, I cannot imagine my life without you by my side.

Even when I get married, my future husband must understand that you are dear to me. So don't get mad at me, but if I ever get married, I will want you to be my man of honor; I won't need a maid of honor because of you."

Audrey does not notice the pain on Jonathan's face. He says, "I don't think I could stand at an altar with you unless you are my bride. Forgive me in advance; I can't do that for you."

Audrey ignores his polite refusal, saying, "Not true; I know in my bones that you would do anything for me, just as I would do anything for you. One of these days," she continues, smiling, "I will tell you how you saved me from myself, but I can't tell you now because you'll get all big-headed, then I'll have to kill you. But, Jonathan, speaking of saving me, why did you save me back at Iwo Jima? Were you scared? And why did you say I was your wife? Just wondering; you don't have to answer, but I liked it when you made me stand behind you."

Jonathan drives slowly past all the landmarks he's never noticed while heading to her home. He considers her questions and wishes that her home was now also his home. Finally, his truck turns into the side streets toward her townhouse. Stopping in her driveway, he answers.

"To put it simply, I love you too Audrey. If anything happens to you, I would not want to go on. Saving you was really saving both of us. Life without you is pointless to me. I know you don't feel the same way, but back there at Iwo Jima, I wasn't risking my life for a friend-girl, bestie, girlfriend, or even my steady. At that moment, I saw you as my wife, the person I swore to protect and defend. Perhaps premature, but I'd die before I let anything happen to you. You may not be my wife yet, but one day…"

She smiles, laughing at herself, undoing her seatbelt, leaning across the center console, and kissing him, saying, "I am so blessed to have you. Thank you for all you do for us."

Jonathan gently grabs her arm before she can get out of the truck. Then, he asks her, "Do you know what Bobby Vinton's most famous song was?"

"I've never heard the name; who is he?"

"He's before our time; just askin'. Have a great night's sleep, my love."

Audrey bounces out of his truck and playfully curtsies and replies, "You too, my love," with a giggle. Jonathan waves affectionately to her as she enters her home. Jonathan's facial expression betrays he is both miserable and happy as he drops her at her townhouse.

Brookstone Church:
The Christening Ceremony of Olivia and Tyler's newborn:

Tyler and Olivia brought a beautiful little girl into the world several months ago. They named her Aria. Jonathan and Audrey are surprised and excited that they are asked to be God parents. Jonathan resists at first, saying, "Aren't God parents supposed to be married? Won't it be awkward if a future event has us showing up not as a couple?"

Olivia and Tyler dismiss that ever happening. Olivia says, "That's not possible; I see in both your eyes that you love each other, and no matter who you say you're both waiting for, no one else will ever do for either of you; you just don't see it yet."

Tyler follows, "I'd bet my 401K that you two will become husband and wife; no doubt about it."

Today, watching the baptism for Aria, as first-time Godparents, Audrey grabs Jonathan's hand with so much affection and adoration that they can feel each other's heartbeat pulse through the other's hand.

She knows that Jonathan is imagining this is their baby, and he is overjoyed as he looks at Audrey with such emotion that she recoils, feeling the depth of his love.

Audrey involuntarily places her hand over her stomach, rubbing it with tenderness. Jonathan glances as she does but dares not acknowledge that he has seen it. As if each has telepathy, he knows Audrey is imagining carrying Jonathan's baby. Her kind smile indicates that she enjoys the thought and the passion they'd feel as they conceive her imaginary baby.

He shocks her as he whispers to her, "Maybe one of these days, just maybe, it will be our baby in your tummy, I hope."

Feeling naked and shocked, she jerks her hand away from her stomach, asking herself, "*How could he know what I was thinking?*"

For the rest of the day, Audrey refuses to look into Jonathan's eyes through lunch and dinner together. She avoids his gaze, and he never forces his glance onto her. Instead, she feels naked, as if Jonathan could reveal every raw emotion she feels into her soul.

Jonathan understands her plight and says without preamble, "It's okay if you check my heart out; it is an open book to you. Look in there all you want; the only thing you'll find is me wanting you and wishing I could extinguish the memory of the girl with the socks. But don't worry, I'm working on it."

Finally, Audrey confesses the truth; he had read her mind, saying, "Okay, Frack; I guess Frick has nothing to hide from you. I give up. Take me home; I'm tired."

South County Bikepath:

JONATHAN AND AUDREY DECIDED MONTHS AGO TO PARTICIPATE IN THE endurance bike run along one of America's most celebrated bike paths.

The path begins on Route 301 in Gambrills, Maryland. On any weekend, hundreds of bikes could be seen pedaling along 424 south to route 2 to Deale and points along the way.

Most bikers like to race, but Audrey and Jonathan enjoy riding at their own pace.

Riding south, they take the somewhat unsafe detour through Mill Swamp Road. No shoulders and wandering cows made this two-mile shortcut always a surprise.

At the end of the road, they join other bikers heading south. Jonathan and Audrey see a produce stand with a crab truck parked next to it. Both see the truck's giant crab logo and pull over with Audrey beside him, asking her, "That looks like Aileen's truck." Audrey, surprised, asks, "You know Aileen?

Before he can answer, Aileen instantly recognizes and hugs him. "Jonathan, it's been a while. How is my adopted son, and where's Chuck? How did your crab soup turn out?"

Aileen doesn't recognize Audrey with her helmet still on. She looks at Audrey and back to Jonathan. "She's pretty. Is she…" Aileen pauses, "No fricken' way! Audrey, what are you doing here with my Jonathan? I thought you said you didn't want to meet him."

Aileen turns to Jonathan, saying, "Audrey is the girl I wanted to introduce you to way back then; Audrey, Jonathan is the guy I thought you'd be perfect with, but you shot me down. So now ain't this something else? Is Audrey the girl you were looking for back then?"

Jonathan says proudly, "No, I never found her; however, Audrey is my best friend, maybe even my girlfriend. I wish I had listened to you then, Aileen; I was so tired of the pointless mating game. I wasn't interested in riding on the dating merry-go-round any longer; it's terrible."

Audrey chimes in right behind Jonathan, touching him affectionately on his shoulder. "Jonathan is an amazing man. He's improved my life; we became friends when we ran into each other in Korea. Before Jonathan, all I did was work and go home. Now I have a full life with a kind and generous man, a friend I adore."

Aileen snaps back, "Get married then. I don't know what you're waiting for; you're never gonna find a better than each other for yourselves. And stop with this friend stuff Audrey; I can see all over your face that you're crazy about him, you're probably in love, and like you were with me before meeting Jonathan, you are too stubborn to admit he's the love of your life." Audrey and Jonathan blush openly hearing this as they wave goodbye to Aileen.

And with that, Audrey and Jonathan merge into the cycle parade before heading back to the starting point and home.

Audrey suddenly scolds Jonathan, "You've been staring at my legs all day; you're making me self-conscious."

Jonathan responds, "Sorry, I love your legs; never seen that much of them until today. Nice!"

Audrey blushes, pushes off, and begins peddling back to Gambrills with Jonathan in tow.

Trader Joe's:

Jonathan and Audrey are shopping at Trader Joe's; she is in the middle isles, and he is at the meat counter. He places salmon, pork chops, spatchcock chicken, and fresh cod in his basket. He meets Audrey coming out of the fresh veggies aisle.

He thanks Audrey for helping him do his weekly shopping.

Audrey responds, "Of course, my friend, and I've already got everything I need for your dinner surprise."

While in line, Audrey tells Jonathan how excited she is to reciprocate and prepare dinner for him. He smiles, answering with a distracted note in his voice.

"I'm looking forward to that. You could serve me a boiled egg, and if you boiled it, I'd love it."

She punches him lovingly in the shoulder, and he responds, "You're violent; you're always beating me up."

Audrey says, smiling, "And you love it." They both laugh.

Jonathan is clearly elated. "Yes, I do. But on a more serious note, I'd like to use my time with you this evening to discuss something that's important to me."

Still laughing, Audrey says, "Don't tell me you've got a rare disease, you're getting married, you don't want to be my friend anymore, you're thinking about suicide." Then, laughing harder, she says, "Tell me."

Jonathan responds without a smile; he seems serious: "Perhaps a slight combination of all three, but we'll talk. What time should I swing by?"

Audrey's Townhouse:

Audrey and Jonathan have just finished a homemade seafood boil with mussels, langoustines, blue Maryland crab, and corn on the cob.

After dinner, they settle into her couch with a little soft music in the background. She turns to him, asking, "Okay, my friend, why so serious?" She punches his arm affectionately. He grabs her fist, pulls it to his mouth, and kisses her loosely-balled fist tenderly. She recoils and says, "Oh, that. Yikes!"

Jonathan begins, "Yep. You've told me a bit about this guy you met in the market, and I've told you about the woman who first moved my heart. You have the right to know the details; I want to tell you everything. Are you okay with that? I've been thinking about it, and I realize the crab truck owner knows more than you; that's not fair to you."

Audrey answers fearfully, "No, God, no, please. You promised me you wouldn't…"

Jonathan plows ahead anyway. "But I do; I think I'm falling for you. You heard what Aileen said; she can see it; why can't you? I already love you; as a friend, but the more time I spend with you… and I swore I never would. There's been someone in my heart for years now, someone I never got to know, and nothing, I mean nothing, could make me give an inch of finding that woman until I found you. There was once a woman named Clair who sort of got under my skin; she had a crazy crush on me. Since I never had a relationship with her, I will tell you about her at another time; she was a self-anointed work-wife. Anyway, Audrey, don't stop being my friend. I won't bring it up again, but I felt like I'd bust wide open if I didn't tell you where I am emotionally; you have a right to know, and I have the right to know you know. Knowing I feel this way about you feels like I've betrayed you, but not telling you feels like I've betrayed me."

Audrey replies, "Jonathan, I'm afraid we're almost in the same weird boat." She rubs his hand, explaining, "There is a man I met—almost met—years ago. This won't make sense because it doesn't make sense to me. Anyway, this guy was my almost first love, and I don't know where he is. It was a crazy thing, but while I love you, I cannot; I will not commit to loving you as you want me to until I know there is no possibility of a life with him. I should have mentioned this to you soon after we met while being arrested for droning." She laughs a bit, "But I so enjoyed your quirkiness that I… well, you know the rest of the story. I think we should cool off and not see each other for a while; that way, you can find your girl and keep your promise, and I can do the same. It would be a shame if we ended up together seemingly happy, and then our respective lost loves popped up. Don't-cha think that would sort-a suck?"

Jonathan is surprised by her openness, and she sees in his eyes that he loves her even more because of it. So she decides to toss him a bone of consolation.

Audrey snuggles up to him, saying, "Don't feel bad because I love you so dearly that when I took a shower at your house after the brake job, I stood there drying off and for the first time in years felt that feeling down there…" she looks at her lower waist and then back to his face, "…that I thought was dead and buried long ago."

She smiles, attempting to lighten the mood. "Come on, buddy, and don't be like that. You know what I'm trying to say. Don't you? Jonathan, you awakened something in me, and I was grateful for your reaction when I came out to eat pasta in your oversized robe. I knew you wanted me, and to be honest, I wanted you too. You will never know how much I respect you for honoring me like that, just as you did in Seoul. I prayed you wouldn't reach for me because I wasn't sure I'd be able to resist. You made it easy for me, even though I know it was hard…" she pauses with a sly giggle that he finds adorable, "…hard on you. Jonathan, let's take a month off and cool off, let's think this through. I just didn't count on you becoming more than my best friend. Let's email and text; I think it will become dangerous for us to be together in close and private proximity now. Oh, my parents have been bugging me to bring my mystery man-friend to meet them. I will arrange a day and time and reach out to you if you're willing."

Jonathan drives off confused, happy, and disturbed by the unexpected twist of fate. Talking to himself as he goes home, he asks himself key questions and tries to answer them.

Jonathan, now alone, speaks out loud, "What was that? Was that a confession, a pronouncement of a pre-goodbye from me, from her? How is this possible? Is this lust or love? Am I just horny? Is she tired of being alone? Do we really care about each other? Would I actually betray my sock-girl and have a romantic relationship with Audrey? Audrey is not a swipe-right, swipe-left girl; she's my best friend, confidant, my everything. So what exactly in the heck am I thinking? And she wants me to meet her parents? I'm not ready for the family meeting. Something is amiss here."

Seventeen

THE KISS THAT WAS MORE THAN A KISS

Jonathan and Audrey set out to spend a month apart, but that plan lasts a full three days. Finally, on the fourth day, neither can take it. Audrey has been listening to Sirius on the way home from work when she hears Whitney Houston's *'Where Do Broken Hearts Go.'* She has listened to the song many times, loves the orchestration, but never really gets the message.

This time she listens to the words and realizes that the song echoes her and Jonathan's exact situation. She is broken-hearted not seeing Jonathan and wants to run into his arms. Audrey curses herself for asking Jonathan for a month's space away from him. She doesn't know that Jonathan, too, is missing his Audrey.

Jonathan calls her first. When she answers, her first words are, "Thank God! I was going crazy missing you. I was about to call you; me and my stupid idea of a month's separation; I can't be away from you for that long."

Back together, neither want to leave the other's presence. The relationship is not over the top; just two people who need and adore each other's company. Things are going smoothly for Jonathan and Audrey.

Both have become comfortable with the friendship they managed to create, build, grow, and sustain. Seeing them together, it has become impossible for friends and relatives to determine the relationship's true nature.

In gatherings, it has become awkward to watch them complete each other's sentences, and their points of view are in lockstep. So it is eerie that Audrey and Jonathan would fight to come to the center even when they playfully argue a point, quelling the disagreement before it gets started.

Then there are the wonderfully intimate moments when Audrey punches Jonathan in the arm with approval, admiration, and something akin to love.

Sitting on the lowered tailgate of Jonathan's truck, Audrey and Jonathan practically fall asleep as they relax, laying back in the spotless truck bed as they talk about everything.

"Audrey," Jonathan begins, "I can't imagine life getting any better. I've never had a girlfriend; I mean friend-girl like you. Every minute I spend with you, I feel my heart will burst with gratitude. Of all the women in the whole-wide-world, I get to spend the precious days of my youth with you. You probably don't understand since you always get to be with you. But, sometimes I can't get enough of you. I don't know what this is, and I know you hate for me to keep bringing it up. We're everything to each other, except lovers. I don't even mind waiting till 'I do' to do the do, but you're driving me crazy. Can't you be a little meaner to me, please?"

Audrey, hearing this, still lying on her back in the truck, speaks up to the sky above them with generous affection in her voice. "Me too, Jonathan. Sometimes I want to be with you like that so much that it hurts, but then you and I both have the same roadblock, your first love with the crazy socks and my guy from the store. If we could only agree to erase them, we'd be free. But, should we kill them, then I'd give you my whole heart…"

Jonathan replies, "You would indeed until he shows up or my girl shows up, and then we'd have to work, really work, to have the relationship we have now that is so effortlessly easy. Can you imagine the pain of belonging to someone else, and then the right one comes along? I'd rather die than hurt you like that."

Audrey sits up on her elbows and turns to him. "But I promise you there will be no man closer to me than you unless that man comes along. So don't believe for a moment that you're out there all by yourself. At this point, I often dream of waking up in your arms as your wife and you as my husband. I've even seen our children's faces, and that little Kenneth is a stubborn little brat, but we love him."

"Kenneth," Jonathan replies. "So you've already named our children?"

"Just one," Audrey replies playfully. "I'll let you name our other children. How 'bout that?"

Jonathan shoots Audrey a salacious little smile, saying, "Does that mean you've thought of sex with me? How was it? Huh?"

"Jonathan Dawson, you're like all men. Is that all you men think about?"

"Yes, it is," Jonathan replies. "Especially when a man has a woman as beautiful as you. I just can't help it, but I'd still love you if you weren't this way. The first thing a man notices about a woman is her physical beauty and face. Then, after being attracted to her, he hopes and prays that her personality matches her aesthetics. If so, he will pursue dating her to determine if her countenance, meaning her ordinary facial expressions that indicate whether her mood, emotion, or character is sustainable; if it is, he will discard all others to woo her with a vision of marriage. You and I went the long way 'round. You became my friend first. We got to know each other as people. Your beauty was irrelevant to me since I fell in love at first sight with the sock-girl. After that moment, there was no room in my heart for anyone new. But slowly, as I got to know you, my heart connected to yours, and I began to at first like you, and then really like you, admire you, to loving you, to being in love with you, and now I am waiting for karma to drop the other shoe, and I hope you're in my Christmas stocking. So, I understand what's going on with you, but I trust that things will work out if they're supposed to. What are the lyrics to that old song from *The Umbrellas of Cherbourg*? '…*If it takes forever, I will wait for you...'* That, Audrey, is where I am. Only you can set me free; only you."

Audrey is now somber, and something in her expression says she is about to cry, but instead, she says, "I'm not being vain, but since high school, lots of boys and men have wanted to and asked to sleep with me for all sorts of reasons, but such a proclamation has never so moved me. If we ever get past these obstacles, you can be assured that you will be the only man to get my goodies, and I hope you can save yours for me. I know that's selfish. I am a virgin by choice, but men are sowers of wild oats. I understand that, but I do not, will not have the ghost of previous men in my bed when I make love to my husband. I refuse to compare my husband's orgasmic response with my 'I-don't-know-how-many' previous lovers' orgasms. Yuck! Not gonna happen. Perhaps I'm naive, but I believe that's how it's supposed to be, no matter what everyone else is doing."

Wanting to end this discussion, Audrey scoots up to the truck's tailgate, saying brightly, "Didn't you promise to take me roller-skating tonight? I haven't been on skates since high school; I brought my old skates; I hope they still fit." Audrey warns Jonathan, laughing gaily, "You better not let me fall during *'couples skate'*." They both smile and burst out laughing.

Jonathan sits up beside her. "You're right, I did promise, but I was having a ball just hanging out with you. So let's make getting there interesting; are you afraid of motorcycles?"

Audrey answers excitedly, "My dad used to have a big bike; he taught me how to drive his; I think it was a *Honda 750 – Four*. I drove it quite a few times, but mostly I rode on the back of his bike. Mom was always scared to ride with him, but I loved it; on a few occasions Dad let me drive while he took the passenger seat. You talk about big fun; it was great, made me want to get a bike of my own."

Now in his driveway, Jonathan electronically opens the garage door to expose his M109 Boulevard. Audrey runs to jump in the saddle as if she is the driver. Then, she twists the throttle, making mouth noises as if the engine is running. Jonathan follows her into the garage, grinning from ear-to-ear.

Tucking their skates into the saddlebags of Jonathan's cruiser, they take off. Audrey rides cupcake behind Jonathan as she lovingly places her arms around his waist. Then, out to route 424 toward Blue Dolphin restaurant, they head to Crofton's Skate Zone. Her hair blowing from underneath her helmet makes the two of them look like a poster for a motorcycle commercial.

Inside the rink, we see them skating 'couples', then 'all-skate' as hundreds hurl around the floor at nearly twenty miles per hour. Still getting her skating legs back, Audrey declines to skate 'Trios' but watches with pride and delight as she watches Jonathan racing around the floor connected to two other skaters hand-in-hand at nearly thirty miles an hour. The roar of the skates against the wooden floor is deafening, but still, she screams his name as Jonathan's group hurls around the floor near her.

He hears her and grins in appreciation for her cheerleading.

These two have no idea that they are in love's death grip, and there is absolutely nothing they can do.

Heading out of the rink, Jonathan hugs her around her waist, saying, "I trust you; you said you've driven your dad's bike. So I will take the passenger seat, and you'll drive. Everything is the same as your dad's bike but with a bit more power."

Jonathan jumps on the back seat, giving her no choice, saying, "My girl can do anything."

Taking the front saddle, Audrey examines the controls and the gauges, revs the engine and tells Jonathan to hold on.

As if she's driven this monster before, she pulls the clutch lever and kicks the bike into first gear. Her right hand adjusts to the feel of the throttle, and then with the smoothest clutch release to the drag point and the precise amount of throttle, the Boulevard lurches smoothly into the night traffic heading north to route 97.

Looking back, she says to Jonathan, "This is frickin' awesome. Oh-my-God, the power! Do you mind if I take the long way back to your house?"

Jonathan lovingly squeezes her tiny waist and whispers into her helmet Bluetooth microphone, "Go for it; I'm all yours."

Audrey adjusts the music in the headpiece and proceeds around the Baltimore beltway to downtown. She parks across from Camden

Yards and the two of them sit there wordlessly watching the Baltimore night skyline and up to the Bromo Seltzer tower on the northeast corner of Eutaw and West Lombard Streets in downtown Baltimore.

Re-strapping her helmet, she takes off, heading south on the Baltimore-Washington Parkway, exiting on the ramp to Thurgood Marshal-Friendship International Airport.

Parking on a ramp with a clear view of the runways, she takes off her helmet, and both she and Jonathan dismount and sit on the grass near the bike.

Audrey leans back on her elbows and says, "This might be the best night of my life, and I owe it all to you. I love to watch planes take off and land. It is so majestic. It's incredible to watch tons of machinery and hundreds of thousands of parts lift into the heavens using the Bernoulli Principle of acquired lift. It cements my belief in God. I mean, if a man could accomplish this, imagine what God does; how he created all of this. Watching the miracles of man astonishes me, reminding me that God invented us. And when I hear music; oh my God! I ask myself, how can eight notes and a few half steps allow composers to create millions of unique tunes, melodies, harmonies, and the feelings they generate?" Audrey turns to Jonathan gleefully. "I have to see heaven. Can you imagine what music sounds like in heaven? Can you imagine the un-invented-here notes and instruments? It must be magnificent. Oh, Jonathan, I want to hear it with you at my side. They say there are no husbands or wives in heaven; perhaps we can be partners forever?"

Jonathan frowns.

Audrey asks, "What's wrong?"

Jonathan answers, "I'm greedy, and if I can't be your husband here, I want to be your husband in eternity forever. And how do you know about Bernoulli's principle?"

Audrey kisses him with a dry peck on his lips, blushing, and saying, "I love physics and anything mechanical. What did you think; that I'm dumb? Nope, I'm a tomboy. You're sweet. Let's go."

Arriving at Jonathan's home, the time is now after 1 a.m. Jonathan says, "I'm not comfortable with you driving home this late; I will follow you."

"No, Jonathan, it will be 2 a.m. before you get back here. Look, I will crash in your spare room; we've done that before, okay?"

Inside, Jonathan makes Audrey a cup of lemon balm tea and hands her a set of his oversized-for-her-frame pajamas. The pajamas swallow her petite frame; after putting them on, she comes out of the spare room for tea; she looks adorable. He is also wearing pajamas and looks like a Hanes model.

While she sits at the table sipping her tea, he says to Audrey, "Don't you dare laugh, but I wrote a song for you. I call it *Lifetime Love*. It's been such a cool day and night hanging out with you. I want to sing it; do you mind if I sing it to you?"

Audrey grabs her cup, heads to the living room, and sits on the couch with her tea.

Jonathan uncovers the Korg keyboard, faces her, and plays a beautiful melody to set the mood.

Jonathan never looks up as he sings and plays. He does not see the single tear of joy streaming down Audrey's face.

As he plays the last cord, he looks up, and Audrey is standing next to him. Her shoulders are slumped down in total emotional surrender.

Jonathan is terrified that he has offended her and stands to face her to apologize. Instead, she reaches up to him, wrapping her arms around his chest, the top of her head just under his chin. Audrey pulls away, placing her lips on his closed mouth. She forces her tongue into his mouth, kissing him more deeply than she ever thought possible.

She will not remove her mouth from his and continues to explore his mouth with hers; he gives in and returns her kiss and affection with unrestrained passion.

She is so close to him that she can feel his excitement and desire for her. He continues to kiss her but discreetly pulls his body away from her as their lower torsos fight to remain together.

He carefully pulls away in agony. He says to Audrey, "We can't. I won't hurt you that way. I want and need you, but I will honor you and wait until our wedding night. I promised that I would never hurt you and even though you think you want what you want in this instant, what you've wanted for your whole life is greater. I will be the man who enters our bedroom together on that special night; I will not be the ghost you remember if it's not me. That, Audrey, is my gift to you."

Looking into his eyes, she gathers her wits. "The song moved me past my principles. I couldn't help myself. I am, and I am not sorry. At that moment, with the words of that song, and the melody, I felt like I was married. You're a remarkable man, Jonathan Dawson."

"Don't go trusting me too much; another minute of the way we were going at it, you might be having little Kenneth in nine months. But, Audrey, there's something else I have to tell you; It's been years since I've kissed a woman, but the way you kissed me tonight reminded me of a girl I used to work with who confessed to having a crush on me. I cooked dinner for her once, and she rewarded me with a kiss so romantic and sweet that I thought about it for days afterward. No, I didn't have the same physical reaction as I did with you, and I didn't sleep with her, but it was an amazing embrace. So now I understand what you mean about a ghost. For a moment, while you were kissing me, I thought about her."

Audrey asks, "Why are you telling me this now?"

"Because up until now, you only let me be your friend and best friend. You insisted on no romance, even though you knew my feelings for you were much greater, but I had to play by your rules. There's no denying now that you have deeper feelings for me than you're willing to admit to right now, but I'm no fool; you like me more than you're ready to let on. Anyway, as long as you and I were simply best friends, who I kissed before you was none of your business, I now want you to know as a point of honesty. Tonight was the kiss that was more than a kiss, and you know it. This other woman lives in another state twelve hours from here. Before the drone incident, when we found each other, I allowed myself to get close to her because I missed you and thought I'd never see you again. But if she's ever here again, I don't plan to hide, duck or evade being seen with you. I love you, not her. She may not be a past lover, but she is and was someone important to me. So I am asking you, are you okay that I have a friend who once asked me to marry her? Tell me now; I don't intend to have drama over this."

"Jonathan, you're a man. I expect you to have a past. Me? I never wanted a past, only a present, and future with the love of my life. As long as you never call me by her name, compare our kisses to your previous smooches, and never cheat on me with her if we ever become an item, then I'm good. I am neither possessive nor jealous. You should know by now that I trust you. By the way, what's this girl's name?"

"Clair."

Audrey kisses him deeply again, ending that conversation. They both laugh, neither ashamed nor guilty, knowing something has changed between them. Instead, their faith is renewed, knowing that God has a plan for them and all they have to do is be patient.

Audrey waltzes into the spare room, singing, "Goodnight, Jonathan."

After she's asleep, he grabs his tea and sits at the keyboard; he turns the volume as low as possible so as not to disturb Audrey. Then, he plays the song he just sang for her. Hearing the lyrics in his mind's ear, his eyes become glassy, overwhelming him with longing and emotion.

Jonathan fights himself. *"Don't play that song; anything but that,"* he shouts in his mind's ears. Finally, but sadly, he succumbs playing Elton John's, *'Something About the Way You Look Tonight.'* The melody is beautiful and haunting.

Audrey hears the tune from the bedroom and comes behind Jonathan, hugging him from behind as he plays. She whispers in cadence with the song, mid-lyric singing its longing words.

Audrey, afraid to face Jonathan, hugs him from behind again, whispering, "I feel the same way. Good night."

Off to bed, both do not awake until 10 a.m. the following day. Then, finally, she stumbles into the kitchen, where Jonathan completes breakfast for her, consisting of home fries, sausage, eggs, toast, and a French Press brewed cup of Sulawesi coffee.

After breakfast, she showers and heads home. Before leaving, she says something so romantic to Jonathan that he cannot shake it for the next few weeks. "Well, honey, we just spent our first night as spiritual husband and wife. Perhaps soon, it will be for real. I don't know everything, but now I know I love you with almost all of my heart; I'll be working on getting rid of the 'almost'. Have a great day, love."

Jonathan grabs her hand, swinging her toward him for a departing hug. She shoulders her purse over her back and returns his hug. Finally, he says to her wistfully, "Are we still on for movie night this weekend, your place or mine?"

Audrey smiles. "Saturday night, my place, you pick the movie."

AND SO ENDS THE BEST DAY AND NIGHT SO FAR OF THEIR ADULT LIVES. Now it is up to fate, Clarence, and Ethan to remove the last obstacles to Kenneth's birth and Audrey and Jonathan's lifetime of happiness.

But the enemy of humankind has been busy plotting against Audrey and Jonathan. Worse still, Ethan, Audrey's guardian angel, is hurt and sulking. He is nowhere to be found.

Wallace, a new assistant angel working for Clarence, knows something is amiss. His heavenly intuition feels the dark forces that want to prevent earth's salvation from environmental cataclysm. So, Wallace begins to pan the world searching for Ethan, the broken-hearted guardian angel to Audrey and Jonathan.

AS FOR JONATHAN AND AUDREY, LOVE IS BLOSSOMING, BUT NEITHER knows that dark days and trying times are ahead. Life and Death for both hang in the balance, and only true love and sacrifice by each can save the other. It all happens accidentally on purpose.

Audrey is not a crowd person. She doesn't mind people so much, but if she can, she always looks for ways to be among smaller crowds. Audrey chooses Sundays at the Farmer's Market because there are fewer people. She attends her health club either early in the morning or mid-afternoon when fewer members are there. Her most unusual effort to be alone is the deal she made with the pool attendant, Arnold, at the Riva Road swim center.

Audrey is not unaware that some men consider her attractive.

However, she hates the unwanted attention men thrust on her, vying for her recognition. Her first visit to the pool is an ugly and embarrassing moment as men stare at her in her plain one-piece swimsuit.

Arnold sees the distraction and offers to allow her to come in at closing for an hour to do laps. He directs her to the employees-only side entrance door. Audrey swims twice a week after returning from Korea. Arnold meets Jonathan and allows him to swim laps with her.

On that fateful early evening, Jonathan needs to run a few errands. He doesn't go with her every time but loves seeing her in her form-fitting bathing suit. Jonathan has trained himself not to react to her fantastic figure. "Audrey, I can't stay today; I've got a little errand I need to take care of. I will meet you back here at the usual time."

Audrey enters through the employee's door, changes, and begins her regiment of laps. Finally, an unforeseen danger almost kills Audrey on the seventh lap set, and only Jonathan's soul connection saves her life.

Arnold always activates the pool's powerful recirculation pumps after Audrey leaves. The pumps run on a low non-suction mode during the day but are switched to hi-power during off-hours. The pumps create a powerful vacuum pulling water into the pool's filters, cleaning the water, then ejecting the recycled water at the opposite end of the pool.

Unknown to Arnold, an automatic timer is installed that morning before his shift, which no longer requires human activation. The timer is programmed to activate after closing hours.

During Audrey's seventh lap, the pumps automatically cycle on. As Audrey swims by the side vent, like an ocean undertow, her 125-pound body can feel the suction as the strong flow pulls her closer and closer to the pump. She strokes as hard as possible, but swimming against the artificial undertow would not allow her to escape easily in effect, swimming in the same place with no forward motion.

Audrey tries breaststrokes, arm-over-arm, and treading water techniques; nothing works. Finally, tired from the feverish effort, she feels herself being pulled down and closer to the pump's intake manifold vent. Audrey protested in her mind, *'I cannot let this thing drown me. I won't!'* She screams in her mind's voice.

Desperately kicking, Audrey begins to tire, and her muscles begin the ache one feels when a cramp starts. She knows she is exhausting the potassium in her muscles. She thinks of Jonathan. *'I can't die; I'm finally happy. I have Jonathan; I love him. I've got to live for my Jonathan.'* Mustering all her courage, she wishes that Arnold would come from his office to check on her, but she knows he is busy with reports and maintenance schedules. Slowly, Audrey's fight against the suction is becoming a lost cause, and as her life flashes before her, all she sees is Jonathan, Jonathan, and more Jonathan.

As dribbles of trickling water enter the corner of her mouth, she tries to spit the chlorinated water out.

Jonathan arrives at Annapolis Mall; his mission is to purchase a friendship ring for Audrey, but as he parks, he twists his face as if something is wrong. Looking around, he can detect nothing. Suddenly in his heart, Jonathan feels a crazy urge to see Audrey right away. He knows this feeling is unreasonable and exits his truck. But just as he gets to the mall's entrance, he cannot shake the feeling.

Jonathan runs back to his truck, driving like a careless maniac toward the swim center only two miles away.

He carefully runs the lights at Bestgate Road, cuts off the 97 north traffic at exit 21, around the loop to exit 22, and runs the light at Bowen's Farm Supply and Truman Parkway.

As if his very life is on the line, he drives over the parking lot and lawn and directly to the side door. Then, leaving his driver's side door open, he runs in to see his Audrey going down under the water with her right hand extended just above the waterline.

Fully dressed, Jonathan runs to the side of the pool closest to where Audrey is drowning, takes a massive gulp of air, and dives in like a torpedo.

Reaching Audrey, he goes under, grabbing her torso with all his might. Now both underwater, he treads for the both of them, his powerful kicks keeping her from sliding further down. Audrey is barely conscious, but she recognizes Jonathan. He pinches her nose with his free hand, places his mouth over hers, and transfers the fresh oxygen he had gulped into her starving lungs.

Forcing himself to the surface, he sucks in more air while still holding her hand. Underwater again, Jonathan places his mouth tightly on her gasping mouth. He again exhaled every last drop of air, filling her nearly depleted lungs.

Audrey calms a bit in his arms, and with powerful side strokes, he pulls her out of the draft of the pumps. Now in the middle of the pool, still treading water, he flips Audrey on her back, her lower torso adrift below the water. Jonathan performs artificial respiration and does not stop until she can breathe on her own.

With all his strength, he pulls her to the poolside and pushes Audrey over the pool's tile lip and onto the floor surrounding the pool.

Jumping out of the pool, Jonathan holds her exhausted body. Her arms are limp, lying against the floor. He grabs a poolside towel and covers her body as he holds her close, transferring heat from his body to hers.

Lifting Audrey's head, shoulders, and lower back off the tile floor, he holds onto her in tears. He would not let her go. Slowly, she drowsily comes back to herself, still in his arms. She lifts her arms, wrapping them around his back and neck.

What she says to him, he is not prepared for. "I tried my best to live for you, our life together, our babies. But, as the water claimed me, I gave up once I knew I would never lie in your arms as your wife. I thought, what's the use of living without my Jonathan? I guess I am a hypocrite after all. It wasn't until I almost died that I realized that I only wanted to live... because of you."

Audrey collapses in his arms somewhere between sleep and unconsciousness.

Still wrapped in a towel, Jonathan picks her limp body up and carries her to his truck, belting her into the passenger seat. Back inside, he grabs her street clothes from her usual locker and hurries to his home, which is closer than her townhouse.

Jonathan enters through the garage and carries Audrey, still shivering, inside, laying her on his couch. He quickly covers her with a down comforter he ripped off his bed. Almost running to the bathroom, he half-fills the bathtub with warm water. He scrambles through his toiletry shelf, grabbing a bottle of L'Occitane Lavender Foaming Bath, and then ensuring the water is perfect, he carries Audrey's shivering body and gently places her in the warming bath. Then, not sure if Audrey is conscious enough to remain alert, fearing she might slip under the water, Jonathan kneels beside the tub, supporting her limp body's weight by holding her left arm wrapped around his right arm to ensure she does not slip under the water while warming her body.

He tries desperately not to gawk at her figure, but the form-fitting bathing suit reveals a female body of such beauty that he forces himself to look away.

Audrey is fully awake in fifteen minutes. He motions to her clothes folded on the shelf, saying, "I'll make us some hot cocoa; come out when you're ready.

Sitting at the breakfast bar for a long half hour, neither said a word, but their eyes spoke volumes. Finally, she rises first and walks over to him wordlessly. Audrey leans his head back and kisses him softly and gently. Then, pulling away, she says, "I love you more than you can know. I'm yours tonight."

She places her empty cup in the sink, slowly walks to his bedroom, pulls off her street clothes, falls into Jonathan's bed, and is asleep within minutes.

Jonathan dares not enter his own bedroom that night, knowing her lifelong wish to remain chaste until marriage. He knows that if he enters his bedroom that night, there is no power on earth to prevent what they both wanted. Jonathan loves her enough to protect the future he knows she wants. Jonathan sleeps on the couch that night; surprisingly, neither speaks of what happened until…

Eighteen

I WOULD DIE FOR YOU, AND I DON'T KNOW WHY

Neither Jonathan nor Audrey has ever claimed to be outdoors people, but if the weather is good, they are always spontaneously ready to do anything that lets them be outdoors. Conversely, if the temperature drops below forty degrees or colder, one couldn't drag these two out. They are known to spend entire weekends at one person's house or the other. Their cold weather tonic is home cooking, binge streaming, karaoke, and dancing. And when they aren't doing that, they love to sit in a room, each engrossed in reading a novel yet loving breathing each other's air. Some might call them boring, but they love just being together.

It is the end of fall when they decide to indulge their passions for the great outdoors—they set their sights on Quiet Waters Park.

There is a mishap that changes the direction of both their lives. While hiking, Jonathan stumbles, spraining, then breaking his ankle. The following events force a disabled Jonathan to try to protect Audrey, but he cannot. Equally surprising to Audrey is that she must, in an instant, decide to give part of her life to save Jonathan's life. This is that story.

Six Weeks Earlier:

AUDREY COMPOSES HER WEEKLY EMAIL TO JONATHAN, WHICH HE usually reads gleefully with just a touch of disappointment. However, today he is happy about Audrey's text suggesting they go hiking.

Jonathan *Facetimes* Audrey, saying, "Good morning Audie, wow, you even look great on this tiny screen; anyway, I got your text, and I feel like taking the day off. *Weather Channel* says tomorrow is going to be a perfect no-humidity day. So, how about you call in sick; spend the day with me at my favorite park? We can fish, hike, paddleboat, lounge around, and tire ourselves out. What do you say?"

Audrey quickly answers, "Okay, if you promise to make me a nice picnic lunch. We will probably need two days to do all the fun stuff. But, if you plan on doing all that, won't we need a day to recuperate?"

Jonathan responds, "Done. I will pick you up tomorrow at 8; is that too early?"

Audrey looks at Jonathan tenderly. She has been doing that a lot since the pool incident, but her eyes always say the same thing wordlessly, *'Thank you Jonathan, for everything.'*

Next Day: Quiet Waters

THEY DRIVE THE WINDING ROAD TO THE PARK'S CAMPSITE. THE SITE OF the statue of the pelican is stunning and majestic. Audrey wants to touch Jonathan's hand but withdraws with trepidation, fearing that Jonathan will misunderstand the gesture.

They spend the day in a flurry of activities that include croquet, archery, paddle boating, and ice skating.

Jonathan, tired, escorts Audrey to the Dogwood Pavilion. He extracts a colorful table cloth and an elaborate picnic basket. Inside the high-end basket are china, flatware, two salads from the local market, a bottle of sparkling cider, two flutes, and handmade cold-cut subs.

Jonathan proudly adds, "And for dessert, I brought my two favorite soft drinks; you have the first choice."

A SIMPLE ACT OF KINDNESS

Audrey extends her hand, saying, "Saratoga and Topo Chico. You remembered our first meeting at the Expo Center. I liked you then but didn't know you, and I was afraid to get to know you."

Jonathan answers, "Audrey, we've been friends for a while now. I think we really like each other. I feel whole when I'm with you. You've said no, and I'll think about it before, but I'd like us to be a 'thing,' as old-fashioned as that seems by today's standard of morality. I just don't want to lose you; you're my best friend."

Audrey replies, "I like you, Jonathan, I do. Ever since Seoul, you're that special friend, but if we go down that path, like all those before us, we'll eventually tire, get on each other's nerves, and possibly lose this 'thing' we have. I couldn't stand that. But, look, Jonathan, I've already confessed that I love you, and I know you love me. So, let's hold on to what we have. Let's not be greedy. I don't want to mess this up. And don't think of yourself as my second choice; you could never be anyone's second choice."

Jonathan smiles, saying, "Let's clean up this stuff, get our gear from the truck, and go for a hike. I know a great trail across the lake."

On their way to the trail, they pass by a wedding just letting out at the Blue Heron Center. Audrey and Jonathan silently envy the bride and groom, surrounded by guests and loved ones. Both look at each other silently. We know what the wishful expressions on their faces mean.

Jonathan and Audrey take the walking ferry across the lake. They are the only two passengers on the ferry. The ferry master hands Audrey her stowed-away walking stick, telling them both he will be back on the hour for the next five hours. Audrey grabs the six-foot-long walking stick, hoisting her backpack and holster-like tool belt around her waist. She glances at her watch, taking note of the time.

Jonathan sarcastically asks her, "What's all this stuff; we're not climbing Everest?" She grins, telling him that she was a girl scout. She points to the embroidered patch on her rucksack. "It's the Girl Scout gold award. I try always to be prepared for anything. Come on, let's go."

Before stepping off the ferry's landing ramp, the driver warns them. "Stay on the main trail; we had reports of critters wandering off their perimeters last year. I also had a report of a couple of coyotes on the trail, but the park manager says it's probably a rumor. So you should be okay; call the emergency number if you get spooked, and I will come to get you before the hour."

They hike up the trail and through the woods, taking pictures along the way with cellphone cameras. Leaning back to get a wide shot, Jonathan stumbles, but he sprains his right ankle and cannot walk so quickly as he catches himself.

Audrey helps him sit on a boulder and takes a bowie knife from her canvas backpack holster.

Hiking about twenty yards away, just a bit off the trail, Audrey sees a stout tree branch, chops it down, and fashions it into a crutch-like cane.

Hiking back to Jonathan, she helps him to his feet, fine tunes the length of the homemade crutch under his arm, and assists him in walking around to where the ferry is to pick them up.

Suddenly, two coyotes cautiously approach Audrey and the lame Jonathan. They snarl and snap; Jonathan attempts to protect Audrey but collapses, hearing his ankle crack, unable to support his weight. He screams to Audrey, "Run to the dock, and I will hold them off. Run!"

Audrey looks at her helpless best friend attempting to get up to protect her. Then, she withdraws the bowie knife from its sheaf and whacks one of the coyotes on the side of the head with the hilt flat side of the blade as hard as she can.

A dribble of blood spurts from the animal's wound; Audrey instinctively uses her body to cover and protect Jonathan. The animal howls loudly and backs away, stumbling to the ground and angering the other coyote, now snarling and snapping alternately at Audrey and Jonathan, still on the ground.

With discerning trepidation, the other coyote comes closer to Jonathan. Audrey circles behind the coyote, carefully pulling something from her backpack, a taser pistol. She aims it, firing it. Two electrodes stab the coyote, causing it to writhe in excruciating pain. Audrey approaches the suffering animal, screaming, "You had enough?"

Standing there facing the two coyotes, one just regaining consciousness, both animals run off back into the woods with the leads of her taser dangling on the ground. She observes, standing at the ready, still screaming at the coyotes with mixed semi-curses. "Get the heck away from my man. I will kill you; do you hear me?"

Still helpless on the ground, Jonathan watches in disbelief as his so-called female buddy has just saved his life at the risk of hers. He is grateful and stunned.

Audrey's 5'4" frame picks up Jonathan's 6'1" body, practically dragging him and the crutch to the waterside ferry dock. She opens her water bottle, washing the dirt and sweat off her hands and face. She sits beside Jonathan, wordlessly consoling him by rubbing his shoulder and saying, "It's okay. I've got you. I won't let anything or anyone hurt you, my dearest friend; not on my watch."

The ferry picks them up, and they head for the truck.

She gently places him in the back seat, extracts an ACE bandage from the first aid kit, and wraps his now swollen ankle. Tears fill her eyes as she completes the bandage.

She pours rubbing alcohol and betadine over his, then her skin, sanitizing the portion where her skin and Jonathan's wound came in contact with the coyote's blood.

Annapolis Medical Center: Emergency Department:

AUDREY DRIVES JONATHAN'S TRUCK, FOLLOWING THE AMBULANCE TO the emergency entrance. The paramedics have informed Audrey and Jonathan that his ankle is broken, not sprained. Audrey jumps into action inside the ER, getting Jonathan registered for the doctors to treat his broken ankle.

Audrey stays with him every step, escorts Jonathan into the men's room, helps him into a stall, and waits for him at the hand washing sinks. Finally, she is shameless as she answers his call that he's done and helps him hobble out of the men's room. She escorts him to the treatment stall just beyond patient registration.

She follows him to X-Ray and back to triage treatment. They

hang a broad spectrum antibiotic I-V, explaining that his skin had a break and want to be sure he's okay.

The managing attending ER doctor interrupts, "Actually, I prefer Mr. Dawson to stay a night or two; the ankle will heal normally, but I am concerned about observing how the antibiotics perform. Also, we're unsure if the animal's blood infected Mr. Dawson's open wound. He could develop sepsis, and I want him here just in case."

Audrey informs Jonathan forcefully, "I want you to stay, just until the doctors are sure. Then, I will call your parents."

Jonathan is transferred to a private room, introduced to his care providers, and given instructions for his stay, "It should be short, possibly a day or two. Animal blood can be nasty stuff; we need to observe your vitals for twenty-four hours at least. Then, you can go home once we're sure you're okay."

Audrey enters the hallway, waiting for the ER staff to tell her what room Jonathan is assigned. Audrey, having Jonathan's cell in her backpack, speed dials number two; she blushes and is pleasantly surprised to see that her number is in the number-one position.

Mr. Dawson answers, thinking it is Jonathan, "Well, Jonathan, this is a pleasant surprise; you never call this time a day. What can I do...."

Audrey interrupts. "Hello, Sir, my name is Audrey Sawyer, Jonathan's friend-girl and buddy. I'm sorry to disturb you, but Jonathan is at Arundel Med. We went hiking, and a coyote attacked him shortly after he broke his ankle. His ankle is fine, but Jonathan got a small scratch, and the doctors want to keep him overnight; they're worried about sepsis. I thought you should know."

Franklin answers, "Audrey, you say? His mother and I will be there in fifteen minutes. What room is he in?"

Audrey says, "They're taking him to a room now. I don't know, but I will ask the nurse and wait for you at the ER entrance."

Entering the ER, Franklin singles out the only person near the entrance who is alone. Allison approaches Audrey. "Are you Audrey? How is my son? Where is he?"

Audrey is steady but shaken, and responds, "Five twelve."

The three enter the room just as the trio of nurses leave, giving

Jonathan last-minute instructions. Jonathan looks at his parents, saying to his mother, "Now don't look like that; I'm okay. And this is not how I wanted you to meet my best friend, Audie."

His dad interrupts, "Your best friend, what's wrong with you, son? Why isn't she your fiancée?"

Jonathan laughs through his pain. "It's a long story; Mom, come here; I need a hug."

Audrey blushes and takes a chair, bowing out of the moment, knowing this is a private family moment.

The family catches up during the next hour, and Jonathan attempts to explain Audrey to his parents. Finally, Mrs. Dawson turns to Audrey, saying, "I'm so glad you two found each other. He's been so melancholy about a girl he saw long ago wearing crazy socks. One day a few years ago, Jon came by the house to tell me he could never move on until he met this girl again. I advised him to open his heart to other possibilities; he refused. I am sure you know how stubborn my Jonathan is. Anyway, I'm delighted he's found such a polite, thoughtful, and considerate, what did he call you, a friend-girl. I never heard that one before, but as long as he is happy, that is all I care about. So, Jonathan, when they discharge you, you're coming home with us; we will nurse your ankle back to health."

Jonathan stops them. "Mom, Dad, Audrey will be nursing me at her place. There will be no discussion on this. Nope, we're not having sex or anything like that, but I love and trust her. Not a word from either of you. Understand?"

Audrey jumps up. "You can't speak to your parents like that."

Jonathan turns to Audrey for the first time and shouts, "My decision is final unless you rescind your offer…"

Audrey is unsure how to respond and looks to Jonathan's parents for a clue.

Franklin is the first to speak. "Don't worry, Audrey; we will visit him at your house; text me your address. Once he's made up his mind, that's it. It ain't worth the fight. Clearly, the boy is crazy about you; I'm just happy to see him over the long-lost crush."

Meanwhile, the flurry of activity in heaven saw angels moving about at such speeds they are hardly recognizable. Then, finally, an intermediate-grade angel, Wallace, bursts into Clarence's office without permission. Clarence is in conference, and his expression is shocked that a lower-grade angel would commit such indignation.

Clarence apologizes to the other senior host. "Please accept my apologies; it seems one of my protégées has no manners." Then, turning to Wallace, he asks, "What are you doing here? What's so crucial that you violate protocol and embarrass me in the presence of other senior council members?"

Wallace catches his angelic breath and speaks in panic tones, "Sir, there's big trouble on earth. It's Jonathan; he's dying."

Clarence answers with disbelief, "What are you talking about; Jonathan can't die; it's not his time. Without him, Kenneth will not exist. If Kenneth and Audrey don't produce him, the earth will not survive its own environmental stupidity. So, slow down and tell me what is going on."

Wallace explains the events, the coyote attack, and how Audrey saved Jonathan. Finally, he describes the infected blood that has Jonathan in a coma. "Sir, he's not expected to live, and if he dies prematurely, Audrey will die soon after that from a severely broken heart."

Wallace further states, "Not long ago, Audrey almost drowned, she would have died, but I couldn't find Ethan, so I violated the rules and sent the call for help to Jonathan directly. He got to her with only seconds left; he saved her."

Clarence asks, "Why are you just telling me this now?"

Wallace struggles to answer. "Sir, both were emotionally drained; Audrey insisted on sleeping with Jonathan in gratitude and love; Jonathan was able to resist but with great difficulty."

Clarence rises from his seat, screaming, "Where's Ethan? He is their guardian angel. He should have been protecting them. Where is Ethan now?"

Wallace bowed; his body language did not want to inform his boss. Finally, Wallace confesses, "Sir, Ethan has been sulking in Sri Lanka. Audrey broke his heart as he was in love with her. You stripped Ethan

A SIMPLE ACT OF KINDNESS

of the knowledge that he was an angel when you assigned him. As an ordinary human, he naturally began to love Audrey. Her blunt rejection sent him reeling and lost emotionally. "

Clarence, using telepathy, consults with the other senior angels. After their huddle, Clarence orders Wallace, "Go down and instantly infuse Ethan with who he is. Get him to the hospital to support Audrey."

Wallace asks, "What if Jonathan dies before...? Can we use temporal adjustment?"

Clarence answers, "Time travel is not allowed; Master's strictest order."

Wallace interjects, "Sir, we estimate that Audrey will die from Cortisol poisoning soon after that if Jonathan dies."

"Cortisol?"

Wallace answers his boss, "Yes, Sir. When humans become stressed, their endocrine systems produce Cortisol to decrease the stress. However, too much of the hormone from too much pressure will, in her case, cause myocardial infarction, and when combined with her desire not to live without Jonathan, she will die in her sleep literally from a broken heart. If Jonathan dies, Ethan will only have less than a minute to naturally restart his heart and use electrophoresis to clean his blood of the foreign life form. But, Sir, everything must go perfectly for this to work."

Seconds later, Wallace appears before Ethan on the island at the southmost tip of India. Without conversation, he touches Ethan, transferring the knowledge needed to work a miracle required in this scenario.

Ethan asks Wallace, "Why was I put in this position? If I had known I was a protector, I would never have developed feelings for Audrey."

Wallace answers, "Clarence has authorized me to tell you everything but at a later date. He will be coming soon to meet with you in person. But, for now, you must hurry; time is short."

Seconds later, Ethan transforms into an ambient form of electrons and gas-like magma, reappearing almost instantly on the fifth floor of the Annapolis Medical Center. Ethan visits multiple rooms on the floor and discovers Jonathan alone in room 512.

Still invisible as an apparition, Ethan sits in the corner like a guardian angel, ready for battle. He knows that he can restart Jonathan's heart should it fail. He knows he can clean the blood, but the sequence of events must be followed precisely, or brain damage could occur. But on the other hand, Ethan knows that he cannot perform artificial respiration; he knows that only Audrey can because the air she must give him is part of the same air he gave her when she almost drowned. This backward exchange is part of the rule of the heavenly *equation of circumstance.*

It burdens Ethan also to know that if Audrey cannot restart Jonathan's breathing, he will suffocate and die. Ethan is disturbed by what Wallace said in Sri Lanka, "If Audrey helps him to restore his life, her life will necessarily be shortened, perhaps by years. You must tell her; she has to know before. It is a bargain she must make willingly."

Ethan ponders the one fact Wallace had mentioned in Sri Lanka. "Ethan, your abandonment of duty could cause irreplaceable damage to this planet. So many rules of heavenly order have been bent; that is how vital Jonathan and Audrey's DNA are. Your hurt feelings could have and perhaps will cause this planet to be lost forever. The elders understand you being smitten by Audrey; she is a one-of-a-kind woman. The council forgives you because you were unaware of your angelic responsibilities."

ETHAN LOOKS AT JONATHAN, SAYING TO HIM WHILE HE SLEEPS, "I'M sorry, old friend; I just didn't know. Forgive me and come back. Audrey needs you."

Ethan, as a spirit, watches and protects Jonathan all night from the wandering evil spirits that would have been pleased to see him die tonight. But, Ethan would not let that...."

Ethan's thoughts are interrupted as he hears voices outside in the corridor.

The following morning, Audrey is en route to the hospital when she receives a call as she turns onto Jennifer Road. The doctor says, "Miss Sawyer, I mean Audrey, Jonathan's numbers turned south overnight, and we're very concerned. Call his parents and get them here ASAP."

Audrey immediately goes to Jonathan's room; his parents enter a few minutes later. Jonathan is breathing shallowly and is unconscious. The life support monitors beside Jonathan's bed show rapidly blinking red LEDs next to his vital signs.

"It's not rabies," the doctor says. "If it were a garden variety bacteria, he'd be up and walking by now. Instead, we think it may be one of the new Methicillin-resistant Staphylococcus aureus, commonly known as the MRSA bacteria strain. We're hoping his natural immunity can manufacture antibodies faster than the foreign strain can multiply. I'm sorry, folks; at this point, all we can do is hope."

Audrey leaps to Jonathan's bedside without hesitation and begins praying. She wraps her arms around him, almost lifting Jonathan off the bed, watching the monitors indicate a further decline. Audrey locks her head in the locks of Jonathan's shoulders, praying. "God, please, not him. You can't have him yet; I need him. He is my only friend and the only person I love. I won't let you have him. Take my life instead. You promised me, God, that Jonathan would always be my friend. God, you know I'd die for him. Take the bargain; the trade, take me. I can't let him go."

The doctor is trying to be professional and compassionate. Jonathan's parents are teary-eyed, trying to console Audrey and hold on to their dying son.

Ethan stands, being careful to remain a spirit. The stress in the room is overwhelming.

Moments later, the monitor makes that awful monotone flat line tone, and the scope shows no heartbeat.

Audrey holds on to Jonathan's body tighter, speaking to his limp body and God. "Dear Lord, we've always been close. I never bother you with my little problems, but I know you're always there. I'm asking you for a miracle. You sent this man into my life; I didn't know until recently how much I need him, and he needs me. Now, God, I'm not threatening, but I will die from a broken heart if he dies. If you restore him back to me, I will work to forget the mystery man of my past; I promise. That's all I have to say, God."

The doctor attempts to pull Audrey away from Jonathan's limp body gently. "It is Maryland state protocol; I must call the TOD. Please, ma'am."

The doctor checks Jonathan's eyes for dilated pupils. Then, he placed his stethoscope on Jonathan's chest, listening for a heartbeat, and turned to the parents with sadness and a head nod from left to right. The doctor finally places his index finger on Jonathan's pulse and under his nose and says to the nurse, "Jonathan Dawson, age 24, died at 8:07 a.m. on this day...."

As Audrey begins to move away with a sobbing Allison's help, both are now crying. Audrey mumbles, "Not my Jonathan. No, God, please...."

Audrey sniffles and turns back to Jonathan's corpse. She weeps and convulses over Jonathan's lifeless body. Then, in a last desperate plea, she says to God, "He saved my life and almost died himself to save me when I was drowning with no hope. If you could send him to save me, let me be the one who saves his life."

No one notices the nearly invisible apparition that formed in the room next to Audrey. But just then, Audrey catches its shape and voice. The voice was familiar; it sounded like Ethan, but the figure was something from a distant memory. Audrey thinks, *'Perhaps the death angel,'* but quickly dismisses the thought as she feels exultant pleasure in the apparitions' presence.

Audrey says to the room, "Jonathan will be back; I'm sure."

The doctor glares at Audrey, saying, "I'm so sorry, Miss; there is no medical method to bring Mr. Dawson back. He has passed away. It is impossible to resuscitate a patient with severe septicemia. I will leave you and your family alone with his body for as long as you need."

Audrey bursts out in tears of joy, almost screaming, "Doctor, we won't need an hour; we won't need even a minute." Audrey shouts toward the ceiling, "Thank you, God, for bringing my Jonathan back to me."

Exactly thirty-six seconds after having his death pronounced by the doctor, Jonathan's vital signs monitor begins a gurgling blip-blip-blip. Then, moments later, they see and hear a full heartbeat.

The apparition speaks softly into Audrey's ear. "Now, Audrey, we've cleaned his blood; now you know what to do. Only you can breathe life back into Jonathan, your actual life. I must inform you that if you give your life force to Jonathan, you will shorten your own life, perhaps by years. It is now your decision. Only you can decide; your shortened life or his present restoration. Don't be afraid; hurry!"

Audrey leans over her dead friend's body and opens his mouth as if to kiss him. And with a single long exhale from Audrey's mouth, Jonathan's chest rises, and normal breathing is restored with coughs and spurts.

Audrey remembers this is precisely how Jonathan had restored life to her body with his living breath; the irony gave her exultant pleasure. She thinks, '*Jonathan blew the breath of his life into me, and now I can return that same lifesaving breath to him.*'

The doctor says, "This is impossible." Audrey replies through her tears, "Nothing is impossible with my God. My Jonathan will be okay."

Later that night, a sample of Jonathan's blood is sent to pathology for express analysis. The results pop up on the doctor's tablet, indicating the impossible; that Jonathan is sepsis free.

No one in that room has ever witnessed a miracle. No one knew that a friend's prayer was more effective than all medicine. Audrey has her friend back. Jonathan never knew he had died, and it was his soul mate, Audrey, who begged God for his life. His parents can tell Audrey wants this to remain a secret between them; they honor her wish but now think of her as their future daughter-in-law.

A few days later, Jonathan is approved for discharge. They send him to orthopedics to complete the necessary work on the broken ankle.

The orthopedic doctor placed Jonathan's foot in a hard shell cast, telling him he would need an in-home nursing and therapy service until he could bear weight.

Audrey interrupts, "No, doctor, I will take care of him until he recovers, and I will bring him to your office for all his follow-up appointments."

Jonathan's Truck: Medical Center Parking Lot:

Jonathan is in the back seat, and Audrey is the driver. She looks behind, her eyes full of tears. She snarls at Jonathan, "You'd better not get hurt! And don't go thinking I'm in love with you; it's not that." She is now sobbing and speaking through her tears. "Do you want to stay at my place or yours?"

He looks at her, smiling. "I didn't know you had such a *potty-mouth*."

Audrey glares at him. "What do you mean? I don't curse. Besides, this mouth begged God to keep…" She does not complete her sentence; instead, saying, "You scared the *you-know-what* out of me. Oops, there goes that potty mouth. I guess you're right. I will do better, I promise."

Jonathan winces in pain. "Oh yeah? You should've heard what came out of that sweet little mouth of yours when you were screaming at those coyotes. I like it; you're human, after all. So, what do I call you now, G.I. Jane? You are one fearsome chick, and I love it. I won't be messing with you. Yikes! You begged God for what? I don't understand; what are you talking about?"

Audrey tells him, "Never mind that. My house tonight; tomorrow, I will pack a few things and stay with you until you're strong enough to move around with a crutch. Let's stop by your place to get some stuff for the night."

With laughter through his pain, Jonathan says, "But, honey, what will the neighbors think if you have a man staying at your place? What about your reputation?" Looking in the back seat at Jonathan, she teases, "Scandalous; maybe I will open the blinds so that everyone will see us. I like it."

Jonathan chuckles. "You're crazy, but I like it."

Nineteen

THE SIDE-STEPPED LOVE, OPIOIDS & FORCED HONESTY

Audrey has insisted that Jonathan stay with her. Her townhouse is spacious, with bedrooms on the second and third floors. She makes him comfortable in the dining room while preparing a bedroom for him.

"Jonathan, this is my study and woman-cave. I've moved most of my lady stuff out, so you should be comfortable on the first floor; no climbing stairs. Now let me give you the tour."

Audrey helps Jonathan to his feet, wraps his arm around her shoulders, and slowly walks him through the first floor. "This kitchen is yours; the spices are in that cabinet, plates over there, and flatware in these two drawers. Behind those louvered doors is the pantry; you can have anything you want in there. I keep the refrigerator stocked with all kinds of goodies; I go shopping every other Monday; if you think of something you need, let me know. I've taken a few days off to get you settled. After that, I will prepare your breakfast and lunch and fix supper when I get home. And don't be shy; I will bathe you every night before bed. The remote is in the caddy, and you have the Captain's choice. Okay?"

Jonathan looks around. "I can easily go to my parent's home; I don't want to put you through all this trouble. And what is Captain's choice?"

"Captain's choice means whoever gets the remote first picks what we look at. I've got cable, Netflix, Hulu, Prime, and Disney with a side of HBO. Whatever you pick, I will look at it with you. Your doctor says you're not to put any significant weight on that ankle before a few weeks, or you could develop a repetitive stress fracture.

"You're my patient, Buster, and I'm your nurse, got it?" she says with a playfully stern affection.

"Why are you doing this for me, Audrey?"

"Jonathan Dawson, you're so silly; you'll figure it out one day. I will pick up your meds from the drug store tomorrow."

The evening progresses, and he cannot take his eyes off her. She trots up the steps to the master bedroom, returning moments later, messy and beautiful. She's wearing satin knee-length KÜHLs, a matching Tankini Set, and her hair lassoed in a scrunchie. She's wearing colorful ankle socks and oversized flip-flops. This is the first time he has seen her legs or her arms since the bicycle endurance ride. He keeps staring at her, unable to focus on what she is saying about what she is fixing for dinner.

Jonathan's reaction to her natural fresh-face beauty causes him to have an involuntary response, and when she catches him staring at her, she says, "What are you looking at, you dirty old man?"

Caught, Jonathan can only smile with an admission of guilt look, mumbling, "I couldn't help myself; it won't happen again."

She says playfully, "Don't say that; sometimes a girl likes being admired, but you're still a dirty old man."

Dinner is great. Jonathan hobbles to the breakfast bar and watches Audrey cut up peppers, onions, shallots, and andouille sausage. She sautés it all in a Caraway pot on a medium flame. She tastes the mix, and once she feels it is perfect, she mixes it into the pasta sauce.

The water has been boiling feverishly for ten minutes when she gently layers the DeCeeco thin spaghetti in the boiling water.

Jonathan sits there watching the precision of each step she follows without a recipe. Then, finally, she turns to him. "Is al-dente okay with you?"

Jonathan nods, 'yes.'

He sits across from her, and for the first time ever, Jonathan wishes that the memories of the girl he had been pining over for years would vanish. He stares at Audrey now as his savior, possible girlfriend, and perhaps even his future wife. Jonathan tries desperately not to say it, but he cannot help it. He apologizes in advance. Audrey gives him a *'What are you talking about'* look.

Jonathan says, "How could anyone look so beautiful slumming, take care of me all day, and then prepare a gourmet meal like this? I must be dreaming. I guess I am a chauvinist pig!"

Audrey blushes and gives him a half smile.

She washes the dishes, and they fall asleep together on the couch, watching television.

The next few mornings, she instructed him to put on her oversized knee-length joggers and escorted him to the bathroom. "I don't want you standing, and I can't catch you if you slip. So I've run lukewarm water for you."

She helps him into the tub and washes him with a loofah. Then, she hands him a washcloth, telling him, "I'm stepping out for a minute; you can scrub the family jewels while I'm out. Call me when you're ready."

She returns, gets him out of the tub, dries him off, and leaves him dry clothes. When he comes out of the bathroom and dresses, she is dressed for work, leaving his breakfast on the table and kissing his forehead, saying, "Goodbye."

Audrey notices that the pain rises and lowers on an unusual schedule.

After a few weeks, she notices Jonathan counting his pain pills. Concerned, she reads the label and learns that they are opioids. The doctor had told her they were prescribing Acetaminophen; Audrey panics, knowing the ramifications of this particular narcotic at the rate Jonathan has been consuming them. She sees Jonathan struggling to maintain his composure, but it is difficult to watch him abandon his naturally kind nature to a person who keeps the bottle of Oxy with him 24/7.

She notices he would start to take the dosage and quickly fight the urge. She knows the signs and cannot allow this to happen to someone she cares about.

One day, she hides his pills to see how he'd react to check her theory.

Audrey has never seen him in a rage before but knows that it is not personal as he first interrogates her about the location of his meds till he runs into her study, nearly in tears.

Audrey knows the signs and calls her boss to say she wouldn't be in for a week or so due to a family emergency.

The following day she allows Jonathan to find his meds. He takes the pills like a thirsty man dying in the desert. Finally, he calms down and returns to his usual composure. He asks her why she isn't going to work.

Audrey responds to Jonathan, "My friend Jonathan is sick and is developing a dependency on his pain meds. He and I are going to break this together. I'm not leaving you, and I'm not letting you have those pills. I will be your pills until we break this together. I will not lose you like this. I've seen it happen to others I know; I can't let it destroy you. You've only got a pill or two left. So be ready for the fight of your life when this prescription runs out. I will hold on to you for as long as it takes. You will not be alone in this fight, I promise. I will be your pain killer until we beat this together."

"I'm scared," Jonathan says.

Audrey holds him. "I know; so am I, but we can do this together. Do you know how you always tell me your girl can do anything? Well, my man can do anything. You can beat this; I've got you."

The first day is agony for Jonathan. Profuse sweat pours out of his body. The pain twists his torso as if strapped to a medieval rack. Jonathan's fingers curl so tight in agony that Audrey cannot hold his hand. Audrey softly sings a song to Jonathan, telling him he is her everything.

Jonathan cannot hold down food or water on the second day and night. He constantly cries with no tears. His eyes are pink with pain, and his facial hair has grown monstrously, making him almost unrecognizable. He begins to sweat and re-sweat, and as each layer dries on his skin, the body aroma she used to admire fills her home with a sweaty odor that even he cannot stand.

On the second day of his fight, even with excruciating pain, Jonathan is drained of all energy and is more unconscious than asleep. Audrey is grateful to see him free from suffering, even for a few hours.

Then, for the first time since Audrey has reconnected with Jonathan, she hears his phone buzz. Expecting to see Mom, Dad, or Tyler on his cell's caller-ID, she sees a name she's only heard a few times, Clair.

Accepting the call, she answers, "Hello, this is Jonathan Dawson's cell; how may I help you?"

Clair answers with puzzlement in her voice, "Hi Allison, I didn't expect to hear you. Have you been well? I haven't seen you and Franklin since I moved to Kentucky. Is Jonathan there?"

Audrey answers, "No, my name is Audrey, Jonathan's friend. He couldn't get to the phone, so I answered for him, thinking it might be his mom."

"Would you tell him that Clair called? I haven't seen him in nearly a year and wanted to say hello."

Audrey's expression betrays a familiarity with the voice on Jonathan's phone. She asks, "Are you Clair Hansley, Jonathan's friend, and coworker? I think you and I have met several times at cyber events. Unfortunately, there aren't that many women in cyber at our level today. Jonathan has told me a lot about you; he says you are a great friend, and before you relocated to Kentucky, you were his so-called work-wife."

Clair answers, "Wow, you know all about me. I guess Jonathan has no secrets from you. How do you know Jonathan? Are you two friends?"

"Not sure what we are," Audrey says wistfully, "Jonathan and I are best friends. I love him, and he loves me, but I don't seem to be able to make the jump from loving him to being in-love. I see him as my friend-boy but he wants it to be more. If you know him well, you know how ruthlessly dedicated Jonathan is. You must be aware of his honesty and penchant for loyalty."

Clair answers, "Yes, I do; Jonathan used to tell me about a girl he met in a grocery store; he fell in love at first sight with her, and while Jonathan and I are close, he wouldn't give me a chance to be anything more than his friend. After he returned from Korea, I thought I had a chance, but things got even worse for me with Jonathan. Seriously, if he wants more from you, and you want him, go for it. I'd love to be in your shoes. He's a great guy and will make a perfect husband. He's honest, loyal, funny and kind; I'd follow him anywhere because of his wisdom and always looking to do the right thing. He's an unusual man. But Korea changed all that for a future I thought I might have with Jonathan."

Audrey now probes, "Why is that? What does Korea have to do with your friendship with him? I don't get it. I've been to Seoul; it's a great place with fun people."

Clair responds with exasperation, "Well, Audrey, it's like this: Before Jonathan went on vacation, he and I got sorta close. He took me on a few outings, he'd never call them dates, and he was fun but would not give an inch of finding his first love from the market. Then, when Jonathan returned from Korea, he called me, saying he didn't want a closer relationship with me anymore. Mr. Dawson said firmly, *'No more kissing, holding hands, or nights alone at our respective homes.'* Jonathan came to see me in Kentucky, took me to Johnny Carino's, my favorite restaurant, and informed me that he had met the love of his life in Korea. He said she made him forget about his market girl and me. He said he would be my friend forever, but this woman he accidentally met in, I think he said Iteawon, was going to be his wife one day. Can you believe that? I asked him about the market girl, and his answer surprised me and made me give up on my Jonathan."

Clair continues, "I don't know if he told you, but I've known Jonathan and his brother since second grade. I had a big crush on him until he helped a kindergarten girl with a bully problem. Then he started walking home with her every day. Years later, I finally got a job working with Jonathan and told him of our history. Anyway, when he returned from vacation, he said that even though this girl he met didn't give him the time of day, and left with no way to contact her, Jonathan believed she was the girl from the store. He made it clear that if he couldn't be with her, he would most likely grow old and die all alone. Audrey, I really love Jonathan and would love to be his wife, but I can't be number three in line waiting for him to return my affection. Anyway, I called to say hello and to tell him that there were no hard feelings. Audrey, let me give you some sage advice. If you are waiting for Jonathan to open his heart to you, forget it. After Korea, not even the sock girl from the market had a chance with Jonathan. He's so cute and nice; I would have loved to have been his wife. When he returns, tell him I called, but don't you dare tell him about our girl talk; he's very private and hates gossip. I hope to meet you again one day."

Audrey politely offers her goodbyes and promises to tell Jonathan she had called.

Audrey knows Jonathan loves her but had no idea she is the woman of his dreams. She feels both honored and trapped, learning from a third party how deeply Jonathan loves her.

Audrey watches Jonathan sleep, realizing more than she is ready to know about him and even her true feelings for this man. Watching him suffer and his dependence on her to get him through this hell, Audrey realizes, still fighting the emotions, that Jonathan is the only man she has ever wanted. Audrey decides that her saving him from the coyotes and the opioids was not for him alone but to preserve the life of the only man she would ever love.

On the morning of the third day, Jonathan begins to return to normal. That night, Audrey, exhausted, lays next to him nearly naked, holding his shaking and quivering body close to hers. He holds her tight, knowing that she is the life raft to a man drowning in the ocean of an oncoming addiction. Still, Audrey continues to hum the haunting tune in his ear. Finally, he, still quivering, asks, "What's that tune; what's that song you keep singing?"

Audrey keeps humming the tune, answering, "It's just a tune to remind you how much I love you." Audrey feels no shame as he caresses her body for warmth from the freezing sting the opioids have rippled through his body. While Audrey is physically beautiful, he thinks nothing of the body he has desired and wanted. Now she is his savior, and her body's warmth sustains him through this, the worst day of his life.

Jonathan begs her for a single pill, but she holds her standing. "I am your pill; I won't leave you. My guy can do anything. We've got this."

Audrey cannot stop thinking about her conversation with Clair. It was as if she could hear Jonathan confessing his love for her through Clair's voice. Audrey asks herself why she is caring for this man. She wants to know what possessed her to defend Jonathan against wild coyotes and why she would trade years of her life to give Jonathan the breath of her life. Her mind cannot answer all these questions easily, but her heart knows the answer and shouts to her, *'You're in love with this man!'* This is not what she wants to hear or think; again, she feels she is being stubborn for stubbornness' sake. It occurs to her that if she does not accept Jonathan's love, Clair certainly would if given an opportunity. Audrey wonders if she is sabotaging her future for no good reason at all.

Jonathan observes her internal battle. He thinks she is considering granting his wish for another oxy pill; he does not know Audrey is evaluating her footing with the man she loves and wonders why she is holding out for a man she has never met. *'Was the grocery store man real?'* Audrey asks herself in her mind. Finding no answer, she answers Jonathan's request with a new love for him she is only just now recognizing in light of what Clair had said.

Jonathan, in agony, knowing Audrey's defiance and iron will, knows it is hopeless to beg. Jonathan knows she would die before letting him go through this alone. He is aching so severely that he screams, "I hate you!" She responds, "I know, but still, I got your back. Say or scream whatever you need to shout; we will get through this or die together trying. Jonathan, I won't leave you alone, ever."

Through the fog of suffering, he remembers Audrey whispering the words of that same song as she continued praying over his body as she held him the night before.

"Dear God," Audrey began the night before. "Please help my friend. He is a good man, and I need you to help me help Jonathan.

You sent him to save me when I was alone and afraid in Korea. You sent him to save me when I was drowning in the pool. Now it is my turn; let me be the shore Jonathan can land upon. I need him, God, he is my only friend, and I love him. Bless him, bless us, and bring him back to me if it is Your will. I pray this in Jesus' name."

That was Audrey's prayer the night before. The following day, the pain, chills, and fever subside. So, what can one say when one witnesses a miracle? Audrey kisses his sweat-filled brow, telling him, "All you are to me," as she sings the song of comfort a little louder to him.

Holding Audrey's now grimy body layered with Jonathan's sweat and vomit, he looks at her, then to the ceiling, saying, "Thank you, Lord, for this woman, my friend, my pal. Amen."

First, Audrey places a plastic deck chair in the bathtub. Then, dragging his weak and limp body to the shower, Audrey musters all her strength to lift Jonathan into the chair. She then steps into the shower, her sheer slip still clinging to her body, glued there by his sweat. Using the shower hose, she tests the temperature of the water and then proceeds to clean and scrub Jonathan's completely naked body.

She has often imagined and wondered what it would be like to take a romantic shower with this man, but there is no hint of sensuality, and she resists the repulsion her senses force on her as she cleans his filthy, soiled body from head to toe.

Telling him to close his eyes, she shampoos his hair, gently admiring the texture of his mane. Audrey turns her head as she uses a washcloth to clean his private parts, wondering how she could be doing something like this for a man that was not even a boyfriend. Finally, she asked herself in her mind's voice, *"If I don't marry him, how will I explain to my husband what I've done for a man who was not my husband or even my boyfriend?"*

Audrey thinks about it for a moment, convincing herself that she would do the same for a brother or her father if they were disabled with not an ounce of shame.

At this moment, she discovers she loves Jonathan more than she was willing to admit to herself.

His strength slowly returning, he opens his eyes from the stupor as he drifts between the shadows of an 'almost' lost battle with addiction. He observes Audrey's near nakedness as she selflessly rinses the soap from his body. He tries to talk. "Audrey, no; this is not fair to you." He wants to push her away but has no strength to stop her.

Audrey turns the shower off, grabs a few towels, and dries him off. She helps him walk to the bed and covers his mid-section with a towel, ordering him, "Now air dry the rest of the way; I will be back to get you dressed in a few minutes." She returns to the shower, tossing his clothes and her nightgown into the trash. She takes a quick shower, washing her hair in a single rinse. She quickly dries and dresses, returning to Jonathan, fresh as a rained-on daisy on a spring day.

Audrey is shocked to see Jonathan sitting up dressed in jeans, socks, and an A tank shirt she brought from his home. Jonathan looks at her and asks, "Did you get the license plate number of the truck that hit me?" He chuckles, wincing with a tiny pain that he ignores.

Audrey rubs his back and tells him the whole story of his slide into near addiction. She explains that it was no fault of his. Jonathan pulls her to him, dragging her beside him. He faces her, wrapping his arms around her, crying uncontrollably. She understands the power of this moment and lets him hold her as long as he wishes, for she knows how much he needs her. What shocks her is her heart now telling her how much she needs him.

Several more days pass, and with each day, the spell of the opioids is broken. Finally, by the upcoming weekend, Jonathan is free of the ankle pain and the manufactured pain produced by his brain, attempting to force him to feed his hypothalamus the drug it had become accustomed to.

Audrey knows he is almost back to himself when he says during the next week, "What was that song you kept singing? It's lovely."

She answers him with a new-to-him tenderness. "Something I want to sing to and for you one of these days; it's called *All you are to me*. It's from <u>Secret Garden</u>."

Seeing her just out of the shower, he says, "You should've waited to take a shower with me."

She punches him in the arm as hard as she can. Jonathan screams. "Ouch, that hurt!" he says, laughing.

For Audrey, it is wonderful to hear him laugh. She's never realized how much she missed that sweet chuckle of his, even though he was being nasty and salacious. Jonathan pulls Audrey to him, hugging her as hard as he can. He would not let go; instead, he pulled back a little. "That's the second time you saved my life. Thank you." Jonathan doesn't know this has been the third time Audrey has come between him and death; the coyotes, MRSA, and now opioids.

Audrey rewards him by saying, "You're welcome, Jon," and gives him a gentle yet moist kiss on his lips. "I'm not sure what I feel, but I think I love you, Jonathan; you know, like best of best friends or maybe even more than I consciously realize right now. I think my heart has a thing for you."

"Me too, Audie," he says to her with a new tenderness in his voice. Both recognize but do not speak of the fact that this is the first time either has given the other a lover's nickname; Jon, and her, Audie. Instead, they both giggle, knowing what this means, for indeed, the opioid crisis has passed, and both are ready to get on with their lives, friendship, and their thought-to-be Platonic love for each other.

A few more weeks go by at warp speed. Jonathan can now support his weight with just a remnant of a limp. Audrey hovers over him, guiding his recovery, sitting with him when he is lonely, and her favorite grooming activity is shaving his face, cutting his hair, and general grooming. At the end of the process, Audrey likes saying, "Now that's my pretty face boyfriend."

Jonathan becomes accustomed to Audrey's doting over him. He especially loves Audrey's strength combined with her straightforward femininity. He has seen Audrey at her worse while taking care of him at his worse. Gone are the barriers that routinely keep a pretentious wall between couples, never wanting the other to see them as they are.

Jonathan winces when thinking about how she wrestled him single-handedly from the grips of opioid addiction with her sheer willpower to sustain him through cold turkey, never leaving his side. He tries not to think about it, but when he looks at her while she does his laundry, prepares his meals, runs errands to his house to get his mail, and struggles to bring home more than the usual amount of groceries to feed him, he weeps openly.

Audrey understands his tears of gratitude. She wipes his tears without saying a word, her Mona-Lisa smile telling him that all is well.

It confuses him because he loves Audrey. It is difficult for him because he cannot distinguish between his love for her as an act of gratitude or the ordinary love a man feels for a woman. He has seen her beautiful frame nearly naked, covered with his filth, as she fought the devil who wanted to kill him to keep him from having her.

Jonathan wants to possess her but would not betray her by asking her to commit an act he knows she also wants but desperately wants to preserve till marriage. He fights the urge whenever she comes near, a desire to have her as his wife before she was his wife. But instead, Jonathan loves her more than he wants her at that moment, refusing to start a flame he knows neither of them can extinguish before a fire of love ignites.

Audrey can feel his struggle of not asking her for what she also wants, and they come to a mental agreement that if they can beat addiction together, surely they could beat the urge to be with each other that way too.

She drives him to the medical office building to confer with his orthopedic surgeon a week later.

The doctor examines him, replacing the bulky cast with a short, flexible model that can be removed while he is at home, sleeping, or doing non-support activities.

THE NEXT DAY, AUDREY TAKES JONATHAN FOR A LONG DRIVE TO Richmond, Virginia. She shows him all the places she frequented when her job sent her here for a year.

She pushes his wheelchair through older historic sections of the city. She insists he sees the museum district and points out the one-of-a-kind eateries in suburban counties like Henrico, where she proudly expresses her pride in the Short Pump section of town. Dinner that night is at Texas de Brazil, a Peruvian-style all-you-can-eat restaurant.

She has booked two rooms on a different floor at the Hyatt. She escorts him to his room and gets him settled. Jonathan glares at Audrey with disappointment reeking from his eyes and pouting mouth.

Audrey ignores him. "We are way too hot to tempt fate. You're feeling better, and it's no tellin' what you'll do and what I want you to do. No-sir-ee, buster. You feel better, and I don't want to be a baby mama, so you stay here, and I will be in my room if you need anything."

Audrey kisses him on the forehead and leaves without looking back.

The next day, they head back to Maryland. She takes him over the new Harry Nice bridge connecting Maryland to Virginia, and they are back in Maryland, avoiding the usual traffic hassle of 95-North.

She takes a strange route back to either his house or her townhouse. Then, without asking for permission, she says, "You've been a terrible son. Your parents have been asking me about you, and you wouldn't let them visit, so I am bringing you to them."

Audrey drives to Jonathan's parents' home. She turns to Jonathan and says, "Now, don't get pissed, but your mother called your cell one day while you were sleeping. Of course, she knew it was me who answered her son's phone. I told her you had recovered but didn't want to break her heart, so I left the opioid thing out. We talked for a long time, and she said you never visit. So we girls arranged this visit so that I could meet her and your dad under better circumstances. She said she forgot what you look like. So here we are."

Audrey turns to him with a *"You're going inside with me, Jon!"* look, and he knows she would not relent. It is odd that he hates pushy women but loves that Audrey instinctively knows when to stop being a feminine submissive partner to become the force he needs when he needs a firm push. She amazes him, and inch by inch, the memories of his market socks girl fade more and more into the abyss of his memories of her.

MICHAEL A. WAY, SR.

Home Of Jonathan's Parents, Franklin & Allison Dawson: Davidsonville, Maryland

AUDREY PARKS HER SUV IN THE DRIVEWAY OF THE CUSTOM-BUILT McMansion. It is again a beautiful day, and his mother, Allison, is waiting on the porch, and his dad, Franklin, comes out as Jonathan is being helped out of the truck with his arm around Audrey and a crutch under his other arm. They walk to the entrance as his mom lunges to hug her son. His mom has tears in her eyes. His dad looks first to Jonathan and then to Audrey, offering her his hug. She falls into Franklin's arms. "This is so much a pleasure to see you both again under better circumstances. I couldn't thank you at the hospital. You two created Jonathan and raised him from birth. He is one of the most wonderful people I have ever met."

The three of them just stare at each other, unable to stop smiling.

Audrey helps Jonathan sit at the kitchen table and then sits beside him with adoration in her gaze. His mom reproaches Jonathan, saying, "You said she was okay-looking; you never said she was beautiful."

His dad chimes in right behind Allison, leaving Audrey graciously blushing. "Son, she's no ten; she's maybe a 12, 14, or something off the scale; you must be blind. His dad turns to Audrey, asking, "What are you doing with a scrub like him?" He quickly chuckles. "Just kidding."

Audrey smiles and says, "He's... I dunno; he is simply the best friend anyone could ever have."

Franklin asks quizzically, "You mean you're not together, like an item, boyfriend-girlfriend?

Jonathan speaks up, "No, Dad; Audrey and I are friend-boy and friend-girl, but we're getting there, maybe, but we do love each other, sort of."

Franklin scowls with near sarcasm. "Oh, I thought you always said you'd only bring the 'one' home." But then, Franklin addresses Audrey; "You okay with that; you guys look like a great couple, and we sure could use a few grandkids to spoil rotten."

Audrey and Jonathan, together and in sync, say: "It's complicated."

Franklin asks Jonathan in front of Audrey, "Son, do you love her?"

Jonathan answers his father, "Yes, sir, I do, but not with ALL my heart."

Allison to Audrey: "How about you; do you love my son?"

Audrey to Allison: "More than you can know, with almost all of my heart. In fact, sir, I would die for your son." Then, interrupting, Jonathan says, "Dad, Mom, I would give my very life to protect this woman, but we cannot marry, not just yet. It is too complicated to explain, but I ask you to trust me; us."

Allison asks her son, "Jonathan, you and I talked a few years ago; is this what this is about; is this about that girl you almost met, the sock girl?"

Allison, now showing understanding, addresses her husband. "It's okay, dear, for the both of them. I understand the circumstances, and if you trust me, honey, then let it go; it is a situation beyond anyone's but God's control. However, you must understand that while they are a great couple and could have a spectacular life together, you must always remember that the heart wants what it wants. So let's have dinner, as I am so glad to be with you. And to you, Audrey, our phone conversations have kept me from missing my daughter, who is away now."

Jonathan asks, "And how is my wandering sister?" Allison shrugs, an *'I don't know'* with sadness.

The evening ends pleasantly. Allison hugs Audrey with tenderness, whispering something neither Franklin nor Jonathan can hear. Then, Allison turns to both men's puzzled faces, saying, "It's our little secret, boys."

Franklin playfully barks at Jonathan, "I'd like to see you back here soon, perhaps with a ring on her finger. I want to talk with you about your long-term intentions with my maybe daughter-in-law."

Jonathan responds politely, "Yes, Dad, we'll come back for a longer visit soon; as for my intentions, don't worry, I'm crazy about Audrey."

Twenty

THEY KNOW, BUT WE DON'T. HUH?

Two Weeks Later:

Jonathan is beginning to walk with his usual gait. His cast has been removed, but he is warned not to step on hilly ground or play any sports. Jonathan has returned to his home but continues to keep company with Audrey, who is almost living there, as she attends to Jonathan's needs.

Audrey, pleased to see him returning to himself, helps him to the kitchen garage entrance. She has rented a wheelchair, telling him, "You need fresh air, and I don't want you re-spraining or breaking your ankle. So I will take you for a walking ride around the neighborhood." She orders him, "Hop in, don't be shy."

Audrey pushes his wheelchair to the community duck pond a half mile from his house, locks the wheelchair's wheels, and sits on a bench next to Jonathan, watching the green and grey fowl fighting over pieces of breadcrumbs tossed in by onlookers. Then, finally, Audrey says, "There's something I want to tell you about. I know you don't like busybodies, and I would never pry, but I answered your phone a few weeks ago while you were fighting for your life. It was your old buddy, Clair. We talked for nearly an hour; she's very nice, and even though we aren't friends, she and I knew each other from a few cyber events we attended. You can't tell at first glance, but she's a beautiful girl. I mean gorgeous. Don't you think so?"

Jonathan tries not to appear surprised, but he asks suspiciously, "Okay, Audrey, what are you getting at? Don't be coy with me; just ask me directly. I told you before that I will never lie to you. Now spill it."

Audrey starts, but Jonathan interrupts with a smile, "Audrey, you're a bit insecure and possibly jealous. What is this emotion from you? I know you love me but are you falling in love with little-old-me?"

Audrey exhales, saying, "Not exactly, but I know this girl, she's purposely plain Jane, but underneath, she possesses a wonderful personality and is physically amazing. She says she's loved you all her life and made great efforts to stay by your side. Clair told me she wanted to be your wife. She said that after you returned from Korea, you informed her that you met the love of your life there and that there was no hope. She said you nicely dumped her. Is Alice Park, the flight attendant, your new love? She told the whole group that she would be your girlfriend. Am I standing in the way of your happiness?"

"Audrey," Jonathan begins. "I've never belittled you, and hopefully, this will be the first and last time I insult you but are you being funny or silly and naive? I can't believe you are asking me an idiotic question like that. I spend nearly every waking moment with you, thinking about you, or dreaming about you and an 'us.' Who do you think I'm in love with? You're crazy for even asking me that, or I'm a fool thinking I will be your husband one day. Unbelievable! Can't you see the evidence? Alice Park, get the heck out of here! I don't believe this."

Audrey is both smiling and pleased, even though Jonathan has spewed a torrent of polite insults. She says, "Then you've loved me since Seoul, and according to Clair, gave up on your market girl because of me. I'm sorry, I didn't know. I didn't get your call after coming home. I thought you took Alice up on her offer. How was I supposed to know you liked me?"

Jonathan stands from the wheelchair and hobbles to where she is sitting, hugging her with his best grin and softest kiss on her cheek.

Audrey replies, "I really didn't know you felt this way. Why didn't you tell me sooner?"

"I felt if I had laid that on you too soon, I'd frighten you away."

"Did you ever love Clair, wanted to have sex with her?"

"I still love her like a friend. Were we a couple? She thought so, but not because of me. The time between Korea and us getting caught droning, I took her on an outing; she called them dates, but it wasn't you, so my heart wasn't in it, but she once forced a kiss on me that knocked my socks off. So let me put your mind at ease, you crazy woman."

Jonathan calls Clair on his cell and places the call on speaker so Audrey could hear.

Clair answered gaily, "Hi, Jonathan. I was wondering when you'd call. I'm not a sore loser; I talked to your girlfriend, Audrey. She's nice. If I had to lose you to anyone, I'm happy it's her. She's cool. Now I understand why I couldn't get you to give me the time of day; I guess with Audrey by your side, you don't need me, but I'm not mad, in fact, I've got a boyfriend now; one I'm sure you'll approve of."

"Hello, Clair, can I get a word in edgewise? How do you breathe?" Jonathan says as both he and Clair laugh. Clair responds, "It's been so long; I forgot about how I over talk you. I met my new boyfriend in Atlanta at a softball playoff game. He's almost as cute as you. Tell me about Audrey. Is she the girl you fell in love with in Korea? She told me she's just a friend, but a woman knows; Audrey is definitely in love with you, whether she's ready to admit it or not. Look, Jonathan, my boyfriend is flying in shortly; I've got to get to Louisville before his plane arrives. Love you, old friend; bye!"

Audrey smiles, "You didn't have to do that; I trust you."

Jonathan kisses the back of her hand, saying, "I know you do, but trust is like cancer. If one doesn't stop the degradation of trust early, it can kill even a great relationship. I never want you to doubt my sincerity, ever. I have no secrets from you. You saved my life twice, and I owe you the comfort and confidence of knowing all you want to learn about me."

Jonathan insists that Audrey sit in the wheelchair; he takes delight in pushing her back to his home, and she admires his tenacity and regained strength. While pushing with one hand, Jonathan strokes Audrey's luscious hair with his other hand.

Back inside, Jonathan asks Audrey to drop by Zips to pick up his black pin-striped suit. He informs her that he will meet her at her place and dress for an internment service he promised a coworker's friend he'd attend.

It is early afternoon; Audrey takes half a day at work and volunteers to go with Jonathan to help support his weak ankle as they walk the internment site's uneven terrain.

Audrey and Jonathan have gathered at the graveside of a Sherman, a friend of Phil, who is a coworker of Jonathan. Sherman passed after injuries sustained in a drunk driving accident. Both place a single rose on the coffin as the minister speaks over the casket.

Mourners are solemn as the ceremony is about to conclude. Then, just as the pastor sprinkles symbolic sand on the metal hull of the coffin, except for three children, all heads are bowed.

Audrey sees the kids first and then nudges Jonathan to look at a teenager and a young girl staring at them ten yards away. The young girl waves to Jonathan. Unsure who the hand waving is directed to, Jonathan points to himself, gesturing, *"Are you waving at me?"*

The internment is over, and everyone is walking to their automobiles. The teenage boy walks ahead of his younger sister. She walks up to Audrey and Jonathan, grabbing their hands and saying, "I always thought you two look good together. I'm glad you got married."

Puzzled, Jonathan and Audrey stare at the young girl, saying, "We're not married, just good friends."

The young girl responds with honesty and hubris. "Well, you should be; you've known each other long enough. I know Jonathan's name from Graul's; miss, what's your name and what are you two

A SIMPLE ACT OF KINDNESS

waiting for?" Her brother calls from the parked car. "Hurry, Joanie, Mom's ready to go."

Audrey answers, still shocked by the girl's rude tone, "My name is Audrey; you must be Joanie."

Joanie trots toward the car and turns for a second to look back at Audrey and Jonathan. "I just don't understand grown-ups; you guys are so stupid, can't see what's right in front of your noses after all these years." Then, pointing to Jonathan, she yells back in a friendly tone, "Thanks, Jonathan, for the tangerine; it was good. Audrey, I love the cool Christmas scarf you wore then. Nice socks too."

Jonathan shrugs off the encounter as mistaken identity. Audrey's expression demonstrates her struggling to remember something long forgotten. Finally, Audrey mumbles, "…Tangerine." She ponders a thought, and they both quickly forget the encounter as they get to her car.

Audrey chauffeurs Jonathan home. She helps him into his house, noting that he can almost support his whole weight and the practically healed ankle. He notices that Audrey has been crying. He asks her, "What's bothering you? Tell me, perhaps I can help."

Audrey responds with defiant strength and openness. "Funerals have always saddened me, but this one made me realize how short and unpredictable life is. It seems we have no control as we plow through life as if we can navigate our way to what we think we want. Yet, amazingly, we humans believe what we want is so elusive. My heart is breaking for that family. I feel their pain so vividly that…" She sobs quietly, allowing Jonathan to hug her.

Audrey's movements appear sad and down, but she tells Jonathan she's okay. While hugging Audrey, Jonathan leans into her with a soft forehead kiss, then the nose kiss to the ear kiss. She reacts with sincere pleasure to the tenderness of each kiss. Finally, Jonathan presses his lips to hers.

She fights to hold her mouth closed with a single tear rolling down her cheek. Audrey realizes where this could lead, but she needs his comforting embrace.

Audrey struggles to be fair as she remembers the first time she forced the kiss with Jonathan the night after he played a song he composed and sang for her. It was a great evening then, and she rewarded him with a wet romantic embrace that he enjoyed and accepted. Now it is her turn to surrender, but she fears what would follow. Finally, deciding to trust Jonathan, Audrey decides to allow Jonathan's full embrace.

Slowly Audrey begins to yield, at first opening her mouth a little as he continues kissing her passionately. Finally, tossing caution aside, she surrenders completely, returning his embrace with a welcoming return kiss that lasts nearly a minute as neither wants the moment to stop.

Jonathan wraps his arms around her, and she around him in a full embracing romantic return kiss. He unbuttons the top button of her blouse; Audrey does not resist, but as he reaches for the second button, Audrey pulls away, her face disheveled, asking Jonathan, "… What are we doing? This is crazy. We can't." Jonathan responds somberly, "I know, but I still want you, but don't worry, I know, and I know why."

Realizing what has almost happened, Jonathan forces her to leave quickly with a lame excuse that lets her off the hook. "I've got stuff to do. Thank you for taking time off to accompany me."

Audrey, still holding his hand, leads him to the front door. He lets her leave but stands at the exterior door, watching Audrey drive off. She silently curses herself, knowing that every fiber of her being wanted what he wanted.

Audrey gasps and falls back against her headrest, realizing she had barely escaped the 'almost'.

A fast week goes by when Jonathan calls Audrey, inviting her for the upcoming weekend's Annapolis Sunset Cruise.

Audrey hears the excitement in his voice as he says, "They've got live music. It's an hour and a half cruise taking us out on the water to watch the sunset and see the lights of the Annapolis Harbor. We will have some lite fare and great conversation and can relax. My coworker, Lydia, who saw you at the expo, wants to join us with her boyfriend. I think it will be fun. What do you say?"

Twenty-One

FRIENDS WITH BENEFITS

Audrey and Jonathan meet Jonathan's coworker, Lydia, and her friend, Thomas, at the Annapolis docks. The evening is lovely for a sunset cruise. They board the boat; the atmosphere is festive as they greet thirty-some other couples. Jonathan wears navy blue gabardine slacks and a linen shirt, while Audrey sports a knee-length jumper that flows with her every step. Jonathan is carrying his and her jackets just in case the Bay weather cooled while on the water.

Jonathan, fascinated by the musicians, leaves his table and goes to the bandstand, where he shakes hands with some of the band members who seem to know him. Then, he returns to the table, smiling, telling Audrey and Lydia he knows some of the band members and wanted to say 'hello' to them.

At the table, the mood is lightly festive and fun for all. Audrey queries as to how long Lydia and Thomas have been a couple. Lydia states with no emotion, "We are not a couple; you could say we're friends with benefits."

Jonathan asks, "What's that?"

Thomas responds, "It means we don't want to pollute our friendship with obsolete dating rules. We are committed as friends with the benefit of having sex if the other is in the mood. So we satisfy our urges and each other without guilt."

Lydia chimes in right behind Thomas, "We love each other as friends and have the extra benefits of occasional intimacy. However, we only sleep with each other, and only at times when I can't get pregnant. Gotta watch that cycle to be safe."

Audrey sighs, speaking with disbelief. "Are you serious?"

Jonathan is equally disturbed, saying, "I could never do that. Why would I want that level of intimacy with someone I am not committed to romantically?"

Thomas quickly snaps back an answer, "Be honest, it's clear you and Audrey care deeply for each other, but you say you're just friends. And you, Audrey, are a beautiful and desirable woman with a handsome and equally desirable best friend, Jonathan. Are you trying to tell us that you've never thought of having a little fun with each other? Are you saying you have never felt the sexual urge to be with her? Are you saying that you truly don't want each other?"

Jonathan answers spontaneously, "Of course, I find Audrey desirable, but we've got circumstances and situations that are more important than getting our rocks off. Right, Audrey?"

Audrey tag-teams with Jonathan, telling Thomas, "It's complicated. I've never been with anyone sexually; I don't know about Jonathan, and it's not a religious thing. I'm sure our reasons wouldn't make sense to you, so let's drop it."

Lydia, unwilling to let it go, fires one more round. "Okay, we can drop it, and I perhaps even believe and understand the bull you're both spouting, but answer me this honestly, and I will drop it."

Before Lydia can ask her question, one of the musicians, Ronnie, comes to the table, asking, "Jonathan, come do a song with us like old times in college, keyboard or guitar; your choice."

Ronnie drags him nearly out of his seat. Jonathan is reluctant, saying, "Only if my girl can come front and center with me." Audrey does not like being the center of attention but agrees shyly and reluctantly rather than continuing the exhausting conversation about sex.

Ronnie escorts them to the bandstand area, telling Lydia and Thomas, "One song, and I promise I will have them right back to you."

At the bandstand, Jonathan helps Audrey to an empty seat at a table near the front, then whispers to Ronnie, '*Can't live without you,*' or '*Can't fight this feeling,*' then sits at the keyboard and begins playing a warm-up melody, *As time goes by*. Then looking behind him to Ronnie, who confers with the band on a choice of songs, mouths '*feeling*' to Jonathan.

While playing, he speaks to the crowd. "I haven't played this for a bit, but I want to dedicate this to my girlfriend, Audrey Sawyer, someone I almost lost but found again, someone I can't fight the feelings I have for her. It's an oldie, but I think a good one if you like 80s rock."

The band joins in as the musical intro begins, and Jonathan, never taking his gaze from Audrey, sings '*Can't fight this feeling*' by REO Speedwagon to Audrey's delight, and the crowd loves it. As the song comes to the last few chords, the attendees give Jonathan and Audrey a standing ovation with some shouting, "Just one more, please. That was great!" Audrey stands with her hands clasped in front of her; she is moved, proud and pleased. The crowd will not stop chanting, "One more." Jonathan turns to Ronnie, asking if they know Michael W. Smith's *Love of My Life*.

Jonathan speaks again to the crowd, "Thank you for being gracious. I've always wanted to sing this to my girl, and now that I've found the love of my life, I'd like to sing *Love of My Life* to her and for her enjoyment. And if you're here tonight with the love of your life, hold each other's hand and enjoy."

The beautiful song sees many on the cruise with teary eyes, shoulder-leaning hugs, and hand-in-hand couples, all swaying to the soothing rhythm.

Afterward, Jonathan escorts Audrey back to her seat, kissing her on the cheek as they walk. Lydia and Thomas congratulate him. After the performance, they all enjoy the balance of their evening. Audrey continues to stare at Jonathan with adoration.

Lydia observes the sneaked gazes between them and returns to the original question. "Audrey, before Jonathan's fantastic performance, let me put it this way, I've been watching how you two are with each other. Even the way you were when you met at the I.T. Expo years ago; you love him, don't you?"

Audrey answers easily, "Yes."

Lydia goes for the kill. "Audrey, do you want Jonathan sexually? Jonathan, do you want her, and not as a one-night-stand? Don't answer me now, but when you are both alone, in the quiet place where you can't lie to yourself, ask yourselves, and at that moment, you will discover that despite your objections, in your hearts, minds, and dreams, you've already been friends-with-benefits. You can't convince me that you haven't dreamt about being with each other sexually; I can see all over your faces that you guys are in love, no doubt about it. And after that public singing confession from Jonathan that he can't fight his feelings for you, please! But for now, Thomas and I will leave it alone."

Audrey is especially relieved to end this conversation. She bids Lydia and Thomas a fond farewell as the boat docks in the harbor.

Jonathan and Audrey move through the crowd to thank the band. Most of the others on the cruise tell Jonathan how much they enjoyed his performance. Audrey and Jonathan head home.

Jonathan and Audrey take what seems like a long drive back to Audrey's home. Getting out of Jonathan's truck, Audrey waves silently to him with a soft whisper of, "Goodbye. I had a great time, and I have loved you letting me take care of you these past few months. On occasion, it felt like I was your wife and you were my husband. Whenever I helped you in your most helpless state, I recited the vows in my mind, *'for better or worse; in sickness and in health...'* It was nice. Jonathan, you made me feel like a queen, your queen, when you sang to me in front of all those people. You have no shame; I hate being front and center, but I liked that. You were amazing. I knew you liked me, but wow!"

Jonathan smiles at Audrey with pain, agony, and longing in his gaze. He reaches for her hand, and she almost touches his hand but withdraws now, knowing the danger that even a single word or touch would spontaneously combust a dangerous flame that neither was prepared to extinguish. Audrey mouths, "Good night, Jonathan," as she enters her home.

Jonathan drives off. He can feel that Audrey is also in pain, both understanding the unanswered question presented by Thomas and Lydia. The terror of facing reality both had sworn to themselves never to broach was now staring them right in the face.

Lights out, teeth brushed, both sit on their respective beds at their separate homes, falling asleep, hoping to avoid the subject they both carefully side-stepped for years.

Like Audrey has always done before bed, tonight, Jonathan feels the need to kneel beside his bed to pray. "God, I'm so confused. What are these feelings I have for her? Is it lust or love? Is it her beauty and body or her heart that I love? I can't do this alone. Guide my steps and grant me peace. So I pray this request for clarity, in Jesus' name, Amen."

And with that, Jonathan crawls up into his bed, thinking of how Audrey pulled him back from the brink of addiction with her love and dedication. He put his right hand over his heart and was fast asleep, thinking about his future alone or his future with his precious Audrey.

Twenty-Two

THE NICE GUY PARADOX IN THE MODERN DATING WORLD

Jonathan and Audrey have seen very little of each other for the last few weeks. Both send 'good morning' text messages but have avoided direct contact. However, their text messages reveal that they both got too close to the flame.

That last text message breaks the hiatus, and Audrey calls Jonathan. "Hi, Jonathan, yes, you don't have to say it. I've missed hanging out with you too. Want to get together? I'd love to see you."

Jonathan's text message: *"You feel like getting your hands soapy and a little dirty? Why don't you come over and help me wash my motorcycle?"*

Audrey's text message: *"I'll be there in just over an hour."*

Audrey dresses quickly in jeans and a light button-down sweater, grabbing her purse and into her SUV. Driving to a sizeable palatial home in Davidsonville, she runs in where she greets her mom and dad, who joke about not having seen her in a month of Sundays.

Audrey's father grumbles, "Listen, young lady, I want you to bring this young man you say is 'just' your buddy and best friend to meet us. I know men and how attractive my daughter is. Your mom and I want to meet this angel-of-a-man if he exists for ourselves."

Audrey shouts to her father. "Dad, I'm leaving my car, taking my bike. See you guys later."

Audrey exits the garage on her crimson red V Star 950 motorcycle, heading out route 50 toward Annapolis and Bestgate Roads to meet Jonathan. Arriving at Jonathan's house, she pulls into his driveway, pulling up next to him as he is washing his motorcycle. He cannot determine who it is through her helmet.

Audrey settles her motorcycle on its kickstand, hopping off, still approaching Jonathan with her helmet on. He does not know who this is and shouts, "Can I help you? Are you lost?"

Audrey tries to alter her voice, saying, "Yes, you can help me; I am lost. I seem to have lost my best friend. Can you help me find him, please?" With this, she pulls off her helmet and, for the first time, gives Jonathan a full 'I've missed you ' smile he has never seen. She comes close and hugs him tightly, saying, "I've missed you so much, my friend; God knows I've missed you."

The look in Jonathan's eyes betrays his confusion, warmth, and expressions of pure joy. "You never told me you had a motorcycle. You ride! And you've missed me too; this might be the very best day of my life."

Audrey laughs. "Let's wash these babies and go for a ride."

Jonathan responds, asking, "You like crabs, don't you? I know this place over the Bay Bridge on Kent Island. You game?"

Jonathan and Audrey joyfully rinse and dry their motorcycles and head for route 50 east to the Chesapeake Bay Bridge. They turn into Kentmorr Restaurant and Crab House off Stevensville Road off the bridge.

At the table, they split the rib-eye and the double crab cake dinner. After dinner, Jonathan and Audrey watch the bay's waters and stroll outside to the waterside sitting area to talk. Jonathan begins. "What don't you do, Miss Audrey? Just when I thought I had you figured out, you ride up on that sweet bike. I'm going to have to marry you."

Audrey admits, "That's what I want to talk to you about. Oh, and before I forget, my dad wants to talk with you again soon; he's going to ask you about your intentions with his daughter, but don't worry; he won't beat you up too bad." She laughs.

Jonathan replies, "Yeah, my parents have been bugging me for us to revisit them soon,… meaning you and me together, as maybe a couple. Mom told me that you and she talked a bit after my broken ankle thing; now, she wants to see us as more than friends. My dad is asking me a lot of questions about you. I can feel the heat coming on, do you?"

Audrey replies, "Actually, I thought about that after the questions Thomas and Lydia asked us on the sunset cruise. It's the reason I've been avoiding you since I did not have a reasonable answer, but I'll go first. Everything she said is true. I react physically when you and I are together and sometimes when we're not. I think about you before I sleep and often crave being intimate with you. We're supposed to be friends, but in reality, I have betrayed that friendship because I wonder and want to be with you like that, but only if we're married, and neither of us can marry the other because our hearts want what they want. Am I making sense to you?"

Jonathan quips, "You are so candid! Dang! I thought I was direct; you put me to shame."

Audrey calmly states, "We have to be cautious. Suppose we go for it and then, as fate would have it, meet the persons we've been looking for soon after that? Can you imagine the pain and suffering we'd go through? That silly Lydia forced me to look at something I swore I'd never peek at. Sooner or later, we will have to figure this out."

Jonathan checks Audrey's facial expression, saying, "You know this is crazy to talk about now; let's choose a better place and time. Deal?"

Audrey does not accept the deal to close this conversation, asking, "Jonathan, one question before we go; it's kind of related to what Lydia said. What do you think about physical attraction because the other person is physically attractive to the other person; does that matter?"

Jonathan asks, "If the question is whether a beautiful woman would be attracted to an average man or visa-versa, I think it would matter to superficial couples. Besides, men are visual. They see first and then pursue, whereas women study and observe character first, and if the guy comes in a decent enough age-appropriate physical package, they can and most likely will make a go of it."

Audrey asks sheepishly, "What about me? Am I attractive to you? Do you think I'm pretty? And by the way, did you ever call that girl, Penelope or Penny, who hit on you at Sweet Frog?"

Jonathan is evasive. "You keep playing around the flame like a moth. Do you really expect me to tell you if I think you're hot? I thought you hated compliments. You shun me whenever I tell you that you look good, like on the bicycle endurance ride." Audrey replies, "that's because you look at me like I'm a piece of meat." Jonathan rebukes her saying, "All men are like that. I can't help it if you're hot to me. Don't be shocked if I burn you.; asking me silly questions like '*am I attractive to you?*' And were you jealous of Miss Sweet Frog? We can talk later after we both give this conversation some serious thought. Come on. And by the way, yes, I think you're pretty."

Audrey punches Jonathan in the arm affectionately. "Will you please follow me to where I left my car?"

Bay Bridge To 50 West To Davidsonville

ARRIVING AT AUDREY'S PARENTS' HOME FOR THE FIRST TIME, Jonathan is moved by the spectacular retired farm grounds and their home. They park their bikes, and Audrey invites Jonathan inside. "Since you're here, will you come in for a visit? My dad has been dying to meet you. He won't bite you... that hard." She giggles, locking her arm in Jonathan's arm.

Audrey takes Jonathan down a few steps off the great room, where her father is shooting pockets on the expansive pool table in his man-cave. She introduces Jonathan formally. "Daddy, may I present my best friend in the whole wide world, Mr. Jonathan Dawson. Jonathan, may I present the first man I fell in love with, my daddy, the best father in the whole wide world, Mr. Graham Sawyer."

Laying his cue on the table, Graham extends his hand to shake Jonathan's hand, saying with a smile and a grin, "This girl's full of it, but I'm sure you know that. Girl, go talk to your mom *sooz* Jonathan, and I can get to know each other for a bit and his intentions toward my daughter; whether they're honorable or not."

Audrey cautions her father. "Yes, Daddy, now play nice; don't you dare scare him off." Then, sternly, she says, "I mean it, Daddy."

Graham places the cue ball on the table's green, and after chalking his cue, aims at the triangle of racked balls on the table. Graham barks at Jonathan, saying, "Son, I will get right to it. For years, all my daughter talks about is Jonathan this and Jonathan that. Everything is Jonathan, Jonathan, and more Jonathan. Are you playing her? She tells her mother she's not sleeping with you, and in my estimation, that's good, 'cause I don't want no baby-momma-drama with her. I believe her, but I'm askin' you directly, are you sleeping with my little girl? Now tell me honestly, she's a big girl, and she's gonna do what she's gonna do, but I raised Audrey a certain way that's not common in today's world. Well, are ya?"

Jonathan replies simply and honestly. "No, sir, we are not having sex, but I want to, and I think she would if I pushed her hard enough, but you see, I love her more than my own life. I can't imagine doing anything that she would regret now, later, or way in the future. I know it's strange, sir, but there is someone whom I don't know, who is dear to me. Frankly, sleeping with Audrey before I'm free of the other girl's memory would dishonor both relationships."

Graham is surprised and comments. "Whoa, son. You say someone you don't know? That's the same silliness that girl upstairs is talking about. She says she's saving herself for some guy she only met once. Both of you are idiots. Damn it! Love's starin' you both in the face, and you won't grab on because of some phantom love. I thought she was BS-ing me when she told me that about you. My daughter is attractive, smart, charming, and feminine, and virtually all my friends' sons what to date her, but it's you, and this phantom is all she's willing to share her life with. So why don't you two forget about what could be and grab what's right in front of you? You both gotta be kiddin' me."

Jonathan rubs the felt edge of the pool table, saying, "Sir, sometimes I feel like I'm kidding myself. I love your daughter so much it hurts, but I'm not sure about being in love. And she feels the same way. You must understand what happened when I met the woman years ago with the socks. I can't explain it, but it was real. But I can promise you this if Audrey ever wants to consider her options of capturing that feeling with someone else, I will let her go and jump off a bridge; just kidding, but I won't try to stop her from pursuing her dreams to placate my dreams."

Bang. The 12 ball reverberates, dropping into the corner pocket. Graham chalks his cue, saying, "I guess I'll have to break the news to her mama that we ain't having no grandkids for a while. I hope Audie doesn't make me wait forever. She's a few years from her mid-twenties; it's not like she can take forever to make up her mind about you or the phantom. Son, you've convinced me that you're nuts, but you've also convinced me that you love my little girl. You young people today are certainly strange. When I met her momma, I knew I'd spend the rest of my life with her. It's been glorious, even with the ups and downs. But Jonathan, let me give you a piece of advice that will do you well even if you don't marry my little girl. When you do marry, you will most likely think that is the pinnacle of love, but you will someday tell your wife this, *'When we married, I thought we were in love, but how I feel about you now 20 years later pales that early love by comparison.* That, son, is how love grows in all its mysterious ways. So I hope you and Audrey get what you want and what you're looking for, even though I believe it is right under your noses, and you can't see it."

Graham shakes Jonathan's hand again and motions him to rack the balls for a man-to-man game of pool.

Audrey left the men earlier, joining Elise, her mom, upstairs in the great room. After a few minutes of awkward silence, Elise makes an offer Audrey cannot resist. "I can see something is bothering you, Audrey; you seem happy and sad simultaneously. Let's go out to the deck to talk privately."

Outside, Audrey asks her mom, "Well, Mom, what do you think of him?"

Elise speaks spontaneously, "He's special. Besides being drop-dead gorgeous, he's tall, respectful, sophisticated, and a bit old-fashioned, but best of all, Audrey, he's a kind man. I like him, do you?"

Audrey gathers her thoughts for a minute; Elise waits. Then, finally, Audrey speaks, "Mom, do you remember me telling you about the man I almost met when I picked up a few groceries for you? I think he's the man, but I cannot remember his face. Jonathan swears I am that girl, but even he has no proof for recollection of my face. Jonathan and I are best friends, and I really love him, but suppose the guy I first fell for shows up; I can't let that happen; I won't. I've only felt my heart move like that just once; now, I feel it almost every day with Jonathan. I've tried staying away, but he possesses me without even trying. I know I'm in love with him, but I keep insisting I love him like a friend, trying to protect my heart. Recently, we kissed a bit. When Jonathan embraces me, both our worlds come to a stop. If I trusted my mind, I would marry him today and sleep with him tonight; but I also trust my heart that wants the other guy. I keep hearing that the heart wants what the heart wants, but I want Jonathan. I've never wanted to sleep with any man, but I want him; I am so confused. What should I do, Mom?"

Elise turns her back to Audrey and then quickly turns to face her. "Audrey, you're the most stubborn person I've ever known, and being my daughter is both good and bad. Sometimes you are unwavering for stubbornness' sake. You know you're wrong about something, but you stick to your guns anyway. That quality about you has kept you safe, but now it will keep you from something most rare; being with the singular love of your life. Most people go through life settling for the next best thing; you get to have the first best thing, Jonathan. Even if the grocery store stranger made your heart flutter, Jonathan makes your whole body feel his energy. Firstly, you were never interested in sex, and now you're talking about marriage and intimacy with Jonathan. And even your dad and I can see how much he loves you. Secondly, I know there's a lot of pressure on young people today for sex, but if you can refrain, wait. Making love for the first time on your wedding day is a memory you will think about every day for the rest of your life. It's that special; I waited to be with your father; I promise you will not regret your first night with Jonathan as his bride. The memories will be the gift that keeps giving even through the rough patches all marriages experience. My advice to you, my daughter, is to examine the reason you're being stubborn. God will reveal the solution. Do you remember when I taught you how to use a needle and thread to darn your Astro club socks with the hole in the toe? You refused to get new socks because the newer ones weren't the same as the original ones. Your stubbornness paid off, and you preserved one-of-a-kind socks that became a precious part of your past in high school. You were adamant about not letting Ethan escort you home; you relented and ended up with a superb friend."

"Mom, what does that have to do with Jonathan? I don't get it."

"Because, my daughter, it was your first lesson showing you when to be stubborn and when to be more malleable. This situation with Jonathan may be telling you to let him into the place he already possesses, your heart. Let God lead you. Take your time, but don't discard the love of your life for the *perhaps* like of your life; you will not get another bite at the apple of true love; you just won't. Enough for now, let's head down to the billiards room to see what the men folk are doing; I don't trust your father not to scare Jonathan away. We can talk again if you want."

Elise stands and hugs Audrey, saying, "My baby is in love. God, I'm so grateful to see this day and with such a fine man."

Audrey and her mom have come down to the billiards room. Graham and Jonathan are talking trash as each takes a shot. Each miss of a pocket by the other brings a loud boyish howl of joking ridicule. The ladies are watching; Audrey particularly enjoys seeing her friend bonding with her dad; her mom is tickled to see her husband's renewed youthful exuberance in an enjoyable and competitive game of table billiards.

They all head to the dining room for coffee, tea, and soft drinks. Jonathan spots photos in exotic frames on the fireplace mantle.

Audrey and her parents are busy talking 'old times' at the dining room table. Jonathan has wandered away from the table, observing the photos on the mantle; he sees what he cannot believe. It is a photo of a young woman standing with 18 other young women in a group shot.

Jonathan sneaks a cellphone picture of the picture and asks Audrey's parents who this woman is wearing a scarf and muffler that partially obscures her face in the photo. Her father proudly states, "That's my Audrey, and the rest are half of her slow-pitch team, astronomy club, and school choir; one of them is my baby girl."

Audrey blushes at her dad's expression of pride. No one knows that Jonathan has seen the socks he fell in love with at first sight in his life all these lonesome years of yearning for the first time. He cannot tell who the girl wearing the socks is, saying to himself, *'It looks like Audrey, but she's so young I can't tell.'*

Jonathan walks from the mantle and whispers in Graham's ear, "Can I speak with you privately for just a moment, sir?" Graham tells the ladies, "We'll be right back."

Graham leads Jonathan out to the expansive multi-acre, exquisitely manicured lawn. Both men jump up to sit on the rough-hewn timber fence bordering the property. Graham starts by saying, "I used to enjoy cutting all this grass by myself; took half a morning to get it done, then one day I decided the fun of cutting was prematurely wearing me out. I thought that time could be better spent. So now, I hired a landscaper who comes by every nine days, and on those days, I take my Mrs. out to breakfast, lunch, a movie, shopping, or whatever, and she loves it. I didn't realize I was stealing precious time I could be with her. I realize that at the end of this life, the only thing I would regret is not having more precious moments with her. She gave me two great children, a life worth striving for excellence, and much more. I don't suffocate her, but I refuse to make her whatever my hobby is at the time, to make her a hobby-widow. And she does the same for me. We don't often talk about love, but when I hear her breathing at night, I fall on my knees and thank God for giving her to me, an undeserving fool. I love that woman. I expect about as much as you love my daughter. Now, what do you want to talk to me about?"

Jonathan begins somberly. "Sir, things in my heart are moving faster than I can slow them down. I like planning and protocol, but what I am asking is this, if, and only if, the moment comes and it's right, I'd like to have your permission in advance to propose to your daughter. I know it's old-fashioned, but I believe in respect. I sure would like to know you'd approve of me as your future son-in-law."

Graham chuckles. "Aw hell, son, are you kidding me? You're the first and only boyfriend she's ever brought home. This guy she knew, Harold, tried to con me and molest her, but besides that, you're it. And, I just plain like you. So, of course, you can propose to my little girl; it would be an honor to call you son. I thought you figured that out over our game of pool. But the ladies are nosey and will pester us about what we're talking about. My lips are sealed 'cause I don't trust her mama not to call Audrey ten seconds after I tell her that you want to jump the broom with our girl. So your secret is safe with me."

Waving back to Graham, Jonathan steers his motorcycle down the driveway; Audrey follows in her SUV. They wave goodbye to each other affectionately. Her mom and dad stand on the front porch's exotic vestibule, waving goodbye. Graham says to his wife, "What a shame she can't see how perfect they are together. I hope they don't miss out on the life God has planned for them because of her reluctance. That boy really loves our little girl. They're an incredible couple; they really are."

Audrey's mother: "Yes, they are, just like us."

Twenty-Three

READING EACH OTHER'S MINDS ON CHRISTMAS

Audrey and Jonathan are both IT Specialists with respectable six-figure incomes. Neither is flashy, extravagant, or arrogant. Both grew up in middle-class homes of modest means. Audrey's only extravagance involves photography, videography, and drone photography.

Audrey still has every camera she has ever owned since elementary school. She even purchased a Brownie camera from an eBay seller to complete her collection.

In the study of the spare bedroom, Audrey has a large glass case she purchased from an out-of-business department store to house her collection of cameras.

When Jonathan first sees the room, being a photographer himself, he is blown away by the collection. He asks her, "Why so many cameras?" He is delighted at her answer.

"I am fascinated with time travel," Audrey begins. "Photography is the only way we have to travel into the past exactly as it was. History, as we know it, is 'his' 'story,' often filled with bias. They say the winners write history. I like the idea of seeing history as it was and making my own judgment. Before I met you, Jonathan, I spent hours on YouTube viewing old flickering videos transferred from film. I love watching New York at the turn of the 19th into the 20th century and wondering what folks were thinking about. I like watching old European videos, trying to figure out the real reason World War One started; it couldn't have just been because of Archduke Franz Ferdinand's assassination. So, photography allows me to capture moments of my today that I think I will enjoy looking back on when I'm old and wrinkly with you by my side."

Jonathan replies, "You're funny, but I love it."

Christmas is fast approaching, and Jonathan has no idea of what to get Audrey as a gift. In the years he has known her, she never put up a tree or celebrated the holiday. Jonathan thinks this strange because Audrey always speaks of God's mercy and blessings at every critical point in her life of success or trouble. Furthermore, Audrey is not the typical churchgoer; she says she can't stand the hypocrisy of fleecing the members by their leaders.

Audrey once spoke of some of her sanctimonious coworkers, whose holier-than-thou behavior while in the church seemed to convert to the vilest raving sinners once out of the church. It confused her, and she prefers to keep her relationship with God private. The only people she ever speaks about her religious beliefs with are her parents and Jonathan more recently.

Jonathan admires that Audrey is not demonstrably religious but is never ashamed to 'grace' her food before eating, no matter how many people are around. The first time Jonathan saw her pray was over her food in Korea, he thought to himself, *'Wow, what a girl!'*

On the other hand, Jonathan is a good man, not particularly religious, but always God-conscious as he moves through life. He has never been known to be offensive and is most often referred to as a kind and caring person.

Jonathan has only three passions; music, cooking and kitchen appliances, and tools. He sat as first-violin in his high school orchestra.

He started buying small kitchen appliances when he was in Junior High. He saved money from his first part-time job to buy a juicer. He loved juicing various fruit until he saw his six-pack abs disappearing.

A SIMPLE ACT OF KINDNESS

Research revealed the extremely high sugar content from three apples, two oranges, and other stuff from the resulting juice. He estimated that each glass of juice added twelve to fifteen hundred calories and unhealthy levels of glucose to his daily intake. So, Jonathan discontinued the juicing but discovered new uses for his juicer.

Jonathan has every other appliance, including several air fryers, a deep fryer, an electronic pressure cooker, immersion cookers, computerized rice cookers, etc.

His other passion is great music. He plays several instruments, including the violin and guitar. He is especially fond of easy listening; country, classic rock, and his favorite, the modern pop and classic orchestras.

Jonathan once mentioned to Audrey that seeing the orchestra perform at the open-air hall in Vrijthof, Maastricht, was on his bucket list. As a result, Jonathan's CD collection includes many of the group's concerts.

By now, in Jonathan and Audrey's friendship, they've exchanged keys and let each other know they are welcome to enter their respective homes whenever they wish.

This came about because Jonathan's job is closer to Audrey's home and visa-versa.

Audrey would often meet Jonathan for lunch, and he, her.

Traffic is awful for Audrey getting back to work on time, and she is gently scolded for being late for a meeting where she is the main presenter. The next time they meet for lunch, he extracts a spare key from his home and gives it to her. "Audrey, take my spare key. If you ever want to have lunch at my place, feel free. Eat anything you want. The alarm code is on the back of this business card. My place is yours."

Audrey responds, "You're funny," as she hands him a little embroidered cloth bag no *bigger* than a boiled egg.

"What's this?" he asks.

"Open it," she says, suppressing the smile behind her gaze.

Inside the bag is the key and code to the lock on her townhouse. Audrey breaks the smile, saying, "My home is your home. Feel free to come by any time; you don't even have to call first."

Jonathan holds the key between his thumb and forefinger, looking Audrey directly in the eyes. He wants to say something about the key but is distracted by her smile. "Do you have any idea how wonderful your smile is? You don't smile often, but it lights up the room when you do."

Audrey blushes graciously. "You make me smile. When I'm with you, I try not to, but you're both my best friend and joy of my life."

"So," Jonathan begins, "if I use this key without calling, will I walk in on you and another man having dinner?"

And as always, she approaches him and punches him in the arm, laughing. He continues, "I'm sorry, just joking around. But, you know, Audrey, we think alike; you're Frick, and I'm Frack; we are a team joined at the hip, and I like it."

Months Later:

JONATHAN HAS NEVER USED HIS KEY TO AUDREY'S HOME, BUT SHE USES his key often. He has come home early to do his laundry on multiple occasions, noting that morning, he is down to his last pair of clean underwear and has very few groceries in the fridge and pantry.

Jonathan, work day done, arrives at his house; he had planned to go for a light grocery shopping trip and to wash a load of white clothes. Instead, he opens the hamper to find it empty. He looks in his chest of drawers to see his underclothes washed, folded, and neatly in their place. Jonathan stands there shaking his head, puzzled. He calls his mother, asking if she has been to his place. His mother replies, "No, Jonathan, I don't even know where the key you gave us is; I haven't used it in years. Is something wrong, dear?"

He strolls around the home up and down. He knows he left in a hurry and didn't have time to make the bed in his bedroom, but now the bed has been made with entirely new linen, and the pillows fluffed; he would never do that.

The pantry in the nook off the kitchen isn't full but stocked better than he left it. It dawns on him that only Audrey has access, but why would she do all this? He calls her at work. "Hi, Audie, you're something else, but you are not my maid; you didn't have to do all this. I appreciate it, but your time is too valuable for…"

Audrey interrupts him, "But I had lunch at your place today and noticed you needed a little help. Besides, if you feel that way, why did you tune up my car, why did you fix the shelf in my closet, why did you install a new shower head with a sprayer just like the one in your bathroom? And who was it that power washed my deck and fixed the toilet float? Need I go on about the stuff you do for me but never speak of? Look, my friend, we care for each other, and as far as I'm concerned, there is nothing I wouldn't do for you. I think that's only fair since you do so much for me. By the way, I've got a little present for you. Come by my place after work." She laughs. "Or were you planning to do laundry and grocery shopping?" She cannot contain her sarcastic chuckle. "See you later this evening; bye, love." And with that, Audrey hangs up without giving him a chance to respond.

Audrey does not know that he had been at her home earlier and set up a Christmas tree. He grabbed garland, bulbs, and assorted decorations, storing them in his truck, not sure if she would like his gift of decorating her living room. For assurance, Jonathan patted the envelope in his pocket, planning to give her a unique and expensive Christmas present along with the surprise of him having decorated her home.

He couldn't wait to see Audrey's surprised face. He has never surprised her and knows she does not like to be in the dark, but the little boy's nature would not allow him to resist.

Jonathan parks down the street past her home, undetected. He sees Audrey park in her driveway and enter the townhouse. His cell phone buzzes to life within one minute, with 'Audie' flashing on the phone's display.

Jonathan answers but never gets to say a word as Audrey screams into her phone. "Jonathan, it's beautiful. It's the most beautiful Christmas tree I've ever seen. I love it, and I love you. You've got to come over so we can decorate it together. Oh my God, I haven't had a tree in forever. Say you'll come, please."

Jonathan does not answer, and it startles her to hear a knock on the door. She speaks into her phone, "Hold on, Jonathan; don't hang up; there's someone at the door."

Audrey opens the door slightly with the chain still on. She sees Jonathan standing there, grinning. She drops her phone. Fumbling with the security chain, she rips it off, opens the door, and jumps outside into Jonathan's arms with genuine tears. "I love it; I hate surprises, but I love this."

Inside she fixes him a quick dish of ramen noodles, saying she's in a hurry and wants to decorate the tree. After eating, he goes out to his truck returning with two plastic tubs of Christmas decorations.

After dinner and decorating, Audrey says, "I have a present for you; it's the first present I've ever given to a guy." Audrey hands Jonathan a blue and white envelope with Stub Hub on it.

"And I have a present for you," he says, handing her a Ticketmaster envelope.

They both open their envelope to reveal identical 'open' tickets to André's concert in The Netherlands.

Audrey says, "You once mentioned this was on your bucket list. Unfortunately, the Strauss Orchestra couldn't perform during COVID, but now is the perfect time for us to go. You pick the date, and I will put in for vacations."

Jonathan cannot contain his pleasure, saying to her, "First, my laundry, and now this; you're something else."

Audrey smiles again. "It was on my bucket list too; now we have two extra tickets; what will we do about them?"

Jonathan jokes, "Not to worry. The Hub will re-scalp them for me; we can use the money for airfare and lodging; we're good. We need only pick a date."

The evening ends with Audrey and Jonathan practicing a Viennese Waltz. Audrey says, "You're a good dancer; how did you…"

"I took dancing in college. My mother insisted dancing makes for a well-rounded man; I just never had anyone I wanted to dance with… until you. Did you know that they let couples dance in the isles at some of the concerts? So we've got to be ready if we get the opportunity."

Audrey hugs him tightly at the door as he leaves.

The look in her eyes wishes that they shared the same home, but she knows he is leaving for her sake and the promise she made to herself.

Another beautiful and surprising day ends with a soft whimper of prayer as Audrey kneels beside her bed, saying once again, "Thank you, God, for Jonathan. Amen."

Twenty-Four

THE TALK – FEELINGS & EMOTIONS

Audrey bounces into Jonathan's home using her key to enter without calling first. As she enters singing, Jonathan makes French press coffee; she says, "I've got a surprise for you, honeybun. Betcha can't guess what it is."

Jonathan says, "I made enough coffee for you; I sort of knew you'd come this crisp Saturday morning. Fact is, if you didn't come here, I was about to drive to your place. You've abandoned me since I got well, and after spending so much time with you, I miss you terribly when we're not together."

Audrey smiles. "Me too. So, do you want to know what my surprise is?" Then, without waiting for him to answer, she continues, "My parents' place is surrounded by miles of old farmland; you and I are going droning today to celebrate our getting arrested together."

Jonathan smiles widely. "You're crazy, but I'm game. You wanna practice that song we've been working on while I charge a couple of my drone batteries?"

Jonathan spins up the Korg and begins to play the duet they've been working on. It's a corny little tune, and neither knew the other liked to sing until Jonathan heard her angelic voice in the shower while he recuperated at her place.

One morning after the opioid beast had let go, Jonathan decided to learn the song's lyrics he heard her sing every morning.

That morning, Jonathan crept to the bathroom door as she was singing. Hearing the tune, Jonathan began to sing an accompaniment he had written to match her song. He sang boldly and loudly; she kept singing her part through the closed door. Still inside the bathroom, Audrey quickly grabbed a hotel-style terry cloth robe and tossed it on her still-wet body.

"You were great on the cruise, but wow, you're really good; I mean, like you should be on someone's record label."

He replies, "I didn't know you could sing like that either. You have the voice of an angel; I could listen to you all night."

They sing the song together from the top, and both are delighted, giggling with unrestrained pleasure that they have found something else they love to do together.

So, as they charge their drones that Saturday morning, they sing several standards they had practiced. They call their singing their special private jukebox. The singing has brought them even closer together.

Jonathan says, "I've got a song I would love to do for you; why don't we go to a karaoke place like those in Korea, and I will sing for you."

Audrey kisses his cheek and says, "And I've got a tune I've been practicing for you; let's do it soon."

Audrey drives Jonathan's pickup to her parents' house. It is a medium-sized estate home surrounded by retired farmland her dad purchased when the soil would no longer support crops. Mr. Sawyer thought of re-energizing the fields, but the cost of nitrogen, fertilizer, and new topsoil was prohibitive. So now the land is a grass field, tree apportioned plot of land that forms a beautiful backdrop to their home.

This land has become one of Audrey's favorite thinking spots. The acreage is so large and can be entered from many surrounding side-roads; she likes to do this because if her parents knew she was there,

A SIMPLE ACT OF KINDNESS

they would make a fuss, asking her to stay for dinner or lunch. This place is like her Fortress of Solitude, similar to Superman's North Pole hide-a-way.

Now parked at her spot, they push the electronic tailgate release from inside the truck. "Today, you and I are droning and having a private tailgate party. First, we will launch our babies, check out what's behind those woods over there," she says, pointing. "And then we'll pull the director chairs I tossed in the back and enjoy the day and each other."

Jonathan tries not to look at her with admiration in his heart for her. He is fearful that he's setting himself up to be the *'simp'* to this woman. Still, his admiration and respect for Audrey overwhelm him, and it bothers him that he agrees to almost anything she suggests without discussion.

"Am I hen-pecking myself?" he asks himself. He answers in his mind's ear, *"Of course not; it's simply that I like and agree with most of her ideas and actions."*

Audrey and Jonathan drone for nearly 30 minutes when the 'low-battery' warning pops up on the iPads attached to their respective controllers. Pressing RTH (Return To Home), the drones shoot up another hundred feet over the distant tree line and begin their flights toward Jonathan and Audrey.

Now directly above them, the drone pair descends at nearly the same rate, Audrey's to the right side of the truck, his to the left.

Audrey and Jonathan high-five each other as the drones softly set down on the grass.

Neither can contain the delight of droning together; they hug and tepidly kiss, ending in a long shoulder-leaning hug.

They do not know that Graham and Elise Sawyer are watching them from the large kitchen picture window.

Inside the house, Graham says to his wife, "I didn't tell you 'cause I didn't want to get your hopes up, but the boy asked me for permission to ask for our daughter's hand in marriage. He said they both had leftover baggage to deal with from a perceived first love, but the boy loves our daughter; no doubt about it. He's a good kid."

Elise responds, "She still wears that sad shell, but I've never seen her happier than when she is with Jonathan. If anyone can win her over, it'll be him. And he's so cute!"

Graham growls. "Ain't I still cute?" Then he smiles. She says, "We're a cute couple," pointing out the window, "just like them. Maybe we will get a grandchild or two after all."

Outside, Jonathan and Audrey have stowed their drones and are finishing the last of the lunch Audrey has prepared. Jonathan pulls out the chairs and sets them up side-by-side. Then, he politely orders her to get in on the truck's passenger side. She does, and he drives off toward the woods.

Jonathan stops at the tree line and says, "I know your bladder is full, and I'm about to burst. So you find a spot over there, and I'll find my spot. I don't want to bother your parents."

Audrey laughs. "You silly boy, get in the truck; I'll drive."

Audrey drives to the other side of the field, where her dad installed a large Amish-built shed. Opening the door, Jonathan is shocked to find a bevy of tools, supplies, and a tiny corner room with the word 'HEAD' paint-brushed above it.

"My dad spends a lot of time out here, and as he got older, he had to use the bathroom often, so he put a head out here. You don't have to pee in the woods, Mr. Dawson. You go first."

Now back at the place where the chairs are set up, both grab bottled water from the cooler and sit out in the afternoon sun, relaxing.

It's almost five minutes of silence when both speak at precisely the exact moment, saying, "I think we need to talk."

It shocks them both that they were thinking the same thing. Finally, Jonathan asks, "Who goes first?"

Audrey says, "I'm a coward; you go first."

Jonathan replies, "You, Audrey, a coward? Yeah, right, I don't think so, but I will go first."

Jonathan gets up and turns his chair to face her directly. "Audrey, my friend, we got too close to the flame while you were nursing me back to health. You'll never know how much I needed you, even when I didn't think I needed you. You saved my life. I'm not going to be coy or BS you. You and I have loved each other for a long time now. But, unfortunately, we've been kidding ourselves by peppering our relationship with nice words like bestie, buddies, best friends, etc. I am ready to admit that I have feelings for you and think you feel the same. But, as badly as I do, I know you want to move to the next step and the stage beyond when we can completely share our lives. I understand why we keep having these fake breaks where one or both of us disappear for a week or two, sometimes longer. But we are both trapped by a memory that each holds on to and simultaneously wishes we could abandon. I know you want intimacy, but I also know you don't want any regrets. That makes sense to me, and I feel the same way. No other woman has touched my heart the way you have, except for the woman I met at the Market that day. Little Joanie thinks it is you, but I swear I cannot remember her face. And now that I know your heart, yours is the only heart I wish to allow to enter my heart. I can't move forward, and I can't move backward away from you, and I can't stop wanting to share my life with you."

He continues, "Audrey, I needed to tell you this to your face. At this point, I can barely distinguish between wanting to love you and the nearly naked body that held me in my worse moments. Is this an animal's lust, or do I really care for you? I get excited thinking about you. I can barely sleep thinking about you. I can't concentrate on my work thinking about you. Is this a feeling of gratitude or affection? I do not know. There, I've said it again."

Audrey sits quietly, contemplating what Jonathan has just said. She is quiet, knowing even a single misplaced word could turn this relationship left or right.

Audrey thinks about her conversations with Lydia about placing a guy in the friend zone. Then, she thinks about the warning. "If you let him stay in the friend zone too long, someone will surely grab him relieving you of his affection for you."

Audrey craves his affection, attention, love, and, more recently, his body. But, having maintained chastity her entire life, she is now faced with the unknown territory of actually wanting to have sex with a man who is not her husband.

She bounces around the idea that Jonathan would be her husband one day, so why not enjoy a sexual relationship now? Then, she thinks of the allegory of opening a birthday present before one's actual birthday. But she feels like she has been on an opioid herself, and she cannot think of anything besides consummating her love for this man. The only thing stopping her is the serendipity of Jonathan's refrain on several occasions and her having the strength to refrain on other occasions when he wanted her.

Both are worried about the looming day when luck will be on vacation, leaving them to the wiles of pleasure within each other's arms.

Jonathan waits patiently for her to reply to his heart's message. Finally, she speaks. "Jonathan, I'll be quick. I believe you are the guy I met at some store. I am still sure I have never been to the Market you mention. But even with that, I can't remember the face of the man. I can only remember how my heart moved as he spoke to me. I don't remember any children, apples, or any of that stuff; I only remember how my heart felt at that moment, and I haven't felt that feeling again until the moment I fell for you. This is why I always talk about premarital sex and the ghost in the bed with my husband and me. I don't want the spirit of anyone when we make love for the first time. How can I do that to you or myself? I won't. I know you're completely free of the woman you met in the market with the crazy socks. Yet, I watched myself slowly and unwittingly replace her in your heart when I cared for you through the ankle injury and the almost addiction. I could feel you forgetting her, and like a movie, I felt myself move into her place within your heart. Perhaps it's because you're a man, but I'm sure you could now be with me forever, and even if you saw her again, nothing would tear your love from me. After you saved me from drowning that day, I want to forget him, but I can't do that for you just yet." Audrey laughs. "Hey, I'm already hooked on a narcotic called Jonathan. Perhaps you can save me, freeing me from the other in my heart. Just kidding! But seriously, Jon, I don't have the confidence yet, that would make it impossible to hurt you; I couldn't live with that guilt even if I thought I'd be happy with the other in my heart. I wish it were you in there."

Jonathan is impressed and understanding. He is about to speak when Audrey interrupts, completing her thought. "This is what I will do. I will pray and ask God to send me a sign; He has never failed me. I often pray for you but rarely pray for my own benefit. Based on my history with God, I'm sure he will answer. Can you be patient with me for just a bit longer?"

Jonathan sings the lyrics of a tune by Andy Williams; "*If it takes forever, I will wait for you.*"

Jonathan stands, pulls her up to him, and they hold each other, dancing beside the truck while he sings.

Audrey's parents try desperately not to peek out the window to see their daughter, but temptation overwhelms them, and as they look, Graham and Elise see their daughter dancing. Elise pecks Graham on the cheek, saying, "Perhaps we'll get a grandchild sooner than we hoped for."

Graham says, "I'm sure of one thing; the boy loves our little girl more than life itself. I didn't think any man could break through that protective emotional shell she kept around her. Good on him."

Audrey and Jonathan pack their stuff, happy to have had this intimate and honest chat. Both are relieved and happy now, with both their cards on the poker table of love. Both are now '*all in.*'

Twenty-Five

THE TALK – SEX, INTIMACY, & CONFESSION AT THE RIVER'S EDGE

Feeling restless and confused about his recent longing for Audrey, Jonathan speaks aloud, reciting Israel's King David's 23rd Psalm, *"...The LORD is my shepherd; I shall not want. He makes me to lie down in green pastures:* **he leads me beside the still waters. He restores my soul***: he leads me in the paths of righteousness for his name's sake. And yes, though I walk through the valley of the shadow of death, I will fear no evil: for thou art with me; thy rod and thy staff they comfort me. Thou prepares a table before me in the presence of my enemies: thou anoints my head with oil; my cup runneth over."*

Feeling a bit melancholy, Jonathan drives to National Harbor to consider his innermost thoughts in the shadow of the Awakening sculpture on the Potomac River waterfront.

While daydreaming, sitting at the water's edge, he feels two hands softly cover his eyes and a voice he's wished to hear, says, "Guess who, my friend?"

He removes her hands, seeing Audrey there. "How did you…"

She interrupts, "You told me when we first met at the Cyber expo that you come here when you want to think. So here I am, here for you. Jonathan, old friend, it's getting so that I can almost feel your thoughts, feelings, and especially your feelings toward me. Now that you've met my parents and talked to my dad, I think we need to have another talk, honest and straightforward, slightly different from our last pow-wow. If we don't have this discussion, I think we're both going to be miserable in the short run and long run."

Jonathan asks, "So, why now?"

Audrey answers, "Back then we chatted a bit under our mask and had an awkward snack-table moment. I didn't know it was you then until later, but I liked you right away."

Jonathan pauses, looking at her and then away to the water. Then, finally, he replies, "Audrey, you've got one heck of a memory. I remember our meeting; I remember being impressed with you, and I thought you were too good-looking to be a computer geek, but then I rebuked myself for being sexist."

Audrey chuckles. "And it's good you did. What did you think of me at that first meeting? I sort of liked you, but at that time, I was preoccupied with a guy I met years earlier, so I only noted you were cute, but nothing beyond that."

Jonathan laughs some. "Well, thank you for at least that much; you're bad, did you know that?"

Audrey laughs. "Yes, I know, and I like that about myself."

Jonathan straightens his face, asking her, "So, what's this serious talk you want to have?"

Audrey becomes somber. "I think it will be uncomfortable for both of us, but I don't think we can navigate our present or future unless we acknowledge the boundaries of…"

Jonathan interrupts. "Yes, I know. I've been dreading this conversation, preferring to hold onto what's so special about us, but I don't know if we've allowed ourselves to fall in… I know we love each other dearly, but I am scared to death trying to sort out the agape or if there is a romantic facet to what we've got. I never intended to love you, but I do, and I can't figure out why it bothers me."

Audrey admits, "I dream about you in ways I shouldn't. And while I don't have an official boyfriend in the romantic way it's seen today, I do think of you as my boyfriend and so much more. I often reprimand myself as I have no business having intimate desires for you; I wasn't raised that way. I only want to be that way with the person I'm in love with and who I intend to share the rest of my life with. I never wanted or cared about hot-girl-summer, I don't have a problem with a body count, but if I do have a count, each body should mean or have meant something more than a freelance orgasm. I'm not prudish, but I am not one for sport-sex, casual hookup sex, or a swipe right with some guy. I think I would do the deed with the man I'm in love with, but I won't just bang some guy to get my or his rocks off. And then there's the possibility of pregnancy, or one or two or three venereal diseases as yet undiscovered and unnamed. A baby! That's a lifelong commitment! Me, a baby mama, no way! I know modern morality approves of anything, but I answer to a higher power. So I just ain't sleepin' with anyone until the time is right. You, Mister Jonathan, almost made me break my promise to myself and God the night you sang that song you wrote for me." She continues with a sly smile and quip, "You're dangerous, Jonathan; very dangerous indeed."

Jonathan replies sarcastically, "Sheesh, could you be more direct? You're making me blush."

Audrey follows without hesitation. "You blush? Do you know how close we came to making love that night? What's unique is that everyone says they are 'making love' when they are actually having raw, animalistic intercourse. Making love is something special, something God ordained to be enjoyed by a husband and wife without shame, regret, or a defiled bed chamber. So many today desecrate God's gift, and it is a gift that consecrates the love between two people and can create an entirely new life. Only God can create life, and He gave that power to us, which we squander for quick satiation of our flesh. Seriously, that night you really kissed me was the most difficult emotional battle I've ever fought. The way you held me, the tenderness in which your tongue explored my mouth, and the gentle breathing that cried out how much you wanted me left me nearly defenseless. When you opened the top button of my blouse, I was overwhelmed by the contradiction of whether I should or shouldn't. My bones ached for you, but my heart still remembered the conviction taught by my parents and the memory of the first man that entered my heart in a chance meeting whom I wish was you. I can imagine myself being married to you and celebrating the birth of the children our love made. And what would I do then if I gave you what I want to give to him first? And the thing is, it's not morality or religious based, it's just a gift that I can only give once, and while I want to give it to you, I want to give it to him more. And if I find him and he and I consent to sex, and he leaves me for whatever reason, I will have no regrets because he was my first love."

Jonathan, now puzzled, interrupts. "You say you can only give a first time; didn't you say to me a long time ago that, *'since neither of us are virgins…'* Did I miss something?"

Audrey smiles, twisting her face to answer. "Oh, I just said that to feel you out about your sexual history, body count, flings, etc. Besides, I am not a super religious girl, but my parents raised me to be careful with men, especially my father. My oh-so-cool father sat me down after I got my first period and explained the bird-and-bees to me very graphically. Of course, I knew most of it from the girls at school, but he said the one thing I will never forget."

"Tell me; I've got to hear this," Jonathan says. "I've never heard of a father having 'the-talk' with his daughter."

Audrey continues, "Dad said, *'Audie, sex today is almost unavoidable, and you will have your temptations. There are so many handsome, good guys out there who will want to bed you down because you're young, untouched, and if I say so myself, you're going to be a beautiful woman, just like your mother. I'm saying, dear daughter; men will come at you with a line and a game to have sex with you. Last week, your first period meant that your body could support motherhood, but your soul may not. Your mother and I have raised you with specific Christian values, but you will have to decide for yourself if you want to live by them. Only you can be the gatekeeper to your values. This is the one piece of advice I can give you to help guide you. You can only give yourself to a man for the first time once and once only in the whole of your life. Every other sexual encounter you have after that will be seconds. You may not know it now, but for every different man you sleep with, he will leave a part of his spirit intertwined with your spirit and your spirit with his. If he has slept with twenty other women, he will leave parts of the souls of those twenty and all those who have slept with them. You won't know who you are in time because of the amalgamation of intertwined energies. Think of it this way, when you make tea, it naturally has a specific taste. When you mix sugar, it acquires a new flavor. Add lemon and honey; the tea has an even more unique taste. Insert a cinnamon stick, and now you've got a really complex drink, but you can never get the tea back to just being honest, simple tea. The same is valid with your spirit; the more men you have relations with, the more you remove the nature of the original you until one day you'll look in the mirror and have no idea of who the original you have become. So, daughter, many will tease you about your activity or lack thereof, but it is your soul, body, and spirit. Guard them well for the most blessed life ever. Choose wisely, my precious daughter.'"*

Audrey continues, "So, Jonathan, my mother walked in and confirmed what dad had just said. Mom told me that she had many friends in high school and college who wished their fathers had stepped up to tell them these things. Instead, mom was teased as a *square* or *goody-goody-two-shoes*. Mother said some of the girls fooled around in college, having sex with entire sports teams and boasting about it, which makes the guys not much better. A few keep in contact with mom, and mom tells me that many of her old friends struggle to forget reminders of all the guys they slept with, most wishing they could erase the memories. A few got pregnant and dropped out, and one had an abortion.

Jonathan responds, "I can appreciate everything you've said, and I love your father's wisdom, but you could've just asked me about my past; I would have told you. Yes, I was a little crazy in college, there are a few things I regret, but most men, even me, are looking to score."

Audrey asks, "And with me, Jonathan, are you looking to score?"

Jonathan answers easily. "If I had never met the girl at the grocery store, sure, you'd definitely be someone I'd like to be with, but after feeling my heart move like that, I lost my desire to be with a woman just for sexual gratification like in the old days of my life. And even though I never followed through on those opportunities, the gnawing desire was gone. So now I only want to be with a woman who makes my heart feel like what I felt that day, and I must say, Audrey, you come pretty close to turning my world upside down. When I saw this woman, I thought she was a mother of three children. I was smitten from the moment I saw her with those crazy leggings and the unique overcoat. I couldn't see her figure, but that face, those eyes, that heart. I never felt it before, and sometimes I think I feel it with you, but that could be because of our lovely pathetic friendship. Unlike you, Audrey, if I thought you'd marry me, I think I could be happy for the rest of my life, but I wouldn't marry you on the chance that you'd meet your mystery man, and understanding how you'd feel, would release your heart to pursue your true love. So you see, nothing is more important to me than your happiness."

With a look of understanding, Audrey says, "I never thought of it that way."

Jonathan responds, "If we became a couple, it would kill me to imagine that in our precious moments of intimacy, you'd be thinking of what it would be like with him, or you were thinking that I'm using your body all the time thinking about her. That would be a horrible consolation prize for both of us. And how would we behave if that happened? How would we face each other while imagining being with someone else? These things are too horrible for me to contemplate."

"Where does that leave us, Mister Dawson?" Audrey asks. "Do you think we should start dating other people? You and I never say we're dating, but we are, but are too afraid to face up to it."

"It wouldn't work." Jonathan sighs. "I can't be with anyone but you at this point. But, it would make it easier on me if you weren't so perfect; could you do that for me?"

"I love you, Jonathan Dawson; some part of me hopes God will give you to me completely in the end, with no ghost, no reservations, and no regrets. But, I will tell you this, ever since we went to that funeral where the kids called us stupid, I have often wondered if my mystery man has died or is married. Then I'd have the closure I need to be with you. Ain't I horrible?"

Jonathan agrees. "Yes, you are horrible." Jonathan smiles painfully and tries to kiss her tenderly on the forehead, but at the last moment, she moves her head up sharply so that her lips meet his. Then, she pulls away, momentarily moistening her lips with her tongue, and moves back closer to his lips with a moist kiss.

Audrey suddenly pushes him away playfully, saying sternly, "You know what else bothers me about us? Do you?"

A SIMPLE ACT OF KINDNESS

Jonathan glares at Audrey with a puzzled *'what?'* look.

Audrey shouts with affection and sternness. "We never argue, disagree, and fight. In a relationship, when everything is honky-dory, life is easy; it is not until you survive an argument that you know how life will go. In the movie *Star Trek, Wrath of Kahn*, what did Mr. Spock say to Lieutenant Savik after she failed the *Kobayashi Maru* test? There was a training exercise in the Starfleet Academy designed to test the character of Starfleet Academy cadets in a no-win scenario. So often, an argument between lovers is a no-win situation; that is what lawyers call irreconcilable differences. I hope one of these days we can have that minor fight and recover. Then I will have confidence that we can both have the tenacity to go the distance. Am I making sense to you?"

Jonathan smiles broadly. "You're a Trekkie; unbelievable. Let's get hitched tomorrow; you're perfect for me."

Audrey returns the quip with pleasant sarcasm.

Audrey and Jonathan often realize that no words have more power to convey emotion than the glances of affection shared, especially when they read each other's minds.

Audrey and Jonathan sit there silently, observing the arches of the Wilson Bridge. Finally, Jonathan begins to stare intensely at the southbound walkway, asking Audrey, "Is that someone up there? Doesn't it seem strange? They're not walking; he or she is just standing there. I think something is wrong."

They both keep looking at what appears to be an indecisive jumper. Finally, Jonathan says to Audrey, "I can't sit here and watch this; I will never forgive myself if… Come with me."

Both in her SUV, Jonathan drives to the emergency lane and stops twenty yards from the person who appears to be pacing about the pedestrian walkway. He gently asks, "Are you okay? Do you need help?"

The stranger looks up, and the headlights of a passing car reveal it is a young woman, mid-twenties, and her face reveals an unspeakable terror.

Jonathan carefully extends a hand, saying, "Come back this way; we can talk. You don't have to do anything you'll regret; come on back."

She snarls back. "How can I regret anything if I'm dead? That's the whole point; to put an end to my regrets.

Audrey steps forward. "You're a pretty young woman; my name is Audrey. This is my boyfriend Jonathan; what's your name?"

The young woman snarls. "Your boyfriend." She adds an expletive to the statement, indicating her disgust. "My boyfriend left me with this bump in my stomach, saying he'd love me forever if I… So I did, and now he says he doesn't want to be a father or a husband and doesn't need the extra baggage of a baby. So he suggested I get an abortion or the morning-after-pill. But, I'm a grown woman; I can't ask my derelict family for help, and I only make minimum wage. Wouldn't it be simpler for my baby and me to end it all here?"

Audrey asks again, "What's your name, honey?"

Audrey and Jonathan sense how critical this is and remain silent for an agonizing minute. The sounds of the cars passing by accentuate the silence when she suddenly answers. "My name is Cheryl."

Jonathan reaches for her hand, whispering, "Cheryl, take my hand; I need a hug."

Jonathan moves toward her, and Cheryl retreats. Jonathan whispers to her, "Not long ago, I stood at this very spot thinking the same thing you're thinking now. Trust me; life gets better." He looks with gratitude at Audrey. "I'm living proof; she's living proof that it can get better, but first you gotta live. Now come on."

Cheryl backs up further away. Audrey walks slowly toward her and then, reaching her, extends her hand. "Let us help."

"How can you help; why would you care? Just go back and mind your business." Cheryl says through her tears. "My situation is hopeless; how can I condemn my baby to a life of poverty, misery, and eternal unhappiness? If I take her out now, she will be with God today."

"You're a Christian?" Audrey asks.

The young woman nods, 'yes.'

Audrey and Jonathan sit on the railing near Cheryl, talking for more than a half hour. Then, finally, Cheryl smiles for the first time, feeling hope.

Audrey is happy to have gotten through to her until Cheryl

retreats, asking, "But if I do end it now, God will forgive me, and my unborn child is innocent and will never have to deal with the suffering I have. So it's a win-win for me and my baby." Finally, she stands. "I'm grateful for what you're trying to do. Please go back."

Jonathan, with a tear forming in his glassy eyes, feels defeated. Audrey says to Cheryl as Audrey turns to accompany Jonathan back to her SUV, "Your baby will be fine, but you will never be forgiven and will die separated from God forever."

"That can't be," Cheryl states; "There is only one unforgivable sin, and suicide is not it. You don't know what you're talking about."

Audrey turns back to face Cheryl with a sharp, punishing glare on her face. "Blasphemy is not forgivable; murder is if the murderer asks for God's forgiveness. So many on death row had converted before their execution to be put to death at the hands of the state, completely forgiven for their sins because they asked God to forgive them before they died. All salvation is a function of repentance; you have to ask God to forgive you. If you jump, that will be attempted self-murder, and if you complete the act, it will be actual murder. Who, then, will ask God for your forgiveness if the only person who can is dead? Do you know how long forever is?"

Cheryl shakes her head 'no.'

Audrey consoles her, saying, "If you don't do this, we can help you find the way to a better life for you and your unborn baby. You have no idea what's waiting for you. Did you know that President Obama, America's 44th president, was raised by a solo mom, Ann Dunham, who gave birth to him when she was only 18? Did you know she earned a Ph.D. later in life? You can too. Suppose you are about to kill a future world leader, scientist, minister, or the best John Doe husband a future person could wish for. You don't have the right to alter future history because you're in pain now. Now get in my car; I will take you to a place of safety where you can think this through. Will you come with us?"

"Cheryl," Audrey continues, "no matter what happens, remember, life is a collection of good choices or bad choices; make yours a series of mostly good choices beginning with letting us help you at this moment."

Audrey guides Cheryl to her car, sitting in the back seat; Jonathan drives. She affirms that Cheryl has done the right thing. "I'm taking you to a great church that will board you for the night. Tomorrow I will contact the Temporary Assistance for Needy Families (TANF) program. They will take care of your prenatal and financial needs. This is my number; just call if you need to talk, cry, and complain about whatever."

Cheryl asks, "Why are you helping me; why do you care? I don't understand."

Audrey answers easily, "Because it's the right thing to do; every life matters. Besides that, a taxicab driver helped me a while ago. He made me promise to pay his help forward; that is what I am doing and I expect you to pay what Jonathan and I have done for you forward one day. Do you understand now how important your life is?"

Later that night, Audrey returns to National Harbor with Jonathan to pick up his truck. Sitting at the exact spot they were before they left to assist Cheryl, they stare at each other in admiration and gratitude, never mentioning what had just happened but grateful to have made a difference.

They sit there for another hour, watching the blue border lights on the Woodrow Wilson Bridge and the traffic and the huge *Roue de Paris* Capital Ferris wheel near the waterside park.

Jonathan asks Audrey a question that's been on his mind for an hour. "You asked Cheryl did she know how long forever is; what made you ask her that, and why?"

Audrey snuggles up close to Jonathan, answering, "It's something my father taught me about life here and life-after-life. He wanted me to make my own choice about eternity. Mom and Dad taught me to be a good person, guided me toward God, but let me make the choice. He told me to make a good choice. He said, *'Think of it this way, take a teaspoon, go all the way east to Ocean City, Maryland. Dip the teaspoon into the Atlantic Ocean and get a spoonful. Then walk all the way to San Diego, California, and drop that one teaspoon into the Pacific Ocean. Now do that until the Atlantic is empty and the Pacific is full. I want you to imagine how long that will take in human time. When you've accomplished it, at that very moment will be the beginning of forever. Do you understand, Audrey?'* So, Jonathan, at that moment, I realized how long forever is and decided I wanted to spend forever with God. I was trying to convey to Cheryl that a single wrong decision here on earth can have an everlasting effect. So I wanted to nudge her into making a good choice with her precious life, just as I have made a great choice having you as the best friend any woman could ever have. So, Jonathan, you'll be my best friend forever and I thank God every night for you."

RETURNING TO HIS HOME, JONATHAN CRASHES INTO HIS BIG COMFY chair. Sipping on a beverage, he hums a tune wordlessly with a smiling somber expression. Finally, he calls out Audrey's name to the open space, and we know he is thinking of her.

Moments later, he jerks up out of his chair and scrambles to his computer. He searches the directory and, finding it, plays a bit, but we cannot hear as the speaker volume is too low. Finally, he grabs a blank CD, and we see the copying thermometer in the explorer window as he copies the song to the disc.

Grabbing a Sharpie and pulling the cap off with his teeth, he writes 'For Audrey' and the date on the writable side of the blank disc and shoves it into a sleeve, placing it on the table where he keeps his keys, wallet, and loose change.

Jonathan plops down in the same chair and falls asleep, dreaming of the girl he can't have.

AUDREY'S ATTEMPT TO COMFORT JONATHAN LEAVES HER BEWILDERED, lonely, and angry with fate.

Leaving National Harbor and unable to settle her mind on what she's experienced, she drives below the speed limit around the late-night beltway, over the bridge they were just admiring, continuing into northern Virginia, across the American Legion Bridge, and into Maryland. She is singing along with the music on Sirius-XM radio's love station number-70 when she hears a song she's listened to her whole life but never really listened to the words; on the beautiful melody and riffs she loves.

Listening to Roy's melodic voice, she finds herself silently weeping. Unable to distinguish between her tears and the weather, she believes it is rain on her windshield. Then, switching on the wipers against the dry windshield, she realizes it is not rain but her tears obstructing her vision of the road ahead.

Wiping away her tears with the palm of her hands, she looks at the display on her radio to learn that Roy is playing. Then, whimpering and gathering her wits, she continues home.

At home, she opens her computer and finds Roy on the playlist. She inserts a thumb drive into the USB port and transfers the song to the drive. Audrey is exhausted and places the thumb drive in her purse. She is dead-tired, deciding to skip her nightly hygiene routine. She struggles to her bedroom, falling face-down into her bed, curled up in a semi-fetal sleep position.

Audrey suddenly wakes up with messy hair in the left corner of her mouth. Too tired to get out of bed, she hoists herself up to her knees on the bed, whispering, "Dear God, thank you for today, and Jonathan, and for the opportunity to help Cheryl. God, I'm too tired to make this long, but you're awesome. I'm not sure what the world would be like without Jonathan. I'm falling for him, and I'm unsure what to do. So guide my steps, God, and good-night."

Audrey again collapses into her bed, falling to sleep for the night, fully dressed.

Her last words before surrendering to sleep are, "Good night, Jonathan; I love…"

Twenty-Six

LIFE'S KALEIDOSCOPE

A kaleidoscope is an optical device consisting of mirrors that reflect images of bits of colored glass in a symmetrical geometric design through a viewer. The design may be changed endlessly by rotating the section containing the loose fragments.

Jonathan and Audrey have been existing inside a living Kaleidoscope. But unfortunately, neither knows that they have been collecting pieces of images that are the solution to the mystery of their love and affection for each other.

Furthermore, Jonathan and Audrey have begun to sense something familiar about each other but are confused about developing new feelings.

Without preamble, Jonathan calls his friend, Audrey. "You're right, and we've never been on an 'away' date. Miss Audrey Sawyer, I wish to invite you on a first date with me to a great little big town in California. We fly there; we don't know anyone, completely out of our element, eating good food and figuring out the universe's solution together; just you and me. What do you say, you game?"

Audrey: "Okay, sounds fun; where are we going?"

Jonathan asks Audrey, "Do you trust me to surprise you? I'm paying for everything; we're flying to southern California, so pack for five days of casual mornings and spectacular evening dining apparel. In addition, we will be walking and touring by day, so pack comfortable shoes."

They landed at John Wayne International. Jonathan and Audrey exit to a Range Rover holding a sign bearing their names. The driver loads their luggage and greets them, "…I will have you in Temecula in less than an hour, and your hotel is spectacular. It is The Inn at Europa Village; you'll love it. As your travel advisor and per your instructions Mr. Dawson, I booked two deluxe suites myself. It is truly five-star. Have you ever been here before? By the way, aren't you two a couple; why two suites?"

Jonathan answers gaily, "Next time we will only need one room; we will be married then. We're sort of an old-fashioned couple."

Audrey leans over to Jonathan and kisses him on the cheek. "I've always wanted to come here. You are indeed a mind reader. Thank you for not putting us in a position where we'd have to fight the temptation to break our vows to ourselves; you're wonderful."

"No, not a mind reader, Audrey; it's what you told me about your bucket list in the back of a cab in Seoul on our way to our respective hostels after Itaewon."

Audrey remarked, surprised, "That was years ago. I don't even remember what I said or even having that conversation. We just met; we were complete strangers. How could you not have forgotten that?"

Jonathan: "I don't know how, but when I first saw you… it was… I'm not sure, but I remember every conversation and everything about you. This trip is just about giving a gift you'd remember me by forever. I never want you to forget me or what we share. Audrey, I feel you're going to meet your mystery man soon; I want to be able to replace the real you I've come to know with actual memories of you."

Jonathan looks away, unable to face her, continuing, "Nope. I'm not trying to get mushy, romantic, or clingy; I'm just prepping my heart for the day you'll have to leave me, or I'll have to send you away. It is so scary how much I feel for you, Audrey. You can be assured that

I will never hurt you or cause you to make a choice not consistent with what is in your absolute best interest. You quite simply mean that much to me, and the odd thing is I didn't know it until your father grilled me about my intentions toward you over a game of billiards. He forced me to face up to my true feelings. He's quite a man and an excellent father who adores his daughter."

Over the next few days, Jonathan and Audrey tour several wineries, take a hot air balloon ride, pick grapes from a vineyard and generally tour the city. It is difficult to determine if they are a couple of friends or lovers.

The evening is still young; Audrey is tired but does not want the evening to end. She inserts her arm into Jonathan's arm, leering at him with affectionate eyes. She says, "You owe me a debt, and I owe you. Don't you remember what you promised me back home?"

Jonathan is puzzled, asking, "I would never break my word to you. Maybe I forgot; what promise?"

"You said you'd take me to karaoke and sing a song to me that reminds you of us. And I've got a piece for you too."

Jonathan chuckles. "You remembered that? You're something else. I was going to save that for our last night here, but let's do it tonight."

Jonathan drives to *Baily's*, saying, "I looked this place up when I planned this trip. You'll love it." Inside was lively with lots of friendly people, and some of the best singers both had ever heard, saying to each other, "We better be good; these people can sing. Audrey, let's be creative; let's sing a duet. Do you know, *tonight – I celebrate my love for you*? I will do Peabo's part. Can you handle Roberta's part?"

Audrey smiles, saying, "I love that song; it reminds me of us and how I feel about you. It's one of the songs I sing in the shower. So let's do it."

Audrey and Jonathan perform the song flawlessly, receiving the only standing ovation from the crowd that night. Midway through the song, lovers from all over the bar come to the dance floor to celebrate their personal love stories. At the song's end, Audrey kisses Jonathan in gratitude for what she says is the best vacation of her life.

The next day, Jonathan drives Audrey to Chardonnay Hills Estates. They make several stops viewing the late 20th Century homes and carefully manicured lawns. Finally, they park the rental car walking some of the tree-lined streets. Many neighbors see them speak, wave, and compliment them on how wonderfully they behave with each other. Some residents asked if they were thinking about moving to the area.

Audrey asks Jonathan, "These are homes; what did you want me to see here?"

Jonathan stands tall, suddenly clicking his heels. "I love east-coast living, but I don't particularly care for our cold, stark winters. So I thought, if perhaps somehow, just maybe, if we do become a real couple, you might like to live your winters here and return to our Maryland home each spring."

"Our Maryland home? Mister Dawson, are you trying to slip me a sideways marriage proposal?"

Jonathan, still serious, peers directly into Audrey's eyes without flinching or speaking. His silence is louder than his voice, and she knows it. She is grateful and apprehensive, feeling the pressure of his affection for her. She lightens the mood by saying, "Come on, let's get *out of* here. What are we doing tonight?"

The hotel concierge tells them of a relatively new winery with great ambiance and free ten-bottle wine tasting on their private terrace after dinner.

Dinner is lovely, and the two wander out to the terrace, now a little tipsy from sampling so many wines. They are both loose and talkative. Audrey dives in with her guard down, throwing Jonathan off a bit.

Audrey twirls to Jonathan. "This has been so much fun; there's only one thing missing. What? Are you afraid to ask me what's missing? I will tell you; romance!" she exclaims. "This is exactly the kind of vacation I want to take with my husband, my lover if I had one. Imagine days and evenings filled with this kind of fun and making love with my love all lovely night. Can you just imagine making love all night, then sleeping the whole of the next morning, and then doing something fun the next day and having a night of nights over and over again? Now wouldn't that be romantic and fun?"

Jonathan looks at her, both wishing it were so and with extreme caution. Audrey is wearing a beautiful, nearly sheer knee-length sun-dress that accentuates a body he's never seen quite like this before.

Her curves, waist, décolletage, and skin have an aphrodisiac effect on him. Yet, he keeps looking at her flawlessly shaped legs as the dress drapes just beneath her knees, and he is in torture. He forces himself to look away with an occasional stolen peek at the 5'4" 125-pound goddess-like beauty in front of him and laments ever becoming friends with her.

Jonathan attempts to redirect his line of conversation by asking a series of questions he is sure she cannot answer honestly. "What do you want, a wedding or a marriage? Do you want to be a bride or a wife? If you have children, do you want a nanny, or will you sacrifice your IT career to become a full-time mother? Just curious; you don't have to answer."

"Jonathan Dawson, are you sizing me up for a future together? I can answer, but my answer is not the modern view."

Jonathan pauses; interest in her answer makes him sit straight up, facing her with his fist under his chin like a student in a lecture hall. She swirls to face him with her somewhat translucent sun-dress shimmering in the evening light. She answers, "Let's take the last first; career or mother? Personally motherhood is the greatest job-slash-occupation on earth. Parenthood, in particular, motherhood, is irreplaceable. I think of a child as a blank audio or video tape. You only get one chance to record an original audio or video image on it. Sure, you can erase a tape and re-record over, but the latent original will always be there and can be extracted. So if I want me and my husband's children to have the best influence, we can only count on us to make the first recording on our child's brain that can never be overwritten by sin, Satan, or the world's influences. Proverbs states, *'Train up a child in the way he should go: and when he is old, he will not depart from it.'* So how can I trust a nanny to be the first to imprint on our children? We only have one opportunity to get it right, just one. And while I'm at it, I hate the term that women say every day, 'my child this, my child that.' That's just crazy. Shouldn't it be our child?"

She continues, "Second question; bride or wife? For me, a bride is a female that takes a vow to become a wife immediately after promising she will. Bride-ness lasts for a day; wife-dom endures forever. The wedding ceremony is wonderful and often extravagant. Wouldn't it be nice if the modern bride spent as much attention to detail for helping to sustain the marriage than fritzing out over the centerpieces on the reception table or her fishtail, sweetheart, or ballroom gown? If one can afford it, get the gown you want, but why spend more for a gown and wedding than one-sixth the cost of a new home or a complete college education. Me? Being the bride to my future husband pales by comparison to being the wife and helpmeet to the man God gives me. And as to the first question, I believe I've answered it in the second answer. I'm an old-fashioned woman, and I'm looking for a man seeking an old-fashioned girl. When I bake a cake, I follow the recipe. When I become a wife, I intend to follow God's recipe for success. So let's look at it this way, 'what God has joined together, let no one tear apart.' Jonathan, did you know you're an idiot? We could have known each other a long time before the accidental meeting when we were arrested for flying drones over Federal property. I cannot tell you how long I waited for you to contact me; I was ready but felt you didn't want to know me better. When I realized that you were never going to call, I gave up on you and went back to pining for my mystery man, which leaves us to where we are emotionally today. It's your fault."

Jonathan is clueless as to what she is speaking of. She extends her hand to him. "Give me your phone." She opens it and goes to the 'memo' icon.

There is only one memo. Audrey orders Jonathan, "Read it aloud."

After determining that it is a memo dated from their time in Korea together, he reads it.

> ON THE PHONE AS A MEMO: *Jonathan, I can't believe what you have done for me. I've always been a sucker for a man with a genuinely kind heart. You are such a man. You are rare, especially for an American male. Thank you for keeping me safe. If you want to see me again when you get home, my number is 410-…-….; I hope you'll want to be my friend; perhaps we can grow a relationship together. All my love and respect – Audrey.*

She says, "I was ready then, but I lost hope when I didn't hear from you, and my defensive mode set in again. That's why I was curt and defensive with you when we got caught droning. But I have come to know you again, and I feel that fate and karma have something in store for us, my dearest friend. Jonathan, I'm not sure what we are, but I am no longer afraid of whatever future we have as friends, lovers, or even husband and wife. You're a terrific guy. Thank you for bringing me here and for paying attention to even the simplest of my whims. You're a remarkable man, and I count myself blessed to have you in my life."

"Audrey, are you saying that…"

"I'm not sure what I'm saying; I'm just saying something has changed between us, and I'm both afraid and happy."

Just then, three musicians enter the courtyard, where they are seated alone. Audrey tells Jonathan, "I have a surprise for you. Do you remember asking me a hundred years ago if I know who Bobby Vinton was?"

Jonathan cautiously nods 'yes.' Just then, the three musicians, one playing the accordion, the other a classic acoustic guitar, while the last a violin, begin to play louder, and sweetly the accordion player sings Bobby Vinton's classic, *'There! I've Said It Again'*.

Audrey pulls Jonathan to his feet, dancing with him to the slow melody of the timeless love song.

After the song and dance Jonathan takes Audrey's hand and walks silently to the edge of the seating area. The music continues for moments after. Jonathan holds her tightly, unwilling to release her. Finally, he pulls away from her somberly, asking, "You arranged this for me?" She responds gaily, "No, for us."

The musicians are about to return to the hotel. Audrey quick-steps to catch the lead singer. She tips him with a wad of cash in her clutch, thanking the three of them. "Thank you so much. You guys were great, and to do so with so little notice. Oh my God, thank you, thank you, thank you."

The musicians smile and walk back to the complex, leaving Jonathan and Audrey alone in the night air. He quietly kisses her right ear so tenderly that she can barely feel it, saying, "Thank you, Audrey.

You're the most thoughtful and kindest person I've ever known. I can't believe you remember me asking you about that song."

Audrey looks up to him. "I remember everything you've said since Seoul. Thank you for appreciating both the song and my gift."

Silent in each other's presence, Jonathan pulls away from her somberly, asking, "Do you know what a Kaleidoscope is?"

Audrey smiles, answering, "Sure I do; I have several at my parent's house in my old bedroom and one in my desk drawer at my place. Why do you ask?"

"Because our lives have become so entangled from a simple twist of life's Kaleidoscope, we see many things differently. With one turn of the device, I see us closer together, and with a slight twist, the optics reveal something entirely different. But one thing is for sure, when I turn in the tiniest of increments, life becomes more straightforward and more purposeful. So I think you and I should spend some time brainstorming, trying everything to remember every clue that could solve this situation."

"What do you mean every clue?"

Jonathan's face turns curious as he answers Audrey thoughtfully. "At the cemetery, that little girl calling us stupid and the thing about the tangerine. I have no idea what she meant, but I bet I can find her by backtracking my friend whose friend died, and I can meet her; I'm sure she thinks she knows something."

Audrey responds, "I get it; you mean like your friend Chuck; he knows something that should be checked out. Unfortunately, I don't have many direct clues, but I remember most of the things you mentioned about your 'store' girl; perhaps I can help you get to the bottom of it. If you tell me where I can find Chuck, I will pursue that one for us."

Jonathan ponders the idea, saying, "It's been a few years, but he was a manager at a little independent grocery store in or near Annapolis last I heard of him."

Audrey questions as to where. "I've only ever been in an independent store once; we like big name markets. As an adult, my parents and I shopped at the big stores like Giant, Safeway, Harris Teeter,

Trader Joe's, and Whole Foods. So I will do an internet search and find this guy."

"Let's twist the heck out of this personal Kaleidoscope until the picture of our lives together or apart make sense. We're wasting our best years betting on a feeling that may never come back or is right in front of us, and we are just too love-stubborn to see it."

Twenty-Seven

FINDING CHUCK

Audrey is at work in a private office. She closes the door and Googles independent grocery stores in Annapolis, Maryland. Audrey calls twenty-eight stores, asking if a "Chuck or Charles" is employed there. Finally, she calls Graul's in Annapolis to the last store on the list. The phone answers, "This is Graul's Market in Annapolis; how may I direct your call?"

"Hi, I'm looking for a manager named Chuck. May I speak with him?"

"I'm sorry, Chuck never worked here; he was at the Cape St. Clair store for many years, but I think he's moved on. I'm not sure where he is. You might try the store there; they may know."

Audrey brings up Waze navigation in her SUV, enters Graul's market, and selects the Cape St. Clair location.

Entering the market, the store's ambiance reminds Audrey of something from the 70s of the last century. She exits her vehicle and stands there, mumbling, "Something is familiar here, but I don't know what."

She shrugs off the feeling and enters the rustic grocery market and approaches the elevated manager's booth just to the right as she enters. A friendly woman motions to Audrey 'just a minute'. Audrey patiently waits and then hears, "How may I help you?"

Audrey responds with a slight smile, asking, "I'm looking for a manager that worked here. I believe his name is Chuck or Charles."

"Ah yes, Chuck worked here years ago. In fact, he trained me; he's a great guy. So, why may I ask are you looking for him?"

The woman comes out of the booth and leads Audrey out of the store, sensing this is to be a private conversation. Audrey answers, "My friend-boy, my buddy used to talk to him often. He is trying to find Chuck, but they don't keep in touch. I know Chuck is very important to him."

"Is your friend's name Jonathan?"

Shocked, Audrey nods, 'yes.' "How did you know?"

The manager, Nancy Collier, asks Audrey to wait outside for a minute. Nancy reenters the store, up the manager's booth, and returns with an envelope. She asks if they can sit in Audrey's car.

Inside the SUV, Nancy holds a blank envelope addressed to Jonathan or the girl asking for Jonathan or Chuck. "When Chuck moved on, he told me a customer's story, a woman wearing socks that he, Jonathan, fell in love with at first sight. Jonathan would call, come by for at least a year asking Chuck if he had seen this young woman. This guy Jonathan was broken hearted because he failed to approach her because he felt modern women hate come-ons from guys they don't know. He was paralyzed by fear. Anyway, at first, Chuck thought it was a joke, but after the fourth or fifth visit, Chuck realized how tortured this guy Jonathan was and made it his business to observe every pretty girl that came in during his shift, but according to Chuck, she never came back. Then, one day, Chuck saw her just as Jonathan was leaving after asking if Chuck had seen her. She came in just after he left, asking for a guy who fit Jonathan's description. Could that have been you? You're beautiful."

Audrey answers, "It couldn't have been me. I don't remember ever coming here; this is too far off my regular beaten path, but thank you for the compliment."

Nancy stares at Audrey and tells her, "No one has ever asked for

Chuck or Jonathan, but I was given specific instructions on whom to give this letter to. Either Jonathan, if he identified himself with a driver's license or the woman who can answer a very specific question written on the back of this envelope."

Nancy hides the envelope, asking Audrey the question, "What are your two favorite soft drinks in order of first and second place?"

Audrey shrugs and says almost rudely, "Nancy, this is ridiculous; I must be crazy to come all the way out here for twenty questions."

Nancy says, "I'm sorry I bothered you," as she exits Audrey's SUV. "Have a great rest of your…"

Audrey turns back to Nancy impatiently, yelling, "Saratoga Sparkling and Mountain Dew!"

Nancy then hands the envelope to Audrey. "With that nasty attitude, I sure hope you're not the girl Jonathan is looking for; he deserves better. Goodbye."

As Nancy Collier is almost at the entrance door to the store, Audrey asks her to wait, "I'm sorry I treated you that way. It's just that it's been a wild goose chase trying to run down any lead. Jonathan asked me to do this. I'm his friend, and I apologize for offending you."

"So you know Jonathan?"

"He's my bestie in the whole wide world, and I'm simply trying to help him find the love of his life. So please forgive me for showing my frustration." Audrey hugs Nancy with a 'thank-you' embrace.

Nancy returns the hug, saying, "I think Chuck works at Mom's Organic; not sure which one. But are you sure you're not the girl of Jonathan's dreams? You certainly fit the description."

Audrey responds kindly with a smile, "Can't be me, I've never been here before today, but I do like the quaintness of the market; it's great."

Audrey drives off immediately, calling Jonathan.

"Hi, Jon, I couldn't find Chuck, but his successor at the store left an artifact for you. I think you should open it privately as it is addressed to you and your long-lost love. I will bring it over tonight after work; I will pick up some Chinese food, and we can talk if you want."

PART THREE

REVELATIONS

Twenty-Eight
FRIENDS BECOME A COUPLE

Jonathan has waited patiently for his friend at work to return from a two-week vacation, hoping to ask detailed questions about his buddy's friend who died.

Jonathan tries desperately to be inconspicuous as he moves from cubicle to cubicle, attempting to learn the name from his friend's network.

After a few days of skulking around, a coworker spots Jonathan in the coffee-teria, asking, "Did you ever learn who it was that Phil lost? I think it was a contractor, Sherman Treesdale, I guess. Phil should be back from vacation next week. I hope this helps you."

Googling Sherman Treesdale, Jonathan learns who he was and how he lost his life when a DUI hit his van one night, killing him and injuring others in the van.

Searching the funeral home's website, he examines every name on the list of those leaving messages of comfort. Then, in a moment, he spots a name that he knows very well; he saw the name of his Pastor Counselor, Jack Campbell. Moreover, the guest book was signed by both him and his wife, Dr. Doris Campbell.

He quickly dialed Pastor Jack's number, asking, "Pastor Jack, this is Jonathan Daw…"

"Well, hello there, my friend; I was thinking about you recently. I trust you're okay. Did you ever find your soulmate?"

"Pastor, that is why I'm calling; I think I have a lead after all these years. I was at the internment for Sherman Treesdale a few weeks ago. I didn't notice you. I want to ask you, were you there?"

"Why, yes, I officiated the interment. Why do you ask? Did you know Sherman?"

"No, sir, but one of my friends at work knew him and asked me to attend the funeral for moral support. Of course, I agreed, but I saw and experienced something extraordinary at the cemetery. Three young people, maybe eight to twelve years old, approached me, asking me if I had found the girl. I've never seen them, and the little girl insulted my guest and me saying we were stupid not to be together. We were confused, but now that I think of it, she may be the answer to a clue that has evaded me for years."

"And what was that, Jonathan?"

"The little girl asked me if my friend that accompanied me was the girl I like. I was befuddled, and she said, *'You probably don't remember; I was eight then. My name is Joanie; thank you for the tangerine.'* I'm not sure what that means, but I have to run it down. Can you help me identify and contact the family of those young people?"

"I tell you what, Jonathan; I know most of those there as I was Sherman's Pastor. Let me make a few phone calls about a girl named Joanie; I will get back to you if I learn anything. Do you mind if I share your story with my wife? I think she can help too."

"Yes, sir, please do. Contact me as soon as you can. Thanks Pastor; great talking with you."

Somberly, Pastor Jack says, "Are you better, son?"

"Yes, sir, I'm great and almost ready to move on if you can help me find those kids."

"I will call you soon, Mr. Dawson."

A SIMPLE ACT OF KINDNESS

The funeral service has focused their attention on the brevity of life like a laser beam. Audrey begins asking probing questions, and Jonathan answers with direct answers, which almost always leads to a verbal volley where she has to answer him.

Both begin to see each other more often, sometimes twice, even three times a week. Finally, they joke between themselves that the absence has started to feel weird. On occasion they'd greet by saying, '*Like a Sad Song*' by John Denver to each other. It was their code phrase because the song's message is about missing someone when the other wasn't around.

They decide to go to White Marsh Park for a walk and bike ride tonight. They have been riding for nearly thirty minutes when they stop to sit on the old wooden bridge.

Sitting next to her, Jonathan asks Audrey, "We do everything together; would you be my real, not pretend, not maybe, but my actual girlfriend? You can break up with me anytime you feel uncomfortable for whatever reason."

Audrey ponders the question and then responds with an answer that even surprises herself.

"Jonathan, oddly enough, I did not realize it until now, but I do think of you as my boyfriend. I don't go out with anyone but you; isn't that dating? Also, I don't cook for any man except you, nor do I eat anyone's food but yours; doesn't that mean I trust you? I wake up thinking about you, and you are the last thing on my mind before I sleep; I've even dreamed about you. I've never had sex, but I have wondered what it would be like to be with you, but not as two horny kids, but more like a romantic married couple; you know, just wondering. So how about you, Jonathan, you ever think about intimacy with me?"

"Girl, you are crazy. Do you expect me to answer that? You're not stupid; what do you think?"

Leaving their bicycles cabled to a nearby tree, Audrey smiles, placing her arm in his arm as they continue their walk around the park. She kisses him on the cheek. "Since we're sort of a couple now, I want to ask you a question I've been wanting to ask you for some time; truth or dare; you game?"

Jonathan nods his head in the affirmative. Audrey weighs in with her first question. "When we talked that girl Cheryl out of hurting herself on the bridge, you whispered to her that you had been there and understood. You used your familiarity with her situation to convince her of the validity of the truth that got her to back off. Jonathan, what did you mean by that? Have you ever thought of…"

Jonathan takes her hand as he continues to walk into the woods along the trail. Finally, he sits down on a huge fallen tree, clears his throat, and speaks directly to her. "Audrey, I was in a bad place a few years ago. It was about a year after Korea. It's my fault because I never used 'notes' on my phone; I never saw your message. Being with you in Korea was a godsend for me. I tried not to like you, but I did. So it was like a double betrayal of myself; first the woman I met in the little market, then you. They say lightning doesn't strike twice in the same place, but my heart was the victim again to a double strike from her first, and you second. My innards were fried. I blamed God for losing the first woman and then again for not having the guts to tell you how I felt in Seoul. I asked myself, *'How can you tell a woman you just met formally in a foreign country that you're crazy about her, especially when you haven't dealt with the issue of the woman before that?'* I felt I had no right to pursue you until I straightened myself out. By then, you were lost forever, or so I thought at the time."

Audrey squeezes his hand, "Are you saying…?"

Jonathan answers, "Yep. I was lost, approaching my mid-twenties with no prospects for real love. Sure, Clair was there for me and others. I could get a girl, but I wanted a soulmate, not a bedmate. Crazy, huh? But it's how I feel; I can't imagine a life sentence with someone who is not my soulmate. The pain was so great that I would've done anything to escape the emotional suffering. One evening at my favorite place to think, I looked at the very spot where Cheryl stood in contemplation of abatement of the pain. I knew the total weight of depression one could not escape; you just want it to stop. But then I saw your face as I saw you in Korea in my mind's eye, and it was your face that lifted me out of that horrible place within me. I remembered my father teaching me the allegory of the 'forks-on-the-road' and biting my bottom lip, vowing to wait for you, Audrey.

A SIMPLE ACT OF KINDNESS

The promise of seeing you again was enough to save me from my torment. Yours is the face that kept me, and now you're my official girlfriend; I think, I hope. So, am I?"

Jonathan never bothers to look at Audrey as he speaks, but when he turns to ask if there's more to her question, he sees a face filled with tears, joy, and appreciation. Audrey holds on to Jonathan's arm, pulling herself closer to him.

An hour later, evening dusk is approaching. They collect their bicycles, leaving the park a closer couple than ever.

As he drops Audrey at her townhouse, he says, "Next time, you have to answer my question."

Audrey smiles, saying, "Deal! But before you leave, you've got to tell me something. I told you what my dad told me when I got my first period. What is the allegory of forks on the road? I've never heard of that."

This time, Jonathan takes her hand and kisses her palm, saying, "You are a fork on the road of my life. My father sat me down when I got my first job at Graul's. He said always give an honest day's work for an honest day's wages. They are hiring you to make a profit from your labor. Don't give your all to become enslaved but don't underperform, which is cheating and stealing from your employer. And most importantly, for the rest of your life, remember the allegory of the forks on the road. I asked what that was; boy-o-boy, did he explain. He said to me, 'Jonathan, my son, you will come across hundreds of thousands of decision points in your life. These decision points are points-on-the-road of life. Do I go right, do I go left? Most are inconsequential, but in every life, there are five-to-seven forks on the road that can destroy or make your life better. Nearly all the forks and decisions can be reversed, remediated, and altered, but that half-dozen are permanent, and you must make those choices wisely. Some of those choices or forks are life-altering and can never be reversed. For example, what college you choose, who you marry, how you raise your children, your choice of career, whether you will serve God or not, how you will eat properly for a lifetime, to have an affair after marriage, who or will you sleep with a woman before you're married. Let's take just a few. Choose the wrong college, and you may miss the best education for what you want in life, or you may miss meeting the love of your life or even the career that ensures your financial stability, all stemming from a single fork along the road of life. Then, will you serve God? Do you really believe you just popped up on the planet? Are you aware of the phenomenal systems put in place by a higher power than us that sustains us? If you choose a life without God, He will allow it, but imagine a life without me as your father. A life without God is even worse; it is often hopeless. Who you marry; now this is a biggie. She will either complete your life or destroy it. She is to be your helpmeet, not your slave. While she is your helper and partner in the relationship, she is equal in every way. Only one of you can lead, the other must trust to follow you, and it is only if she knows you trust God for guidance can she truly trust and follow you. Only she can bear your children, and without her, your seed and lineage dies with you. Marriage has no strength unless you choose the right mate and the right mate chooses you. That choice will determine how you raise your children; you two alone can shape the world's future through your progeny. It is a big fork and a big responsibility that cannot be undone if you choose poorly. Divorce will free you both of the bad initial choices, but the ramifications of the bad choice will bond you in a unique mental slavery for the rest of your life. Teach your children the allegory as my father taught me. And my father's father taught him and now passes on the allegory and wisdom it contains to benefit your children, who will be my grandchildren. Son, do this, and you will have the best life possible.'"

Jonathan kisses her hand again, saying, "You are the correct fork in the road for me. Without you, there will be no other."

Audrey is so moved that she cannot face Jonathan. She opens the passenger door, saying, "Wow, you sure lay a lot on a girl. Good night, my love."

AUDREY AND JONATHAN HAVE BEEN CHECKING THE WEATHER FORECAST for weeks and excitedly text message each other, saying, 'Tonight's the night. Your place or mine?' is what both see looking at their phones.

Both love stargazing and playfully argue which type of telescope they prefer. Audrey is proud of her Celestron Newtonian telescope. She likes it because it has a long tube and excellent direct optics, meaning you look into the lens directly at the object in the heavens.

Since grade school, Jonathan, an astronomical geek, owned the top-of-the-line Meade LX-200 Schmidt Cassegrain. He likes it because it's masculine, beefier, and great with GPS computer tracking and skewing capabilities.

Jonathan is surprised by Audrey's interest in astronomy, telling her, "I never heard of a girl loving stargazing." Audrey quickly snaps back, "I was vice-president of the Jupiter Club back in university; we even had club uniforms, pants, unique jackets, and thick wool socks for cold winter nights."

As for scopes, Audrey always cites the classic Jupiter Club answer as they playfully argue. "Newtonians are better for viewing near space objects. Maksutov-Cassegrains are better for observing planets and details of the moon. Therefore, Newtonians are better backyard telescopes."

Tonight, both agree that Audrey has the best view of the easiest to see near-field objects from her deck. Tonight is to be a full moon with not a cloud in the sky. The light pollution is annoying, but they both have become adept at avoiding the annoyance. They also have planned to practice 'hand-dancing', which both love as much as synchronized dance.

The moon is glorious through her telescope. They take turns skewing as the moon passes out of range and the earth rotates.

Audrey steps inside her home, returning to the deck several minutes later with two cups of tea. Jonathan has removed the cover from the propane fire pit table. They sit in the warming glow of the bluish orange flame, staring at each other warmly.

Audrey says, "Okay, last time was my question to you. Now it's your turn; ask me anything."

Jonathan smirks a bit. "Can I have two?"

Audrey, with wit, says, "How about one and a half questions since my first to you was tough and personal?"

"Audrey, why is that since I've known you, you virtually never smile. Why is that? You have such a great smile."

Audrey gives Jonathan an exaggerated perfect smile, answering, "Since the seventh grade, whenever I smile, boys always bother me with protestations of how much they like me. They only like me because they think I look okay. No one ever bothers to see the 'me' inside of me; I'm not some idol or *Helen of Troy*. I can't see myself; it is only the person on the inside of me that I know. I somewhat smile around my family, Ethan, and a few coworkers, but unless you're blind, You, Jonathan Dawson, are the only person I smile for. You light me up from the inside just thinking about how kind you are to me. Sometimes I can't wait to see you, but I am cautious about letting you know for fear that you'll take me for granted, and then I may end up on the edge of a bridge, missing you. I am taking a risk exposing my hand to you; you now have the power to destroy me, and me, you. I have to trust you for my happiness as you already trust me. I'm answering this way because I'm never evasive, and I never lie. The truth is always the same while lies shape-shift like a chameleon. I don't want to use my brain power to remember what lie I told to whom. It's easier to be truthful. Now you know why I only smile at you, my love."

Jonathan is shocked by Audrey's answer, stammering. "Are you saying you love me, and I'm the one that makes you smile? Is that what you're saying?"

"Yep, Jonathan, I've loved you since you let me stay in your hotel room in Seoul. I knew then that you would never hurt me, and even though you didn't know it then, I let you into my heart, and sometimes I miss you when I'm with you, thinking of times we were apart. But, seriously, Jonathan, there's nothing I wouldn't do for you."

Jonathan touches her hand, asking, "And If I asked you to marry me, would you?"

Audrey's response stuns Jonathan with how easily she answers. "Yes, I would if you could free yourself of the memory of your market girl, and I could free myself of memories of the guy that first touched my heart. I cannot imagine anything crueler than fate tossing a wrench in our life together if one or both of us came face-to-face with those two. Can you imagine how awful that situation would be?

But I will tell you a little secret; I've been working on getting rid of my heart's first flame in favor of you, and the more time we spend together, the easier it becomes. Yet, some weeks go by, and I have to jolt myself into thinking about him. How about you; do you feel confident enough to forge a 'forever' with me without regrets?"

Jonathan never attempts to ask a second question as her answer to his first is more than he can digest. He admires Audrey's openness, but this is too much.

They eat a quick snack. Back inside, they spin up an R&B CD and begin to practice hand-dancing. He twirls her around the floor, and she laughs gaily, enjoying him leading her.

Next, she jerks him closer to her as she whispers, "I'll lead now."

Jonathan releases the stiffness of his dance posture, responding to Audrey's every move. He loves it when she turns him, catching his torso in her arm's grasp, holding him affectionately, and then releasing him to lead her.

He looks at his girlfriend, eyes filled with respect, love, and warmth. Jonathan cannot believe that this happiness was possible for him, and for the evening, he is free of the thoughts of the girl with the colorful socks and wishes to spend the rest of his life with the woman twirling in his arms.

Twenty-Nine

DREAMING OUR LIVES AWAY; DREAMS & IN DREAMS

Jonathan has waited patiently for Pastor Jack to call him but is careful not to pester him; The Pastor is perhaps Jonathan's only solid lead to finding a child he and Audrey saw only once.

Audrey continues the relationship but pulls back a bit, realizing the futility of expecting a long-term relationship. Audrey has been so busy with life, her job, and an upcoming formal meet and greet she must attend at a country club.

Knowing he already has plans, she calls Jonathan and agonizes over asking for a favor. Finally, speed dialing his number, she goes for it. "Jonathan, I need a huge favor. My car is in the shop until this afternoon, and I need to get to the hairdresser…"

Interrupting her, Jonathan says, "What time do you want me at your house; I'll take you there and wait."

"No, I just need a ride there, and if you're willing to wait, you can help me with a diva problem that's been bugging me; or if you're busy, I will catch an Uber back; it's just that I can't get a ride-share that quickly from here."

Jonathan replies, "On my way."

The drive to the salon is short and quiet. Neither have had much to say since the night of star gazing where unexpected declarations were made. And California is so romantic both feel uneasy and happy about this new phase of the relationship. Then, finally, Audrey breaks the ice. "I guess we got too close to the flame in California, huh?"

Jonathan glances, giving her a longing smile. "Our talk down at the Harbor and stargazing made things awkward, I think; I mean, the conversation made the feelings worse and better simultaneously."

Jonathan reaches into his glove box, extracts a CD, and hands it to Audrey. "It's a song I like that reminds me of something you said to me that night. Play it when you're alone; it mirrors part of our talk."

Reaching into her purse, Audrey extracts the thumb drive, saying, "Pure irony; I did the same thing for you. There's a song on this that reminds me of our situation. I hope you like it. Play it when you're alone; I don't think I could stand to listen to it with you. It's a little bit heartbreaking."

Jonathan wanting to change the subject asks with no emotion, "You mentioned you had a stack of mail for me. And how did it go with finding Chuck?"

Excitedly, Audrey says, "Not too long ago, after you surprised me with the California vacation, I played Sherlock Holmes and found a lead to Chuck. It took a while and a lot of phone calls, but I finally found Graul's, met Nancy, Chuck's replacement, and perhaps struck gold. She was great, but I had to apologize for offending her when she asked me several annoying identifying questions. I found a letter she gave me for you or your sock girl; I think she suspects I am your long-lost love. That would be nice, but I don't remember being at that cute little store. I accidentally stuffed the letter in with the other mail I picked up for you."

Audrey reads off the various senders' names through the small stack of envelopes. "Hmmm, let's see; there's BG&E Verizon, Valpak, Jet-A-Way club, your bank statement," she paused, asking, "You still get paper statements; that's interesting." Jonathan, still curious, asks, "What else you got in there?" Audrey smiles, saying, "Ahhh, here it is." Then, pulling the envelope out of the stack, she apologetically says, "I wasn't trying to hide this from you. I was somewhat hurt, and a bit scared realizing this letter's contents from Chuck might lose you to me forever. I know how much you want to find your sock girl."

Jonathan gives Audrey a warm smile and says, "Not to worry; it would take a lot more than misplacing a letter for you to upset me. Besides, I'm not looking for my sock girl anymore now that I've found you. What more could I want? What else is in that stack?"

Audrey blushes as she continues thumbing through the envelopes and then pauses. "You will not believe who you got an actual live letter from. Who mails letters anymore? It's from Clair Hansley; now my curiosity is up. I talked with her when you were recuperating; I only mentioned you weren't available. I didn't mention the coyote and the opioid thing."

Jonathan pulls into the salon's parking lot snaring a prime spot in front of the entrance. He unbuckles his seatbelt and pushes the seat back and says, "I will relax here and read my book while waiting for you. Audrey, don't rush; take your time and enjoy yourself. I'll be right here when you come out. We can read the letter together later."

"No, no, please wait for me inside; they'll serve you coffee while you wait. Please come inside. I want to introduce you to my salon friends and show you off to them. I've been bragging about you for years now, and they don't believe you exist; they think I'm a young spinster; this is a perfect occasion to shut them up. That's the diva problem I'm having."

Jonathan asks with a wry expression, "Did you set this up? Is your SUV really in the shop?"

Audrey admits, playfully ashamed, "It is a partial setup; I probably could have gotten an Uber, but these chicks are always teasing me about not having a man. Will you do it for me? Will you be my pretend boyfriend, just this once?"

Jonathan replies forcefully, "Pretend? I thought we settled this; I am your boyfriend!"

Audrey giggles. "I know, but I mean the smiling, kissing, sex thing; they think I'm a spinster."

Jonathan for once, punches her gently on the shoulder. "I thought you didn't care what others think?"

Audrey says solemnly, "Yeah, I don't, but I like the way my stylist,

Anton, does my hair, I've tried other salons, but these catty women are relentless with their high school mean-girl antics. I just need…"

Jonathan places his hand over her mouth. "I got this."

Inside the salon, Jonathan takes a seat in the waiting area, where he is served a coffee and pastry. Audrey robes and goes to the wash station, then the drier. While under the dryer, four of her so-called salon buddies come in laughing gaily, asking each other who the handsome man is up front. Each makes semi-lude suggestions in earshot of other women and Jonathan, who can hear them.

Candice says, "Humph, I'd love to take him home to mama." Salina goes farther, saying, "The heck with mama, I'd take him straight to my bedroom."

The helper lifts the hood on Audrey's dryer, telling her she's almost ready for cut and styling. Deidra is being shampooed and cannot participate in the jeering, but gives Candice, Salina, and Juanita a 'thumbs up' as they begin their usual tirade of teasing. "So, Audrey, what did you and your boyfriend do since we last saw you? And why are you here today?"

Audrey ignores their insinuations, saying, "I'm attending a company formal tomorrow; I needed a touch of elegance."

"And what about your mystery boyfriend; did you ever find him, or are you still looking? Foolish girl, you better just grab the next best thing. You're a pretty girl; any man would love to be with you. Hey, there's three guys out front waiting for haircuts and manicures; why don't you approach one of them? The tall one is especially cute."

Audrey plays it down. "No need; my man should be here soon."

Salina says, "Yeah, right. Uh huh," with laughter.

After a while, the stylist completes Audrey's hair and then escorts Jonathan to see the finished product. Audrey is seated in front of the full-length mirror, and the other girls are amazed at how wonderful her hair looks. Just then, the man they had all been swooning over is escorted back to Audrey. Jonathan looks at each woman with a charming smile and says hello to them individually. Then, the stylist directs him to Audrey's station and says, "What do you think?"

Jonathan stands there with a look of sheer delight and amazement at Audrey. He has never seen her hair like this, and without hesitation, he pulls Audrey up from her chair and gently spins her around to face him full on. She looks up at him, smiling; he looks at her as if his eyes are consuming her entire being while Salina, Candice, Juanita, and others look at the two of them with contempt, admiration, and jealousy.

Pulling her closer, he gently kisses Audrey, who returns the kiss. He pulls away to look at her again and then kisses her again. "My God; you're stunning. Are you ready? I already paid at the front desk. Grab your stuff, and let's get out of here." He turns to the ladies still looking on. "Have a great rest of your day, ladies; I hope to see you again." He waves to them, saying, "Bye."

Jonathan walks wistfully, holding Audrey's hand to the parking lot. The ladies inside are still watching them through the plate glass windows of the salon.

They see his luxury pickup truck exit the parking area; Audrey never looks back at them but looks at Jonathan with gratitude and love. She thanks him. "Thank you, Jonathan; you didn't have to do that; your presence was enough."

Jonathan turns to her. "Did my kisses feel real?"

She nods 'yes.'

Jonathan replies, "That's because they were real. It all overwhelmed me when I saw you, your hair, eyes, face, and body; I couldn't help myself; I was losing my mind dealing with you. I want you, but the *'I-can't-have-you'* is killing me, no, us; I know you feel it too. Our relationship is insane. Who ever heard of two people play-acting what is real? Who does that? I am trying not to love you, but I love you so much it hurts, and I know you feel the same way. We are in one helluva mess here; you better help me navigate this, or I'm losing my mind. You said we are a couple, but I want to be a full couple with no baggage. If we ever have to split up, Yikes! This situation will be tough on us both."

Audrey touches his hand gently and simply says, "I know, I know; me too, me too."

Back at her home, she invites him inside for a drink. He declines. "No, that would not be wise, especially today. I don't believe there is a power on earth that would keep from happening what we want to happen if I go inside today."

Audrey reluctantly agrees. "But can we at least sit here and read the letter Nancy got from Chuck to give to you? I don't know what it says, but it could make things better… easier; don't you think? And I'm sure you'll want to read Clair's letter in private."

Extracting the letter from the center console, he hands it to Audrey, asking her to read it aloud as he's afraid of what it might say, dashing their futures permanently.

She carefully extracts the letter, showing Jonathan Chuck's notes on the back of the envelope. She begins to read:

To Jonathan – my friend

Jonathan, if you're reading this, then I have left the store where you have known me for many years. It's great having a person like you demonstrate an interest in an average guy like me. This letter is to tell you that I have been on the lookout for the girl you say is the girl of your dreams.

I know how it is to miss out on a lifetime opportunity. I had to drop out of college because of family obligations. I will never become the me I want to be now, but I'm all good, and my family is great.

I've subconsciously scanned every woman that matched your description of the woman you've loved for many years, and I have not seen her. I only hope you two connect and form a permanent bond, as I've never seen you happier than when you're talking about her.

You should know that I once caught a glimpse of her, but she was gone when I got to the parking lot. Not so sure it was her, but my other managers said she walked through each aisle as if she were looking for someone as she did not look at any products on any shelves.

At first, we thought she was a shoplifter waiting for an opportunity as she had no hand cart, shopping cart, or anything but a shoulder-slung purse. However, after wandering the store, our security person said she only purchased one item before she left; water in a blue bottle.

By the time I was informed, I only caught a momentary glimpse of her, and she was gone.

Jonathan, I hope this helps, as you deserve all the joy and happiness in the world.

A SIMPLE ACT OF KINDNESS

I have been recruited by several markets and don't know where I will be going, but I will let my trainee know if you want to contact me directly.

To my friend's soulmate:

You don't know me, but my friend Jonathan saw you once and fell in love instantly, which I believe is impossible. Anyway, he asks me about you; he has described you in exacting detail, saying your image was carved in his heart's memory from the day Jon saw you with three children he hoped were not yours.

His name is Jonathan Dawson, and he is a good man. If you're interested in knowing him, please reach out. If not, know that someone you never knew loved you at first sight. Again this is crazy because love, at first sight, does not exist, but he swears your two souls are or were a match made somewhere outside this universe.

I apologize for intruding into your life this way; I can't imagine you miss your opportunity to at least know one of the most decent and kind men to walk the earth.

May your life be happy, and should you and Jonathan re-connect, all I ask is that you invite me to the wedding or make me a Godfather.

Best always,
Charles 'Chuck' Mathis.

Jonathan and Audrey look at each other for the first time with the promise of hope. Audrey speaks first. "I honestly don't ever remember being at that store, but everything lines up. Even down to the Saratoga. Did you discover anything from the search for the little girl at the gravesite?"

"No, but Pastor promised he would call me. So, for now, let's just cool it. I think a resolution is coming soon, one way or the other. My family, especially my mom, wants to see you again; she says you saved my life. What is she talking about? Those coyotes weren't enough to kill. You and Mom are keeping secrets; I can feel it." Jonathan does not want to leave; he prods her. "Right now, we better call it a night."

Audrey asks, "The letter from Clair, tell me what it says later. I know it's private, but my woman's curiosity wants to know." Audrey gives the letter from Clair to Jonathan. He returns it, echoing his earlier sentiment. "Didn't I say I have no secrets from you? You read it."

Audrey opens the envelope and reads it aloud as she holds Jonathan's left hand.

'My dearest Jonathan,

You always admonished me on the power and gratitude one must have for unanswered prayers. You made me play that tune by Garth, and I thought about the lyrics so many times, missing you and what I thought was my dream; you as my husband.

It broke my heart when I was sent ten hours away from you to Kentucky, but I was grateful every time you visited me to ease my pain. I was mad at God for not giving you to me, especially since I had a crush on you for as long as I can remember.

When you cried on my shoulder about your sock girl, I was hurt but let you talk, hoping you would turn to me for romantic comfort; you did not. I thought I had a chance after our first outing/date. I often think about how I forced my kiss on you. I still remember the shock, but you let me kiss you so as not to hurt me. How noble you are. I thought I had you after we went rock climbing. I cleaned myself up for you as you're the only man I wanted to see me as attractive. I loved the expression on your face when you looked up the wall and saw my booty and legs; your reaction was unmistakable, and I really thought I had you. It was nice to see a genuine desire for me in your eyes, yet you still held on to your virtue, disappointing me once again.

After you returned from Korea, you told me we would never embrace again. What you said to me about the woman who stayed in your hotel and who you fell instantly in love with hurt me more than you can know. At first, I imagined you and her having sex; it killed me. That is until I realized that you would never sleep with a woman you are not married to. Still, I knew there was no hope, so I wrote the included poem and am sending it with this letter.

Now, Jonathan, here's the good news. I attended a softball championship in Atlanta and met the most wonderful guy in the world besides you. He's handsome, funny, witty, super intelligent, and a gentleman to the core, and based on the number of times he's visited me, I think he loves me. He asked me to be his girlfriend, and I said yes.

I can't wait for you to meet him; the next time we're in your neck of the woods together, I will present him to you. You're gonna be shocked, I promise.

I'm really happy now, and I thank you and God for unanswered prayers.

All my agape love forever,

Clair – your former work-wife (lol)

P.S. It feels strange to write a real letter, but being cyber suspicious about everything, I didn't want this communication floating around in the cyber ethersphere. So, sometimes old school is the best.

C.U. Soon – c.h.'

Audrey hands the poem to Jonathan, and he unfolds it preparing to read it to Audrey with a twinge of sorrow. Audrey stops him before he could read a word. She looks at him, absorbing what Clair expressed in her letter: "Jonathan, you really do love me, don't you? Love at first sight in Korea? You dumped Clair when you didn't even know me?"

"I didn't know you, but my heart knew you instantly. Let's read Clair's poem; she calls it lost love found, that's a strange name for a poem."

He scans it and then reads it aloud to Audrey.

Lost Love Found

    Grade school brought us together long ago
    My heart felt attached to yours, I, too young to know
    That the feelings of spring you planted in my heart
    Were sown with seeds of a girl's wish, that we'd never be apart
    Time gave me hope as I followed you to manhood and beyond
    Granting me a glimpse of a future lover, I could care for because of his charm
    Best of friends we became, I pledged myself to make you my man
    But the unknown girl with the socks, came one day and ruined my plan
    You wept on my shoulders hoping to make things right
    My heart grieved lost love, as it faded into a loveless night
    Fate and cupid have abandoned my wish
    And left me empty and void, without even a hint of bliss
    And now in pain, I wish and bid you, a graceful farewell
    knowing my life will continue as only faith can foretell
    Be well my love, I bid you no harm
    I am grateful for every moment I spent in your arms.
    Thank you for trying to love me so

Even though in the end, your answer was no.
I know for you Jonathan, that you will find the love of the ages
I too, will inscribe your heart, name and love in my life's pages
Be well my love,
Clair

Audrey is moved and somber, understanding that Clair's dream was lost because of Jonathan's steadfast love for her and not Clair. Audrey stands to enter her home but turns back to Jonathan, who is still sitting. "I will never forget what you did for me at the salon. You have my gratitude forever. And by the way, you're a fantastic kisser; I could kiss you all day and night; you taste good."

Audrey walks back down to Jonathan and leans over, kissing him on his right cheek. She cannot stop staring at him. Finally, he turns to her, suddenly asking, "What? Do I have something on my face? Why are you staring at me?"

Audrey sits on a deck chair on her porch. She leans back in her seat, emotionally unable to face Jonathan, still on her stairs.

Finally, she says, "Jonathan, how are you making even the simplest things so pleasant for me? What you did; what you've done for me is…" Audrey pauses, unsure of her following words. "Jonathan, would you…" waiting again. "Never mind."

Jonathan cuts her off. "Would I what? There is nothing on earth I would deny you; ever. No, Audrey; it's what you've done for me. I am so frightened by the joy I feel when I'm with you. It's difficult to explain, but it is real. You've reached into my soul with some kind of magic salve. Sometimes I am terrified just imagining you not being in my life. It's crazy. I try not to think about it; the fragility of our current relationship. When I think of you out of my life, I experience anxiety and panic attacks. I've never had a panic attack in my life, never! Why do you think I'm still sitting here? I get anxious whenever I have to part from you."

Audrey leans forward in her chair, and he turns to face her. "Jonathan, do you remember me mentioning that you saved me from myself? Do you remember me telling you that and that I'd explain one day?"

Jonathan looks over to her, silently nodding, 'yes.' "Yes, I remember; I figured you'd tell me when you were ready. I racked my memory, trying to figure it out, but I was lost. You've done more for me than I deserve. No one's counting, but I owe you. The swimming pool thing; is that what you mean? You'd do the same for me, you did do the same thing with the coyotes."

Jonathan comes up to the porch, reaches across to the arm of the chair, caressing her wrist, bringing it to his face, kissing the back of her hand.

Audrey again goes silent. Jonathan knows this is a reflective moment for her, and he honors her silence by not saying a word.

Moments seem to creep by like molasses. Finally, Audrey looks at him directly and then speaks. "The coyotes and near drowning were saving each other from something else. I'm saying that you saved me from MYSELF; there's a big difference. Jonathan, let me tell you a story. You spoke of anxiety and panic. Did you know that while in Korea, I was never alone as the PGP employees took excellent care of me? The night we went to Iteawon was a Friday night. When I saw you at the dumpling place, my heart moved and fluttered like it did when I saw that guy years ago. I tried to remember how this could happen. At first, I thought you were one and the same person, but I couldn't remember his face, and there I saw your whole face for the first time with my heart doing flip-flops in a foreign country. Even though I didn't know it was you, the first time I saw you, we both wore N95 masks, but I recognized your kind eyes. I tried to ignore both you and my unreasonable feelings. I snuck a peek at you every time you were distracted; I didn't want you to catch me looking at you. It was like an instant crush, something I had never believed possible. With the guy in the store, I was moved by his kindness, which is why I probably can't remember his face. In Korea, I was moved for the first time by your good looks; it was crazy, at least for me it was."

She continues, "As the crowd thinned, you and I spent more time with each other until we were finally together alone, one-on-one, just you and me. But, Jonathan, don't think awful of me, but I wanted to sleep with a man, you, for the first time in my life; worse still, a complete stranger. As fate would have it, I was locked out of my corporate apartment, and you tried everything to find a hotel for me. When you insisted I stay in your room, I was terrified, panicked, and pleased. Outwardly I clung to my virtues and upbringing; Inside, I screamed, now! I have never stayed in a man's hotel; that's not who I am. Yet, you were so kind and gave me the master suite. I thought to myself, *'No guy is this nice. What's his game? When is he going to make his move? Will I be able to resist?'* I felt profound anxiety, knowing that if you approached me sexually, I knew I had no power to resist; I thought I would give in instantly. The gaggle of emotions overwhelmed me. I scolded myself, knowing that I wanted to break my promise to myself to be a virgin on my wedding night, and here I was at the mercy of a man I wanted to sleep with. My virtue and conviction were out the window at that moment. And after you told me in the cab that you were the guy I met at the I.T. expo, I was helpless because I felt even more comfortable sleeping with you since now I knew you weren't the stranger I thought you were. I actually looked forward to making love with you, even against my upbringing and better judgment; I decided to do it if you asked me. I was prepared to kill my own rules and inhibitions to be with you; I was helpless, I just didn't care. I wanted you and was both proud and ashamed of myself for how I was acting. The things I imagined us doing were crazy, at least for me. And even after you went to sleep on the couch, I came out to take your shoes off. I tried to be quiet, but part of me wanted to have you accidentally wake to take me where I both wanted to and not to go. I'm sure you get my drift. I can't believe I'm saying this stuff to you. I watched you from the cracked bedroom door, praying for you to stay asleep and hoping you'd wake to satisfy the aching I felt for you. I left without waking you that morning, knowing that if you were awake, I dreamed of making the first move, fearing both your rejection and acceptance. It was like I was being torn in two. I'm telling you this now because when you kissed me at the salon, I had a physical reaction I haven't felt since that night. So, Jonathan, you preserved my virtue and my promise to myself in one of the most difficult emotional battles I have ever experienced. You saved me from me, and I thank you."

Jonathan, again, knows this is a moment for silence.

Now moving to the seat next to her, Jonathan is finally free to speak. "Audrey, I did want you that night in Korea, but I could not bear the idea of a one-night-stand with the woman I instantly fell for. I knew that you could be the one for me from the moment I met you. I cursed the memory of the sock girl, and by night's end, I was lost in the spell of enchantment for you. I cursed myself again for being so modest. Why couldn't I be like other guys? But at that moment, a lifetime with you was far more important than a single night with you. Do you understand what I'm saying? Until we are entirely free from this temptation, you and I will have to save each other intermittently. There will be times when you will have to put the brakes on us and times when I will have to refrain. However, the real danger will be when we both want the same thing more than we want to wait. So, Audrey, now that we've been to confession, I feel better. Obviously, after what you've said, I can't come in; way too dangerous. I'll see you later."

Still unsure of the control of his desire for Audrey, Jonathan leans over as he stands and whispers into her hair, "Good night, my friend."

Down the stairs and hurriedly into his truck, Jonathan drives off, never looking back, thinking of her shocking and candid confession.

Driving home, Jonathan inserts the thumb drive Audrey gave him, and it plays Roy Orbison's *In Dreams*. As he listens to it for the third time in a row, the words choke him up, leaving him missing his buddy whom he has just dropped off.

Inside, Audrey plays the CD of Kenny Nolan's *I like Dreaming*. She sobs on the second pass, realizing that they both dream of each other for a reality that neither is sure they can have past their heart's original objections.

She dials Jonathan. Still driving; he answers, "Hi, babe, what's up?"

She replies, "It's a good thing you left; I just played your song; several times. You're lucky you drove off before I heard it."

He replies, "I played '*In Dreams*' four times and couldn't take it anymore. To be accurate, you're lucky I drove off before I heard it. Sweet dreams tonight, my love. Good night."

As Jonathan reaches to disconnect, he hears Audrey's voice, but it is too late; he is too quick and ends the call.

Driving, he asks himself, speaking out loud, *"Jonathan, Audrey sounded like she was about to say something; you hung up on her. It's probably nothing, or she'd call back. Maybe I should call her back, but if I do, we could end up... Nah, better leave that alone, Johnny Boy; we're both too hot now. Suppose she wants me to come back?"*

Jonathan wrestles with himself, finally giving in to call her back. Five tortured minutes pass; he smiles, hearing her voice. "Jonathan, what's up? Did we forget something?"

Jonathan answers with reservation, "I thought I heard you say my name just as we hung up."

Audrey relaxes. "Oh, I was going to ask something of you, but then I thought it would be an imposition, especially after all you've done for me today. If I ask, you'll think I'm shallow and vain; I couldn't stand that."

Jonathan responds, a little irritated, "Either you don't believe me, or I'm not convincing enough. But, Audrey, my love, I don't want to repeat this; there is nothing you cannot ask of me. Don't you feel the same way about me? Is there anything I could ask of you that you wouldn't do even if it meant your discomfort? Now just tell me what you want. I'm your genie in a magic lamp; your slightest wish is my command."

Audrey has never heard that tone in Jonathan's voice, and she knows he is serious. He considers her reluctance as a sign that she believes that he does not love her completely. It feels both awkward and exhilarating hearing Jonathan asserting himself.

Finally, she submits. "Yes, Jonathan, I'm sorry, but I am so used to being self-sufficient. I've never had someone treat me the way you do. As a result, I sometimes feel I'm taking advantage of your affection for me. Okay, I'll do better. I got my hair done today because tomorrow evening I have to attend a formal corporate event for my job. My company wants all the technical staff there for a dog-and-pony show. I hate this stuff and thought if you go with me, we could make a boring event something fun. I got a ticket for you a month ago but was afraid to ask. But I'm good; I'll make an appearance, then sneak out to the powder room and never come back."

Jonathan is intrigued. "Audrey, you're a silly girl. But, of course, I will go, sweetheart; count me in."

Audrey says, "But it's formal; you can't rent…"

"Not a problem Audrey; I own a bespoke Kingsman for after six and a Charles Tyrwhitt tuxedo for weddings and other hi-end occasions. Where is the event being held?"

Audrey tells him, "Hold on, I think it's in Severna Park; let me look at the invitation; Yep, Chartwell Golf and Country Club."

Jonathan replies, "Since it's a formal event, we should take your car."

Audrey stops Jonathan. "No, no, no, since they're making me go, I'm spending the company's money; I already rented a car and driver for tomorrow just in case I have a glass or two of champagne; my only vice. I even got my hair done for them. Can you be here at four? The event starts at six."

ENTERING AUDREY'S TOWNHOUSE, JONATHAN IS STUNNED AT THE goddess standing before him. In all their years together as friends, he has seen her in jeans, slacks, and sundresses. On some occasions she wore skirt and blouse. Most times when he picked her up from work, she often wore what she called her 'uniform' consisting of business casual dresses or two-piece suits.

Today, Audrey looks amazingly beautiful. She's wearing a formal designer after-six dress. It has a scallop-trimmed sweetheart laced neckline, a fabulous lace bodice dotted with sparkling accents, a draped waist detail, and an A-line chiffon skirt that drapes gracefully to the floor with her beautiful legs barely visible through the translucent lower dress.

Audrey's beautiful legs descend into two-inch heeled black satin pumps that match the dress's alternate color and are equal to the beauty of her legs. The outline of her body catches Jonathan off guard as he stares with his mouth open at her subtle curves and perfect chest. Three-quarter length embroidered lace sleeves cover her delicate arms. She's holding a satin clutch, bringing the vision of a goddess to life.

Jonathan turns her around to view her as if she were a sculpture in a museum.

Audrey rarely wears make-up and is one of those women whose natural face is even more beautiful with only a modest hint of nearly invisible makeup.

Now seeing his girlfriend with almost impossible to see touches of shadow, blush, and powder takes his breath away. Her perfectly French manicured natural nails shimmer with a gloss, not a shine. Crowning the whole package is her hair. The luxurious female mane moves and shimmers with the light.

Audrey knows that her hair is a significant female asset; she refused to wear it in an up-do. Instead, Audrey's just below shoulder-length hair bounces as she walks, and each curl is an exclamation point of glory to her angelic face.

The mutual admiration society continues as he enters her home. Standing there, Audrey gawks at how fine her boyfriend is. Jonathan had primarily been dressed in business casual or jeans for the entire time she knew him; tonight, he looks like he stepped off the cover of GQ or Esquire.

Audrey spins him around, saying, "Fella, you look good enough to eat."

Jonathan keeps staring, saying, "Wow, you clean up real nice. Let's take a selfie before we leave."

Audrey sets up the self-timer on her Nikon DSLR and runs back to stand next to him, saying, "I set it to burst shot. It will take ten pictures in a row three-to-four seconds apart. So let's do something fun for the camera."

Their poses for the camera are fun and spontaneous. Then, with her arms around him, the camera fires. The next his arms are around her. Then, an exaggerated kiss to his cheek, then a shot of her fixing his tie. Finally, she slips her arm interlocked with his. With only three shots left, Jonathan pulls her to him, kissing her on the mouth and holding his embrace through the sound of the last three clicks.

And when the camera is done, Audrey wraps her elegant arms

around Jonathan and continues the kiss for a minute more. Finally, they part lips, smiling and embarrassed. She says, running to the powder room, "I'll be right back; got to redo my lipstick."

Jonathan smiles, saying, "I'm leaving your lip balm on me as my souvenir. You taste good."

Out of the powder room with a damp towel, she wipes her lipstick off his lips, and then he escorts her out the door, down the steps, holds the limo's rear door open for her, then gets in behind her. The driver politely says, "You guys look great, but seat belts, please."

Chartwell Golf & Country Club

ENTERING THE VESTIBULE, AUDREY IS MET BY HER BOSS AND A FEW coworkers. No one has ever seen Audrey at one of these events, and most are stunned at her appearance.

Audrey looks at her place card and leads Jonathan to their assigned table. Each table is formally set up with several plates, various glasses and flutes, and a spread of flatware on either side of the bone china service ensemble.

Arriving a bit early, there is only one other couple seated at their table for now. The woman, Charlene, speaks first. "Audrey, it is wonderful to see you here." Charlene points to her husband. "Audrey; this is Ben, my husband."

Audrey only nods with an acknowledging petite smile. Jonathan, a bit disappointed, rises from his seat and walks over to Ben and Charlene, saying, "Ben, may I present my girlfriend, Audrey." The two men shake hands. Ben and Jonathan compliment each other on the venue and each other's formal wear. Jonathan says to Ben, "You're wearing a Montblanc Timewalker Automatic Silver Dial Watch; a wonderful timepiece." Ben asks, "You must be a watch guy?"

Jonathan says, "At last count I had one-hundred-three, the Omega Speedmaster Chronograph Automatic with the Black Dial is my favorite, but tonight I decided to take the Sturhling Original for a spin." Both men stand there enjoying something they have in common. Jonathan notices Charlene's obvious dislike for Audrey and comes to his girlfriend's rescue.

Charlene glares at Audrey; Jonathan senses the moment's awkwardness, asking Ben, "Would you two excuse us?"

Jonathan pulls Audrey's seat out, allowing her to stand. He says, "I want to meet everyone; come on."

With Audrey on his arm, Jonathan makes his way through the crowd as if he knows everyone. First, he introduces himself warmly, saying various forms of how lucky he is to attend with Audrey. By the third introduction, Audrey finds herself speaking freely and beginning to enjoy the crowd.

Halfway around the ballroom making rounds, Jonathan spots Lawrence, a contractor to the Federal agency Jonathan worked for.

Lawrence shakes hands with Jonathan, grins at Audrey, and begins a revealing conversation.

Jonathan speaks first. "Larry, I haven't seen you in a year. What are you doing here? You did a great job on the big data thing your people handled for us. Thank you. I got a lot of accolades for hiring your company; you did not let me down."

Larry replies, "Forget about big data, Hadoop, Python, and all that. Who is this with you?" Then, Larry turns full on to Audrey, introducing himself. "Hello, my name is Larry. I worked for Jonathan for a few years. Are you the long-lost girl from the market with the socks? He's been looking for you forever, and now I see why."

Audrey shakes Larry's hand. "I'm Audrey, and no, I'm not the market girl, but I plan to replace her."

"Holy smokes, Jonathan," Larry bellows. "Audrey, you're a lifesaver. This dude was so unhappy with everything. I tried to hook him up with a dozen women; he was never interested in anyone but this girl he found then lost; he used to tell me about her over lunch. So now I understand why he stopped calling. Not being superficial here, but Audrey, you're a knockout. Jonathan, how did you get this girl? She's amazing. Audrey, how did you pry his heart loose?"

"Well, Larry, I sort of lost my way too; right guy, wrong place. So then I met Jonathan at one of these less formal events, we exchanged a few words and went on with life."

A SIMPLE ACT OF KINDNESS

Audrey puts her arm in Jonathan's arm, saying, "Then I accidentally met my Jonathan in Korea. When we returned home, we were independently arrested for droning on Federal property in Laurel, and, well, the rest is history."

Larry asks, "Are you two serious, thinking about living together?"

Jonathan answers with the least condescending tone he could muster, "No, we aren't planning on living together, but I do want to marry Audrey when the time is right."

Larry politely recoils. "Oh, right. I forgot you're one of those old-fashioned dudes; you'd never shack up or try before you buy. But that's good. I was raised that way, but the world sort of turned me away from my parents' view of the world, but hey, do your thing."

Audrey and Jonathan move through the ballroom easily; they are stopped by many of Audrey's coworkers who introduce themselves to Jonathan first, and then saying 'hello' to Audrey. Jonathan is not surprised knowing how standoffish Audrey could be at work, but he also knows she is surprised that so many knew of her reputation and greeted her warmly. Some she knows well, many she is only acquainted with. Jonathan takes note of the awkward introductions and uses his charm to side-step the moments, allowing everyone he meets to feel at ease. Jonathan makes it easy for Audrey by saying to various couples some version of, *"So nice to finally meet you. Audrey has mentioned you."* Jonathan leads Audrey to the dance floor, where several couples are dancing slowly to the live music.

Jonathan had taken dance in college, and Audrey has been a natural dancer since glee and thespian club in junior high. The two of them make it look effortless as they move elegantly around the dance floor.

Audrey and Jonathan are so good that the other nine couples slowly leave the dance floor as if on cue, leaving the two best dancers to the floor by themselves. Jonathan is tall, fit, and handsome. Audrey is just under his chin, and her beauty matches his charm.

Audrey feels embarrassed being the only dancers on the floor. Her expression begs Jonathan to let her return to her seat as she does not like being in the spotlight. Instead, Jonathan holds her tightly, reassuring her that he is, as always, proud of her. He tells her he understands and will help her through the awful glare of being in the center of attention amongst her friends and coworkers. He whispers in her ear, "I've got you; I love you. Did you forget; my girl can do anything." And she forgets about the accidental audience and melts confidently into Jonathan's arms as he leads her.

The band concludes the semi-up-tempo tune, and everyone applauds, saying, "One more for the house!"

The band immediately begins the instrumental version of *The Last Waltz*, one of Jonathan and Audrey's oldie favorites. Audrey perks up, forgetting about everyone, whispering, "I love and adore you" to Jonathan as he leads her through the graceful waltz-like moves of the Engelbert Humperdinck hit.

Their dance moves the crowd, and soon, the floor is packed with others swaying and swooning to the grand tune. While dancing, Jonathan sings in a whisper, the lyrics into her ear; Audrey cannot stop smiling, saying, "You are so romantic; I love it."

Audrey feels confident and happy for the first time, saying as she dances, "Jonathan, I'm so happy you came. You kicked me out of my shell; I feel like a better person when I'm with you and especially when I'm around you with other people." She pauses, asking, "Can I lead you?"

Jonathan releases his leading arm to Audrey's guidance as she whisks him with moves he has never experienced. He is delighted, saying, "Where did you learn those moves?"

Audrey answers easily. "My parents loved to dance as far back as I can remember. Mom and Dad taught me some of their moves from the time I was eight till I left for college. So, Jonathan, can I ask you a question?"

Jonathan nods 'yes.' Audrey asks, "You told Larry you wanted to marry me. Was that for my sake, like at the salon? I'm just asking for clarity's sake. You sort of suggested the same intention in California when you showed me our future winter home."

Jonathan stops dancing and escorts Audrey outside the ballroom to the beautiful grounds. He finds a secluded place, takes off his jacket, and places it on the outdoor seat for her to sit on. He sits next to her and says, "Audrey, I've loved you since Korea. My life is so much richer because of you; I only hope I've done the same for you. Since I'm laying all my cards on the table, let me tell you where I am, so that you can determine where you want to be in my life. When I sort of met you at the Expo, everyone wore masks, but my heart pounded as it did for the woman I met at the market. If it weren't so dumb an idea in Korea, I would've stayed there with you and never returned. That way, I would be assured of never meeting the girl with the socks from the market. Then, the drone thing. You were snarky and mean, but my heart was still pounding. And then we had coffee at Starbucks that day, and I got to see the real you. At this point, I have betrayed whatever I felt for the market girl because it is you I want. I was extremely reluctant to tell you this because I felt that if you believed I could forget market girl so easily for you, then you would most likely believe that in some distant future, I would dump you for the new so-called market girl. I cannot prove it, and I won't try to convince you, but I am 100% sure that you are the girl I met that day, but I also know that you don't know it and until you do, this is where we are. I also know how stubborn you are. So, being aware of all that, the only thing I can do is wait for you."

He continues, "And I will tell you one more thing, Miss Audrey, if I only wanted your body; you and I both know we could've done that a long time ago. But I also know that while we crave each other physically, we both want the right to each other without shame or guilt. So, do I want to marry you one day? Yes, but only when you're ready. Like the song says, *'If it takes forever, I will wait for you.'* Is there anything else you wish to know?"

Audrey says, "Yes, one more thing. Where did you get this super cool social personality? You were like a butterfly in there. I'm so proud of you, my almost-husband."

Thirty

TANGERINE JOANIE

When Jonathan's phone lights up with Pastor Jack's number, two months have passed. Answering it immediately, the pastor gets straight to the point. "Jonathan, the girl's name is Joanie; she's eleven or twelve and was here from Seattle for her uncle's funeral. I talked to a zillion people to learn her whereabouts. I spoke with her parents, and they are willing to meet you in their home as long as you give them proper notice. Their daughter Joanie has spoken about the incident to her parents for years but they thought it was an imaginary story since they visited their maternal grandmother in a little town near Annapolis. Write this down; this is the number of her grandma here in Maryland. Her memory comes and goes, but I think you should contact her first, and if that pans out, you and your buddy should fly out to meet Joanie for confirmation. This woman may be precisely the lead you need. Because Joanie called you both stupid, you may have been best friends with the girl you've searched for for years. Now ain't that something else? And my wife thinks so too. She had a patient matching your lost love's description seeking to find you or move on years ago. When we compared notes as you permitted me to do, well, Jonathan, I think we're on to something extraordinary, my friend."

Joanie's maternal grandmother lives in a lovely home on the cliffs of the Severn River. Jonathan drives up the driveway, where a middle-aged woman is pruning the walkway gardens. He gets out, and before he can speak, she says, "You must be Jonathan. I never get much company these days. Come around through the side gate to the back porch; I prepared some iced tea and fresh scones for you."

Following her inviting instructions, Jonathan gasps at the panoramic view of the Severn River opening up before him, commenting to her, "This view is breathtaking."

Grandma responds with pride, "I love this place and this view. Why go on vacation when you live on vacation? People pay good money to enjoy a panorama like this; I get to see this for free every day."

Jonathan gets straight to the point. "Ma'am, I hope you know the woman you mentioned in your phone call. Unfortunately, I never knew her name and never had the opportunity to properly thank her for helping me out that day at Graul's Market."

Jonathan carefully inquires, careful not to give her any leads, hoping to collect as much unsolicited information as possible. "Do you know Chuck, the manager?

"Of course, I know Chuck, he always carries my groceries to the car for me, and he lets me use the store's employee-only restroom as I have grandma's weak bladder." She laughs. "By the way, my name is Edna. Please call me Edna. So you say you met my granddaughter Joanie at a funeral, and she called you stupid. That is one bright and precocious young lady. That little girl has no filters whatsoever. Now, what is it you want to ask me?"

"A few years ago, I was in the store, and I saw three children standing with a young woman. She was wearing these unusual colorful knee-high socks. I thought the children were hers, but she didn't look quite old enough to have been the mother of the oldest one. I have been trying for years to find her; I've had no luck, but I tracked her to you by finding someone who knew of Joanie and said you might know who that woman was. Do you?"

Edna ponders the question and answers slowly, "You'll have to forgive an old woman's memory; I'm actually not that old, but I remember I had to pee something crazy, and I wasn't sure I could hold it. So, Chuck gave me the key to the restroom, and I asked a woman; I don't remember what she looked like; she was very pretty; I'm sure of that! You don't see faces like hers around here much. So, anyway, I asked her to keep an eye on the kids until I returned from the restroom. I took a little longer than I expected, and when I came out, she immediately left the store. I thanked her, and she smiled kindly and left the store. Then, as I was leaving with the kids, some guy walked up to the children, offering them… Hey, now I remember; it was you! As I remember, you gave the kids apples and an orange or tangerine. Well, ain't that something! The kids said you were the nicest man. Joanie said you were only nice to them because you were hitting on the young woman; I guess little Joanie had you figured out. So tell me, what did she say to you at the graveyard?"

"Joanie said that my female friend and I were stupid for not realizing that we were the same people in the store. The trouble is, my friend Audrey has zero recollection of that event or even being at the store. It was many years ago, but there is nothing that ties Audrey to that day."

Edna studies Jonathan's face, answering, "My memory for faces is not that good, especially after time passes. Do you have a picture of Audrey?"

Extending his phone, he shows Edna a picture of Audrey. Edna responds, "She's pretty, but I don't remember her; I was more interested in the bathroom than making new friends. I wish I could help you, but I don't recognize this girl. All I remember about her is that she wore a tan coat; she had pretty hair under a fur hat. Sorry, that's all I remember."

Jonathan nibbles his scone. "Your daughter in Seattle, Samantha, has agreed to let Audrey and I meet Joanie; we're going to fly out soon."

Jonathan and Edna sit there for an hour more, talking about growing up and growing old in the area, how things have changed, and the horrible Bay Bridge traffic during Ocean City's summer season.

Jonathan bids her goodbye, promising, "Whatever I discover in Seattle, I will keep you informed. Thank you for your time."

Edna responds with a surprising promise. "Make you a deal; if you find that girl, marry her and promise to have a family, I will give you this home for ten dollars."

"Why would you do that? This property with that view of the river is a million-dollar-home?"

Edna answers succinctly, "And your love for this girl is a million-dollar-love. Before my mister Frank went home to Glory, we shared the best of the best of times here. It would be great if you and your lady could succeed us living and loving in this house. I ain't doing it for you; I want to honor what my husband and I learned and loved in this home; an old-fashioned love story. Be safe now, Mr. Jonathan, and good luck."

Leaving Edna, Jonathan calls Audrey. "Grandma was very nice, but she does not recognize your picture. I think we need to fly out to Seattle to meet Joanie; are you game? Great, then I will pick you up at your place tomorrow around 10 a.m."

Gaithersburg Regional Airport:

JONATHAN GIVES AUDREY ALL THE DETAILS HE LEARNED FROM EDNA, including little Joanie's precocious nature. Then, he drives into the airport grounds and up to the hangar where private jets are stored. Audrey asks, "Are we taking a private plane; who's the pilot?"

Jonathan answers Audrey, "A good one; I've flown with him before; you'll like him."

Approaching the private jet, the hangar attendant shouts to Jonathan. "Good to see you again, sir! She's all checked out and fueled for a two-leg trip to Seattle. Have a safe trip."

Jonathan escorts the wondering Audrey up the steps of the jet. She heads for the comfortable cabin seats. He stops her, saying, "Nope, you're with me, up here," pointing to the cockpit. She watches with admiration as Jonathan goes through pre-flight-check and taxis to the runway ramp. Finally, she hears the tower clear him to take off. He looks at her and asks her to ensure she's strapped in. With that, Jonathan guides the plane to the runway, puts his hand on the throttle, and then places her free hand on his as he advances the throttle levers, causing the twin jets to roar to life.

The large multi-function LCD screen shows the air speed indicator increases with gut pulling acceleration. Jonathan says, "Hold on; you may feel a bit queasy for a few seconds as we rotate off the runway." She hears him say, "Rotating." Next, she feels the craft lift off the runway heading into the northwestern sky. Still holding his hand, she cannot stop staring at his confident demeanor as the craft reaches cruising altitude. Finally, she whispers to him, "Dude, I'm gonna marry you. I can't let another gal grab you; you're mine."

He turns to her, whispering, "I sure do hope so."

The flight out is quiet and peaceful. Audrey, still stunned by her man's ability, asks, "How long have you been flying; is this your plane? What don't you do?"

Jonathan chuckles. "No, very few could afford this jet. I joined a jet membership club with less than a hundred partners. I think you saw the monthly invoice from *Jet-A-Way Club* in my mail that day. So, we all own a little piece, and depending on our share input, we fly when we need or want to. It's like a timeshare that flies. If I have to travel more than 500 miles or want to impress my girlfriend; just joking, I reserve it for a day or two."

Jonathan laughs. "Seriously, Audrey, I am not a fan of the big airports, TSA lines, taking off my shoes, random searches, bag checks, and overpriced airport food. My private plane is a Beech King Air 350. And no, I'm not rich; I couldn't afford it until some of the stocks I invested in during my college years blew up. My first was an old Navion I kept at Freeway."

Audrey touches his hand affectionately, saying, "So, you know how to pick stocks too; I'm so lucky to have you. I dabbled in the market a bit too; I'm doing okay."

He looks over at her with affection and a smile. Minutes pass silently as she observes the skyline. Finally, Audrey taps Jonathan's arm excitedly, saying, "You will never guess who I got an email from; I forgot to tell you." She did not wait for his response. "Cheryl, the girl who almost killed herself that night."

Jonathan responds with curiosity, "Tell me; is she okay?"

"More than okay; she's engaged!"

Jonathan interrupts her, "Audrey, hold that story; I'm going to land to refuel; I want to hear the rest when we take off." Grabbing the microphone, he says, "Central Illinois Regional, this is November-7406-Whiskey-Xray requesting landing vector for refueling."

Back in the jet, refueled, Jonathan asks Audrey to place her hands on the wheel. "I want you to feel how it feels to take off. You ready?"

Speeding down the runway, Audrey mimics Jonathan's pulling back on the yoke, loving the sensation of leaving earth for the sky.

Back at cruising altitude heading west, Jonathan continues the prior conversation. "You say Cheryl is engaged. How is that possible? It's only been six months."

Audrey turns almost sideways to face Jonathan, saying, "She enrolled in TANF and qualified. She was required to take a family care clinic. She met a single father there. His name is Brayden. He's two years older than Cheryl. He and his girlfriend had a baby out of wedlock. Ten months later, she left the baby with him and never came back. After a year, he learned she died from some kind of designer drug overdose. Brayden was all left with an infant to raise alone. Cheryl and Brayden hit it off, and after what she called a few poor-man's-dates, they decided to make it official. Her last line in the email was, *'God turned lemons into lemonade; that is oh-so-sweet. Tell Jonathan thanks for saving my life, and I will definitely pay your kindness forward to you, Audrey. Thank you both for a simple act of kindness.'*"

Jonathan inhales deeply, feeling extreme pleasure knowing that he and Audrey had saved a life. They are both deeply moved wordlessly. Audrey holds his throttle hand until she shares a sandwich and a Mountain Dew with her man somewhere over the Midwestern states.

The jet's GPS indicates they are now over Nebraska approaching Montana. Audrey comments, "I still can't believe all you do; you are a true renaissance man. You are so modest, always talking about you don't deserve me, with your list of professions and hobbies; you

A SIMPLE ACT OF KINDNESS

deserve a better woman than me. You could have any woman. Why me?"

Jonathan puts down his sandwich and confidently answers Audrey. "You're the best woman I've ever known. I have a history with you and personal interactions; I adore you and respect your abilities and kindness. With my market girl, I only saw her face; your face, I'm sure. But nothing could be more perfect for me than the you I've come to know. You're amazing."

Audrey blushes with an appreciation for Jonathan's matter-of-factly compliment. She relaxes and then hears the cockpit speaker crackle to life. She looks alarmed and sits her sandwich and soda aside.

Suddenly the cockpit speaker squawks again. "November-7406-Whiskey-Xray, this is Billings ATCT. Descend one-thousand feet twenty-nine thousand and come right to 3-1-5 northwest. Over"

Jonathan grabs the microphone, saying, "Billings ATC; November-7406-Whiskey-Xray acknowledging and executing; over."

He looks at Audrey, saying, "You can do this; I'll help. Now take your control wheel and hold it loosely as you did on take-off."

Audrey shrieks, "Are you kidding me? That was just holding the wheel; I've never flown a plane."

Jonathan takes his hand off his Control Wheel, saying, "You're my co-pilot here and the co-pilot for our life together when we tie the knot. My girl can do anything. Just trust me and do as I say."

Audrey timidly takes the yoke, following Jonathan's instructions. Then, pointing to the large screen, he says, "Audrey, this is the compass, and this part of the screen is the artificial horizon. Turn the wheel slowly to the right until this reads 3-1-5. Now, as you do that, push the wheel very slightly forward until this," he points, "the altimeter reads 29 thousand feet. You can do it. Now loosen up your arms and go for it. I trust you with my life."

Audrey carries out Jonathan's directions precisely. She is frightened and thrilled at the same time. Audrey smiles as the jet banks smoothly to the right, and the altimeter shows a gradual decrease in altitude. She pulls back on the yoke, levels the jet out as it reaches twenty-nine thousand feet, and hears the squelch from the cabin speaker again.

The air traffic controller says, "November-7406-Whiskey-Xray, perfect execution; Great flying. You've got several heavies around you, one above and several below on approach to Salt Lake International; we wanted to give them and you plenty of room. Maintain this heading until your next turn to your downwind leg and final approach into King Airport. Have a nice day."

Audrey is drunk with pleasure and surprise.

Jonathan pats her on the back and says, "See, my girl can do anything. Now keep this heading, and I will take over shortly."

He exits the cockpit to use the restroom while Audrey pilots the plane. When he returns to the pilot's seat, she says, "My turn; be back in a flash."

Audrey, back in the cockpit, kisses Jonathan on his cheek before retaking her seat. She is reticent and reluctant to speak.

Both finish their sandwich halves and sodas, and they intermittently gaze at each other. Audrey's gaze betrays her desire to say something, but she does not know how to broach the subject troubling her.

Jonathan looks at her, saying, "Come on, spill it. I know when you want to tell me something. What is it; you don't want to be with me anymore?"

Audrey stares thoughtfully. "No, that's not it; I want you even more than you know. But I want to talk to you about our marriage."

Jonathan says, "That's an improvement; at least you're thinking about 'our' marriage. I feel good, so, what's up?"

Audrey ignores his sarcasm, asking, "Have you ever heard the expression 'Happy wife – happy life'? Do you know what it means?"

Jonathan states, "I hear it all the time. It means that if a man makes his wife happy, he will have a happy life. So, what's wrong with that? I intend to make you a happy wife. I want to please you to demonstrate my love for you."

Audrey says, "You recall my diva friends from the salon? Have you noticed that I don't have many female friends? Do you know why?"

Jonathan stares blankly; Audrey continues, "Because women are so catty and cunning. To the average woman, that phrase means that if the man doesn't do what she wants when she wants, she will make his life miserable in many unfair ways. Men don't know it, but women usually use no lovin' and no conversation; the angry silent treatment, as standard weapons to have their way. These acts will snap a man back into serving her and getting her way. This type of woman uses her feminine wiles and his desire to sleep with her to control him. Before long, he will do anything to keep having sex with her. He becomes booty-whipped."

"And why are you telling me this?" Jonathan asks.

She answers, "Because a man cannot lead his family if he is worried that she may cut him off. It leads directly to a loveless marriage where she is happily in control, and he must walk on eggshells to please her. I'm telling you this because when we're married, I want you to lead our marriage precisely as you explained to me. I want you to be the front wheels fearlessly, and I will provide the propulsion. But, I never want you to feel you can't use your best judgment on our behalf. As I watch you fly this jet, it becomes clear that I have trusted you with my life even to board this airplane. I am saying that when you are my husband, I will trust you to pilot our lives and I will willingly be the jet fuel that makes us go. Today taught me that I 'want' to be your co-pilot for life. Sure, I may argue, fuss, pout and shout, but I want you to know that still, you must lead. Like you told me way back when, as long as you are never disingenuous, I will never make you beg to be with me, and I will love you all the days of my life. I promise."

Jonathan is stunned. She continues, "I know I'm being stubborn about not remembering your face, but if you believe it was me that day in the store, then I will trust you. If you were only trying to bed me down, you could've done that long ago; I already want you. What I want now is to clear this last hurdle so that we can start our lives together. You will never have to live under the implied torture of a 'happy wife-happy life.' You have my word."

Jonathan replies, "I know; that is why I have entrusted my heart and life to your care. And I swear that I will never intentionally hurt you, and I will be the first to apologize if I accidentally offend you.

Likewise, I will never cheat on you, embarrass or shame you. That is my heart's wedding vow to you."

King County Airport - Seattle, Washington

LANDING AT THE AIRPORT IN SEATTLE, JONATHAN escorts AUDREY to a Range Rover SUV just outside the private plane aviation hangar. He speaks to the attendant, asking him, "Fuel her up for our return trip; we will be back tomorrow morning." Jonathan turns to Audrey. "You ready? This little girl lives in Cottage Lake. I'm scared to death of what she may say. So far, it's looking good for us, but I just want us to be sure. I hope she gives us what we need to be sure. Her grandmother doesn't remember you, but I will talk to your father if Joanie does, asking him…"

Audrey says, "I'm hopeful too. I wish I could remember, but I don't remember being at that store ever, except for when the manager gave me Chuck's letter to you. I would know if I'd been there, I would for sure. What do you want to talk to my dad about? What are you two up to now?"

Jonathan ignores her, laughing at her naivety.

Arriving at the modest home in Cottage Lake, Audrey and Jonathan enter the house, met by Edna's daughter, Samantha. "Mom called and said you'd be coming. She's informed me that my Joanie is the key to some mystery between you two. Before I let you meet her, can you tell me the nature of the mystery?"

Jonathan attempts to speak, but Audrey, trying a softer approach sensing Samantha's apprehension, speaks first. "You see, Samantha, Jonathan here, and I have been friends forever, but he doesn't remember me, and I don't remember him from the beginning. The only person in the entire world who witnessed our love-at-first sight moment is possibly your daughter, Joanie. Jonathan and I are pretty close, but only as friends. We want to take it to the next level but are afraid that we may meet our respective intendeds after building a life excluding all others. So you see, our future stability in our happiness depends upon us knowing for sure if we are the people we each saw for just a second and fell in…"

Samantha speaks, "Now that's a mouthful. If you two love each other and want to make it official, why not forget the past and go for it? People do it all the time. So, what's the big deal? You're a nice enough couple. Great love is where you find it, and it sure seems to me like you've found it in each other."

Both Audrey and Jonathan are silent, realizing that Samantha has no intention of allowing Joanie to speak with them. They stand to thank Samantha; they are obviously saddened. Samantha senses their disappointment, saying harshly to them, "Nobody ever loved me like that. But, aw hell, what the heck?" Turning to the back room of the house, Samantha screams, "Joanie, get your butt out here; some folks want to speak to you."

Joanie comes out of the room with her nose buried in a tablet. She enjoys saying to her mother with a touch of sarcasm, "What is it now, Mom? I'm busy."

Joanie looks up and instantly recognizes Audrey and Jonathan. "Whoa, this is too cool; the supermarket and graveyard couple. What are you doing here? You two aren't mad because I called you stupid at the cemetery? Are you?" Laughing, she continues, "I can't believe you guys are here all the way from the other side of the country; wow! Did you take my advice and get married?"

She continues with a mocking tirade, "You, mister, looked at her in the grocery store like you lost your mind. You couldn't take your eyes off of her. And you, Miss Audrey, you looked like a deer caught in headlights; I thought you were paralyzed or something. Then, when grandma went to pee, you two seemed too scared to talk to each other. I liked him because he bought me a tangerine. On the other hand, you, Miss, just left my brothers and me like you were scared to death. Silly girl, he's a good-looking guy; can't you see that?"

Audrey interrupts, "How do you know all of this? You said you were just a little girl."

Samantha interrupts, "Joanie has Hyperthymesia. It is an extremely rare ability that allows Joanie to remember nearly every event of her life with great precision. She never studies and aces all her exams. She's scary and sassy."

Audrey says, "Are you sure, Joanie?"

"Of course, I'm sure. You were wearing a tan-colored coat, a sort-a Christmassy scarf, and a cool hand-knit hat. You have the cutest nose that I wish I had, but what I like the most is those crazy-colored knee socks you were wearing. So cool."

Audrey rebuts, "I don't have socks like that or a hat or scarf. I don't even like hats."

"Look, Audrey, I don't know what you have or don't have, but I know I saw you at Graul's Market way back when. There are two kinds of faces I will never forget; unique faces and angelic ones like yours. Is there anything else? I gotta go. Again, you guys are so stupid; even I can see; I saw it that day at the cemetery; you guys love each other, and you were made for each other. Audrey, if you can't see how much he loves you, and you, Jonathan, if you can't see how fearful she is that she can't remember meeting you that day, then you both have a problem. You're both gonna miss out on something really special; true love. I hope I'm not that dumb when I grow up!" Frustrated, she turns to her mother. "Can I go now?"

Joanie has left the room; Samantha shrugs her shoulders helplessly. "That's all I can do; I can't answer any more of your questions; I wasn't' there. My mom only remembers snippets. So I suppose you two will have to gamble and tie the knot. My guess is that you're 80 percent who you think you both are to each other. That's better odds than most of us get to meet our perfect match. I wish I could help you more. Please have a safe trip back; I have to get dinner on for the family."

Thirty-One

IN HER OWN WORDS; THE RECORDING

A month has passed since Audrey and Jonathan met with Joanie and her grandmother. Both have become more emotionally affectionate with each other since. They openly kiss each other when they meet or departed. It is clear that the 80 percent Joanie pronounced has given them both the confidence to allow more affection and the nature of their feeling to leak out.

Audrey and Jonathan receive the same phone call from their counselors, who want to invite them both to dinner at their home. So Audrey picks up Jonathan at his job and drives to Dr. Campbell's home.

It is a simple dinner of meatloaf, broccoli, rice, and a simple dessert. Nevertheless, it is clear that dinner is a precursor to why they are politely summoned.

The evening with the Campbell's concludes with the counselor playing a voice recording made during one of Audrey's semi-hypnosis sessions. Listening to the recording, Audrey and Jonathan hear in Audrey's voice and words a vague reference to her remembering being in the market the day in question.

"*Session 4a: A conversation between Audrey Sawyer and Dr. Campbell dated...*"

"*Seriously, Dr. Campbell, the only time my heart was moved by a complete stranger occurred in a random grocery store in or near Annapolis, which I only frequented once. I discovered this unnatural feeling that frightened and scared me as it moved me in unexpected ways. He was handsome, but physical beauty is only skin deep and temporary, but a person's heart will always be the same person's heart. That's the love my parents have; that's the love I want, and only that love.*"

Dr. Campbell stops the voice recorder and turns to Audrey. "Except for those ridiculous socks, I believe you may be the persons you're both looking for."

Audrey and Jonathan depart their home. Audrey drives Jonathan and he heads back to his job to pick up his truck. Audrey coasts to a stop at the next traffic light; Jonathan asks, "If you're not too tired, will you take me home? Then, if you're free in the morning, you pick me up, and I will chauffeur you to work? They gave us a lot to think about, and I don't want to drive with my head in a fog."

Audrey offers a suggestion. "Can I stay at your place tonight? My head is spinning from listening to the tape she played. I can barely concentrate now, thinking that you may be my guy. Dr. Campbell's evidence was compelling, but I don't own it yet."

Jonathan offers her an alternative. "Are you sure? You and I are ninety percent there. We've lost nearly all our former inhibitions; we are openly affectionate, and we smooch all the time."

Audrey is way ahead of him. "Yes, I know, and I love kissing and hugging you. But I also feel safe with you. You're my circuit breaker, and I am yours. I know how much you want me, but I also know you will respect my wish to wait until we are married. Am I right?"

Jonathan says, "We've been lucky because one or the other of us was in the state of mind to press the brakes. But tonight, I can feel you want to throw caution to the wind and do it. But how will you feel in the morning? Will you have any regrets? Will you hate me?"

Audrey answers, "All excellent points, but still, I trust you even if I don't trust myself with you. Makes sense, doesn't it? You've never lied to me, not kept a promise or been evasive with me. So give me your word; we won't do anything we will regret in the morning, okay?"

Jonathan is silent as she continues the drive to his house. He says nothing, and neither does she.

Parked in his driveway Jonathan finally answers her, gritting his teeth. "I won't make love to you; you have my word."

Audrey asks, "What took you so long to answer?"

Jonathan answers quietly, "I'm a man; you figure it out."

Audrey smiles, "I already have figured it out, Mister Dawson; I will sleep on the futon in your office; you take the bed."

Inside, both are dead tired, and while she brushes her teeth, Jonathan throws his clothes off and onto the recliner in his bedroom. He is in bed and fast asleep before Audrey completes her nighttime hygiene sequence.

Audrey exits the bathroom, looking for Jonathan. After a quick look around Jonathan's house, she calls his name softly but cannot find him.

Finally, Audrey gently peeks into his bedroom, observing that he is asleep. Audrey closes the door and then finds her way to his study, where she folds out the futon, dresses the bed, kneels to pray, and is fast asleep in minutes.

The house has been pin-drop silent for hours as both slumber peacefully. Audrey starts a little tossing in bed. Suddenly she sits up, looking around. The place is still quiet, and she thinks about what the pastor and the counselor revealed.

Missing Jonathan, she creeps to his bedroom, observing his sleep depth. Then, comfortable that he will not wake, Audrey stealthily enters his room, gently pulls back the cover, and slides into bed with Jonathan.

After a few minutes, she pulls the blanket up to her chin. She is a side sleeper and faces away from Jonathan. She is almost asleep when Jonathan starts mumbling her name "Audrey." She smiles, knowing he is thinking or dreaming of her. Still sleeping, Jonathan turns to face the back of her frame and unconsciously places his arm around her waist and 'spoons' her body.

Audrey relaxes into his arms, falling asleep with the man she loves holding her the whole night through.

Audrey and Jonathan awake simultaneously as the morning sun

breaks through the window. Both are clothed in their pajamas, yet they look under the blanket to learn if they are naked.

Breathing a sigh of relief, Jonathan kisses her as he plays with her hair draped on his temple. "Good morning, love; what are you doing here?"

Audrey responds, "Hi Jon. So this is what it will be like to wake up next to you."

They are unashamed and pleased that what could have happened did not. Jonathan looks at the clock and says, "You take the big bathroom, and I'll use the other. Whoever gets dressed first will start breakfast. We better hurry."

They exit Jonathan's house and into Audrey's SUV, driving to work. Audrey smiles, saying to Jonathan just before dropping him off at work, "So, that's what life with you will be like; I like it."

Jonathan pecks her cheek and then jogs to the government computer center office complex.

Audrey drives away with a smile so bright, forcing her to look in the rearview mirror at a face she's never seen smile; hers.

Thirty-Two

WHEN HARRY MET AUDREY; AGAIN

Audrey is slowly facing the reality that Jonathan is, in fact, her first love, but only based on evidence and not innate knowledge and memory of the events. Still loving Jonathan, she, with trepidation, agrees to meet first again with Jonathan's family, then both families hoping to solidify the words she heard herself say to Dr. Campbell so long ago.

Jonathan is on his way to get ice cream with Audrey when he suddenly remembers he is supposed to see his younger brother Harry's slow-pitch game at the Bowie-Baysox baseball field. He has promised to stop by to see his brother's team. He turns to Audrey sheepishly, asking, "Do you mind? I'd hate to disappoint him."

Parking at the edge of the field, Audrey and Jonathan walk hand-in-hand to the bleachers, observing it is now the top of the seventh inning with Harry on the mound. Screaming as he walks to the center front bleacher, Jonathan screams, "Go Harry, strike him out!"

Harry sees his brother, smiles approvingly, turns toward the batter, and throws a whopping underhand fastball; the umpire screams, "Strike three, you're out." Harry's dugout erupts in applause.

As the next inning begins, the other team is taking the field. Harry darts over to the bleachers. On his way to Jonathan, Harry stops and signals to someone in another section of seats. Harry screams, "Come on over, hurry." Harry reaches his brother giving Jonathan, his big brother, a loving bear hug and an enormous smile and says, "You made it, bro; I thought you forgot me. I've got a surprise for you. Then, looking at Audrey, Harry says, "Well, well, who is this? You didn't tell me you had a girlfriend?"

"Audrey, this is my little brother, Harry; my favorite person after you."

Harry laughs with joy. "You mean you've replaced me; shucks, big brother, I don't blame you; she's beautiful. But wait till you meet my girlfriend and best of all, you know her."

Moments later a beautiful young woman approaches the three of them who surprises them all with her jaw-dropping beauty and their recognition. Jonathan, stunned, looks at first to Harry, then to Audrey and immediately gets out of his seat to greet and hug his brother's girlfriend. To nearly everyone's shock, it is Clair Hansley. She kisses Jonathan on the cheek, saying, "Hi, Jonathan. See, I told you I had a surprise for you. Your little brother is my boyfriend."

Clair turns to Audrey, saying, "You're Audrey. I didn't get to know you all that well at the conferences we attended, but I know of your wonderful reputation. I so enjoyed talking with you over the phone. I hope you kept our little secret from Jonathan."

Audrey looks Clair over with wonder and then says, "Clair, I remember you, but I never knew…"

Clair cuts her off. "That's because I only dressed up for Jonathan. Little did I know that in the end his little brother and I would fall in love?"

Harry turns to Jonathan. "I hope you don't mind that I'm dating Clair? She's the best thing that ever happened to me. She's kind and understands me and I love her. I'm not breaking any 'bro' rules here, am I? You're not mad at me? We wanted to keep it a secret until we could meet in person."

Just then, the current inning is about to end. Harry announced gaily, "But, look, I have to get back to the dugout. Can you hang around for a bit after the game? I've got some other news for you myself."

"Sure, we can wait. We're going over to Pop's for ice cream; Why don't you and Clair join us?" For the balance of the game, Jonathan finds himself sitting between two women, Audrey and Clair; one girl he loves and wants to marry, the other who used to love him and wanted to be his wife, but now loves his little brother. Jonathan thinks to himself, "Life is stranger than fiction; who would've thought?"

An hour later, the four are entering the Pop Pops Creamery; Audrey spots a booth, asking Jonathan to bring her a banana split. Clair asks for a strawberry milkshake. Jonathan says to Audrey, "Hey, let's grab a table outside; we can watch traffic and planes taking off and landing at Lee."

Seated between two brothers on the picnic table, the four talk old times about their mom and dad when suddenly, Harry says, "Audrey, you look familiar; have we met?"

Audrey is struck by how handsome both men are and says, "No, I would have remembered you." Clair catches the glimpse from Audrey's perspective, saying, "Audrey, you're right, they're both different but really good-looking guys." Harry and Jonathan blush appreciatively.

"Audrey, I'm sure we've met. Where did you go to college, high school, junior high?" asks Harry. "I never forget a face, especially a pretty one."

Audrey names each school. "College; the University of Maryland, high school Roper, junior high, Whitehall Grade."

"Okay," Harry says. "Hmmm, Whitehall; let me think. Okay, I got it. What church do you belong to, or did you attend? I know I know you!" Harry names seven churches, and she laughs.

Audrey replies, "Nope, none of those churches. Sorry."

They are now enjoying their ice cream as Jonathan brags about all the things he and Audrey have done. Harry particularly enjoys the story of them being arrested for droning on federal land. Clair is delighted to see that there were no jealous sparks as she was unsure as to how both brothers would react to the knowledge that they sort of shared her affection between them. Clair relaxes watching them talk old times with enormous love one could feel between the brothers.

Suddenly, Harry stops eating and shouts, "I got it; I know where I know you from. You're not going to believe it, but you two met even longer ago than you know. Your fairytale relationship was fated to love before you were born. This is wonderful, this is unbelievable!"

Both Audrey and Jonathan look bewildered, Clair is not, for she knows the events surrounding their first meetings. Clair keeps quiet and smiles. "This is too good, too juicy. Oh-My-God. Bro, Miss Audrey here was in Miss Job's kindergarten class, I was next to her, and after that idiot Ronald stole and ate her radishes, you came over from where you were planting tomatoes, punching him, and you asked me to share my radishes with her. This is unreal; you were her knight in shining armor, and she asked me personal stuff about you for nearly a year until we went to different first-grade classes. Audrey, do you remember?"

Audrey looks stunned; she stares at Jonathan and then at Harry. Then, stammering, she says, "Yes, that happened; I remember the incident, but not Harry's details. I remember crying because it took forever to grow those radishes, and that guy just grabbed mine and ate them. I was so mad that I didn't notice anything else. I sort of remember a boy in my class and his big brother helping me, but I can't remember if it was you. I am definitely sure his name wasn't Jonathan; his name started with a 'K', I think. But the rest of it must be true because the other details are exactly what happened."

Harry, now almost finished with his ice cream cone, slurps it from the side. "Not only that, Audrey, I remember my brother walking you home from school every day until he graduated, and you're the girl my other neighborhood buddy, Ethan, took to walking home after that."

Audrey gives Harry a wide smile. "Ethan and I were friends for a long time. Whenever I needed advice from a man, before your brother, I could always depend on Ethan; he's the best!"

"Is Ethan giving my brother competition? Oh, and the 'K' was for Kenneth, Jonathan's middle name. He didn't want the other boys to know he liked a kindergarten girl. It was our secret. I remember Ethan, but I'm not sure Ethan and Jonathan were ever that close."

Audrey continues with sadness, "Ethan has never met Jonathan; I haven't seen Ethan much in the last few years. He is a great guy."

Audrey has a quick reply to comfort Jonathan. "Yes, he is a great guy, but no one is competition to my Jonathan. Jonathan makes me want to get married sooner than later these days." She looks at Jonathan, sliding her arm into his arm. "I guess we were fated to be friends and family after all. It looks as if we've been part of each other's family for almost the entirety of our lifetimes. Maybe *I am* the girl from the grocery store. Who knows? Clair, I've heard much from Jonathan about you, and even though you and I were acquainted before, we could become sisters-in-law. Are you and Harry thinking about becoming…?"

Harry sighs. "Yes, Audrey, that is if she'll have me, but I'll have to wait on you two. Dad kids me saying that as older brother, you have to tie the knot first. But as soon as you do, we will be down the aisle right behind you a few months later." Switching the subject Harry says, "Man-O-man, Audrey, I've heard about this grocery store girl forever. Big Bro here just won't let it go. I'm surprised he's told you about her. That girl, my brother swears, is the love of his life. Audrey, I think if you'll settle for being a close second, well, you two would be an amazing couple. I've been trying forever to get him to move on with his life, and after meeting you, I definitely believe he should forget about her and grab on to what's right in front of him, you!" Jonathan sends his brother a laser-cutting glare, telling him, "That's enough!"

Audrey jumps in, defending Jonathan. "No need, I understand your brother. In some extraordinary and awkward way, Jonathan and I are in the same boat, paddling upstream with no clear destination, that is, until lately; we just might be coming into port… together."

Harry catches Jonathan's drift and drops the subject with another subject. "Mom tells me that we are all going to Audrey's parents' house for Thanksgiving this year; is that true?"

Audrey nods. "Yes, that's true. My dad has taken a liking to Jonathan and has imposed his come-together-ness on the Dawson's; I think it will be nice, especially with Clair there too. So, Harry, what's your news?"

Harry responds, "Willow teaches English as a second language in Korea. Weren't you guys there not long ago? Talk about coincidence. Before I met Clair, I dated her friend, Alice Park a few times when I was in Canada; she knows Willow and I think she's met both you and Audrey in some place called Iteawon. I'll tell you more later."

Audrey and Jonathan give each other a *'what's going on'* look of confusion and move on.

Outside the ice cream shop, they all hug and part with joy and restoration on their faces. Jonathan mentions, "Audrey, talk about surprises. Are you okay? Does Harry dating my old work-wife bother you?"

"No, Jonathan, that doesn't bother me, what bothers me is realizing how close I came to never re-meeting you or have you in my life. I know you're not vain or shallow, but I had no idea that Clair was that drop-dead gorgeous and fun to be around. I'm surprised you didn't latch on to her; she's got it all and she's beautiful."

Jonathan kissed Audrey. "But she doesn't have the one thing I need and want most; your heart. I fell in love with your heart, not your body."

Thirty-Three

THE FIGHT & HEAVENLY INTERVENTION

Audrey and Jonathan are preparing dinner at his place in preparation for a quiet meal and Netflix binge Saturday evening date. Audrey has been exhibiting an intermittent sour attitude toward Jonathan for days. He tries to comfort her as he works to discover what is bothering her without prying.

"Audrey, is there something you need now, something I can do or get for you?"

"No, Jonathan," she growls. "You are the problem."

"May I ask why? What's the problem?" he asks calmly.

"Oh, I don't know. Why don't you just leave?"

"But this is my house; I've got your key; I will go to your house."

Audrey becomes angrier and angrier the calmer Jonathan is. Finally sobbing in desperation, she walks to him and gives him a back-hug. "I told you, Jonathan, we are getting serious now. Don't you realize that we may be officially together one day, and I mean soon?"

"And?"

"The *Kobayashi Maru* test I mentioned to you that night on the Potomac; we still haven't fought; this is hopeless."

"So, you want to fight to see how we fight, right? What about that fight we had on marriage vows after that wedding we attended just after the drone incident?"

Audrey aggressively states, "That wasn't a real fight; besides, you let me win that one. Look, Buster, I've known you for years now. Although we agree on most, and what we don't agree on, we fall all over each other looking for a compromise. Can't you see how dangerous this is to the stability of a relationship?"

"But, Audrey, I assume you know that I want to please you, and I assume that you want to please me. So we fall over each other trying to make each other happy. Doesn't that sound like a formula for a successful life together to you? Why do you keep going back and forth? Are we getting closer or further apart? I'm just about sick of this game you're playing with my heart"

Audrey pouts, saying, "Why, yes, it is a great formula for success, but still, I don't want to wait till we're married to have a real fight."

Jonathan replies innocently, "Give me something to fight with you about, and let's go for it. What do you want to fight about?" He pulls her close and kisses her forehead. "You're impossible, Audrey, and I love you. So sue me for wanting to please you. I'm done with this stupid conversation."

Audrey scowls at Jonathan. "You're done and you say you love me? You can't be in love with me; we're only friends, best friends of course, but you promised me no more than simple platonic loving. How dare you say that to me?" Fighting the urge to giggle, she loses and chuckles, trying desperately to regain her angry demeanor.

Jonathan ends this conversation forcefully, becoming more serious. "Audrey, stop playing head-games with me. The front wheels of this relationship are now taking over. I suppose you think I will have this conversation again after all we've been through. In that case, changing brakes, kayaking, shoveling snow in the freezing cold, the salon kiss, our sunset cruise, becoming Godparents, finding Chuck and Nancy, Joanie, California, Seattle, sleeping in each other's arms, you sliding into my bed, you saving me from addiction and coyotes, me, you from drowning, conversations with both our parents, Richmond, getting arrested together, South Korea, me protecting you, et al. If you think we're not in love with each other, you're crazy, and I'm a fool. I'm not having this silly conversation a minute longer. If you don't want what we have, then walk away. I would die for you, and if that displeases you, then I'm done. I refuse to force myself on you because I need and want you; I'm not doing it. Either you love me, all of me, or not. You promised I wouldn't have to walk on eggshells around you. What do you think you have me doing now? I'm not tip-toeing around you because I love you, and I refuse to apologize for wanting to please you. Geez, what do I have to do to let you know I'm all in?"

Frustrated, she gently coos. "I was only teasing you; I didn't mean to hurt you."

Jonathan answers with a touch of charming sarcasm, "Stop putting me through this ridiculous emotional roller-coaster. Now you've got me angry. Just stop it; this is insane. Can we please have a no-drama dinner now? I've never seen you so agitated over nothing. Don't you trust my feelings for you; that they're real? I refuse to fake an argument with the woman I love. Geez!"

Audrey studies Jonathan as she sets the table, realizing that she has provoked a discussion that needn't have occurred. She is torn between being apologetic and angry because Jonathan has put her in her place. She wants to test the water by being defiant, but for the first time, she fears that he could actually withdraw his love from her. She asks herself about her stubbornness for defiance's sake, or should she submit to his plea, his passion, and her heart for this man?

She finally settles on an insincere apology. "You are impossible; I don't know why I bother with you. I'm sorry, Jonathan; it's just that you have never set boundaries. A girl has to know how far to push her fella. Sheesh, I know the limit now. I've never seen you riled up; I didn't know…"

Jonathan almost snaps back at her. "You didn't know what?"

Audrey says, "No one has ever loved me; I guess I didn't believe you; or in an 'us'. It won't happen again."

Jonathan sits beside her, taking her hand. "Audrey, there is nothing more important to me than you. When I thought I'd never see you again after Korea, I thought about the unthinkable. The pain of a broken heart is indescribable. If you think losing a dog or pet is excruciating, imagine how we'd feel if we lost each other. For the last time, Audrey, all a man wants is peace and security from his wife. I know you're not my wife yet, but you will be. So please stop this nonsense or kick me to the curb. Are we clear?"

As he pours wine into her glass, Jonathan quips, "You know what they say, *'It's a thin line between love and hate.'* So let's never cross the line, ever. But, again, can we eat now? I'm starved."

They enjoy their simple meal of salmon, asparagus, and petite whole red-bliss potatoes and retire to a night on the couch, binge-watching Netflix with popcorn.

CLARENCE DECIDES TO SUMMON ETHAN FOR A PROGRESS REPORT. Ashamedly, Ethan admits he broke the rules but blames it on Clarence since he had no idea of his purpose, only of his affection for Audrey.

Clarence explains the criticality of the situation and suggests an intervention would be needed to assure providence would bind Jonathan and Audrey's two separate hearts together into one spiritual heart. Now understanding the big picture, Ethan offers solutions for Clarence to consider.

Ethan's ideas include the use of dreams, temporal manipulation, or having the spirits of Audrey and Jonathan observe their first, second, and third meeting in guided teleportation to the scenes of their various fate-bending moments in time.

Clarence reviews Ethan's plan, saying, "Good idea, but will they believe it is real? You know how difficult it is for a human to recall a dream for only a few moments after waking. If they don't remember, it will confuse them, driving them further apart due to suspicious doubts. So, what else do you have, Ethan?"

Ethan states proudly, "Temporal manipulation or time-travel has been used successfully. We can place their spirits in the three original timelines, allow them to keep their present memories and experience the re-memories in simulated real-time. Once the events conclude, they will now have the new memories combined with the old memories, creating an amalgamation that proves who they both hope they are. So, boss, what do you think?"

"Let me think about them; I will get back to you."

"Remember, Clarence, Jonathan and Audrey are having dinner at his place soon; it could get pretty steamy. But unfortunately, both seem to have become lost in their feelings. I'm sure they will end up together and happy, but while the mission will be accomplished, there will always be the lingering doubt of 'what if?' Don't they deserve better?"

"You're right; let's decide on a work plan; Ethan, you do the heavy lifting, and I will back you up."

Ethan frowns. "Yes, boss."

Ethan folds his arms, bows his head, and prays silently. Then, in an instant, Clarence appears before him, saying, "That didn't take long; did you come up with a solution?"

"Clarence," Ethan begins, "Yes, I have an idea; you said to run it by you; that's why I asked you here."

Clarence and Ethan sit on the banks of the Chesapeake at the old Sharps Island lighthouse at the end of the southernmost tip of Tilghman Island. The old fourth-order Fresnel lens lighthouse hasn't flashed in decades but is picturesque as it leans in the bay; it is one of Ethan's favorite thinking spots, only accessible by boat or angels.

Clarence interrupts, "Can we get to the plan, Ethan? I like lighthouses too, but…"

Ethan somewhat ignores Clarence's impatience, showing Clarence inside the living quarters of the old structure. Giving Ethan a bit of latitude, the two angels hang out on the perimeter railing that surrounds the beam tower. Ethan explains, "In a time before GPS, buoys and the like, lighthouses served two purposes; illuminating waterways made treacherous by close to shore hazards and rocks as seagoing vessels left the open ocean and pulled into port. Some had fog warning apparatus for low visibility warnings. I like them because they are majestic and guide humanity along life's rocky shoals like us.

If only they would listen to us. Most lighthouses also include fog signals such as horns, bells, or cannons, which sound to warn ships of hazards during periods of low visibility."

Impatient, Clarence shouts, "Enough, Ethan! What's the plan with our couple?"

Ethan instantly snaps back to reality, stating more as fact than asking for permission. "I will use the two-step on them. Audrey and Jonathan are spending more and more time with each other and at each other's respective homes. They are semi-intimate and almost did the deed a few times, but their internal search for 'the' each other neither knows is the correct each other they are looking for. The only factor keeping them apart is their dream of meeting the other person in time. Now, here's the catch. Both are equally divided on finding their original persons from the past. They suspect but do not know. They want each other so intensely that it would take a nickel's worth of effort for them to consummate their love before they're married. The next time one or the other spends the night at the other's home, I will induce a dream into both their subconscious, revealing to Audrey that Jonathan is the man she's been looking for. I will simultaneously introduce the same thought in reverse into Jonathan's brain that Audrey is the sock-girl he's been seeking. This will realign their passions, now believing they are indeed soul-mates, but because of their *doubting-Thomas* personalities, they will dismiss the dream and never mention it to each other. But they will become closer and drop some of their inhibitions on intimacy; this is why we must move to phase two quickly if they are to maintain and do things God's way."

"And…" Clarence asks.

"They are planning a Thanksgiving dinner with both families this year. Of course Audrey knows me as Ethan, the human; Jonathan has only heard of me but both trust me, especially Audrey. I will review a few particulars of history with them, authenticating my veracity. They will be stunned and disbelieving as they should be. I will take them through the portal to Whitehall Elementary, Graul's Market, Seoul, and the night he sang the song he composed for her. They will be observers of their own past lives in simulated real-time. I will then bring them to their present and reiterate what they have seen and are beginning to believe. Next, I will whisk them to their wedding with a tiny fraction of their wedding night. I will show them the birth of their son, Kenneth. I will show them attending his college graduation with their other children in tow. I will show them their mid-life and empty-nesting years. Finally, I will tell them that Kenneth will win the Nobel Prize for his work in reverse weather technology. I will bring them to their present and answer their singular question, *'Why us?'* I will tell them that God loves a good and proper love story which perhaps has not existed since he planted original lovers in the Garden. I will tell them that they are an old-fashioned living love story hewn from a simple act of kindness."

When Ethan stops talking, he turns from facing the Chesapeake back to the lighthouse to notice that Clarence is not crying but is in tears, granting Ethan full approval of his plan. "The master will be pleased."

Thirty-Four

ARIA'S INTERVENTION

For many centuries, the expression, '*Out of the mouth of babies*' has indicated the unfettered wisdom in babies and children. Aria becomes Godchild to Audrey and Jonathan soon after her birth. No one could have guessed that this child would wordlessly change the course of future history between Audrey and Jonathan. Who knew?

Aria: Playing House

AUDREY AND JONATHAN ARE EXCITED WHEN THEY BOTH RECEIVE THE same text message from Olivia; "*Hello, Godparents. Tyler and I haven't been on a date in a year; you know, baby duties. Can either of you babysit Aria so we can go to a movie and a cheap date?*"

Jonathan and Audrey answer within seconds. "*Absolutely YES; tell us when.*"

Jonathan calls Tyler and sets a date for the upcoming Friday, saying to Tyler, "Look, buddy, we will come to get Aria and the dog. You and Olivia should make an evening, overnight, and next morning of it; we've got you."

Arriving at Jonathan's house that Friday afternoon, the neighbors leer and look at Audrey holding Aria's tiny hands. Jonathan follows with a small suitcase and a leashed golden retriever named Cuddles.

Inside the home, Jonathan and Audrey watch Aria waddle around the living room, examining everything with curiosity and wonder. Finally, Jonathan picks her up, holds her above his head, then back to eye level. He kisses both her chubby little cheeks, and she giggles with joy.

Aria wraps her tiny hands around Jonathan's index finger, gurgling with smiles and laughs.

Carrying Aria on his hip like a bag of potatoes, Jonathan heads for the kitchen and warms Aria's bottle with his free hand. Audrey is mesmerized watching him. While the bottle is warming on the stove and holding Aria, Jonathan rubs Cuddles' head and directs him to an empty bowl on the floor near the breakfast bar.

Audrey watches with intensity and curiosity as he sits Aria in her collapsible hi-chair and places kibble and water in the feeder for the dog. The bottle, now warm, Jonathan tests the bottle's temperature on the back of his hand and then proceeds to feed Aria after lifting her out of the chair. Jonathan returns to the couch next to Audrey and feeds Aria.

Audrey is smiling and watching, forcing Jonathan to say, "What?"

Audrey takes Aria from him and continues to feed her. She cradles the baby in the way only a mother could, saying to Jonathan, "I'm gonna love being your wife; you're amazing, and best of all, you have no idea how wonderful you are."

The morning and afternoon are mostly wordless and comfortable. Audrey and Jonathan take the baby out in the stroller with the dog in tow. The neighbors look pleased and surprised to see Audrey and Jonathan as mother and father, many making comments indicating their surprise and admiration. Those who ask are surprised to learn Jonathan is babysitting, saying, "Oh, that's cool, but soon, very soon, you guys will be doing this for real with your own children."

A SIMPLE ACT OF KINDNESS

Later that night, Jonathan straps on a baby carrier harness and takes Aria to the duck pond several blocks from his house. Sitting Aria on his lap, he gives her oyster crackers to toss in the pond. Aria is delighted to see the few ducks flap over to where the ducks push and shove to eat the crackers.

Audrey joins them a few minutes later, meandering beside them. Aria reaches over to her; Audrey takes her from Jonathan as Aria continues to take crackers from Jonathan's hand while sitting in Audrey's lap. Audrey says to Jonathan, "You really do love this child," to which Jonathan says, "Yes I do. I've never been a Godparent before; feels very special."

The next day, Olivia and Tyler come to get their family. They both look refreshed and appreciative.

Back inside, Audrey and Jonathan hug each other, admitting that neither said much to each other during the previous twenty-four hours. Audrey makes coffee for both of them and leads Jonathan to the dining room table. She says, "I know you want to talk to me, and I want to hear it and talk to you. Do you want me to go first or…?"

Audrey does not wait and speaks first. "Perhaps we have some sort of telepathy between us, but I can answer all your questions before you say a word. I promised you I would never lie to you a long time ago, so here goes."

Jonathan stares, surprised. He knows what he has been thinking but believes Audrey can't have a clue.

Audrey continues, "Yes, we may not have made it official, but spiritually, we are husband and wife. The familiarity of last night and this morning is uncanny; it felt so natural to be with you, our Goddaughter, the dog, and just us. I watched you sleep with Aria asleep on your chest. You held her as if she was our child, and I know what you were dreaming about. I saw the future you want for us; I could see and feel you imagining our lives together. I almost felt sorry for you as I realized how much you wanted me. I know it sounds like a one-way street, but it's not. I regret accidentally forcing you to forget your sock-girl. If she materialized before us right this second, I don't believe you'd give her the time of day. I saw it in your eyes, and my heart felt you abandon and forget her. You now fear that you're out there all alone in love. I know you only want me, and you're hoping I will make what we experienced last evening permanent for us. Before yesterday and this morning, we were in the same boat; today, you feel like you're all alone as there is no trace of anyone but me in your heart. You are terrified that you'll be lost and alone if I don't commit to an 'us'.

She continues, "I love that you love me; now I must adjust to the new place I've taken in your heart now that you're in love with me. So I ask myself, what exactly is my footing in this relationship? It's not like I'm looking for someone better; no one is better. You've heard me talk about a ghost in my marriage. I didn't realize this until last night, that my guy from the market, while not a sexual spirit, is an emotional ghost, which is wholly unfair to you. We were equally yoked as long as we both had someone in our hearts. Now, because you are free and I am not, this becomes a lop-sided love between us. I will die if I lose you. Can you be patient a bit longer? The clues we've uncovered are pointing to something circumstantially true but not evidentially true. There is no one else for me; can you be patient just a while longer?"

Jonathan winces in pain as she perfectly struck each note of his emotional state. He wants to tell her she is wrong but cannot refute a word she said. Finally, unable to look at her, he moves beside her, leans back, and speaks to the ceiling. "Audrey, you and I being in the same boat was a safety valve; it gave me the ability to understand both our points of view. Having Aria here like that gave me a foretaste of the life to come. She represented something purely created by you and me; our love, passion, and gift to each other. So you are correct about the sock girl being out of my heart, but not for the reason you think. Hearing your voice on Dr. Campbell's voice recorder, the letter from Chuck, and finally, after meeting Joanie, I am sure she will never be found because I am sure she is you. Even Harry and Clair have moved on; why not us? You say the circumstantial proof of identity; I say verified evidence. I don't need to see your heart to know that it's your heart. Hearts don't see; they feel. I'm not afraid of losing you, Audrey; I'm just impatient to begin our life together. But I am afraid of you losing me. So I will wait, and you will feel no pressure from me. Not as a threat, Audrey, but this can't go on; it's tearing me in two, so if you cannot commit sooner than later, I will still be here, but I won't see you as much; it is the only way I can survive. Come to me whole in your own time, or leave me. The gift you gave me last night to see us as a family is enough. You should also know that the recent forced argument we had hurt me more than you realized. It bruised my heart to speak to you like that. I've never cursed at you and I did then. It scared me making me believe that perhaps I am not the guy you want. I want you, but I was forced to consider that I was forcing my affection on you. I don't want you by force; I want you to be with me because you have no doubt, because you want me. Again, I'm all-in, are you? I can't be out here all by myself."

Audrey takes the slow drive back to her home, thinking of her stubbornness, their futures, and a sad effort to peel back the layers of doubt and indecision about a man she loved wholeheartedly. It never occurred to Audrey that Jonathan could or would withdraw his time with her while still loving her.

Panicking as she realizes the implications of what Jonathan's heart has said to her heart combined with what his mouth said the last time they had dinner, she pulls off the road, rebuking her foolishness and calls Jonathan.

He answers, "Hey, babe; you okay? What's wrong?"

She holds her breath. "Jonathan, my ears heard what you said, but my heart just informed me of something else. I'm not that far away, can I come back, please, please say yes."

Arriving back at Jonathan's house, he is on the porch waiting for her. She leaps out of her car, running up the steps and into his arms, sobbing. "My heart says that your heart said if I don't get my act together, I am going to lose you. It said that I am the only person interfering with my own happiness. Despite overwhelming proof, my heart screamed at me for being proud of my stubbornness. My heart called me a selfish jerk for my half in/half out behavior."

Jonathan hugs her to assuage her panic, saying, "Audrey, calm down; don't panic. It's true; my heart implied it was done with you, but I can't so easily let you go. My heart wants me to abandon you and move on, but I can't just yet. You're part of me, you are what makes me get up every morning, and while loving you, I have no bad days. But Audrey, ever since our flight to Seattle, the joy I feel with you is tainted with a feeling of sorrow I can't quite put my finger on. It feels like you don't want to commit to me, to us. Perhaps you like me being around you. Sometimes I think you like the idea of us together, but not with me as your husband. I think about our first argument over wedding vows, and perhaps I offended you in a way you can't get over. Or, you're holding out hope for someone else, someone better. I feel like I'm a fill-in boyfriend, not your intended. By now, you should be my fiancé, but it often feels like you're playing games with my heart, patience, and very being. I don't want to rush you, I know you must be self-convinced, but while trying to convince yourself that I am the guy from the store, you are ripping my heart to shreds. But still, take your time; remember I promised, *'If it takes forever, I will wait for you.'*"

Audrey kisses him, saying, "Promise you won't change."

Jonathan says with compassion, "Okay then, perhaps Aria brought us both to our senses. Come on in; stay the night, we'll sleep on the love seat, your head on my lap like we used to. I don't think either of us wants to be alone tonight."

Thirty-Five

FRIENDS NO MORE

While neither Jonathan nor Audrey would ever admit to it, after babysitting Aria nearly a month ago, they are now a de facto couple. The kisses and touching willingly shared by both betrayed that they had crossed the bridge from friends to best friends, to boyfriend and girlfriend, and with just a whisper of a push, they would become lovers despite their desire to remain chaste until marriage.

A week ago, they spent the day and night together at Jonathan's home. Audrey could not stop humming the song melody Jonathan wrote and performed for her.

Her coworkers want to tease her but refrain. Why? Because in the years employed there, no one has ever seen her with little more than a polite corporate smile. Today, Audrey cannot stop smiling, almost giggling as she thinks about her man.

It pains her when she suddenly snaps back to reality, thinking about the man in the grocery store. She thinks, *'He was wonderful, and there was an instant heart-to-heart connection, but now I have a 'real' connection with Jonathan's heart and he, mine.'*

Today is Friday, and tomorrow Audrey and Jonathan plan to spend the entire day together. She giggles at the thought that Jonathan said they'd be playing Mr. and Mrs. Dawson for the whole day. She strokes her hair, wishing it was Jonathan stroking her hair like he did when he kissed her.

She remembers their early pecks on the cheek. She almost cries thinking about the first time he kissed her forehead with such affection. Then, as time moved on during the time of their budding friendship, Audrey remembers the first four-way kiss. First, Jonathan softly held her face, kissed her forehead, cheeks, and finally, a dry kiss on the lips.

It frightens Audrey to feel her body react in a way it has never responded to anyone. She is both embarrassed and ashamed of her femininity, not believing these biological reactions are possible. She is grateful that Jonathan seems to move past his doubts after the Aria effect.

She trots outside the building opposite the doors where the cigarette smokers congregate. Standing alone, she almost bursts out in tears of joy, thinking of Jonathan dryly kissing her many times. Then, on several memorable occasions, Jonathan tried to slip his tongue into her tightly closed mouth. Finally, she laughs aloud in exultation, remembering the first time she opened her mouth to him, surrendering to his full-on embrace. She cannot believe the feeling of oneness with another person she felt at that moment.

So, it was from that moment on, if they are in a private place, their kisses are passionate and sweet, with each instinctively knowing how to please the other. It is strange that both know that the other hates outlandish public displays of affection without ever speaking of it. The most affection these two ever show publically is holding hands.

Jonathan is passively angry with himself for allowing himself to fall for Audrey. He is a fun guy but has rigid principles about his morality.

Most people really like Jonathan because he is never condescending toward others; he hates folks who are hypocrites attempting to show off their so-called morality.

Occasionally, he would join his coworkers at an after-work get-together. Jonathan has vowed never to drink hard liquor; two generations ago, some of his father's family were alcoholics and messed up their lives. His parents, who also did not drink, shared the tenacious family history with Jonathan, Willow, and Harry to protect and forewarn them of the dangers of excess of anything.

At a local watering-hole with coworkers, Jonathan often orders sparkling water, wine, or a lite beer; he stays away from hard liquor and exotic spirits. So, Jonathan is delighted to learn that Audrey imposes the same restrictions on her life.

Today feels special because the plan is to spend the day with Audrey doing everything and nothing. Both love to cook and decide to get groceries for lunch he plans to prepare for her and the dinner she would prepare for him.

After picking her up Saturday morning, Jonathan says to her, "Let's go to this neat ancient grocery store I frequented as I grew up; they've got fresh everything. It's in Cape St. Clair."

"Sounds nice; where is St. Clair?" Audrey asks.

Jonathan answers, "It's just out 50 east, a smidgen over the Severn River Bridge."

Audrey sits back, enjoying the ride, saying, "There's something familiar about this; I've never been here, but I'm having a feeling of having already experienced the present situation: a sense of real déjà vu. I think I came here not too long ago and met Nancy, who gave me Chuck's letter to you. This is spooky."

Jonathan parks, and they enter the store, where various store personnel hardily greet him. "Jonathan, it's been years. Your mom was here a few weeks ago. Hey, did you ever find the girl you were looking for?"

Jonathan answers, pulling Audrey to his side, "Nope, I never found her, but let me…" Holding Audrey close with a proud look on his face, he says, "Audrey, this is one of my oldest friends, Thomas Watson. Tom, Audrey is my girlfriend…" Jonathan looks at Audrey for a sign of disapproval or approval as they have never publically called each anything other than best friends.

Not seeing a sign of disapproval but a slight blush on Audrey's face, Jonathan continues boldly, "Tom, this is Audrey, my honey, the love of my life."

Tom shakes her extended hand and turns to Jonathan. "Dude, how did you get her? She's nice."

Audrey and Jonathan blush appreciatively. Tom is suddenly distracted by another customer's questions.

Jonathan picks up the supplies he needs, and Audrey does the same, saying they'd meet at the deli counter.

Audrey stands there with her hand basket, waiting for Jonathan. When he arrives, Audrey is looking around with angst and wonder. She says to Jonathan as he arrives, "This feels so weird; that feeling is coming back to me, but I swear I don't know why."

Jonathan is about to answer Audrey when Nancy Collier, the floor manager, walks up to them with a smile, saying, "Audrey? It is you, Audrey? Do you remember me? We met when you were here searching for Chuck? Did the letter he left help?"

Audrey snaps out of the cloud, remembering Nancy. "Yes, I do remember. The letter…" Audrey turns to Jonathan. "This is the woman who helped with clues to Chuck. Nancy, this is Jonathan, Chuck's friend and my boyfriend."

Nancy hugs Audrey, asking, "So you found your mystery man? You did good."

Audrey says, "It's a long and complicated story, but while I can't remember the face of the guy I met here that day, it all feels right today and my Jonathan is, well, he's the best. Thank you for your help that day."

Nancy moves to help another customer; Jonathan can sense the confusion that Audrey is feeling. Everyone but her thinks that they are the 'it' couple she has searched for. She wishes that she could just remember Jonathan's face, even though everything else points to the truth that he is her mystery man.

Jonathan tries to assuage her feeling of déjà vu by saying, "What you feel is me projecting on you from my past. You and I have such a unique simpatico that we can touch each other's souls. Audrey, you're standing on the very spot where I met the sock girl who I now know is you. That woman I know in my heart was you, was standing here with three children wearing a tan coat, nice pumps, and the coolest socks. I looked her in the eye, my heart beating so fast I thought it would explode. All I could do was show her my socks, stare at her face, and swallow with my heart now in my mouth. I needed to be honest with you since we are moving forward; this is where it happened, and ironically, you let me call you my girlfriend for the first time in the very spot where I wanted her to be my girlfriend. I will never forget the impression she left on my heart, and I can't remember her face anymore; you've replaced her. I hope this confession does not offend you. I needed to face this place with you for me to move on with you, giving you my whole heart. I pray you understand."

Jonathan, while talking, never notices the tears and simultaneous smile on Audrey's face. Then, for the first time, she initiates what both swore never to do; she puts her basket down and puts her arms around Jonathan, kissing him passionately in full public view of passersby without regard to who sees them. Tom sees them and gives them a hearty 'thumbs-up.'

As she pulls away from the embrace, Audrey says to Jonathan, "Let's go back to my place, my handsome and gallant boyfriend."

Neither Jonathan nor Audrey say much as they leave Cape St. Clair. Both continue to stare and smile at each other. He stops at her dry cleaner; he waits while she bounces in, coming back shortly with two women's suits, slacks, a sweater, and a comforter. Then, seeing her struggling with the bulky blanket-in-a-bag, Jonathan jumps out, grabbing the bag by the handle and putting it in the back of his truck.

Next, they stop for gas at Sam's Club. Audrey pumps the gas while he leans against the side of the truck, admiring her. Next, they beat the light to get to Trader Joe's. This time he runs in, returning with organic muffins and loose Arabica coffee beans.

The last stop is at the motorcycle accessories store near Edgewater. Audrey drags him out of the vehicle and pushes him reluctantly into the store. She asks, seeing the owner, "The best and lightest gloves you have." She shoves his hand to the manager. "What size do you think he will need?"

Jonathan looks confused. Audrey quips, "I've seen those beat-up gloves you wear. I want to keep my man's hands nice and smooth."

After Jonathan tries the soft leather gloves, Audrey smiles and hands her credit card to the owner.

Almost home, Jonathan turns to her, saying as a question, "My man?"

Audrey looks straight at him. "Yep, my man. That's what you are."

Back at her home, Jonathan prepares lunch while she is on the couch, watching something on Hulu.

Jonathan serves her on a lap table. She smiles, "This looks…" she tastes the food and continues, "delicious."

Lunch is over, and they are relaxing. Jonathan says, "Let's go out on the deck; there's something I want to tell you about 'your-man'."

Audrey gaily says, "Oooooh dark secrets, all right, let's go."

Jonathan gulps hard and hopes that she would not be disappointed or insult him as he is about to reveal his sexual history with her.

They step outside the townhouse to the private deck over the garage.

Sitting on the Adirondack Patio Chairs, both get comfortable. Jonathan takes a swig of the water she brought. Finally, Jonathan musters his courage, saying to Audrey, "We're getting pretty close here, and I'm not being presumptuous, but there is something about me you need to know since we are moving beyond being pals. It may affect how you see me or even if you want to be my… perhaps one day be my lover."

Audrey looks a little shocked. "Whoa, Buster. Who said anything about us being lovers? I just said you're my man, my boyfriend; I didn't say anything about doing the nasty."

Jonathan nervously drinks more water. "Can you please just let me finish? Can you do that?"

She laughs. "Testy testy testy! All right, go ahead."

Jonathan turns to face her full-on. "It's not that I'm against sex, but I don't intend to have sex with anyone, including you unless we're married. Of course, I could have gotten laid many times before, during and after college. Even Clair, long before she knew Harry was available if I pushed her a bit, but I think there's something noble about having one sex partner for a lifetime. And trust me, I want you like that, and I think you know it. So I'm willing to wait. But who ever heard of opening a Christmas gift before Christmas? What joy is there to a wedding night when you opened the gift years earlier? I hope you can understand my feelings."

Audrey looks sly and sultry as she pulls off her t-shirt, wearing only a sports bra. She snuggles up to him, rubbing his chest. "So there's nothing I could do to…?" She pauses, rubbing his chest with her palm. She leans into him, kissing him.

Jonathan becomes frightened and alarmed as he tentatively returns her kiss and suddenly pulls away, staring at her with passive shock and obvious desire in his eyes. "Didn't I say no? What are you doing? Of all people I thought you'd understand. You can't force yourself on me like that, knowing how I feel about you."

Getting up from his seat Jonathan barks at Audrey with a bit of outrage in his voice. "Are you kidding me? I'm leaving. I want you, but not like this; didn't you understand a word I said? Have you been lying to me about your…? I'm surprised that you…"

Audrey bursts out laughing. "Calm down, big fella; I was just testing you. I know your will power; I was in no danger from a man like you; my hero."

He interrupts, "You little tease; that is so cruel."

She responds, "I had to know if you were being truthful. I've known guys to use that reverse psychology line all the time; I had to be sure. And after seeing how gorgeous Clair is, I wasn't sure I believed you. You know how you men are, always thinking about sex." Then she kisses him gently. "I'm a virgin too, but not for any noble or high-faluting reason, I simply can have a 'first-time' only once, and I want it to be with my husband, and if it happens to be you, that'll be just fine by me. Besides, your restrained behavior with Clair in the past made me know I was safe testing you. Now wouldn't that be awkward if you did become intimate with Clair, not knowing that one day she'd be your brother's wife? Ouch! That's reason enough to avoid premarital sex."

Jonathan asks expectantly, "Now that's a thought, Yikes! So with respect to me, are you saying...?"

Audrey stops Jonathan, saying, "Slow down, my friend; we both have unfinished emotional business, but I've been feeling really good about an 'us' ever since California. So there's no denying that something is happening; we just have to be patient and wait for a sign. That excursion we took to that store today, and you were sharing about the girl you met way back when, meant the world to me. To trust me with that scenario moved my heart in a way I cannot explain. You, Jonathan, laid yourself bare and stood emotionally naked before me. Do you know what that means to a woman? It validates the connection, a connection between us that is rare and unbelievable. So, it requires courage for a man to share one's sexual history with his girlfriend. No man would allow himself to be that vulnerable to the woman he loves. Even if chaste, most men would prefer to let their women believe that they had some heroic macho body count. And for you to tell me that about yourself in such intimate detail is the most monumental show of trust and unapologetic humility that I have ever seen. Did you know that the man who touched my heart in the grocery store years ago did so with a simple act of kindness..." she pauses, "but I honestly don't recall being in that store or Cape St. Clair before meeting Nancy; it couldn't have been... I should be able to remember something. Even after hearing Dr. Campbell's voice recording, I don't remember." Audrey stops, now confused. "Anyway, thank you for trusting me. That couldn't have been an easy confession. Let's go back inside; it's getting a little chilly."

The rest of the afternoon and evening is even better. The couple alternate between binge-watching a drama series and a Redbox premium movie. Between television and conversation they practice dancing for an upcoming competition. They eat the meal Audrey prepared and walk slowly around the neighborhood, holding hands.

Afterwards, they are sweaty and exhausted. Both take turns in the shower, then plop down on the couch, relaxing as a couple in each other's arms.

Sleep soon overwhelms them as Jonathan sleeps seated on the couch. Audrey falls asleep soon thereafter, falling sideways onto Jonathan's lap, waking him. He strokes her hair, now draped over his knee with tenderness and softness. He looks down at her angelic slumber, dreaming of the day he could call her his own.

Thirty-Six

DREAMLAND; DREAMS BECOME REALITY

It is a month before Thanksgiving. Jonathan and Audrey are beside themselves with an unusual joy that has become usual. Both want to pull at the thread at the edge of their happiness to consent to full intimacy, but dare not tamper with it, deciding to simply enjoy the desire without the act.

Audrey's parents ask that Jonathan's family join their family for Thanksgiving dinner. Audrey accepts without asking Jonathan, knowing that he would do anything to please her just as she would do the same to please him.

At Audrey's townhouse on that Saturday, Audrey and Jonathan sit beside each other with their laptops open. Christmas shopping online has overtaken physical shopping a year earlier.

They come up with gift ideas written on a legal pad. Then she checks Amazon while Jonathan checks Wal-Mart and Target, both making a decision based on best price, fastest and cheapest shipping.

Tonight is their third shopping session; they agree to deliver them to her address and plan to wrap them before Thanksgiving to distribute to the family at the combined holiday dinner.

Jonathan orders two gifts and has them sent to his home. Audrey notes it, saying, "Are you sneaking to buy a present for me? I know what you're doing. What did you get for me? Tell me," she says like a curious child.

Jonathan answers, "You'll have to wait, but I have one gift for you that requires, I mean, will require a retail visit."

Audrey wraps her right arm around his waist and tickles him, attempting to force Jonathan to confess what he has planned for her. Finally, after ordering gifts, Audrey sits quietly on her recliner. Jonathan sits across from her, neither saying anything. The silence is deafening, yet they watch each other with unmistakable eyes of pleasure.

Jonathan warns, "I've been out several times trying to find the perfect gift for you. Unfortunately, Weather Channel is calling for snow overnight; we may be trapped here."

Audrey responds gleefully, "Then I will have you all to myself, and you won't be able to get away from me pestering you."

Jonathan rubs her hand, kisses her forehead, and says, "I can't think of anyone I'd rather be stuck inside with other than you. I only hope I don't get on your nerves. Before you, when I've been snowed in, I put on my sweats with holes in the legs, an oversized non-matching sweatshirt; I don't shave or comb my hair. I make breakfast and lunch and don't clean the kitchen until dinner time. I binge watch K-Dramas and Sci-Fi; sometimes, I sit at the piano for hours thinking about the 'you' I wished for before I knew you. Basically, I am a slob during cooped-up situations, whereas I am normally meticulous and neat."

Audrey draws closer to him. "Me too, and on some occasions, if I sleep too late, I'm sometimes too lazy to shower. I can't believe how similar we are. When you're my husband I'd like to spend all day in bed with you."

Jonathan's expression of delight needs no words. He smiles appreciatively.

Two days later, the snow falls. Audrey barely makes it over to Jonathan's house that morning. The weather is too bad with slippery and dangerous roads to return home; she prays she can make it to

Jonathan's house safely, a much closer and preferable destination to be with her honey.

Since their more formalized relationship, Jonathan always keeps his pantry and refrigerator generously stocked. Jonathan and Audrey do as they predicted they would do; they binge, eat, play music, and talk with each other endlessly.

The following morning, Audrey suggests shoveling the driveway.

Jonathan answers, "That driveway is two-hundred feet long; we'll be dead doing that by hand, and my snow blower wouldn't start last time I tried to use it."

Audrey goes through the kitchen side door and down two steps to uncover the snow blower stuffed in the corner of the garage. As Jonathan warned, Audrey plugs into an outlet and presses the electric starter, but the motor fails to start.

Audrey grabs mechanic's disposable gloves, and then drags a rolling stool to the left side of the blower, removing the carburetor using tools she found on Jonathan's well-stocked workbench.

Five minutes later, Jonathan joins Audrey in the garage. Audrey has removed the carburetor, disassembled the float, and cleaned the float bowl. She has doubled the gloves to protect her beautiful hands from gasoline. Jonathan had no idea she is so handy and mechanically inclined. He stands there watching her wordlessly with deep admiration.

Audrey asks, "Do you have a piece of cardboard, the type that shirt makers insert into a new men's dress shirt?"

Jonathan returns a minute later with the shirt insert. He watches Audrey as she lays the old gasket over the cardboard and etches the original gasket shape and design by tracing the outline. Jonathan is amazed watching her use a single edge razor blade and a hole punch to make a new replacement gasket."

Audrey, seated again on the rolling stool, pushes herself to the left side of the snow blower. She reattaches the carburetor, primes the engine, then presses the start button. At first, the motor spins but does not start. Finally, the engine coughs and roars to life after the third try. She points to the garage door, waving off the choking exhaust; Jonathan opens it.

Audrey pushes the machine to the garage's opening, runs back inside to get a coat, hat, and gloves, and proceeds to clear the driveway. Jonathan just stares at her, saying to himself, "I'm going to marry this girl; she's one of a kind, Unbelievable."

As Audrey cleans around the vehicles, Jonathan moves them to the just cleared spots. Seeing her shiver, he takes over, plowing to give her a break. They alternately tag-team with the snow blower until together, they completely clean the entire driveway.

Returning to the now closed garage, they drop all but their underclothes on the floor just outside the door leading to the kitchen. Both stand there, shivering. Jonathan glares at her; she responds, "Men! You're all so nasty."

Inside, Jonathan says, "You take the big shower; you smell like gas and exhaust fumes. I'll do the same; I can't stand how yucky I feel. And wash your hair too; I love playing with your hair." Audrey punches him in the shoulder, laughs, and obeys.

Clean and frumpy, Jonathan looks for Audrey, feeling that she has been away too long. His face twists with concern, thinking she has fallen in the shower. He peeks in, and the shower stall is empty. He looks out the window, and her SUV is still in the driveway.

Searching the house, Jonathan enters his study, where he finds Audrey dressed in sweats, hair wrapped in a towel, lying face down on the small daybed. He walks over to his angel and looks at her sleeping. Then, Jonathan quietly backs out of the room, enters his bedroom, and takes a nap. Cleaning the driveway has exhausted them both.

Neither Audrey nor Jonathan realizes how tired they are; they sleep and do not wake until the following day.

After a quick meal and a few phone calls about work, Audrey and Jonathan dress warmly and stroll the neighborhood snapping pictures of snowmen in front of Jonathan's neighbor's home.

Jonathan lights the fireplace and Audrey joins him in front of the crackling fire. "Audrey, do you remember the first song I played and sang for you?"

Audrey appears puzzled, "You've sung so many songs to me. Hmmm, hold on, let me think. I got it," she screams, "you sang, *'If it takes forever, I will wait for you.'*"

A SIMPLE ACT OF KINDNESS

Jonathan smiles. "I can't believe you remember."

"How could I not? You're the only person that has ever sung for me, Mr. Dawson."

A few days later, all the gifts are delivered mostly by FedEx and Amazon trucks. Audrey makes hot chocolate and plays music on the Music Choice app. Together they sit on the floor in front of the fireplace like Santa's workshop, wrapping each gift with care and love. Jonathan prepares the name labels for each gift box; Audrey places the colorful labels on the boxes with a color-matching stick-on bow.

And as usual, they fall asleep on the couch, Audrey's head, as always, on his lap. Now both asleep, a shadowy image appears behind them as a vehicle drives by outside. The headlights of the passing vehicle shine through the near window, exposing Ethan standing silently above them.

Carefully placing his hands on both their heads, Ethan prays silently, imparting in an instant, the dream state scenario he has created with Clarence. The dream begins.

Thirty-Seven

INFUSED DREAMS & FUTURE MEMORIES

Neither Jonathan nor Audrey know what is about to occur within their respective dream states as Audrey sleeps on his lap and he gently strokes her hair.

The evening has been wonderfully filled with the joy a couple feels just breathing each other's air. Jonathan and Audrey dance, sing, prepare, and eat dinner together, enjoying the fruits of perfect companionship. Now they are tuckered out and asleep on the couch with the television on.

Ethan appears standing over them, almost as an apparition.

The Bible states in Acts 2:17:

'And it shall come to pass in the last days, saith God, I will pour out of my Spirit upon all flesh: and your sons and your daughters shall prophesy, and your young men shall see visions, and your old men shall dream dreams'

As they sleep, neither Jonathan nor Audrey knows that this is that night and a prophecy to be fulfilled.

Ethan stands over them silently. He looks at his oldest friend,

Audrey, missing their one-sided relationship; the next moment, he thinks of the scolding by Clarence and snaps out of it. Ethan knows the mission, since it is he who proposed it.

Angels use the infusion method to protect their human *protectees* from danger their conscious mind could not quickly assimilate and act upon.

Standing above the sleeping couple, Ethan gently enters the hypnotic ramp into the subconscious of Jonathan and Audrey. "May the peace of the Lord be with you both as I impart His message to you for your benefit and His perfect will. Open your minds to receive what you will need to advance and protect you as you both journey into a timeline that must be. Be blessed both of you, always and forever."

And with that, Ethan proceeds to prepare and narrate the story of Jonathan and Audrey's historical past, specific events in the present, and a hint of the short and near-term future chronology.

Clarence has explained the history of manipulating bloodlines like Adam and Eve, Moses' birth and purpose, Noah's purpose, and Lot's family's departure.

So, Ethan prepares to communicate using what humans would best understand as telepathy. But unfortunately, although humans are capable of receiving telepathic communiques, they cannot transmit it to others.

Humankind has learned to communicate via speech, allowing careful thought before speaking something dangerous or hurtful.

Some, through history, have known this but were unwilling to share the knowledge. Whenever a human acted on intuition, that person knew when to accept divine guidance. Those who ignored that so-called little birdie on the shoulder, did so at their peril.

Ethan watches them sleep cuddly on the couch, standing over Jonathan and Audrey. Observing how Audrey's hair falls across Jonathan's knees causes Ethan to feel a twinge of jealousy, but he recovers his composure and thinks only of his mission.

Ethan folds his arms, bows his head, and prays silently again. "Let's get this right this time; Clarence expects my best."

Projecting directly into Audrey and Jonathan's temporal lobe,

Ethan remembers the mechanics of dream-casting from Clarence, who said, "Dreams form in the brain's temporal lobe. Timing is everything."

Seeing the moment is perfect, Ethan begins projecting into their brains simultaneously. "The product of your combined DNA will produce a mind that will have the capacity to intuit and understand the knowledge imparted to him in the future. This extra-earth-received information, combined with his secular education, will allow him to know how to reverse the damage humans have propagated on the carbon-based life forms, humans, of this orb called earth. And now I will introduce you both to the clarity of your history, present, and snippets of your future."

He continues, "Audrey, when you were a child of four, you first fell in love with agriculture when Miss Job had you plant, harvest, and eat radishes that you produced with your own hand. You will give this love of nature and the environment to your son, Kenneth, who will change the world in his time. You learned to hate the bully and love the benefactor who saved you that day. Your classmate, Harry's big brother, the man whose lap you sleep on now, was your savior that day. Jonathan protected you, shared his tomatoes with you, and walked you home every day until your education cycles no longer coincided. It was I, Ethan, who at that time, did not know was your heavenly protector, guardian angel, who picked up the safety baton and protected you through high school. Your half the DNA is essential for what must be to save the planet."

Ethan pauses, seeing Audrey and Jonathan jostle and move as they sleep. This being Ethan's first dream injection, he does not know the subject's moving around is expected when the dream download rate is faster than humans can absorb and assimilate off-world data infusion.

Ethan paces about until he sees them calmly reenter deep sleep, but is cautious to ensure he completes the mental infusion before the REM stage begins. He remembers Clarence telling him that the injection would not be executed until REM starts, and the infused thoughts would be the subject, title, and execution of the soon-to-occur dream state.

He is observing that Jonathan and Audrey have comfortably fallen back into a deep sleep. Ethan continues infusion along the same timeline; he pauses to check his internal chronometer for precise timing.

"Audrey, you did not see Jonathan again until you completed college. Jonathan, like all little boys, you did not like girls when you were a second grader, but you began to love Audrey as you carried her books while walking her home every day. Do you remember the fifth grade when you were sick with the flu, you were so weak that you couldn't get out of bed, but you protested to your mother that you had to go. Your mother refused until you told her you had to protect your friend, Audrey. Finally, your mother drove you to school just before dismissal. You were shaking and sweating in the back of the car as your mom beckoned Audrey to get in the car. Audrey saw you nearly unconscious in the back seat, and your mother explained to Audrey why she was there to pick her up."

Ethan speaks into both their minds, "Jonathan's mother said to you, Audrey, *'Jon said he could not leave you without protection.'* Audrey, Jonathan pleaded with his mother, saying, *'If something happens to Audrey, I will never forgive myself because she is my best friend.'* His mom said, *'I didn't know my son had a friend-girl. He must really like you.'* Jonathan didn't know it then because it creeped him out that a fifth grader would dare to like a girl in the third grade. But he liked you and talked about you all the time; Harry was the only person who knew what he was talking about."

Ethan infuses more. "After Jonathan graduated, he never saw you again; he gave you his number Audrey, but you never called to thank him; it broke his heart. He wondered what happened to you throughout college, but forgot what you looked like during his sophomore year. He tried desperately to remember your face, but the flood of pretty college girls and your changing appearance, Audrey, you left him with no way to reconnect to the memory of the girl he grew to love all those years ago. We, your angels, believed it was a lost cause and sent you both to the same market to be there at precisely the same time. For Audrey, we constructed the ruse of your mother not having all the ingredients for a meal; for Jonathan, we made you think of your old buddy, Chuck. You both arrived at the same time, but because you had matured and filled out, neither could recognize each other as former best friends. But, and it's a big but, your hearts knew each other instantly. Jonathan's heart saw your heart, Audrey, and once again felt the only love he had ever experienced from a woman, the only exception was his mother's love for her son. You both recalled the events to your friends as a feeling of your heart fluttering. It was your souls reconnecting. Audrey, Jonathan did not recognize you, but his heart did. He spoke of your socks and tried to entice you into a conversation by talking to Joanie and her siblings. Frightened by what you felt, Audrey, you hurried out of the store, never understanding that you had just met your soulmate. Both your hearts knew the other, but your conscious minds did not. So you've held off from becoming a real couple for fear of meeting that heart again, not realizing that the hearts you both want is inside you."

Ethan continues, "Aileen at the farmer's market; we had nothing to do with that. We saw and hoped; Aileen tried everything to get you two together; she intuitively knew your two hearts would be perfect to and for each other, but still, you resisted her best efforts. Audrey, it was me, Ethan, who came to you at the carwash as Charlie Darwin. You were about to stray from waiting to find Jonathan. Charlie's, I mean, my advice, was designed to keep you on course to find Jonathan. It worked! And I got a nice lunch out of it; thank you. You two frustrated a lot of angel-power to maneuver you to re-meeting at the I.T. Expo. And even after re-meeting, you resisted falling in love and separated until Seoul, South Korea. In Korea, we moved heaven and earth to match you two up again and again, yet you failed to keep in touch to develop a relationship, even though that is what you both wanted. In a last-ditch effort, we arranged for you two to go droning independently. Again, the arrest we engineered was our best effort, and finally, you became friends. Friendship was all you'd participate in as you both continued evading the fact that you were falling in love. Instead, you both kept holding out for a love already right before you. So, here we are; you, Audrey, are asleep in Jonathan's lap as he holds you as the dearest thing to him, except for both of you loving my boss more. Guys, stop searching and trust your hearts; you could've been married long ago, but then again, your stubbornness will also be the glue to sustain you through the upcoming rough times. Don't be afraid, and you will never lose your love for each other; your interest will change as you get older, but your steadfastness will hold you to each other until your occasional disagreements pass. One or both of you will always give in to the other for love's sake. As you remember your journey, nothing will separate you. You will have a wonderful family, and Kenneth, your firstborn, will save the world, supported by your other children. Audrey, you will be attractive your entire life; Jonathan, you will be fit, but hormone levels will cause your hair to be thin, but you will not be bald. Embrace aging as there is a great reward for you both when this life is over. I will meet you on the other side to show you what a glorious life looks like. This earthly life is nothing; trust me, your minds cannot begin to conceive of the world God has prepared for you. I must bid you both goodbyes for now. But, of course, neither of you will believe this dream occurred. One day soon, however, one of you will gently broach the subject, admitting to each other that this dream did happen, and after that day, you will be free to live as man and wife for the rest of your lives here on earth."

Ethan ends the dream infusion, touching them both on the head and saying, "Audrey, I've loved you all my life. Jonathan, please take care of the most precious earthly jewel in existence. May you both achieve all your dreams for your future. Goodbye."

And with that, Audrey and Jonathan enter REM sleep. Their closed eyes dart about as if they see so much they have never seen before.

Jonathan wakes first. Rubbing his eyes and looking down, he sees Audrey still asleep on his lap. He sits there, staring at her for long minutes as he pulls strands of hair from her face to her ears. Jonathan loves looking at her face, especially when she sleeps. He once mentioned to his mother, "When she sleeps, she looks like an angel."

Moments later, Audrey starts and then is fully awake. She sees Jonathan looking at her and asks, "What are you smiling about?"

Jonathan answers without hesitation, "The most beautiful heart I've ever seen."

Weeks zip by, and for some reason that neither can understand, they are happier, more loving, and unashamed by their affection for each other.

Both notice it, but no one says it; they no longer refer to each other as friends. Finally, when Mateo sees them at a local pub, he says, "There you are, the two best friends in the world." Mateo is shocked when Jonathan puts his arm around Audrey, kissing her in a crowded room. Jonathan replies with a chuckle, "Best friend? Nope, she's my girl." Audrey returns Jonathan's kiss with loving and discreet affection. Mateo glares in approval and disbelief.

Jonathan and Audrey never talk about their dream that next morning or for the next few weeks, but both know something is different. Neither do they comment from that night forward about his grocery store girl with the socks nor her kind man who purchased fruit for children he thought were hers.

Audrey and Jonathan are closer in every activity after that night and freely share emotions. Pecks on the cheek have graduated to dry kisses on the face or lip. Dry kisses have moved from dry to moist when they are alone and celebrate full romantic embraces for countless moments of romantic feelings for each other.

Jonathan has been happy but feels he is hiding something from Audrey. He invites her to a cozy romantic dinner at Grace's Mandarin in National Harbor. Audrey thinks they are going to the Awakening, Jonathan's thinking spot and the place where he and Audrey realized Cheryl was attempting to kill herself.

She is surprised when they park, and Jonathan escorts her into the fabulous three-story restaurant.

Seated, Audrey accepts Jonathan ordering for her. After the main course, he orders hot plum wine as the table is cleared. He says to Audrey, "There's something I want to tell you about."

Audrey rubs his hand, asking, "Why so serious? What's wrong?"

They sit at the table for long silent moments. Then, finally, Audrey asks again with compassion, "What's bothering you, Jon? You've been a bit melancholy for a few weeks now. Is it something you want to talk about?"

Suddenly Audrey grabs her chest with fake panic, screaming, "OMG; you want to break up with me. No, don't leave me." She cannot contain her suppressed polite laughter.

He responds, "You're silly, Miss Sawyer, but..."

He ponders a thought, and then, unable to contain his emotions, Jonathan speaks earnestly. "Audrey, can I share something extraordinary and possibly bizarre with you?"

Audrey gets up and moves her chair closer to him, reseating herself and holding his hands. She never says a word, but her eyes tell him, 'yes.'

"Sweetheart," he begins; Jonathan has never called her that term of endearment. When he caught the pleasure in her eyes, it gave him the courage to continue. "Audrey, my love, have you ever had a dream so real you could not distinguish between memory and real life? Not long ago, I had a dream about us. Of course, I can't remember it all, but I do know that I was visited by a, I dunno, something that traced part of our lives; things I don't remember or are not true. But I think we're the missing pieces of each other's lives that we've been looking for. Do I sound crazy? Anyway, since that dream, I've become freer with you, and everything we do feels so natural. I'm probably overstepping boundaries, but I think we're supposed to be something special. I can feel the change in your heart too. I know it's scary, but I'm unwilling to miss out on you for fear. Audrey, I'm all in. I'm laying all my chips on the table; I love you more than my own life, and when you tell me, you feel the same…"

Audrey massages his hand, responding, "And don't think I haven't felt the change in us; it's been incredible, and I'm almost there. Can you give me until Thanksgiving? I want to confirm something I dreamed about too. I always dream about you and us, but this dream was unique; I saw our whole lives, from kindergarten to Korea to now and even our future. I've seen our children. It is a glorious future if it's true, and I want it; desperately! I've got an idea; if you are willing to be patient a bit longer. Will you do that for me, Jonathan?"

They leave the restaurant happier than when they entered. It is as if both know the long struggle to be together is almost over. Like a mid-spring day, love is in full bloom.

Both have crossed the bridge from something they knew not what, but whatever it is, it is beautiful for both. And while they independently shared the same dream, both realize a new love as they are now living a long wished-for dream of their own.

Thirty-Eight

THANKSGIVING WITH THE SAWYERS

Audrey is helping her mother prepare a Thanksgiving feast for an evening of enjoyment with the Sawyer and Dawson families and friends. This gathering will be the first time Jonathan's entire family meets Audrey's family. Of course, everyone knows the story of their extraordinary friendship; Mrs. Sawyer and Mrs. Dawson thought this meeting of the families was long overdue.

The doorbell rings, and Audrey's father lets Mateo in with a hearty greeting. It is apparent that they have known each other for a long time. The doorbell rings again as Mateo and Graham head for the family room. Mateo continues to join Elise and the other guest; Mr. Sawyer opens the door and is shocked to see a young man he remembers from years ago and the young man's guest, Clair. Graham greets them. "Harry, the last time I saw you was years ago when you were a teenager. Look at you, and you're all grown up. And who is this beautiful young lady with you? She looks familiar."

Harry steps back and lets Clair enter first and says, "Mr. Sawyer, may I present my sweetheart, my girlfriend, Clair Hansley." Clair extends her hand to shake his hand, but he pulls Harry and Clair to him, giving them a group family hug and saying, "You're both welcome here. Harry, your brother and Audrey are already here in the family room."

Clair and Harry enter the family room, greeted by everyone's broad smiles, hugs, and grins. Jonathan puts his brother in a playful headlock, kissing his forehead and laughing, saying, "Haven't seen you two since baseball and ice cream." Jonathan looks at Clair and Harry with admiration and brotherly affection. Finally, Jonathan pulls Clair aside, whispering to her. "It's all right. I hope you don't have hard feelings about us. I just couldn't give you my heart back then, and I'm sure you know by now that my brother Harry is as good as it gets. He is a man of great integrity and a great brother. He will make you a terrific husband one day. He is simply the best. Do you forgive me for hurting you?"

Audrey watches the exchange between them and, seeing Clair smile, feels comfortable that all is well.

Clair whispers back to Jonathan, "I'm grateful you rejected me. I thought I loved you back then, but I didn't realize that I was not in love with you until I had been forced to be away from you. Then I accidentally met Harry, and even though I didn't know he was your brother for almost a year, I fell for him; hard. Then, as he told me about his family, I realized you two were brothers. So I decided to tell him about you, and he told me the most comforting thing I'd ever heard. He said, *'Clair, my brother is a special person any woman would fall for. There is nothing to regret. So many girls and women have been smitten with him, but from the moment he told me about Audrey after he returned from Korea, I knew she was the only woman for him. So do not consider me your second choice; consider me another choice, and if you choose me, I will love you for all the days of my life.'* After that, Jonathan, nothing else mattered. Harry and I have already discussed marriage and decided to keep our plans a secret except from your mother until you tie the knot with Audrey. We don't want our announcement to distract everyone from the day I know is coming for you and Audrey."

Jonathan kisses Clair on her temple and says, "Thank you, Clair, you're going to be a wonderful sister-in-law."

Clair grabs Harry by the arm, Audrey grabs Jonathan, and the four of them stroll into the family room to join everyone else, where Audrey's dad is cajoling Mateo about Audrey. "I'm glad to see you, boy; Mateo, it's been way too long, considering you and Audrey have been friends since middle school."

The two walk back to the kitchen. Audrey is glad to see one of her oldest friends. She laughs. "What do I have to do to get rid of you, Mat?" He blushes, glad to see her.

Mateo helps set the table and then squats down in the rocker, talking old times and recent achievements with Graham.

Thanksgiving Dinner with two families, The Dawson's and the Sawyer's

EVERYONE COMES IN; AUDREY ACTS AS THE COAT CHECK GIRL, TAKING each coat and hat and storing them in the large closet adjacent to the entry foyer. The Sawyer's home is nearly six thousand square feet.

Franklin, Jonathan's father, comments, looking around, "Wow, Graham, this place is huge; I love it."

"Thank you, my old friend. The farm that was here sold at a fire sale price too good to pass up, we were originally planning a much smaller house, but the home would've appeared tiny on this plot. So, Elise and I decided to retire in place rather than building or buying over and over. After that decision, it made sense to add an elevator and mother-in-law suites just in case. We prepared a room for everyone, so if you want to stay overnight, there's plenty of room for everybody."

Frank responds, "That's smart thinking, Graham. I didn't realize we were neighbors. Our place is back off Governor Bridge Road; we love the peace and serenity."

Graham continues, "Lots of time has passed since we were neighbors in Dunkirk. It is amazing how that little town has become so cosmopolitan. Ain't no little town no more."

Franklin comments, "When we first looked there, the property was four hundred dollars an acre; now you can't touch it for less than three-hundred thousand an acre. I have no idea how kids today afford that." I'm so glad our kids have good jobs; we love being empty nesters."

Audrey waltzes over to Graham. "Daddy, do you want me to move back home?"

"No, darlin', I don't. I like not to have you telling me not to leave dishes in the sink of my house," Audrey's father retorts.

Graham looks over to Jonathan. "Boy, if you marry this girl, don't ever think about leaving the kitchen a mess."

Jonathan gives his potential father-in-law the perfect response. "Don't you worry, sir, I won't."

Graham and Franklin chuckle. "That was a trick question, son. So, you two are thinking about getting married. I thought you two were just friends."

Clair jumps in, saying, "Harry and I have suspected such for a while now. Whenever Jonathan talks about Audrey, it is as if he's already married. I think they are two peas in a pod."

Jonathan answers succinctly, "Yeah, I guess it's sort of obvious. I thought we were to be just friends, maybe even best friends, but the fact is, Mr. Sawyer, Dad, I love Audrey; we didn't know how much until we spent the day with an infant named Aria."

Graham and Franklin dismiss the Aria statement, staring at each other. Then, finally, Graham says, "I think we met briefly when the kids were around seven and ten years old. It was at one of those kiddie zones with moon bounces; stuff like that. Jonathan was maybe eleven or twelve, but he would not leave the side of a pretty girl about eight, nine, or ten."

"I thought it strange that Jonathan never left her side, and whatever event or activity she tried, my Jonathan was right there with her. Do you remember it or me?" Franklin pulls out his phone, saying, "This is the latest iPhone, but I always transfer data from old to new phones." Franklin pours through the older videos, saying, "Ah hah, I think this is it." Then, Graham shows the footage, asking, "Is this your son, Jonathan?"

Both watch the video, suddenly seeing images of dozens of children screaming and playing and a glimpse of Graham surrounded by

A SIMPLE ACT OF KINDNESS

other parents. The video shows a young boy with a younger girl sitting in a corner, engrossed in a private conversation.

Graham shouts, "That's them. Is that Audrey?" Everyone gathers around the tiny screen, blown away by the proof of how long Audrey and Jonathan have known each other.

Everyone moves to the dining room, taking their seats at the spectacularly festive Thanksgiving table set by Elise, Allison, and Audrey. Jonathan and Audrey blush; Audrey says, "I remember the boy I sort of liked; he walked me home every day, but I don't remember that particular event, but that's me for sure."

She punches Jonathan in the arm and kisses him, saying, "I guess we were fated to be lifelong friends or something after all."

Graham looks across the turkey, asking his daughter directly, "Is there something you haven't told us? Mateo, Harry, Clair, what's going on? Your sly smiles say you know more than the rest of us."

Audrey, sitting next to Jonathan, places her fork on the table. She looks at everyone seated individually. "I've loved Jonathan since we accidentally," she looks at Jonathan, "well, maybe not so much an accident, but it was this instant thing. He was so kind and protected me in Korea without really knowing me. He had me at his mercy and never took advantage. I was too hung up on a man I met long ago at some store I can't remember. Anyway, I missed him but had no way to reach out. Then we got busted by the cops flying our drones illegally. I didn't know he was there, nor did he know I was there, not until we ended up at the police station together. We reconnected, but I only wanted a friend, not a boyfriend. I told him, and he remained my friend for years. The more we did together, the more I loved him. I tried everything I could not to love him. I even friend-zoned him, but his affection for me was steadfast. It annoyed me at first, but then I began to feel comfortable in his love and resented him for breaking down my barriers. After that, we attended a funeral internment together, and a little girl, Joanie, called us stupid for not being together. Joanie claimed that Jonathan was the man I met all those years ago. Still, I couldn't remember. Unbeknownst to me, Jonathan and I had independently sought clues of my identification of him, and he traveled cross country to chase leads that would lead him to confirm that I was the girl he fell in love with at first sight. And the strange thing is, I don't believe in love at first sight, but that man in that store that day frightened me when I felt my heart move in his presence. So, with time and patience, Jonathan has replaced that man, but I want Jonathan to be that man. As of now, I'm only missing one piece of proof. If I find it, I will give my… well, he already has my heart, but then I will feel no apprehension. I even dream about Jonathan as my husband. Recently, I began to believe that Ethan, my friend from high school, is some kind of angel engineering all this, but the fact is, I do love Jonathan with all my heart."

By now, the moment is solemn and joyous. The ladies tear a bit while everyone else comments some version of, "We didn't know you two were that serious. This is wonderful."

Clair is the only person not surprised. She feels she has to admit what Jonathan, Audrey, and Harry knew of, but the rest of the family did not know. Clair feels that now is the time to put all the cards on the table so there would be no confusion or gossip later on. Clair speaks clearly with solemn honesty, "I need to say this for the sake of what may become our family's cohesion. I've known Jonathan since first grade; I had a big crush on him, and we worked together, but with Audrey in his heart, there was no room for me. I wanted you all to know that I didn't know he was Jonathan's brother for a year when I met Harry. By then, we had already become a couple. Audrey and Jonathan know this, but as I hope to join the family one day, I did not want there to be any misunderstanding. I'm saying I once liked Jonathan, but I love Harry."

Everyone is quiet and nods in full agreement and deep respect for what Clair has announced.

Audrey responds, "Clair is my sister from another mother. We are so much alike, have the same careers, and both of us like the Dawson brothers. And best of all, we've all known of each other practically forever. Bravo, Clair."

Jonathan says, "What Audrey has said is not even half of it. Mom, Dad, did you know that I met Audrey when she was in kindergarten and Clair a little later? Harry was Audrey's classmate, and when she was bullied, Harry asked me to protect her and share something I had grown in my garden patch with her. Mr. Sawyer, did you know that I walked Audrey home from school every day until I left for the seventh grade? I think your wife knew. By the time I got to college, I remember the feeling Audrey had given me, but I couldn't remember her face. And then I saw this woman in Graul's wearing a tan coat and the craziest coolest knee-length socks I've ever seen. I tried to make conversation with her, but it flopped, and I never saw her again. That is why I held off from committing to being anything more than friends with Audrey."

Audrey's mother asks, "Did you say crazy socks and a tan coat?"

Audrey interrupts, insisting, "I've never owned a tan coat and fashion-high socks; I'm too conservative for the socks you guys are raving about, but I love the sound of the coat. I think I will buy a cashmere coat for the winter. Anyway, that's our story; a story without an ending, so we continue as friends who love each other; two ships circling the harbor of love never to find a port to dock."

Dinner proceeds, and everyone is having a good time. Jonathan and Audrey's eye contact now has confessed their feelings; the table's ambiance is joyously subtlety intense.

Elise stands and walks to the fireplace, staring at those who remain seated.

Suddenly, the room goes silent.

Now at the mantle, Elise picks up the photo Jonathan saw long ago after playing billiards with her husband. She asks Audrey, "Who are these girls, and why are all but two of them wearing these colorful socks?"

Audrey answers, "They are members of some of the clubs at school, including our college astronomy club I belonged to; you remember, Mom? That was taken maybe a few years ago at the observatory when I was a junior at College Park. We called ourselves the Jupiter Club."

Audrey's mom interrupts, correcting her daughter, "No, dear, your group was called The Astro Club, and it was one of your high school extracurricular activities. This photo is a group shot of two other clubs and your astronomy club."

Audrey looks puzzled, asking, "Mom, are you sure?"

Jonathan inspects the picture and asks Audrey, "Which one of these ladies is you, Audrey?"

Clair walks to the mantle. Seeing the picture, Clair says, "That's me when I was in the chess club. Unbelievable; talk about fate. We've been part of each other's lives forever, wow!"

Audrey's mom answers before Audrey can respond. "The girl in the Astro Club jacket in the middle; she was vice-president, and the club uniform included colorful knee-high socks; it was something the Astros chose as club colors."

Audrey suddenly remembers something about the photograph, blurting out, "Oh my God, the guy in the store, when talking to the kids, commented on my 'socks'." She continues, "But I don't even have a coat like that."

Audrey's mom interrupts, asking Audrey to go to the hall closet and retrieve the only item in a plastic cleaner's bag.

Audrey retrieves the garment bag, bringing it to the table. Inside the bag from Zips Dry Cleaners is the camel-colored cashmere coat, scarf, and knit hat Jonathan saw that day in the store.

Audrey's mother explains about the grocery run for shallots and potatoes and how she got soaked in the rain, how her mom lent her a coat offering to have her coat cleaned, but Audrey never came by to pick it up; that was years ago.

Audrey examines the clear plastic dry cleaner's bag and notes the date stapled to the claim ticket is years old.

Audrey leaves the dining room without a word and heads upstairs to her old room. Inside the room, she rumbles through her old drawers and finds the Astro Club socks. Audrey suddenly remembers her mom teaching her how to repair the hole in the toe since replacements were no longer made. She then slips on the coat, socks, and hat. She returns to the table nearly in tears, sees the flashback in her mind's eye, and looks at Jonathan, almost sobbing, saying to herself, "Oh-my-God, it was you; it was me."

Now back at the dinner table, she says to everyone, "Now I remember; I attended an Astro Club reunion that day; I wore my old socks as all the girls did. But, Jonathan, it was you; it was you all this wasted time. It's you."

A SIMPLE ACT OF KINDNESS

Jonathan chokes up, seeing the vision of what he would've given his life to see again. It was like being transported back in time. His heart pounds in cadence with Audrey as the full recognition becomes complete.

Standing in front of him is the girl he fell in love with at first sight. Of course, he knows it is Audrey standing before him, but still, he struggles to remember that girl's face that day, long ago.

And while neither Jonathan nor Audrey can clearly recognize each other from past visual memory, their hearts pound in recognition of the other's heart. Finally, Jonathan stands, looking at his future bride, his prize, and he knows the wait is over as he observes the same expression in Audrey's eyes.

She walks toward Jonathan wearing the outfit he first saw her in. She grabs and clings to him with all her might, melting in his arms, sobbing.

Audrey pulls away and looks at him. Then, she walks to the fireplace and back to him again. "I can see you now, the waist-length coat, the black leather gloves, the way you looked at me and played with those adorable kids. I remember it all now."

She glances at Harry and Clair and then back to Jonathan. "It was him, back in kindergarten, it was… Dad, Mom, I remember now; Jonathan walked me home for four years to protect me from Rodney, the bully; it was him all the time. God kept bringing him into my life, and I kept pushing him away because I was well… waiting for him… Him!"

No one has noticed Audrey's mother disappear from the room. Soon after that, Elise reappears, saying to Audrey, "This is a picture your father took of you two on the last day Jonathan walked you home. You were in the fourth grade, and Jonathan was in the sixth. You look so different now, but you were both adorable and best friends back then. Your father used to joke that you would marry him one day. Well, who knew?"

No one says a word.

Then, for the first time, she kisses Jonathan tenderly and publically in full view of her family. Punching him in the shoulder, Audrey says, "Why didn't you tell me you were my guy?" Everyone applauds the discovery, confirmation, and embracing kiss that follows. Everyone at the table knows that the love ship has finally docked with two happy passengers.

Audrey's father proudly states, "Well now, sealed with a kiss."

Jonathan sheepishly states, "Audrey, I tried to convince you, but you just wouldn't believe me."

Harry says to his father with glee plastered on his face, "See, Dad, I told you they'd be together, but you didn't believe me. I knew Big Bro loved her."

Mateo, with a fake sour note, says, "So, this is why I couldn't get you to be my girl from middle school till you went away to college. I tried everything, but all you could do was talk about Kenny."

Graham asks, "Huh, who's Kenny?"

Audrey explains the name Harry introduced her to his big brother, who was in reality, Jonathan.

Harry explains that Jonathan asked him to use his middle name, Kenny, because of how uncool it would be if his classmates thought he was hanging out with a kindergarten girl. But, of course, this would have been a major embarrassment to an eight-year-old boy from a young boy's perspective. Clair laughs, saying, "Yep, that's Jonathan for sure."

Jonathan clinks his fork on the wine flute and pulls a ring box out of his inner sport jacket pocket, asking for everyone's attention.

Jonathan, turning to Audrey, says, "I've been praying you'd accept this ever since our California vacation. I hoped you would recognize my heart. Now that our hearts have met formally…"

Jonathan drops to one knee in front of Audrey. She recoils at first and then takes a step back to him. Jonathan looks up to her tear-strewn face, saying, "Audrey Sawyer, will you accept me, my last name, my family, and give me the honor of making our lives complete forever; will you marry me, my love? Nothing on earth could make me happier."

Audrey drops to her knee, hugs him, and together they rise as Jonathan presents a diamond ring, and Audrey accepts as Jonathan slides the ring on her finger; they are both in near tears.

The parents, brother, Clair, and friends are exuberant. Mateo pats her on the back. "You go, girl; you deserve nothing but the best. My job is over; he is your protector for life now."

Audrey's father displays a single tear, saying, "Now this is something to be thankful for, especially on Thanksgiving; two families becoming one, amazing!"

During the months after Thanksgiving, Jonathan surprises Audrey with a romantic trip to New York. While there, they see a show, enjoy fine dining, and take a boat tour around Liberty Island.

Audrey thinks she is on their way back to Maryland, but Jonathan has arranged a special gift for his newly minted fiancée. Audrey is amazed when the Lincoln Town Car parks in front of Kleinfeld's, only to be met by Randy at the door. Inside, her family and friends' entourage is already seated; Audrey is overwhelmed with joy. She selects 'Carolyn' from Randy's collection.

Soon after returning home, Jonathan escorts her to the Wedding Cake Factory in Laurel. After browsing their extensive catalog, they sample selections presented by the patisserie, at an informal, impromptu wedding cake tasting. Finally, they select a cake and leave.

The year before their wedding flows by. Arrangements are made and booked; old friends are invited, and dress fittings and matching bachelor and bachelorette parties occur. As promised, Chuck is one of Jonathan's groomsmen, while Harry wins the best man spot. Mateo is also a groomsman. Audrey chooses Clair as her maid-of-honor since she knows that one day, Clair would soon be her sister-in-law. Clair is more than a friend as she helps Audrey navigate through everything along the way to her wedding day. Audrey never had a sister, but grows to love Clair more in so many little ways. Audrey thanks God for giving her a sister in the person of Clair.

Jonathan convinces Audrey to forgive her salon buddies, Candice, Salina, Deidra, and Juanita, who have taunted her for years and invited them to be bridesmaids. He convinces Audrey that forgiveness would release bad juju that he feels would infect their life together. Audrey dislikes forgiving anyone who has hurt her, but she loves

Jonathan, deciding that his character on this subject is a trait she wishes to emulate.

The wedding rehearsal dinner is attended by hundreds of guests and family who flow in to see the couple many have heard about. Jonathan and Audrey are happy to see so many relatives and friends from many years ago. Both Audrey and Jonathan apologize to many in the crowd for carelessly neglecting to keep in touch.

Then, only a few dozen participants are allowed at the wedding rehearsal itself. When Audrey's father practices walking his baby girl down the aisle, he has to stop and sit on a pew to gather himself as he is overcome with joy that his daughter is to be given away by him the next day. He apologizes to the rehearsal participants, saying that Audrey is still his little girl, telling all of how wonderful a father-daughter relationship they have. Finally, he asks the crowd, "Can you imagine having the best daughter in the world? I did, and now I am giving her away to the man she deserves."

Audrey, proud of her father, pulls him aside, saying, "Daddy, when I walk down the aisle, I want to do something different and unique for my Jonathan, but I will need your help to pull it off."

Graham's interest piques, asking her, "What would you like to do? How can I help?"

Graham and Audrey sit on a back pew out of earshot of everyone. Audrey is moving her hands, explaining something to her dad. Graham nods his head in understanding and suddenly bursts out saying, "That's wonderful! A splendid idea. I told you back in junior high that you had the chops. Count me in."

"She's still my daughter, but now I have a son." Graham Sawyer turns to Jonathan. "Take care of my little girl, son; she's one of a kind."

THE END

Epilogue

And so it came to pass that Audrey and Jonathan were wed at the Brookstone Church in Davidsonville, Maryland. It was not an exotic or expensive wedding but a modest ceremony that captured the spirit of Holy matrimony. Clarence permitted Ethan to attend in a human form not recognized as himself; most thought he was an out-of-town friend and guest.

Audrey's father could not contain his tears as he sat with his daughter in a private room off the main lobby. He had never noticed her beauty and said, "My God, Audrey, you truly are beautiful." He asked Audrey to stand and turn around as he gasped with pride at the stunning *Fenoli* gown she wore.

Everyone was seated in anticipation of the bride's entrance. Audrey and her dad came to the rear vestibule and the majestic doors opened in unison; two ushers rolled the traditional linen runner from the doors to the altar. As the last foot of the runner was completed, a beautiful music interlude began. Those in the crowd whispered, "That's not the traditional *'here comes the bride'* Bridal March. What's going on?"

Moments later, Audrey, and Jonathan's godchild, Aria, holding another young girl's hand, seemed to float down the center aisle, both dropping mixed-colored rose petals before the bride's entrance.

A female's voice rang out from the church PA system. No one recognized the voice but Jonathan, who spontaneously teared up hearing the lyrics of *'All you are to me'* from Secret Garden.

Jonathan knew the song but didn't realize until this moment that this was the tune Audrey sang as she held him as he sweated and nearly died on the third day of breaking away from the devil of opioids as she held his sweaty body as his pain killer. He remembered the melody, and the words soothed him through his worst moments.

No one knew where the voice came from; many thought it was a prerecorded singer, but as the rear doors burst open again, everyone saw Audrey singing from beneath her veil as her father slowly escorted her to her groom; his soon-to-be son-in-law.

The song concluded just as she and her dad reached the first pew and waited for the minister.

"Who gives this woman to be wed?" Asked the pastor.

Graham stepped forward, placing his baby girl's hand in Jonathan's waiting hand. Jonathan, still teary-eyed, held Audrey's hand as he trembled in gratitude. He mouthed, "I love you" to his bride, to which she mouthed back to him, "You're my everything. I love you, Jonathan."

The vows they had argued over when they first became friends were read by the pastor and recited by Jonathan, except that he added before saying 'I do,' "Audrey, I swear that you will never feel subservient or less than loved. You have my word. I do!"

Audrey added an extraordinary unrehearsed promise to complete her vow. "Jonathan, thank you for waiting for me. I swear I will love you all the days of my life. I will be your co-pilot forever."

Harry was Jonathan's best man, while the crowd was amazed to see a middle-aged Mrs. Paul Skylar, formerly Miss Job as Audrey's kindergarten teacher and now second maid of honor next to Clair as the first maid of honor. Audrey visited her old school, searched Google, and scoured the Internet, learning that Miss Job was now Professor Skylar, a tenured professor at a Florida university.

Audrey flew to meet her regaling Miss Job, her kindergarten teacher, with the fantastic tale of love that began with her radishes.

Standing between the bride and groom was Pastor Jack, Jonathan's counselor during times of great confusion. It took no wrangling to get him to officiate as he had been part of their lives since Audrey and Jonathan found each other as friends

There were speeches from family and friends who had known them for years at the reception. Mateo, Lydia, Tyler, and Clair, made wonderful anecdotal speeches that were both funny and warm.

Silent tears fell as Cheryl, accompanied by her husband, Brayden, and his young daughter, Patricia, spoke. Cheryl told the story of her suicide attempt by saying, "...I thought there was no hope for me, and then suddenly, Jonathan and Audrey saw me, stopped me, and changed my mind. They saved me and my unborn baby's life, and God did the rest. Audrey insisted I pay it forward; I swear I will continuously, and as proof of my oath, I named my newly born daughter after you; her name is Audrey."

Just before the newly minted bride and groom exited the reception hall, Audrey tossed her bouquet. Jonathan was the envy of the men as he enjoyed sensually slipping the garter off his wife's beautiful right leg and throwing it into the crowd of men. But, to no one's surprise, the Sawyer and Dawson families felt the irony was perfect as Clair caught the bouquet and Harry won the toss for the bride's garter.

The newlyweds approached the vestibule when suddenly Ethan appeared as himself before them, wishing them a fond farewell. Oddly, no one in the crowd seemed to notice Ethan's sudden appearance.

As they entered the limo, Audrey and Jonathan kissed each other privately for the first time as husband and wife. Both were startled to see Ethan materialize before them. Ethan was semi-solid, grinning and invisible to the driver.

Ethan spoke as the limousine pulled away from the circular driveway, the driver taking the newlyweds to Jonathan's old house that was now their home. "Guys, you've known me or of me forever but never knew that I was sent as your guardian angel. Remember that verse in Hebrews 13 warning, '*Do not neglect to show hospitality to strangers, for thereby some have entertained angels unaware?*" Well, here I am." Ethan smiled and ordered them, "Now don't say anything; I'm talking now."

Ethan became more solid, almost frightening them. He morphed himself, becoming more substantial like the Ethan Audrey had known for years.

He completed his thoughts. "Audrey, I apologize for making you uncomfortable all those years ago. I fell in love with you while walking you home from school after Jonathan graduated; I thought I was like anyone else; a boy who liked a pretty girl. You are amazing; you even got an angel to fall for you. So, after that, my boss yanked me back to… Anyway, he explained why I was placed here, my mission, and all about you two. I hope you forgive me." Ethan shrugged his heavenly shoulders. "I didn't know I was an angel on a mission. Anyway, as you start your lives together, I want to give you a few last pieces of advice and guidance. Oh!" Ethan paused. "You didn't know it was me that came to you in the dream you both had some time ago; when you fell asleep in Jonathan's lap, that was me. My instruction was to get you two past your apprehension about falling in love, to open you guys up to what you really mean to each other. I understand from my boss that your type of love is extremely rare. Most today fall in lust, not in love. Most have sex the first or second time they get together. Hormones and orgasms get in the way of each knowing the other's heart as the Master planned for human intimacy. You two have been together for years and have never been intimate with each other, almost a few times, but you restrained yourselves. Good on you. Now that you have the God-given rights to all He has given you, enjoy your whole lives together, including a robust life of intimacy. As I told you in your dreams, your first son's name is Kenneth, and he will grow to love and protect the environment. Protect and love him. Another like me will be dispatched to guide him if he needs it later in life. He is important. Now lastly, my warning is to you two directly; you are both remarkably strong-willed and stubborn. But, unfortunately, neither of you easily changes your position on disagreement, especially you, Audrey. Your hard-heartedness has protected you, but it can destroy your marriage and break Jonathan's heart one day. The Master was pleased that you accepted Jonathan's advice to forgive and allow those who ridiculed you at the salon to participate in your wedding. You won't know for years, but your forgiveness will change their lives for the better, all because you chose to forgive. That was huge, and He is so proud of you. He will never override your free will, but you should know that that simple act of kindness and forgiveness did not go unnoticed. Again, good on you."

He continued, "The enemy you cannot know of will use your stubbornness to create an argument that seems worth putting it all on the line but is not. After I leave this limo, I cannot observe you nor intervene in your lives ever again. "Your lives now belong to you. I am saying, Audrey, that Jonathan loves you more than his own life. He will give in to any argument you have if he thinks it will please you. Many human females become accustomed to using this emotional tool on their men; they inadvertently destroy their husband's ability to lead his family. Please don't do this; there are precious few men who will cherish you as he does. Audrey, the enemy, will subconsciously supply you with a toolbox of other emotional weapons that one can scarcely imagine. Strategies like coldness, aloof conversation, lack of communication, and going to bed angry with each other just for starters. Chief among them is intentional alienation of affection, meaning no intimacy until Jonathan concedes to your wishes, even if you are incorrect. He will not be able to lead under this kind of emotional duress effectively. You will force him first, into adulterous thoughts, and the enemy will set the trap that could pull your husband into actual adultery. And while Jonathan will pay for his sin, you, Audrey, will also be punished for torture and the abuse of a gift God has granted to be given freely to each other and only with each other. Remember my words; the power of the success of your life together is in your hands. Audrey, you must always remember what you told Jonathan on your flight to Seattle; you promised him that you would never trap him in the *'happy wife – happy life'* syndrome. Just don't do it! Keep your word. Jonathan, you are nobility and have a natural resistance to sin. You do not have a wandering eye or desire to be with anyone other than Audrey, as evidenced by your resistance to Clair; it will always be this way; you fought to be with her; it was a noble fight, and you both won. Yet, this is both judgment and a curse. Why?

Because with her at your side, you have no reason to seek anything from another; there is no other for you, for she and she alone holds the keys to your heart and you hers. She is your female dove, and you, her male dove. As human mourning doves, you two are bound for life. I beg you both to learn to compromise. Admire each other, praise each other often, and pay attention to the other's interests even if you don't like the other's interests. Then, you will sense what each other needs, and you will learn to adapt your wants and desires to mellow and compromise for the sake of each other's affection. Jonathan, you are the head of the household, but you are not a dictator. You lead and guide, but Audrey makes the whole thing go. Jonathan, your life is motionless without Audrey; Audrey, your life will go in circles till the useless end without Jonathan's leadership, but you must allow him to lead; he will never force you to do anything, ever. Don't be afraid; Jonathan will never lead you astray. Trust his guidance as he is guided directly by God."

He then said to Jonathan, "Jonathan, just as God grants us free will, so you must do the same with your helpmeet, Audrey. If you don't, Jonathan, she will cease to love you, and then a mundane, boring, hateful relationship that resembles a marriage is all that remains. Jonathan, Audrey, I hate to pull rank because you have free will granted by the Master, but you both owe me; you owe Him. Jonathan, you died in the hospital after you broke your ankle. Infection set in, and under the non-interference directive, there was nothing anyone could do. But Audrey begged God in your hospital room after you died to save you. The doctors pronounced you dead, and you were. No heartbeat, no breathing; you were gone. Audrey lifted you off your bed, praying. She offered in sincerity to trade her life for yours. It moved the Master, it moved me, and I was authorized to restart your heart, cleanse your blood, but only Audrey could breathe the gift of life back into your dead lungs. The Master loves her and made the exception to grant her prayer, for both of you, but only if she gave years of her life in exchange; she did so willingly. Such an act does not often occur since the *equation of circumstances* cannot be easily altered. Audrey's love for you has altered what was supposed to be after the coyote attack; your death. Cherish Audrey for the rest of your life just as she offered her life to God in exchange for yours. It is because of her that you are alive today. No matter how angry you become, remember that Audrey traded years of her life so that you may live. God allowed you both a life… together! Do you understand? Audrey, you should know that the *equation of circumstances*, with sacrifice from another, your full lifespan has been restored to the originally appointed time. Jonathan, Audrey was never going to tell you, but I will reveal it because it will help you be the best husband you can be. When you were recovering at her home, you became addicted to prescription narcotics. You were unable to escape the grip opioids had on you. Audrey went through hell to wrestle you back from the brink. She held you while she was nearly naked, warming your cold, filthy body against her body. She held you for three days. She bathed, fed, and slept with you, never leaving you alone. You could have become an addict if it were not for her and her devotion to you. Always remember what she did for you. You must never mistreat or dishonor her; Jonathan, this is your debt. And Audrey, this cannot be used as a weapon to subdue him, but a footnote to both your lives, a footnote that binds you to each other till one or the other leaves this planet. And to you Audrey, finally, you were supposed to drown in the pool that day. The enemy does not want you two to succeed. You should know that Jonathan felt your cry as you were dragged under by the pump's draft. Jonathan broke traffic laws to get back to save your life. You were supposed to die, but his heart's connection to your heart knew you were in trouble. You both hold each other's life in the other's hands."

Ethan, now an apparition, leaned forward to touch their head and began to pray but stopped, saying, "Oh, one last thing; the Master purposely made it difficult for you two to bond. The incredible fight and struggle you endured to be together will ensure you both remember what effort it took to become a couple. He wants you to remember the struggle in case either of you ever feels you want to give up."

Ethan returned to his pre-prayer-state, praying, "Master, thank you for my time with these two. To feel agape love convert to romantic love is amazing. Now bless these two as they travel the wonderful but temporary life here. And if it is Your will, allow me to see them again on the other side many, many years in earth-time later. Jonathan and Audrey, I leave you now in charge of each other. May God bless you forever."

He faded away into nothingness, leaving Audrey and Jonathan numb. Audrey gathered her wedding dress around her knees and ankles, speaking first, "Did that just happen? Tell me something, Jonathan; anything."

Jonathan, nearly speechless, stammered, "If you just saw Ethan as an angel reciting chapter and verse of our lives, past, present, and future, then we witnessed the same thing. Why didn't you tell me I died and all the rest?"

Audrey took his hand, kissed it, and said, "Even though we were only friends then, my heart knew I couldn't live without you. If you died, then I would die; it was a great bargain I would do again and again and again, my husband."

Neither Jonathan nor Audrey ever knew that it was he, Ethan, who offered his own demotion by two steps in an angelic petition to the council to restore Audrey's entire lifetime. He made the bargain with Clarence, saying, "If I wasn't sulking in India, I could've prevented the coyote attack before it happened. Some guardian angel I am."

Clarence accepted his voluntary demotion that gave Audrey her life's duration back.

THE LIMOUSINE BACKED INTO JONATHAN AND AUDREY'S DRIVEWAY. The driver ran around to the rear door, opening it for Jonathan to exit first. Outside the limo, Jonathan extended his hand; Audrey reached for his hand as her gown fell softly to the driveway. She looked up to what was formerly his home, now their home as husband and wife. The driver congratulated them and drove away.

Jonathan carried his bride across the threshold, kissing Audrey as he stepped inside.

Six months before the wedding, they had agreed to keep his house

A SIMPLE ACT OF KINDNESS

instead of her townhouse. He asked her to spend whatever she wanted to redo the house as she wished.

On the night soon after he proposed, he said, "I want you to make my home our home. Redo it in any way you wish, and this is where we will live and love after we're married until you want your next home large enough for our family."

Audrey gratefully accepted his offer and the two of them met with designers, architects, and contractors. They finished the home a month ahead of schedule. Today, Jonathan carrying her over the threshold in her gown was the first time either had seen the completed project.

Jonathan had dreamed of this moment for years. Finally, he was with his bride, alone. A gentleman to the core, he didn't want his wife to feel like an object of his lust. Still standing, his wife in his arms, he let her down. Jonathan restrained himself, resisting the emotions, knowing how much he wanted her. She commented, looking around, "Oh my God, this is so beautiful."

He kissed her, saying, "Hi, Mrs. Dawson, let me show you around our new home."

Audrey looked at him as if that was the last thing she wanted. Instead, she grabbed his hand, saying, "Come with me; there's only one room I want to see first."

Inside the master bedroom, she turned her back to him, almost demanding, "Get me out of this gown." Before he could undo the last button, she tore off the wedding dress and ripped his tuxedo jacket off, pushing Jonathan to the bed, saying, "Do you know how long I've wanted you, my husband?"

Jonathan sat up on the edge of the bed, startled at her aggressiveness as he was prepared to be as gentle as possible, but Audrey, not having it, tossed her gown to the floor, grabbing both Jonathan's hands. Now sitting on the edge of the bed, she pulled him close to her with playful affection. She unbuttoned his tuxedo shirt, saying, "We made it, but I have a confession and compliment I must give you on this, our wedding night. It's important that I know that you know something about me. Thinking back, Jon, I've loved you since Korea, and as I mentioned before, you saved me from myself. Seoul was the first time I ever wanted to toss my morals out the window to have you like this. When I took your shoes off while you slept, I recognized your crazy earth-tone socks, but I could not connect them to my grocery store guy; I just liked them. Now I know it was you all along. But Jonathan, that night in Seoul, my passion was lust, sprinkled with love and admiration for you rescuing me, but still, you saved me from me. Here I was, for the first time in my life, wanting to sleep with a man, and he passively rejected me. I didn't know at the time that God was saving me for tonight through the special gentleman you are. Amazing! I left you a note on your iPhone, and later, when back in the States when I didn't hear from you, I assumed you didn't want me, and you weren't really saving me from anything. After re-meeting you in America, becoming friends, then best friends, I realized that what you did for me in Korea was a simple act of kindness; you are a good man. As we became closer and closer, I knew you wanted me, but again, you being aware of my desire to wait till marriage caused you to help me keep my promise to myself. That couldn't have been easy. I want you to know that ever since the almost drowning, I've wanted you. I offered myself to you that night, but you preserved my original wish to wait until my wedding night. What man would do that? After that, all the meals we've done for each other, the brake job, becoming DC tourists, Aileen, the kiss at the salon, droning, you with my dad, the formal at the country club, stargazing, skating, and so many other occasions, there hasn't been a single moment when I didn't want this. And the worst and best desire of all was the night you sang the song you wrote for me; it almost got us. I told you that night that I was yours; you refused to accept my offer despite the agony and hunger for me I know you felt. I became so dependent on your promises and your unique integrity that I knew you would preserve this night for me as I had dreamed it. And so, here we are; our wedding night, our first time. I hope I please you for a lifetime, my love."

The evening and night was long, filled with intermittent passion and occasional naps. Audrey could not get enough of him, nor he her. They explored every facet of loving each other with the other's pleasure as their only goal.

That night, their first night as husband and wife, was beyond both

A SIMPLE ACT OF KINDNESS

their expectations. And even though this was the only first night they'd ever know, if one were to ask them, every night for years to come was still their first night.

Finally, in the wee hours, well after midnight, they both slept in each other's arms.

Waking the following day, neither could do anything but smile. There was no guilt, shame, or ghosts of past lovers, for theirs was a pure love unadulterated union blessed by God.

Audrey's first words that next morning after kissing her husband stunned Jonathan. "I've loved you my whole life. From the moment you protected me in kindergarten and when you walked me home. Then, as we grew into adolescence and young adulthood, my eyes could no longer recognize you, but my heart…" she said, touching her chest, "my heart always knew your heart. I've been 'in love' with you since before Seoul; I've wanted you like this since you awkwardly proposed to me after our argument on wedding vows and you kayaked alone without me. If I could go back in time, I would've married you at the Lincoln Memorial. Instead, I fought your love, never wanting to serve you, but I love God, and you were right; you are my gift, property, and life's love. I promise to love, honor, and sometimes obey you." She laughed. "I will never neglect you for anything or anyone."

Jonathan just stared and said, "Loving you was never about sex for me; your heart was the missing puzzle piece to my heart. Sitting in a room with you filled my being with, I don't know, I only know when I'm with you, the world is right. I will never hurt, dishonor, or betray you. I will tell God every day how grateful I am that He gave us to each other. I can't find the words now but know this; you are my life, my wife, and you will never regret choosing me to be your husband; I swear this to you, and not through our passion of the moment, but because it is true. I love you with my whole heart."

The evidence of their joy could be observed with the unfinished breakfast every morning for weeks as the two still couldn't get enough of each other and hurriedly ate in a rush to return to wedded bliss.

Mr. and Mrs. Jonathan Dawson kept those vows for life. They retained and grew the love they had for each other year by year. Those who knew them in later years called them *Frick & Frack* as they were as 'in love' on day-one of their marriage as they were in year fifty of their union. Audrey and Jonathan epitomized the expression in the vows, *'What God has joined together, let no one break apart.'*

AUDREY AND JONATHAN LIVED IN JONATHAN'S FORMER HOUSE, NOW their home, for two years. The lovebirds loved their home, and every day was a honeymoon.

Speaking of honeymoon, they flew to the concert in the Netherlands. The conductor was informed of Audrey and Jonathan's love story. He invited them front center row and had the orchestra play the melody of the song Jonathan had written for Audrey years earlier.

Audrey and Jonathan returned home to Maryland even more in love than either thought possible.

As the newlyweds approached the front door to their home, they both noticed a small envelope taped to the front door addressed to Mr. & Mrs. Jonathan Dawson. Jonathan handed the note to Audrey, motioning for her to open it. The envelope was not sealed but the outer flap was folded under the body of the envelope. She opened and asked Jonathan, "Who's Willow?"

She read the note before he could answer.

Dear Jonathan,

Little sis, Willow here. I heard from my friend, Alice Park, that you married the girl of your dreams; lucky you. I didn't want you to think I'd forgotten you. You were an amazing brother, and even though I'm lost in my own world, I wanted to offer you and Audrey my sincerest best wishes.

Perhaps one of these days I will see you and meet my sister-in-law. Sorry I missed you in Korea; I hear she's amazing, and I'm happy for you both. I left a message for mom and dad too. Tell Harry I love him. Have you met Clair yet? She's wonderful.

All my love - Willow Dawson

Not wanting to spoil their homecoming, Jonathan preemptively said to Audrey in his kindest voice, "It's a long story; I will tell you what I know some other time. For now, let's get back to being married folk."

Audrey kissed him tenderly as he carried her again across the threshold with the expression of a lost-love-found in both their eyes.

It was in their second year of matrimony at that home that Audrey became pregnant. Both knew who was in her belly and couldn't wait to meet their son, who would save the world. They often joked with each other, talking about how much fun it was making the baby in her womb. Both laughed with sublime pleasure, hi-fiving each other.

Audrey was home alone when the postman had her sign for a large certified envelope. The address indicated it was from a prestigious law firm on Governor's Row in downtown Annapolis. Audrey called Jonathan, asking for permission to open the envelope.

Jonathan said, "You never have to ask; I have no secrets from you. Sure, open it. I'm only ten minutes away. I hope no one is suing us."

Even though Jonathan never had secrets with him, still she preferred he had the right to open mail addressed to him.

Home from work, Jonathan kissed his bride, asking about her day and she his. Audrey handed him the still closed envelope. Pulling out the sheaf of papers, he read the cover letter aloud.

Dear Jonathan & Audrey,

I heard you and your sock girl got married. Joanie called me, telling me you two are not so stupid after all (LOL).

I am writing you to keep a promise I made to you, Jonathan.

It has become too lonely in this huge house since my husband passed. My daughter, Joanie's mother, has invited me to live with her in Seattle. By the time you get this, the house you admired so will be empty and cleaned out.

I hired a general contractor to restore the house to its original condition, and now I am giving it to you and Audrey for the sum of ten dollars as we agreed to the afternoon we had scones and tea on my, now your deck.

Please mail a check for $10 to the Seattle address; the money will make it legal. I love you guys, and I love the fact that the home that Frank built for me and for our love to grow will now be yours.

It's the least I can do since your story reminded me of what we had and will have again when I pass.
May God bless you & Audrey as He has blessed me.
With gratitude and love to a loving couple… so rare.
Edna

Jonathan showed Audrey the deed of trust. The post-it notes asked them to the attorney's office to sign and notarize. The keys to the house were enclosed with the papers.

Helping pregnant Audrey into the SUV, Jonathan drove her to the home on the Severn River. Audrey had never seen it. Jonathan talked about it once, but only in passing.

Into the driveway, Audrey gasped. He carried her across the threshold, where she was stunned and impressed by the newly renovated home. Jonathan walked her past the rooms to the huge country kitchen and out the door to the deck that wrapped around the entire rear of the home.

Seeing the view of the Severn River from the porch of the house, Audrey wept openly in Jonathan's arms. Jonathan held her, knowing that God had found favor with them, and he would serve Him for all the days of his life.

Jonathan whispered into Audrey's ears as she continued to weep. "Thank you, God, for this woman, this home, and this life; for everything, Lord. Amen."

A Simple Act of Kindness, An Old-Fashioned Love Story

I hope you enjoyed my story. May you find the love of your life & Soulmate

Michael A. Way, Sr.

Acknowledgments

God, I thank you for allowing me to be Your scribe. As I read and re-read the manuscript, I often thought, *"Mike, you didn't write this!"* So much of this book is not consistent with modern morality but aligns perfectly with God's will and His intentions for love between man and wife. This novel is not to shame anyone but offers a reasonable path to the best romantic love life you can imagine, whether you are religious or not.

Editor: My editor is a woman with remarkable talent. My editor plowed through my manuscript the way a lawyer cross-examines a hostile witness. She took a great manuscript and crafted it into a nearly error-free novel.

Interior Design: Brady Moller, to put it quite simply, is a genius. If you enjoy the novel you hold in your hand electronically or as a printed book, the look and feel are because of Brady. This document, originally a Microsoft Word document, was transformed into a crafted presentation with a feel that matches the power of the story. Before

Brady, I never thought of words on a page as art, but as you flip through these pages, art becomes an understatement. In addition, the theme of doves at the beginning of each chapter subliminally demonstrates that the best human love stories are similar to the love Mourning doves share. Thank you, Brady.

Cover Design: With little more than a one-page synopsis, Emmanuel Ebirehri produced a cover design as if he read my mind, a technique that captures the most crucial moment in the novel's love story. I don't have enough words to describe his patience and expertise in guiding me through the best way to present my story. I've heard it said, *"you can't judge a book by its cover",* all my life. NOT TRUE! Emmanuel Ebirehri's work stands on its own, and if you like the cover of this book, you'll love the story even more. I promise you that the further you read as each chapter unfolds, you will find yourself looking at the cover, reflecting on what you've just read.

MY CHEERLEADERS

Jamie: You are my Audrey in real-life and my absolute best friend. Whenever I was at my lowest, you held me up; at my best, you cheered me on. Additionally, your insights were precise and added a wonderful texture to my female protagonists. Your bright, funny, straightforward wit and brutal honesty made you a joy to work with. Your matter-of-fact wisdom shows up on many of this novel's pages. You're amazing!

Allison: Your preliminary advice before the first word was written helped shape the novel's direction right out of the gate. And I thank you for the beautiful foreword you wrote; you are indeed an otherworldly friend. I wasn't sure men and women could be friends until I met you.

Friends: You know who you are. You guys and gals have been with me through it all—just a quick note to thank you all warmly.

Printed in the USA
CPSIA information can be obtained
at www.ICGtesting.com
JSHW020830250524
63393JS00001B/5

9 798986 774305